HEX,
BLOOD,
& RITUAL

ALSO BY ANDREW FORREST BAKER

MORE FROM THE HEX'D SERIES

HEX MAGIC : BOOK ONE

HEXUAL AWAKENING: BOOK TWO

GREAT HEX: HEX'D BOOK THREE

NOVELS

THE HOUSE THAT WASN'T THERE

LESSER GODS & DEMONS

WHERE THE BIRDS FLY SOUTH TO (COMING SOON)

SHORT STORY COLLECTIONS

WE TREMBLE AS WE SINK

ROAST

HEX, BLOOD, & RITUAL

ANDREW FORREST BAKER

Parlyaree Press
Atlanta, Georgia
www.parlyaree.com

Library of Congress Cataloging-in-Publication Data
Names: Baker, Andrew Forrest, 1980, author.
Title: HEX, BLOOD, & RITUAL / Andrew Forrest Baker
Description: First Edition | Atlanta : Parlyaree Press, 2025
Identifiers: LCCN: | ISBN: 978-1-961206-20-5 (paperback)
Subjects: LCGFT: Novels
LC record available at https://lccn.loc.gov/

Design by Parlyaree Press

Front Cover/Title Typeface is Rosella Solid.
Interior Text Typeface is Baskerville, designed in the 1750s by John Baskerville and cut by punchcutter John Handy.
Interior Ornaments from Espiritu, LTC Flourons, & Bodoni Ornaments.

Paperback ISBN: 978-1-961206-20-5
Ebook ISBN: 978-1-961206-21-2

For Sean.

ANDREW FORREST BAKER

HEX

BLOOD &

RITUAL

HEX'D BOOK FOUR

PROLOGUE

Vampires aren't real, I told myself, repeating the phrase over and over as if it were a spell I was committing to memory. As if it were something that would only be true if I could find solace in the words, and the only way to find solace was by letting the words lose meaning.

But looking at the body—pale and gaunt and nothing like the vibrant woman I'd seen only a few hours before—I wasn't doing a very good job of convincing myself. After all, a year ago I hadn't thought the Fae were real. I hadn't known that were-creatures were the remnant tales of when witches once had the power of transmogrification. Hell, four years ago, most of the world hadn't believed witches existed. But here I was: at a worldwide convention for witch business owners. And so that nagging voice that often accompanied my power—not usually vocally per se, but there— screamed at me to be open to the possibility.

The body was posed like she was sleeping. Slumped against the window, her forehead pressed the glass as her feet curled beneath her on the floral banquette. If I hadn't known better, if I had just been passing by, I might have assumed she was in some French-inspired New Orleans reverie, so entranced by the streetcars making their way up and down Canal Street, by the lights of the city after nightfall, she couldn't bring herself to look away.

But there was no life force within her. None my magic could discern anyway. And her reflection in the glass brought her hollow, vacant stare back to my gaze with the eerie, empty understanding of a Victorian porcelain doll. Her skin was gray—not the dull, pale blue of the recently dead when blood was present-yet-still within the veins, but bone gray—as if every flow of energy within her had vanished in an instant. Her lantern-jaw was as slack and stiff as a proto-expressionist painting. Then there was her neck.

Nearly hidden by the rearranged coif of her hair, two tiny wounds, spaced about an inch and a half apart and damp with coagulation, screamed like a calling card along her jugular, proclaiming: *You know what did this. You are right to be afraid.*

The hotel staff were nonplussed as they milled near the elevators further down the hallway, redirecting anyone who stopped on the floor to continue on with the brightest smiles they could endeavor while their nervousness danced on the rising and falling syllables of their language. I couldn't blame them though. I didn't know how to react either. Every ounce of me wanted to call my lovers back in Atlanta, but they were dealing with their own shit after our surreptitious journey to the Fae Realm left our affairs out of order. Besides, getting the Moral Authority of Witches involved was the last thing I wanted to do. On the other hand, they'd probably be much better at dealing with something like this than the local police.

"We have not been able to contact Mister Yaisien, but I have notified Mister Linnegard of the situation," the hotel manager snarled as he approached my pacing body before the... body. "As the whole of the Crow's Court has been rented to the BOG Convention and its constituents, we have determined to keep the situation in house."

Damn, he was a smarmy man. Thick in stature and accent, his face seemed forever flushed with the heat of New Orleans and the pinch of his squinted eyes. His midnight blue suit was exquisite and expensive but ill-fit to his body. And the amount of product he used to keep his cowlicks down left his hair heavy and shiny as it plastered itself into a helmet on his forehead.

"But the victim is human," I insisted. "She wasn't here for the convention."

"And whose fault is that?"

I cringed as my eyes darted from his thin, unsympathetic eyes to the young woman still prone atop the banquette. Waiting.

"There is nothing more to be done at this moment," he continued. "As such, Mister Cullen, I believe your presence here is no longer required."

I knew he was dead wrong. Not that I wanted to be the one in charge of a mess like this, but every fiber of my being was telling me there was more to come. More than the BOG Witches or even the MAW were equipped to handle. More than I was sure even the most magically-inclined of us witches could handle.

Something threatened to uproot centuries of our perceived understanding in its violent, blood-soaked carnage. It was here already, waiting in the darkest corners of the city, ready to make its presence known.

CHAPTER 1

New Orleans smelled spicy—like paprika and red pepper; magnolia and sex—as I stepped from the backseat of my Broomer onto the placid hustle of Magazine Street. Like every Southern city, there was a heat which drew the vowels long in sentences and left everyone with a dewy complexion. But unlike the Atlanta streets I was used to, where modernity and commerce quickened folks' steps to a hurried pace, NOLA kept things slow and casual. I'd waited nearly forty minutes for my ride to pick me up at the airport, and though she chatted the entire way to drop me off, I really only learned two things: that she'd seen a huge uptick in fares thanks to the BOG Witch Convention, and that I bore a remarkable resemblance to the fella who'd exposed magic to the mortal world.

Truth was, I was in town for the Business Owners Gathering of Witches myself, I'd just chosen to stay in the Irish Channel instead of the busy Central Business District hotel where all the festivities were taking place. I'd found a great rental house on OccultList BNB. A bit off the beaten path and a few blocks south of Magazine Street in the Irish Channel, it had its own spelling quarters—neutralized between each witch's stay so their magics didn't interfere with any spells the next tenant wanted to cast—and a private backyard green space even the swankiest of hotels could not truly provide no matter how hard they tried. Plus, even though it was a bit away from the main events at the Historic Crow's Court, and further still from the attractions and the music of the French Quarter, I wanted to support my fellow witches. And, being my first time as a BOG Witch, I figured I might end up relishing a quiet space away from the festivities.

The other truth—the one I kept quiet with a blushing nod and a face averted to watch the roadside ongoings—was that I was the witch she was thinking of: the one who exposed magic to the world. Most magical folk loved me for it; a few hated their actions were now scrutinized; and still others couldn't care less one way or the other. Most non-magical people were indifferent; but a few—whose numbers were growing—hated me and every other witch alive now that they knew we were real. I never knew which I was going to get, so I preferred to steer clear of the infamy. That hadn't stopped me from attending one of the largest witch gatherings sanctioned in the United States though.

I was a bit nervous as to what to expect, especially facing it alone, but my coven and boyfriends back in Atlanta had encouraged me to go. Cernun was even watching my shop for me while Learco had bought me an elaborate suit and enchanted mask for the famous masquerade ball that closed every convention. I felt odd leaving the two of them behind to deal with the fall out of our recent run-ins with the Fae, but they'd insisted I deserved the break. And no one I had ever met was better than Learco at prioritizing methods or cleaning up magical messes. Whether that was because of his experience as the head of the Southeastern Division of the Moral Authority of Witches—the not-so-dark-anymore organization formed centuries ago to keep the magically-inclined in line—or those experiences had given him the job, I wasn't sure. I did know

I was hoping he'd get the position back when he spoke to Leland Hyde on Monday, and that was a strange thing to think. I hated the MAW with every tendril of my power, but having met the Fomóraiġ and the Tuath Dé, I could appreciate the resources of his connections to the organization. Plus I knew he was working to change it from within. But witches were a stubborn lot.

I breathed deeply to swallow the wafting scent of green and floral and sea, of swamp, decay, and fried sugar, as I jostled my rolling suitcase down the alternating brick then concrete then tiled sidewalk. I'd only been to New Orleans once before—way back in my early twenties—but even then I had felt the sheer power inherent in the place. A lot of witches attributed it to the ley lines which ran beneath its soil, or the fact that sacred geometry was used to construct the city (thanks largely to the crescent shape of the delta), but I had a feeling it was more than that. Nature had given the city an abundance of gifts, an ongoing cycle of birth and renewal, and I thought we could all feel it in our bones, inherent and instinctual as the magic passed down through our bloodlines. I felt it creep into me, exciting my extremities and tingling within my aura without me even accessing my power. It was no wonder the Business Owners Gathering of Witches had chosen the place for their headquarters and yearly gathering. I also assumed, with the MAW HQ'd in Salem, they had a bit more of that southern fried freedom down here.

Or maybe not.

The sticker next to the lock box proudly displayed the letters MIM/MAW.

"Well, fuck," I mumbled as I scrolled through my phone to find the code to get inside, "that definitely wasn't mentioned in the listing."

Not that I was planning to do anything shady, but the Magic In Monitoring charms the MAW was hocking seemed pretty invasive. I'd refused them back at my Atlanta shop, HEX—the Herbal Emporium Xpress—even though the drop in my insurance rates would have been amazing. I'd refuse them again anytime they were pitched though, especially now that I knew I had a wild magic inside of me that differed from the usual witchy fare.

The inside of the house was cute, if a bit kitschy for my tastes, but it would definitely make a nice home base for the next few days. The picturesque front porch with its brick steps, arched valances, and dual rocking chairs off to the side had given way to a long, open living room. Its polished wood floors gleamed in a beautiful red hue around a lush—if too-small-for-the-room—shag rug, and, though the fireplaces were bricked over ages ago, their mantles added a gentle touch of old world character. The sofa was one of those super plush types my parents loved—too large for the space and a bit overwhelming against the smaller charms of the older home—but I had to admit it looked comfortable. And the crown molding still held a delicate nuance despite years of paint slathered over paint.

It was the wall art that got me. Nearly everywhere I looked a new-wood-made-to-look-old sign which sported punny little phrases—"In My Defense, the Moon Was Full" or "Of Course I Can Drive a Stick" next to a broom—stared back at me. Machine manufactured figurines showcased black cats with bristling fur or straw-haired vixens in pointed hats atop every open surface. They were a far cry from the hand-carved totems I sold back at home, but for a space that relied on passers-through to pay the property taxes, I supposed the cheaper decor made sense.

Past the living room, the pass-through led to a combination dining room and kitchen that looked clean and well-stocked. "This Witch's Favorite Brew" was hand-painted above the coffee pot, and a binder next to it was filled with the "house rules" I'd get around to reading at some point. Beyond that, a small hallway led to the laundry pantry, the spelling quarters, a locked closet proclaiming "Owner's Stuff: Keep Out or Get Boils," and what I assumed to be the bedroom before the backdoor to the yard.

I'd get to those in a moment. What concerned me more was the sound of running water and the sing-songy humming pouring from the other side of the closed bathroom door.

As the water shut off, I dropped my suitcase as quietly as I could and slowly backed the few steps into the kitchen. I wasn't sure what was coming out of that shower, but I definitely wanted more space to turn than the hall offered. My eyes squinted as I pulled at the power swirling in my gut, guiding a bit of it to my hands. It wasn't enough to trigger the MAW's monitors, but there was plenty more where it came from if things went that far. The butcher block next to the kitchen sink also had a number of knives if things went even farther.

Magic sparked in my palms as the bathroom door opened, undulating through the phases of green I held inside of me in warning.

"Whoa, easy there, tiger!"

The man was beautiful. His blond hair, sun-bleached to nearly white, dripped the remnants of his shower down his smoothly shaved face. Broad shoulders tensed above the expanse of his pecs, nipples pert and hard as the water serpentined the path of least resistance between his muscles. He nearly lost his towel as he jumped back, afraid of the power I was displaying.

"I didn't think anyone was here yet," he continued, regaining his composure with a sly smile I assumed had gotten him out of a lot of sticky situations. Or into them. "You must be the OccultList tenant, Darragh. I'm Chester."

His towel slipped as his hand extended out, but— unfortunately—he caught it with the other.

"I live in the guest house out back. Just past the garden. The water pressure out there is shit, so I figured…."

I let the power recoil within me as I eyed his outstretched hand suspiciously.

"The listing didn't say anything about a welcoming committee," I huffed.

Not that I minded the view. I just hadn't anticipated sharing.

"I was meant to be out of town too," he frowned, pulling his hand back and readjusting the terrycloth around his waist. "But things fell through."

I squinted. I was pretty good at spotting a liar, and he definitely wasn't telling me everything. But maybe he was one of those guys who'd never had to. Beauty went a long way with most people.

"I promise I'll get out of your way. You won't even know I'm here. I just need to—"

He reached past me to grab the plaid button-up I hadn't even noticed draped across one of the kitchen table chairs. He looked even better close up, and he smelled of lilac and tobacco.

"Sorry," he said as he brushed against me, the wet of his body leaving traces of him across my chest. "I'll go now."

He didn't bother to dress, keeping the towel wrapped tight around him to highlight the orbs of his ass as he padded down the hallway to the backdoor. Opening it, he looked even more majestic in the bright sunlight cascading through the trees.

"Don't report me to the owners, please," he begged. This time there was total earnest in his eyes. "I promise you won't see me again."

The *unless you want to* was implied as he nodded and let the screen door slam behind him.

I stood, staring down the hallway to the backdoor for a moment, my brain unwilling or unable to complete a thought. Maybe I was just on edge. My life had been a roller coaster of new creatures, new magics, and new worlds lately. I could feel all that change working its way toward suspicion within me. But I'd never been the type to shy away from strangers. Or to distrust them from the start. And no matter what the MAW or the Fae had put me through, I didn't want to begin being that witch. I was sure Chester was a nice guy. He was certainly nice to look at.

I shook my head to wash the stillness from my body, and glanced at the clock above the stove. Its broom handle minute hand was rounding close to 1pm already. So much for a relaxing lunch in the sanctuary of my private garden before the hubbub of the convention. Between the wait for my Broomer and the surprise ADU tenant, I was already going to be late. I stashed my bag in the bedroom, taking a moment to shove the "Home is Where The Cauldron Bubbles" throw pillows from the bed to the nearby chair, and checked my phone. It was a twenty minute wait for the rideshare or forty-five minutes by foot to the hotel.

A walk will do me some good, I told myself as I hitched the chain lock on the backdoor and made my way to the front. *I need some of that sweet New Orleans magic to clear my mind.*

"Ah, Mister Cullen!"

The receptionist was alert and wide-eyed, her voice holding the perfect mixture of contempt and excitement necessary to work the front desk of a high end hotel. She had to be welcoming while also showing the property was above it all, and that mixture bubbled within her like a potion. Though I wasn't sure how she knew my name.

"Uh, yeah," I stuttered, trying not to sound taken aback or out of breath from the brisk pace I'd established on my journey there. "That's me. How did you—?"

"It's my job to know every one of our patron's names," she interrupted, her smile not breaking as her eyes scanned my wardrobe and the remnants of sweat on my brow. "Shall I show you to your room to get cleaned up? Sign in for the conference has already begun, and the reception begins in… eleven minutes."

I blushed a bit as I looked down at my wardrobe. It was nothing fancy, but I quite liked the heavy threading of my lightweight brown slacks, the simple floral embroidery of my button-up. Although it was the same outfit I'd flown in, I hadn't planned to change before arriving anyway. Besides, this was a business owner's gathering, and this was definitely something I'd wear—and had worn—to work. Albeit beneath the flowing robes I'd commissioned for myself and my staff. Maybe I liked a bit of kitsch, too.

"I don't have a room here," I said as I regained my composure. "I rented a house for myself off site."

Although, maybe I *should* have stayed at the Crow's Court. The lobby of the hotel was glamorous, if a bit old fashioned, with blue lapis marble flooring, inlaid oak tables polished to a gleam topped with Victorian vases filled with a witch's garden of herbs and florals, and gold gilded ornaments as far as the eye could see. I had a feeling they were actual metal and not just painted. It wasn't exactly my style, but it was definitely a classy place.

Of course, it didn't have any hot naked guys stumbling out of the shower.

Well, not on this floor anyway.

"I suppose that explains why you don't have a bag," the receptionist frowned, rapidly hitting the keyboard of the computer in front of her with way more letters than any search should have required. "It says here we have you in the… Yarrow Tooth Suite. Five days; four nights."

Her demeanor changed a bit as she said the name of the suite, switching from service to awe with slightly less contempt on the vowels.

"That must be a mistake," I insisted. "I never booked a room here."

"There's no mistake, Darragh."

A third voice joined our conversation, and I turned quickly to face him, catching the subtle shock on the receptionist's face as I spun.

The man was tall—taller than Cernun—which put him at 6'6" or 6'7" easily. Or maybe it was the top hat perched over his walnut brown hair that made his height seem massive. I'd always thought top hats looked kind of magician-y, like a harbinger of fake power from an out of touch practitioner, but on him, it actually looked regal. His angular face dove to a small mouth and hooked chin with his nose carved in the middle like a talon. His thinness was exasperated by his height, but I could see a toned firmness beneath his silk-black shirt and the matching, well-pressed slacks that shone against his olive skin. There was an austere sternness to his body that somehow worked to make him seem exotic and sexy. Or maybe that was the joy that danced within his amber eyes.

"You do prefer first names, isn't that correct, Darragh? Not all that formal surname shit," he grinned, reaching out to wrap my shoulder in his arm and guide me away from the reception desk. "Pay no attention to Kara there. I personally booked you the suite. Paid for, of course, by the Council. It is yours. Whether you choose to use it or not."

We stopped before the elevator bay, and he stepped into an open car without me, nodding to the attendant before smiling back at me.

"I do think you'll use it though, Darragh," he grinned, tapping his shirt pocket with two fingers and a double rise of his eyebrows. "The nights at this convention tend to grow long and dark."

With that, the doors closed, and he was gone. I found a room card in my own shirt pocket that I hadn't even realized he'd slipped there. Maybe he was a magician after all, that strange man who had not even told me his name. But what the hell was the Council? And why the hell had they given me a room?

My brows furrowed as I heard the click of high heeled shoes tripping across the marble floor. I turned to find Kara marching toward me. Except she was timid now, more demure, and she refused to look me in the eye as she spoke.

"You will find the Yarrow Tooth Suite on the twenty-second floor, Mister Cullen," she said, all the vitriol gone from her voice and replaced by… was it fear? "Check in for the convention and the opening reception are taking place in the fourth floor library. I've called ahead to let them know you've arrived."

She kept her eyes averted as she reached out to call another lift for me.

"If you need anything at during your time with us at the Crow's Court, please do not hesitate to call the front desk, and one of our staff will see to it immediately."

The bell dinged, and she turned away, clicking quickly back to her perch behind the gold-plated oak of the front desk. The BOG Witch Gala was certainly off to a strange start. Hell, my entire visit to New Orleans had been a bit unnerving.

At least the elevator operator was smiling.

"Going up?" he asked as the doors closed, pushing the button for Four and pulling a lever for show.

The fourth floor was just as elaborate as the first. Ornate embroidery swam over lush fabrics. Gold and platinum metals were embedded with jewels. All was polished and proper and tilted in pleasant presentation. And that was just the witches.

I marveled at the sight of them, dressed to the nines, moving in practiced strides that said "I belong here; I belong everywhere" with each soft pad of their well-soled shoes, and smiling those smiles that said "I'm better than you; I'm better than everyone." Perhaps I *was* extremely under-dressed.

It took me a moment to make my legs move. Sure, I'd expected some of the witching elite to be milling about the corridors, leading panels on marketing to today's hip spell caster or holding roundtables on witchcraft in the digital age, but, looking around the room, I didn't think a single fingernail had met the soil during yesterday's Ostara festivities. I wasn't sure they even knew how to plant a seed. I guessed they took the "Gala" portion of their moniker quite seriously.

I skirted the crowd to make my way to a folding table draped in black cloth. Behind it sat the only other witch dressed like me, albeit in all black, but her clipboard and her earpiece told me she meant business. Her short clipped bob reminded me a bit of Learco's old assistant Samara Byrne, but her expression was more exasperated than stern.

"Name?" she asked when I cleared my throat.

Finally, someone in this town who didn't know who I was already. Between the Broomer driver, Chester, Kara, and the mysterious man downstairs, I was starting to think a memo had been circulated.

Her finger traced her roll until she found me, and a quick slash of her pen marked me as present and accounted for. She fished through a box hidden by the tablecloth and handed me a sleek, steel pin for my lapel. It took me a moment to realize the tree rising out of the swamp engraved on the triangular shape was actually the gnarled-fingered witch's hand so many human films and stories had given us, the bony fingers that beckoned children to their deaths amidst a castle of candy or a cabin of gingerbread cookies. I chuckled as I fixed it to my shirt. At least they still had a sense of humor about their acronym and our kind.

"A schedule of events has been sent to your room," she informed me. "One should have also arrived in the email we have for you on file. The welcoming reception ends at 4pm sharp, followed by a short speech from our founder, then a break for dinner on your own. The evening soiree at 9pm is black tie. Classes and lectures begin at 10am tomorrow. Your schedule and assignments will be on your itinerary."

"Heard," I smiled, trying to be friendly. Trying to prolong our conversation so I didn't have to face that crowd. Not that she was especially friendly. Efficiency had catered that out of her. But at least at the check in table, I wouldn't need to attempt small talk with all those downcast eyes behind me.

"Complimentary Sazeracs and Vieux Carrés are available at the bar in the main hall," she smiled curtly, ushering me away.

At least now somebody was speaking my language. I was sure they wouldn't compare to Aunt Paulina's Old Fashioneds, but the Crescent City definitely demanded I get some liquor to my lips. And a Sazerac wasn't all that different than my drink of choice. It just had the rich, bitter spice of absinthe coating the glass.

I felt entirely out of place. Not simply because of my garb, but because everyone around me seemed to know each other from past meetings or the daily wheelings and dealings of their work. I'd throughly intended to do more research on the event as a whole—to read through the mountains of emails they'd sent; to check out the carefully curated galleries on the BOG Witch website—but preparing for Ostara (and then being trapped inside the Fae Realm) had put the kibosh on that. Oh well, at least the bartender's smile was genuine.

Glad I'd thought to pull some cash from the ATM at the airport, I shoved a twenty into the tip jar as he passed me my glass. The crystal was thin, but heavy in my hand, and the little broomstick stirrers were a nice touch on the presentation. I was certain they were the product of one of the attendees. Witch manufacturing—with all the symbolism humans had used to denigrate us for centuries (though, in all honesty, we'd played our hands in it too)—was booming since magic had been revealed. And it wasn't just for Samhain anymore. In a way, all the broomsticks, black cats, pointed hats, and wart-green noses were our way of taking back ownership of those ideas, of proudly proclaiming who we were.

The sharp aroma of citrus and anise filled my nostrils as I raised the glass to my lips. I took a moment to savor the smell before the liquid swept my tongue with its sweet and bitter courage. It amazed me how one simple ingredient swap could change the whole of the potion. Like how switching sage for skullcap could turn a protection charm to a sedative. Bartending itself was a lot like witchcraft. Knowing how to mix the ingredients properly could make or break the spell. Of course, with bartending, all the spells had the same final intent. It was more about the tastes you took to get there.

"Darragh Cullen! As I live and breathe!"

A familiar voice whined through the hubbub of the crowd, and I nodded my approval to the bartender before I turned to face her. Serena had been a regular at HEX when I'd first taken over and, according to Uncle Gardner, for about a decade before that. One of the few real witches who came through amidst the humans looking for love spells and healing crystals, she was fond of her flowered peasant shirts in oranges and browns, her flowing hippie skirts that always seemed to have more folds than the fabrics should allow, and her strappy leather sandals with golden buckles. Her hair, frizzed to a halo by the Atlanta humidity, had been the brown of fresh baked bread, and she'd never worn so much as a swipe of mascara.

Now, she'd traded in her earth witch ensembles for the sleek black uniforms I'd seen all around me, but at least she'd kept the same flowing silhouette. The brown of her hair had also turned gray, and a thin layer of pale makeup hid the wrinkles she'd once so enjoyed.

"Hi, Serena," I smiled, grateful to have someone I recognized in the room, even if she was twenty years my senior. "I don't think I've seen you in the shop in ages."

"Well, you wouldn't, would you?" she guffawed. I was glad, despite the makeover, her personality was the same. "'Round the time of your little… revelation… I decided to jump up on that magic broomstick that was entrancing the nation. Turned my little Blue Ridge cabin into a healing and meditation retreat. Changed my name to Calendula Hawthorn to appease the yokels, and never looked back. You'd be surprised how much mortal white women are willing to shell out to sit bare-assed in the woods under a full moon with an actual witch!"

I'd heard of the C.H.H.C.'s before, but I'd had no idea Serena was the witch behind them. She had several Healing Centers adorning the Appalachian and Rocky Mountains in the US, and there was a rumor two were being planned for the Alps. Even though MAW sanctions prevented any actual magic being performed there, at least on the "indwellers" as they called them, humans flocked to them like locusts. And I thought that was a good thing. Finding out magic was real had reignited a lot of the world's interest in nature, even if a good portion of that attraction was in the *what can nature give me?* sense.

"It looks like you've done quite well for yourself, Calendula," I smiled, committing her chosen name to memory as I spoke it.

"Call me Dula," she whooped, clasping her hand around my bicep and drawing closer as I took another swig of my drink.

"Dula," I smiled, chuckling as I added the "o" she no doubt intended the laymen at her retreats to hear. Not that it mattered. She was already off and running on a conversation all her own.

"Life is great! I spend most of my time naked by a mountain stream telling blonde girls I can see their third eye when it's actually just the banking apps on their cell phones that's keeping me interested. How's that uncle of yours, kid? You know, if he hadn't fallen in love with Bill, I had a potion or two meant for his lips. Always so handsome, he was. You look a lot like him, you know. When he was younger."

I blushed as I cleared my throat, downing the last of my drink and eying the bartender for a refill. Dula spoke a mile a minute, not even pausing when she asked a question before spieling through another phrase. I guessed all that time in the mountains—speaking slowly, serenely, and saintly—led her to unleash when she was away.

"I'm on the eighth floor, by the way," she cooed. "In case you're in search of a potion of your own. Time, it does its number on us all eventually, but I've found a spell or two to keep up. 'Course, you may have brought those strapping men of yours for company. But the more the hornier is what I always say. I think the three of you—"

"Sorry to interrupt," a handsome man said, reaching between Dula and me and breaking her hold on my arm as he grabbed the Sazerac the bartender had placed out and put it in my hand. "Dula, you look well. If you don't mind, I need to have a brief word with Mister Cullen here regarding... well, the weekend's festivities. Darragh, if you'll follow me."

He turned without waiting for a response, walking purposefully through the crowd. I apologized to a seemingly starstruck Dula and promised to catch up with her soon before I followed. I had no idea who the man was, but I was intrigued. Plus, his ass looked amazing in his slacks as he walked, and, oftentimes, that was all it took to lead me into trouble.

CHAPTER 2

He looked even better in the sunlight. His black hair's slight curl was swept back perfectly, presenting the sparkle of his rich brown eyes. High cheekbones made his thin nose sharp and showcased the stretch of his smile. The other witches present moved inside as he stepped onto the balcony, and he leaned against the railing with a casual ease as he waited for me to approach.

"It seemed like you could use a savior," he grinned as I stepped out, clinking his coup glass against the rocks cup in my hand. "Dula has a tendency to go on and on at these things. I can't blame her though. It's really the only time she gets to let her hair down as her public persona is so… light and measured."

"I appreciate it," I chuckled at his kindness, taking another sip of my drink as I joined him at the rail. "I do actually know her though. She was a regular at my shop, even as far back as when my uncle still owned it."

"Ah, yes," he smiled. His eyes didn't seem to blink as they took me in. Odd yet enticing, it felt like he was seeing all of me. "The Herbal Emporium Xpress. I hear it is one of the finest of its kind."

I almost asked "You do?" but I assumed the words to be

another nicety on his part. Still, I couldn't stop my lips from scrunching and my eyebrows from raising. It was his turn to laugh at me silently calling him out.

"Perhaps it's the store's owner whom I hear is one of the finest," he grinned. "Alongside his coven, that is. A Cullen, a Clarke, and a Kyteler. Those are some of the finest witch names outside of the old world. And to have them practicing together…."

I blushed. It wasn't the first time I'd heard that. Nor was it the first time someone had been interested in me for my connection to the head of the Southeastern Division of the MAW and the only heir to the Kyteler line and fortune. Still, it never hurt to play along.

"It seems like everyone here, except for the woman with the clipboard, already knows my name," I smirked. "And I've yet to get a single one. Other than Dula's."

"Did you not study the photos in the event's directory?" he asked.

My eyes went wide. Oh shit. Something else I had gotten wrong on my first day. I hadn't even seen a roster come through.

"Relax. I'm just playing with you." His grin grew larger as my wide eyes returned to normal. "We did once use name tags before we decided that was gauche. My name is Mehrdad Yaisien. It is a pleasure to officially meet you, Darragh Cullen."

His hand was soft as I took it in mine, and I felt the slight pulse of his aura as he pursed his lips. He let his handshake linger, sliding the tips of his fingers along to meet mine when he finally pulled away. We stood in silence for a moment—me awkward; him at ease—as he sipped his cocktail and I finished my second. All it took was the lift of his finger for a server to appear with a tray holding two more.

"I see you've gone for the Sazerac," he said as a sip of my third drank began to wash the nerves from my body. "Brave choice, considering the absinthe they use here is the real deal. But I had heard tale that you are a brave one."

Make that three missteps. Real absinthe—the kind writers and singers and artists had told stories about for centuries, not the watered-down mass marketed affairs most bars in the States kept on their shelves—contained a decent quantity of wormwood. The plant, potent in potions and sachets, and a beautiful, airy addition to any witch's garden, was said to have hallucinogenic effects on everyone, though witches were especially susceptible. Of course, I knew that the green faeries folks once claimed to see were actually real. And I had a connection to them. A Fae presence was the last thing I wanted, especially in the midst of all these BOG Witches.

"So," I asked, taking a fake sip as to not draw suspicion, and lowering my glass quickly to change the subject, "what have I gotten myself into with this weekend?"

"Whatever your heart desires," Mehrdad purred. "The lectures and classes are a poorly attended formality to ensure the weekend is a tax write off. Most of the time, the speakers don't even show. The greased palms and the lubed connections happen at the parties—of which there are many, official and otherwise."

His aura pressed against mine again as he spoke the words "greased" and "lubed," and I smiled. Of course such a large gathering of witches would have an orgiastic element to it. We were highly sexual beings after all. That was part of the reason my boyfriends and I had an understanding when it came to our extracurricular activities. That and the love and trust we had for one another. I imagined it was also why the BOG Witch Convention and Gala was planned for the day after Ostara when we were all still on our Spring heat high. Perhaps it *would* be a great weekend.

Mehrdad mistook my silence for apprehension. I felt it as his aura withdrew, and he quickly added:

"Beyond that, you are free to explore all that New Orleans has to offer. There's a casino next door. Mugwort and wormwood are mixed into the tiles there to ensure no witchcraft or cheating. But it's still fun to roll the dice. There are also lovely cemeteries spread like coffee shops across the city, though gathering herbal ingredients is frowned upon. Of course, right across the street begins the Quarter. I think you'll find the establishments at Bourbon and Saint Ann's exceptionally invigorating. Are you staying here at the Crow?"

"I rented a house in the Channel," I said, then sent my own aura out to whip against his so he'd know I wasn't a prude. And that I was interested. "But, apparently, I have a room here as well."

"Is that so?" he purred. "I live here in the city, yet I always secure a room in the hotel as well. You never know when you may need quick access to a more… private space. On site or off."

I shivered in the heat as our auras twined together, adjusting to the rhythms of each other's energy, falling just short of equalizing to keep the vitality potent. It was an erotic experience—aura mingling in and of itself. It was the anticipation, the foreplay, the act, and the promise all rolled up into one. Mehrdad's brown eyes seemed to glow red in the sunlight, and he squinted into mine as I mimicked his force.

A throat cleared from the door of the balcony, and I turned to find the witch who'd checked me into the event tapping her foot against the threshold. Our auras fell as Mehrdad checked the exquisite gold watch on his wrist. Four o'clock sharp.

"If you'll excuse me, Darragh," he smiled, floating away with a purposeful gate but eyes proclaiming reluctancy.

Damn. The check-in witch wasn't kidding when she said the reception ending was "sharp." I shook my head to clear it of the intensity I'd just experienced and smiled out over the hustle of Canal Street a few floors below. I guessed the weekend wouldn't be so bad. But now I really wished Cernun and Learco were with me. The three of us together was the only thing I could imagine making Mehrdad's implied promise more exciting.

It was a promise, right? Not just a welcome extended by another randy attendee? Even in the massive crowd of witches, I was sure I'd see him again.

Maybe sooner than I'd thought.

A hush fell over the room as I stepped back inside from the balcony, and I followed everyone's eyes to the far side of the ballroom, not exactly surprised but amused to see Mehrdad take the spotlight on the small platform stage.

"Gentlewitches of all and no genders," he spoke, careening into his preprepared welcome speech with the same sultry cadence he'd used with me on the balcony. I didn't think he was pushing his aura out on the crowd though. Or, if he was, I wasn't included in its reach.

As he settled into a soft series of remarks meant merely to tick the boxes on some IRS Schedule C form, I let my eyes scan the crowd. I found Dula right away, tucked off to the side and still chatting away to someone who was trying her best to look attentive to Mehrdad's words while being too polite to tell Dula to shut up. I also recognized a few other faces from seeing them pop up in various news stories, but I couldn't have assigned a name to them if a wand was at my throat.

There was no sign of that mysterious man from the Council— whatever the hell that was—who'd "personally paid" for my room. Maybe the Council was the organizing committee, and that was simply a service they gave to new attendees. Though I figured I'd probably stick with the house I'd rented in spite of—or perhaps because of—Chester, I wanted to at least say thank you. I'd been so flustered in the lobby, and I knew appreciation and acknowledgement went a long way in the business world. Or any world really. And I'd had experience in multiple.

I did manage to find one other witch who'd missed the black wardrobe only memo though. I was glad I wasn't alone in that. Still, my everyday casual wear paled in comparison to his ensemble. The red velvet of his suit, crushed and draped across his shoulders like a cape, should have been hot in the southern humidity, but he seemed calm, collected, and suave. Somehow, I didn't think it was the AC that was keeping him cool.

Feeling my eyes on him, his own shifted to meet my gaze, followed by the rest of his face as he turned his head to smile in my direction. His features were angelic in that haunting sort of way: narrow and smooth but with a wisdom in his eyes, as if age had passed over his skin and settled itself in his mind. His irises held the same tinted amber the Peychaud's bitters had turned the whiskey in my glass. His lips grew thin as the length of his smile increased. He winked, then tilted his head toward the still-speaking Mehrdad, and I blushed.

"I trust the weekend festivities to be an invigorating experience for all involved," Mehrdad was saying. "And, if it is your first time here with us, just remember to pace yourself and drink plenty of water."

The sporadic chuckles and woos let me know he was being humorous, but he wasn't joking. There was a near glossy-eyed reverie amongst the attendees as they thought back to past experiences at the convention. What the hell had I gotten myself into?

When the welcome speech adjourned, an excited babble rushed like water across the group, and they pushed toward the exit, throwing themselves like waves against the elevators to start their preparations for the events. I hung back, keeping toward the rear of the room to give the space time to clear.

The Man in Red grinned once more as he passed me, his

burnt umber eyes crinkling as he flashed his aura out to mine. It scraped its way against the edges of my being, and I shuddered.

Although every witch's aura was different, vibrating at varying frequencies which could tell another witch as much about their personality as it did their power, we could usually adapt our own to meet and measure the other's. As part of the ebb and flow of the natural world, our auras were as malleable as the elements themselves: solid, but ready to get a little wild when needed or tamed if it was called for. The Man in Red's aura felt like nails scraping across my skin. And not in the good way.

My brow furrowed as I looked up to meet his eye. The bewildered expression on his face—there only for a moment before he regained his silky composure—told me he felt it too. He tilted his head in question, but I quickly turned away as he was swept off in the midst of his entourage. That was probably for the better. If the reason behind the grating was the newly-realized-and-therefor-clamoring-for-attention wild magic deep inside of me, that was an explanation I wasn't prepared to make.

"I see you're already making friends," Mehrdad beamed as he saddled up beside me, nodding to his adoring fans as they went by. "Cal is fairly discerning when it comes to his harem, but I caught him making eyes at you."

"I'm just new and shiny," I demurred, blushing a bit as I shrugged my shoulders. "Who is Cal?"

"Cal Juventus. As in the shoe designer."

What the Moirai did for witch clothing, Cal Juventus did for footwear. His eccentric designs were always next level beautiful and always well beyond reach of my wallet. I'd found quite a few pair that caught my eye, but always soothed my inability to afford them with the fact that I was either at work, at Aunt Paulina's, or in the garden: none of which were really places those fancy shoes fit. Although, judging by the glorious attire of the last remaining witches trickling out, I really could have used a pair for the Convention.

"Legend is," Mehrdad continued, "his family, once upon a time, enslaved a hundred leprechauns to do the cobbling in their shoe factory which is what built the company to what it is today. Of course, we both know leprechauns aren't real. Still, it makes for nice lore."

I laughed meekly.

Truth was, I'd been in the presence of several *leiprea-ceann* and their *clobhair-ceann* cousins only a few days before when my coven and I had been trapped in the Faerie Realm. But it was better to keep their existence the stuff of fable. The fewer folks who knew the reality of the Fae, the less mischief those creatures could create when some errant witch accidentally invited them back to our world. Still, the wink Mehrdad gave me told me he may know more than he was letting on.

"Humans do love a good tale," I smiled.

"Witches, too," Mehrdad nodded. "I assume you'll be back for the ball at midnight."

"I… uh… yes," I stuttered. "I haven't even seen the schedule yet. I was about to head up to my suite to grab it. But I'll be there. Is this… is this the masquerade ball?"

The musical quality of Mehrdad's chuckle seemed to make the sconces planted equilaterally down the hallway brighten.

"The masquerade is the final event on the final evening," he purred. "Tonight is more… foreplay."

I blushed and bit my lip.

"I'll be there," I promised.

"Lovely. If you don't mind my asking, what room are you in?"

The mischievous smirk on Mehrdad's face said the question implied more than simple curiosity.

"The Yarrow Tooth. Something named the Council booked

it for me."

His expression shifted so quickly from impressed by the suite name to disgusted by the Council and back to staid and calm, I almost didn't register the change. I pursed my lips and frowned.

"What the hell is the Council?" I asked.

I watched Mehrdad's eyes swim as he searched his business acumen for a diplomatic answer. But there was worry there. I could see it bright as sunlight.

"The Council," he hemmed, speaking slowly as he chose his words with care, "consists of a group of… rather… supercilious attendees. Extant since just prior to our last convention, they've all but expressly attempted to wrest control away from me and my team in favor of a more… discerning membership roster. If they've paid for your room, I would assume it's because they want something from you."

What would a group of high-and-mighty business folk want from me? HEX was doing well, but it was one small shop along a quaint Atlanta street. We didn't even sell our goods on our website. And I was sure all those companies had their own finger's in the MAW's cookie jar, so my connection to Learco would have been irrelevant.

"Or perhaps I am simply vexed by their attempts to usurp me," he continued, reading my wondering as reservation. "Still, when dealing with witches, I find it always best to consider the spell-not-yet-cast while their glamour is on display."

I nodded. It was actually good advice. Growing up, my mother liked to impart something similar. *Be attentive*, she'd say. *When one summons water, the fire to evaporate the mist is never far behind. When one calls the flame, water is ever waiting to extinguish the spark.* It was her reminder that magic was all about balance. That we were meant to work with nature, not against it, in our intent and our goals. That whatever element was the brightest on display, all the others were there too, even if we couldn't directly see them.

The sentiment was the same. Of course, she hadn't been nearly as jaded as Mehrdad obviously was by the rest of witch kind. But, I supposed, making it to where he had on the ladder of the witchly business world, he'd learned to watch his back where magic and capitalism converged.

The throngs of witches had slowly escaped until it was only the two of us left at the far end of the hall. The witch who'd checked me into the welcome party watched the two of us with an expectant expression, tapping her fingers gently on her watch as she insisted to the elevator attendant it would just be a moment more.

"I will see you again at midnight, Darragh Cullen," the BOG chief smiled as he began to walk toward the lift. "Rest up 'til then. We do have a tendency to go all night."

I decided to forego the suite—if the Council wanted to woo me, it'd take more than a good view and some high thread count sheets—and head out into the city. However nice it had been to be surrounded by my own kind, the pulsating energy that prevailed at the convention was a lot for one afternoon. The heated song of New Orleans, sung from its bricks and its balconies and its Big Easy temperament by both the locals and the tourists—myself included—would better align me to the true magic of the place than any amalgamation of witchly ongoings. Plus, in light of Mehrdad's warnings, I wasn't quite ready to steel myself against group of magicker-than-thou entities. The MAW and the Fae were enough on that front. I didn't need to add the Council to the mix.

The shift from air conditioned serenity to the thickened, condensed atmosphere was palpable as I stepped through the gold-plated doors, and I shivered a bit as my body adjusted. My ears opened to welcome the sounds of a city alive. The low hum of the Crow's Court's orchestral nuance was replaced by the syncopated jazz of the trolley, the vendors, and the actual trumpets of the very real jazz bands careening through the streets from blocks away. Even the clanging clash of the slot machine handles as the doors spun at the casino next door added to the song. This was what life sounded like. I let it wash through me until the wild magic in my gut vibrated at the same pitch.

"Are you staying at the Crow?"

I turned to find a young woman—no more than twenty-three—smiling up at me in wonder, her blonde hair made wild by the bayou's humidity as it wafted from the slower moving waters surrounding the town. A dewy sweat dappled constellations across her brow and cheeks then settled down her back where the tattered rucksack she had slung over her shoulder rested. Her clothing—cut-off denim shorts that clung tight against her upper thighs and a pink ribbed tank top with an airbrushed alligator sipping on a hurricane—was a little threadbare along the hems, and the straps of her sandals were worn and water-stained as they stretched to buckle across her feet. But her smile was bright, and her blue eyes were those of a human who truly believed in magic, even if she did not possess any herself.

"I tried to get a room there," she continued. "But they were all booked up for some convention. Wouldn't even let me in the lobby. Is it really as beautiful inside as everyone says?"

"It is ornate," I admitted, smiling as she nodded and did her best to see through the tinted windows that lined the lobby. "Not sure if I'm actually going to stay there though."

"Man, if I had the chance…" she started, eyes growing distant and wistful for only a moment before they returned to their Pollyanna state. "I kind of just wanted to see the lobby, you know. They say it's like glimpsing the royalty of old New Orleans."

I grinned. The Crow's Court certainly had splendor. But I preferred the weather-worn houses in the Marigny, the cracked marble and concrete of the cemeteries from which rue and resurrection ferns sprung, the sun-drenched and forgotten plastic beads that wrapped the higher branches of the oaks and magnolias. To me, that was the "royalty" she was searching for. Still, I understood a pining for decadence.

"Where are you coming from?" I asked, trying to make small talk as she continued to shuffle her feet against the sidewalk.

"Baton Rouge," she lied.

Or maybe it was a half-truth. The state capital may have been a stop on her travels, but the dirt under her fingernails, the exhausted defiance that teetered just beneath her smile told me the road had been much longer for her. Too, her accent planted her roots within the midwestern cornfields rather than along the banks of the southern Mississippi River. Having spent a large part of my life hiding my magic and my queerness from the outside world, I'd become fairly adept at spotting the meandering journey of someone running away from something. I also had a tendency to take in strays as my friend Madison—a stray themself of a sort—had recently pointed out. But this girl's smile, her unhindered energy, proclaimed she wasn't about to let whatever she was escaping from define her. It was admirable.

"Well, I… uh…" I stammered, nodding toward the French Quarter across the street as a way of saying goodbye.

She nodded quickly, frowning as she adjusted the bag still plastered to her shoulder. The empathy on my back felt as heavy as her bag looked.

I remembered how scary it had been to set off on my own once upon a time, and that was with so much being handed to me by my family. This young lady was hiding it well behind her bright personality, but she was facing a much harsher reality than I ever had. I made a quick wish to the elements that she would find whatever path she was searching for.

"Do you think… maybe…?"

Her words forced from her throat with a rallied bravado, and I turned around from my exit to look her in the eye as a timidness overtook her.

"Could I maybe stay with you tonight?" she asked.

The words were soft and desperate and hard for her to speak. But days—or maybe weeks—on the road on her own had forced a Tennessee Williams-esque reliance on the kindness of strangers. Even if I was a strange man in a strange city.

"Just for one night," she added, eyes scanning the sidewalk as she avoided my own. "I can't pay or anything. But I've got a job lined up as a waitress on one of the riverboats starting tomorrow. I could maybe send some cash once I get some money flowing."

A heavy sigh forced from my lungs as I eyed the dejection beneath her smile. She deserved a night of luxury, a glimpse at the life she was running toward. Besides, the room was paid for, and it was the Council's credit card tied to the incidentals. If nothing else, this act of compassion was simply further proof to them that I couldn't be bought.

"I'm not staying here," I smiled. "But I do have a room. It's yours for the night."

The excitement on her face was all the reasoning I needed as I held open the door for her to enter. It felt nice to do a good deed, better still to help out another soul. That was part of why I wanted to turn the backroom at HEX into a learning center for young witches. If I ever got around to it. And was able to get sanctioning from the MAW. But that was another story. For now, if I had an unused room that had already been bought and paid for, who was I to turn away a young human woman in need of shelter?

"No. Absolutely not."

The receptionist nearly snarled as she shook her head quickly, the sharp edges of her bob whipping color into her cheeks.

"I'm sorry, Mister Cullen," she continued, "but that is against our company policy."

"It's against hotel policy to let folks sleep in your rooms?" I pressed, knowing full well I was goading her frustrations once again but not caring. "I have a room. And... uh...."

"Amy."

"Amy here is my guest," I said, meeting the receptionist's forced smile with my own. "I am simply asking for an additional room card so that she may come and go as she pleases."

All the reverence she'd had earlier in the presence of the Council member was gone as Kara clapped at her keyboard and fumed.

"I'll just go somewhere else," Amy sighed, picking her dirty rucksack up from the marble floor and heaving it back across her shoulders. "I really don't want to be a bother."

"No," I insisted. "I have a room here that I am not using. It shouldn't go to waste."

"The Historic Crow's Court is not a homeless shelter, Mister Cullen."

"Nor am I asking for it to be," I shot back. "Whether Amy is unhoused or not is really none of your business. My room is paid for. Your business is to see her to it."

I wasn't generally so forceful, but something about Receptionist Kara rubbed me the wrong way. Still, I kept my words calm and measured, my tone low and precise, my anger bubbling just below my surface. I'd obviously learned a thing or two about that kind of power from Learco. He had an uncanny ability to toss his weight around with the simple utterance of a few syllables. It's part of why he was so good as the leader of the MAW's Southeastern Division. I was happy to use the tricks I'd learned through observation to stand up for someone else. Still, if the room had been for me, I probably would have cowered away at the first glare from Kara's eyes. Amy certainly looked like she wanted to.

"Can I be of assistance?"

He was short with an accent as heavy as his waist and a suit too thick for the southern Spring heat heaving down outside. His morning ritual must have involved an entire tub of pomade, but no matter how hard he tried to style and freeze his hair, it couldn't quite cover the bald spot on his crown or the receding angle on his forehead. It was also incredibly clear his question was not directed to me.

Kara scrunched her nose as a smug smile spread across her lips.

"Mister Landry, Mister Cullen would like us to allow this… vagabond access to his suite for the night," she growled. "I have informed him it is against hotel policy, yet he is insisting."

I sighed, but held my ground. This was obviously the boss, and I had to hand it to him for sticking up for and with his employees—that was an admirable trait and one I preferred in a good leader—but I appreciated moral kindness a hell of a lot more. Amy may not have been able to afford a room, and she may not have been dressed to the nines like the other folks staying along those gilded halls, but it wasn't like I was all that tailored either. And, like Amy, I certainly hadn't paid for the room myself.

Mister Landry nodded as he turned to face us. Well, me. They were both acting like Amy didn't exist.

"Mister Cullen, as a member of the weekend's festivities, I am sure you can understand our policies involved in keeping all of our guests safe and secure throughout their stays at the Crow's Court. As such…."

His voice trailed off as his eyes shot past me. I followed his gaze to find Mehrdad beelining toward us from the elevators, his assistant in tow.

"Is there trouble?" he asked as he met us, his voice bright yet full of warning.

"I was just explaining to—"

"I was speaking to Darragh," he snarled, cutting off Landry with a curt, clipped smile.

"I was just explaining to these fine folks that my new friend Amy would like to use my room for the night," I smiled, mimicking the hotel manager's words with a sticky sweet sarcasm. Then, remembering his distaste for the witches who'd gotten the room for me in the first place, I quickly added, "The one the Council paid for."

The amusement in his eyes was exactly what I'd been hoping for. I stayed quiet as he ordered the hotel manager to see to my needs, throwing in a couple threats about moving the Gala's business elsewhere in the coming years, and laying it on thick as he welcomed Amy to the Crow's Court for the evening. It must have felt amazing to wield that kind of power.

"You know," he said as we waved goodbye to the young woman and the hotel manager as he personally escorted her to my suite, "it's quite droll of you to turn the tables on the Council like this. I knew we were going to get along famously."

"I was just trying to do a good deed," I laughed. "The rest was just a bonus."

Mehrdad nodded, the mirth in his eyes telling me both had delighted him. He nodded as his assistant, whose name I still hadn't learned, ushered him toward the door of the restaurant across the lobby where several impatient witches were trying to seem obvious as they watched the scene.

"As your quarters are now occupied," he purred, turning slightly over his shoulder as he walked away, "should you not want to escape to your off site accommodations after the Ball tonight, you are welcomed in my personal suite."

CHAPTER 3

"Mads says 'you and your strays.'"

I chuckled at Cernun's words through the receiver as I made my way southwest on Magazine Street, heading back to my OccultList BnB. I could hear from the background noise that HEX was fairly busy, and I knew I should've let him go, but, damn, it was good to hear his voice. Especially after my first few hours in the Crescent City.

"Tell them I thought the same thing," I smiled.

The sun had long dipped behind the taller buildings of the CBD, making his way toward the horizon with a vibrant vigor and exciting the atmosphere with his own magical aura. The pinks and oranges found only in the most exotic of fruits, those harvested from the places where the sun liked his magic to linger, tinged the sky around the buildings to make even their brick and concrete façades assume a tingling glow. I could feel the pulse of the city quickening as it spread around me. All the nocturnal inhabitants were rustling in their robes, ready to break free as the humidity calmed and the music accelerated. *This* was what I'd come to New Orleans for. This magic. This life. The BOG Witch Convention was just a convenient excuse.

I really wished my boyfriends were with me.

"You know," I cooed, lowering my voice a tad to stop any prying ears from eavesdropping, "now that I know the lay of the land here, I could probably arrange a little portal action if you and Learco wanted to stop by for the night."

Cernun's sigh was dreamy as he considered the prospect even though we both knew it wasn't truly feasible. I had managed a portal for us back in Atlanta, but that had only spanned a few miles. There was no guarantee I could command the 425 miles between our cities, even if I could spread the threads of reality as The Mórrígan's crow flew. And I certainly didn't want to risk any of us getting lost to that abyss.

"It's a nice thought," Cernun purred, "a *really* nice thought. But it sounds like you've already got your hands full down there. And you're going to need all your energy focused elsewhere."

That was true too. Using my wild magic to perform Fae spells did take a lot out of me. But my recovery time *was* lessening. Still, it was risky.

"Tell him I looked up Mehrdad Yaisien online, and I fully expect all the details upon his return."

I laughed at Learco's words as they ambled through the line, and Cernun whispered "to the stars and back" to me before he passed the phone to my other partner.

"Did you hear me?" Learco asked. "Measurements too, if you can get them."

"I'll be sure to break out a ruler," I quipped. "Any news on the MAW front?"

I hated to bring up a sore subject and break the mirth, but I needed Learco to know I was there for him, even if I was partying in a different city. Particularly since he knew my feelings about the organization.

"My meeting with Leland is set for Monday morning at nine," he huffed. "But Rafael tells me the higher ups aren't too pleased with Mister Hyde's cavalier dismissal of me. Especially since the only grounds were me not showing up to a meeting on account of being kidnapped. As far as Rafael knows, it's already overturned. And Hyde has to be the one to apologize."

I laughed again as I imagined Leland Hyde, the Moral Authority of Witches' resident witch hunter—the guy they sent out when we truly turned bad—groveling to Learco, his thick Bostonian accent swallowing the consonants and yanking out the vowels as his faced fumed as red as the sun now cresting the swamp.

"Make him suffer," I offered.

"Oh, I plan to," Learco giggled. "Speaking of suffering. I hear your home away from home has an unexpected guest."

"Chester," I huffed. "Human by the feel of it. Unless he's really good at hiding his magic. He came tumbling out of the shower when I let myself in before I'd even put my bag down. Says he'll stay out of my way the rest of the weekend though."

"Uh huh."

"What?"

"Details and measurements," Learco repeated. "Details and measurements."

I truly was so lucky to have such amazing—and encouraging— boyfriends. And I was glad things were shaping up nicely for them back in Atlanta. Those Faeries had done a number on our lives, but it did seem like common sense and right were prevailing.

Our prolonged goodbyes lingered in the thick air as I slipped my cell phone back into my pocket and turned onto the street for my OccultList BnB. I figured I'd have just enough time to relax, grab a quick bite, and take a prolonged shower before I made my way back to the BOG Witch Ball. I knew my rental shower could never compare to the one Cernun had decked out for me in my apartment back home, but it was just what I needed to wash the stickiness of my arrival from me prior to the night's festivities.

And Chester had definitely seemed to enjoy it. My mind flashed to the sight of him—his mussed, white-blond hair dancing like a halo atop his chiseled features; water carving its way through the canyons of his muscled torso; the way his thin, terrycloth towel arched ever so slightly toward me as he startled at my presence. I guessed if I couldn't have the property to myself, at least I had someone nice to look at in the absence of my lovers. Of course, he'd promised to stay out of sight for the rest of my trip.

It seemed like he was making good on his promise. The house was empty when I let myself in, and I smiled as I rummaged through the kitchen for a snack. I hadn't had the chance to hit up the grocery store yet, but I was sure there'd be something left behind by a past tenant. I was wrong. But I'd seen a cute little local pub back on the main street, and the witch's broom of the clock promised enough time to get showered, dress, and grab a bite before I hit up the Ball.

I took the opportunity the pull the suit Learco had purchased me from my suitcase and shake it out before I hung it in the closet. Tailored perfectly to my body, its green fabric—the color of my own magic and laced through with the blue and gold of Cernun's and Learco's—would definitely stand out when I wore it to the closing masquerade ball. And the magicked mask that accompanied it—stylized to look like the witch rendition of the Green Man and spelled to conform and mold to my face— would truly quell any whispers about my attire. I'd actually met Cernnunos recently—intimately—and the mask looked nothing like him. But no one needed to know.

It was a shame I couldn't wear it to the ball tonight, but I had a feeling the BOG Witch crowd would view repurposing an outfit as taboo. And I did bring the loose-fitting, flowy shirt and pant set from Moirai—the pinnacle of witch couture—with me just in case. It wasn't the black uniform they seemed to prefer, and it felt a little early to break it out, but the green and tan asymmetrical ensemble fit me well and would certainly impress. Plus the forest hue of the top really made my eyes pop. I laid it out atop the bedspread to admire as I pulled off my shirt for the shower.

Three quick raps sounded against the window glass on the backdoor outside the bedroom, and I furrowed my brow in question as I popped my head out. A wide-eyed Chester, blushing a bit as his eyes traced my nude torso, held his palms up and shrugged. I shook my head to hide my smile as I unlocked the deadbolt and opened the door to the back stoop.

"I know I said I'd stay out of your way," he blurted, pushing through the words and his accent so quickly I almost didn't catch them, "but I felt really bad about invading your space earlier."

"It's fine," I nodded. "Truly."

"I— I wanted to make it up to you." Chester blushed again as he stepped aside, revealing a sweet picnic setup in the middle of the backyard. "I put together a supper. If— if you're hungry."

This time I didn't hide my smile. He certainly was full of that sweet southern charm. And he looked sexy in the dimming light of day.

"That's really not necessary," I said.

I was hungry, but I wasn't sure I wanted to open the proverbial door to anything more than fantasy with Chester. It was bound to get messy in more ways than one. But after tonight, I would have my suite at the hotel to escape to if things at the house proved tenuous. Plus, the spice wafting on the early night breeze was enticing.

"Let me grab a shirt," I conceded.

"It's still warm out," he said. "You don't have to if you don't want to."

His eyes traced my chest as mine had followed his earlier. It felt good that I wasn't the only one caught up in imagination, even if we never acted on it. There was something hot in just the anticipation and exaggeration of what ifs. I rolled my eyes and ducked back into the bedroom to grab a t-shirt from my suitcase before I rejoined him on the back porch.

The aluminum, two-seater café table out a little ways into the garden had been draped with a blue fabric that looked more like a top sheet than a tablecloth. At least I assumed it was aluminum, being in the garden of a witch-owned house. The sturdier wrought iron of most outdoor furniture created a bit of a dead zone for magic, so most witches avoided the metal outside of their cauldrons where they needed the power contained to the manufacturing of the spell anyway. Atop the table, a covered dish steamed from beneath its lid, offering an almost floral scent to the spice atop the lush green of the yard. Two tapered candles sat at the center beside the dish, and wide bowls of rice rested at each place setting.

"Shit," Chester groaned as he patted the pockets of his denim shorts. "I forgot the matches."

"No worries," I smiled. "I've got it."

A quick thought paired with an under-my-breath utterance of *adhaint* flicked a flame to ignite the wicks, and Chester beamed as he pulled my chair out for me. It was feeling an awful lot like a date, but a part of me figured it was just southern hospitality at play. At any rate, the meal smelled delicious.

"I hope you like crawdaddies," he blushed, pulling the glass lid from the serving dish and placing it gingerly on the table between us. "My family fishes them over in the Atchafalaya Basin, so they're super fresh."

I inhaled deeply as the rush of steam wafted like clouds to dissipate within the cooling air of evening. The white meat, free of their pepper red tails, bobbed deliciously in the blonde roux. He spooned a few heaps over the rice in my bowl before serving himself and sitting down just as the sun finished its descent.

He was even more enticing in the candlelight.

"It looks spectacular," I replied to his expectant stare.

"Thanks," he blushed. "I figured we got off on the wrong foot, and you deserved a little bit of what New Orleans really means."

Sweet but with a kick, the first bite tasted fresh as it coated my tongue, and I couldn't help but grin as I washed it down my throat with the chardonnay he'd paired with the étouffée. A spell in and of itself, the meal warmed me from within to let me meet and relish the heat of the city.

"I grew the Holy Trinity myself."

"Oh, I'm not much for religion," I shrugged, spooning another bite and kicking myself mentally for denying his attempt at conversation.

Chester laughed.

"I'm not either," he said. "Just the doctrine of the soil. Folks 'round here call onion, celery, and green peppers the 'Holy Trinity' on account of them being the basis for pretty much every meal."

He used his spoon to point to the swath of tilled soil a few feet off from the ADU he called home. Even in the darkening night, I could make out the sprouts of an assortment of edibles already springing up from the ground. I liked a man who knew how to get his hands dirty.

"Gotcha," I laughed. "My boyfriends built me a greenhouse on my roof back in Atlanta, but my seeds just went in right before I hopped the plane here. So, you know, it's nothing like what you've got going on."

The blush in Chester's cheeks was highlighted by the glow of the flame between us.

"I've always had a bit of a green thumb," he demurred. "Plus, it gets warmer here earlier, so I had a head start."

His face turned inward as he took another bite. I could tell something was on his mind, but I let it slide as I went back to my meal. Chester was a damn good cook. Maybe having an unexpected guest wouldn't be so bad.

I swallowed a few more bites before reaching for my wine glass, cocking my head at the turmoil on my companion's face.

"What?"

"You said 'boyfriends.' As in multiple?"

"I did."

Chester pursed his lips and nodded as his eyes swam back to his plate.

I was right. He had thought of this as a date. I felt flattered, especially since he'd been the one in the buff when we'd met. I decided to throw him a bone.

"Cernun and Learco," I continued. "They're great guys. I think you'd like them. I think *they'd* like *you*. But they stayed back home on this outing."

Chester nodded, his face brightening a little but confusion still metered in his eyes.

"You're sort of like your own Holy Trinity then, huh?" he asked, and I grinned.

"I guess so," I smiled. "But every Holy Trinity needs a little bit of extra… spice here and there."

At that, he laughed, and the non-magical spell he'd been trying to cast settled back in over the garden. I wasn't sure if it would go anywhere—hell, I wasn't sure either of us really wanted it to move beyond the excitement of flirtation—but the ambience itself was definitely fun.

"So, you said you have family nearby?" I asked, breaking our lingering gazes and letting us get back to the food and the wine.

"Sure do. We got a camp over in Butte La Rose," he grinned.

"Camp?"

"House. Most folks 'round there call them camps. It's… not a big place. Over there in St. Martin Parish. I mean, it's still home, but I wanted something… bigger. For a bit anyway."

"I get that," I smiled. "I grew up on a farm a few hours south of everywhere and hightailed it to Atlanta the minute I was old enough. I go back when I can though."

My smile grew wistful as I thought about home, faltering a little when I realized how long it'd been since I'd actually been back. In fairness, there'd been a lot going on, but I still needed to make a plan to see my parents as soon as I'd gotten this trip under my belt. Alongside as whatever else this trip placed under my belt as well.

"Have you always been a witch?"

Chester's question brought me back to the garden, the words rushing from his mouth like flashes of fireflies in the setting sun. He looked embarrassed to have asked, but the glint of sincerity on his features proved the question was in earnest.

"Well, yeah," I smiled. "It's kind of something you're born into. It's in the blood."

He nodded, frowning a bit as his spoon swirled the food left on his plate.

"So magic's not something you can learn?"

He was even cuter when he was disappointed.

"Is that why you came here?" I asked. "To New Orleans? You wanted to learn magic?"

Chester shrugged, crossing his arms over his chest as he leaned back in his chair. The garden had succumbed to the night, leaving a haze around his skin as the candlelight burned in his eyes.

It was kind of sweet, his dejection. Over the years since magic—*real* magic—had been revealed to the world, I'd met my fair share of chasers. People were naturally drawn to power, and a lot of those people wanted that power for themselves. That wasn't necessarily a bad thing though. Hell, it was what had kept places like Marie Laveau's herbalist and midwifery establishment in New Orleans thriving for two centuries. It was what had kept HEX alive and a roof over my head too.

Most chasers, once they found out they wouldn't suddenly be able to fly or turn invisible or manifest mountains of money like a hoarding dragon, relinquished their quests and saddled back with a slightly lessened admiration. Others got mad, joined hate groups like the Defend Mankind From Magic organization Cernun's adoptive family had founded, or took to social media to simultaneously declare us frauds while claiming we were secretly performing all those tasks they'd so desired to do for ourselves. It could be a bit of a mindfuck.

With Chester though, I didn't get the impression that either path was really where he was headed.

"There was this girl," he sighed, letting his arms fall into his lap as he started to open up, "Félicité. We dated for a while back in high school. And for a little while after. Way before anyone knew magic was really real. But she always said she was a witch. That she came from a long line of Voodoo priestesses. Is Voodoo the same thing? As witchcraft, I mean?"

"Depends on who you ask," I smiled, leaning forward and placing my elbows on the table exactly like my mother had always taught me not to do, trying to show him I was interested in his story. "Personally, I think it is. I think it all comes from the same place. Words, rituals, ingredients—they may vary, but it's the intent behind it all, the core of the natural elements that guide all witches, whatever it is they call themselves."

My own practice centered around an Irish-Euro-centric tradition because that's what I'd been raised in. Learco's upbringing had trained his power around Lucumí and Afro-centric rites. He tended to use Yoruba words when he spelled. And

Cernun, having grown up without a direct family line to teach him, had garnered a mixed mash of Southwestern Indigenous, Latinx, and European leanings as he traveled the country looking for his roots. But we'd always known—and most witches and the MAW agreed—our power came from the same source. The part I couldn't say out loud though—the part that really drove it home for me—was spending time with the Fae folk and knowing they'd once happily assumed the guises of gods under a variety of names. Of course, I knew they weren't truly gods. And I knew their power and ours came from somewhere beyond the both of us. The fact that I had some of it inside me, a piece of that wild source, had shocked the Fae as much as it had me.

"Well, anyway," Chester sighed. "We got pretty close. I was all but certain I was gonna marry her after graduation. We were going to build our own camp. I was going to grow the herbs she needed for her practice, and she was bound to be the premiere medicine woman in the whole of the parish. But she told me her parents said we couldn't be together. That she needed to keep the line strong, so she had to marry someone with magic."

"How Shakespearean."

Chester winced at my attempt at empathy so I quickly added, "A lot of old families are like that. And while we do *learn* our magics in the sense of how we put things into practice, our *power* is innate. That's something that can't be taught or given or conjured."

Though people have tried, I thought. My brow furrowed as I remembered my old protégé Aiden and his attempt to steal my power through blood magic. That was not something I was *ever* going to go through again, no matter how cute the wannabe witch was. Still, Chester's disappointment was palpable.

"I do believe that there is a spark inside everyone," I smiled. "We are all natural beings, after all. Some of us get the power. Others, like you, get a green thumb and a way with plants; a charming smile; an intuitive sense of combining elements to cook a perfect meal instead of a potion. Magic is all in how you look at it."

Chester's mood brightened slightly as he rolled his eyes.

"Félicité's parents sure don't view it that way," he growled.

I chuckled at his smirk and took a sip of my wine as I watched the glint of determination spread back through his body. I couldn't have been the first witch to tell him I couldn't teach him power. But this guy had set his mind to a task and he wasn't about to give up. I got the feeling the quest had begun to supersede the goal, had taken on a life of its own outside of his at least ten-year-old high school romance. I could feel him readying himself to pounce on the next witch who rented out the OccultList BnB.

"If you don't mind my asking," I said, pouring another glass of wine for myself and offering the bottle to top his off, "are you and Félicité still in contact? I mean, you are gorgeous still, but you're well into your thirties. High school was a while ago."

"Emails every now and then," he laughed. "She's married. Two kids. But I came here to learn, and I made a good life. I guess the 'what if's just kind of stuck with me. And this"—his hands waved across the remnants of the romantic meal he'd prepared— "just became a thing that I do. I still love her, in that old high school sweetheart way, but I know we'll never be together."

"So this was all for some old dream?" I chuckled. "And here I was thinking you were trying to seduce me."

I shook my head and smiled as I kicked myself mentally. I really needed to stop thinking every hot guy I met wanted to meet the underside of my comforter. It was bound to get me into trouble. Of course, it had also gotten me into a lot of good trouble too.

"Oh, I was."

Surprised, my eyes locked onto Chester's. His mischievous grin, the same one I'd seen when he'd tumbled nude from the shower, was even sexier in the candlelight. I squinted as I cocked my head, wetting my lips as I took him in. His cheeks were flushed—from the heat or from blushing, I wasn't sure. As he leaned further back against his chair, his shoulders broadened to showcase the expanse of his torso, pecs heaving beneath his shirt as he breathed in the night.

"It's been nearly two decades since high school," he purred. "I may have a few of the same desires, but in all that time, don't you think I've required some—how did you put it?—spice?"

The scent of his sex mixed with the floral aroma of the city as the heat calmed to a simmer with the evening air. Or maybe that was the oaky musk of the last few sips of chardonnay.

I scanned the night sky above us to lock in the moon's travels. I still had a little bit of time before I needed to make my way back to the BOG Witch Ball. And I could think of no better precursor to that party.

I grinned as I rose, pausing a moment to finish the last few drops of my wine, and thanking the man for a fabulous meal. The clean, earthy grunt of the garden around us was intoxicating—the garden Chester had planted with his own strong, thick hands. I let my fingers linger on his as we shook hands, and his eyebrows jumped as he pulled my face toward his.

"It was nothing," he whispered, his breath hot and sensuous as it brushed across my cheek. "Just a little lagniappe. A little… something extra… to make up for my intrusion before."

My eyes caught the bulge in his pants as it jumped, growing large and tight as the fabric of his denim stretched to accommodate his girth. *Speaking of something extra,* I thought. Although there was nothing little about it.

I felt my own pants fight to constrict my excitement as I stood there, bent at the waist, frozen mere inches from his lips. Fuck, he had nice lips. In my mind, ours were already touching, building the anticipation as we shed our clothing to the grass, forming their own spell as our bodies pressed to one another's beneath the starlit New Orleans sky.

CHAPTER 4

The carnal fantasy was hotter than the steam as I showered to prepare myself for the Ball. I could understand why Chester had wanted to use it earlier, and I kicked myself for not letting my kiss reach out to his. Or inviting him in to get ready with me. But even though we'd stopped short of sex, I knew I'd see him again on my trip. He had, after all, offered me a ride on the back of his moped once I was all dressed for the night.

I hated that I couldn't help him with his magical pursuit. Unlike some others—cough, Aiden, cough—I had met in the past, his desires seemed to stem from an altruistic place. Most things that started in love did. And even though Félicité was long gone, the hope Chester was still holding onto seemed kind of sweet. I'd need to reiterate to him that there were all kinds of power. That, even though the power he was looking for wasn't attainable, all kinds of magic could still be found.

I laughed at myself as my mind flashed to more images of us fucking, then shut off the water to stop the flow of the fantasies.

"I'd invite you in if I could," I said.

Chester looked even better in his thin leather jacket. Thick thighs held tight to the idling moped on the curb in front of the Crow's Court, and he grinned as he fixed the spare helmet he'd let me use to the seat. A quick, under my breath spell tamed my hair from the helmet head, and his eyebrows waved as he watched it fall into place.

"So there's really no way to learn magic?" he asked.

"Not that I know of," I sighed. I just couldn't bare to squash all his hope. "But there are other types of power in this world."

"Uh huh," he laughed, pursing his lips.

I could tell we were both thinking the same thing, and I shook my head to bring myself back to the present.

"I'd better get going."

"Have a good night."

I took a few steps toward the door, then stopped to tell him I didn't mind if he wanted to use the main house while I was staying there, but his moped was already puttering away.

The night receptionist smiled as I entered—a genuine smile, not at all like Kara's—and I nodded as I made my way to the elevator bay. A gaggle of witches, all dressed to the nines, stood waiting for the lift. I was glad I'd decided to wear my Moirai outfit. It helped me to fit right in with the well-dressed crew.

As we ascended to the tenth floor ballroom, I considered hanging back to visit Amy in my twenty-second floor suite, but the poor girl looked like she had needed her rest. Besides, depending on how late the party went, I figured I'd probably be coming down to breakfast around the same time she was leaving to start her new job on the boat. Plus, I'd offered her the room as a kindness. Imposing—or expecting gratitude—was not really part of that deal.

"Did you hear they invited Darragh Cullen this year?"

My ears perked up at my name, and I gave a sly smile to the elevator attendant—who'd obviously been given the same dossier of guests as his daytime counterparts—when his eyes met mine.

The witch speaking had a few years on me, but something—I wasn't sure if it was spell or scalpel—had taken years off her face. Her auburn hair, set in exquisite curls, was pulled high to show off the inset ruby earrings that dangled from her lobes. A velvet dress which matched the earrings perfectly swept gracefully from her shoulders.

"Who's that now?" her companion asked, total disinterest in his words as he busied himself with scraping imaginary lint from his suit jacket shoulders.

"You know," she huffed, turning to tweak his lapels and bring his attention to her where it belonged. "The witch who exposed us."

"Oh, that old farce."

From my perch at the back of the elevator car, I could see the other witches present shift and raise their eyebrows at his words. I wasn't quite sure what he meant, but apparently I'd been a topic of discussion within some of the more elite circles. I supposed that made sense. Cressida Troy, one of the richest of our kind in all of Atlanta, had known who I was well before I'd met her. But I was surprised to see the chat pushing past my own city limits.

"You don't think he exposed us?" the woman asked, grinning now that his focus was solely on her.

"Do I think a single witch has the magic to lift a moving SUV from the road with four humans inside of it? As much as I believe faeries will fly out of my ass," he smirked. "The Moral Authority was obviously ready to make us known. There must have been ten, fifteen agents performing that spell. And the grainy camera phone footage hid them all."

"Sounds like someone's a bit insecure about the size of their power, Carmichael."

A third witch spoke up, and a giggle swept the crowd. Even I laughed.

In truth, that magic had been spurred on by adrenaline. At least that's what I'd always thought. Now though, knowing there was a string of wild magic—the type of magic that had branched off into witch and Fae and fae-knew-what-other types of power—twined within me, I wasn't so sure. I still had a long way to go before I knew what all that meant, what all I could do. And with no real teacher to be had, I knew there'd be a lot of trial and error.

"Oh, shove it, Stevens," Carmichael growled. "You mean to tell me you think that was real?"

Stevens shrugged.

"What do you think, Lily?"

"I'm not sure," the witch in the red dress admitted. "But I do know the Council has taken a shine to him. I hear they even paid for his suite. They wouldn't do that if there were not some merit to his craft, don't you think?"

"The Council are fools," Carmichael spat.

"You're just upset the Collectors didn't want you to join their little club," Stevens grinned as the elevator dinged and the attendant began to ratchet the doors open.

"I'm just saying," Carmichael huffed, rolling his eyes as he led his entourage from the car, "if the Council truly wants to overthrow Yaisien, their collection needs more than witches like Darragh Cullen."

His still open mouth snapped shut as he came face to face with Mehrdad's grin, but the smirks on his companions' mouths were still obvious.

"Conrad, Lily, Noah," Mehrdad beamed, layering his voice with the gritted spice of southern decorum, "so happy you could join us again this year. And Darragh! You're looking quite dashing tonight."

The chagrin of the trio was evident, even as they tried to hide their slight turns to take me in. I grinned as I kept my eyes trained on our host, pushing out a slight but ardent burst of my aura to meet his, making sure it brushed the gossip mongers along the way. It'd been quite a while since I'd used an aura push in a non-sexual way. Since magic had been revealed, we'd reverted to simply asking when we were not sure of one's magic rather than pulsing our power out in greeting. But I'd never been one to shy away from a measuring contest. Plus, when Mehrdad returned my thrust, I was no longer sure I could claim it non-sexual.

"Would you give me the honor?" he asked, extending his hand as the trio shuffled their way into the ballroom, the care they were taking to not seem obvious making their eyes on us even more so.

"Don't you need to stay to announce the guests?" I asked, smirking yet enthralled by the lust in his eyes.

"Layla can handle that," he grinned.

I nodded but didn't take his hand, choosing instead to walk beside him as one of his sharp-footed assistants moved to take his place on the welcome committee.

The party was as decadent as it was subdued. Witches, hundreds of them, cloistered about in their fine garb, sipping fine cocktails, and hammering out the finer details of their dealings with their various boards and vendors. Cut flowers—red dahlias, Peruvian lilies, amaryllis, and anemones—were spelled to full bloom and floated as centerpieces above each table. Candles burned and flashed from above the dancing area, adjusting their flames to form dancing constellations above the polished wood of the floor. A jazz band in the corner blew their hearts through trumpets and clarinets, pushed their souls through their fingers to their keyboards, to fill the air with the lively music of the city. And yet…

No one danced. No one laughed. Even Dula, who seemed physically unable to wipe the smile from her face or cease the words from her mouth, held a dour expression as she nodded along to the fourth quarter figures of a man I recognized from his ads as the leading real estate agent in the Greater Salem area.

"I thought these events were known for their hedonism," I chuckled, raising my eyebrows to Mehrdad as he steered us toward one of the bars.

"I imagine the tales of our debauchery are greatly exaggerated outside of this hotel," he smirked, holding up two fingers and pointing to the bottle of my favorite whisky. "But it is still early."

I smiled at his promise and licked my lips as the bartender began to mix two Old Fashioneds. The witch had really done his home work on me. It kind of made me wonder if the Moral Authority had a file they'd dole out to the highest bidders. Still, I couldn't help but find it sweet.

The cocktail was excellent—even if no one's anywhere ever compared to Paul's—and I relaxed a little as the warmth of the whisky coated my tongue through the coolness of the stirred ice.

"How is your subletter settling in?"

The wicked gleam in his eyes proved my intuition about Mehrdad had been right: he was more than happy to supply a bit of inconvenience to the witches who wanted his organization as their own. I imagined, for the witch elite, the games of black cat and newt, of risk and reassessment helped to maintain a bit of frivolity within their otherwise busy days. Or, at the very least, the power plays of their social scenes helped to alleviate some of the fluster of the power plays of their businesses. Mix that with an annual gathering to show off whose cauldron had the most bubbles, whose broomstick had the most baubles, and whose nose had the largest wart, and there were bound to be some interesting evenings. So what if I felt a little like a pawn on their chess boards? It was obvious I'd made a good showing to the boss in my very first play.

"I decided to leave her be," I shrugged, shifting my eyes so he'd know I was in on the joke. "Figured I'd check on her in the morning after she's had the chance to enjoy all the Council has to offer."

"I hope you encouraged her to take advantage of the room service," he grinned. "The Crow's Court's Almas caviar is not to be missed. Ensure she takes a kilogram or two for the road."

My laughter erupted from my throat before I could catch it and turned several heads to our direction. Dula's eyes brightened as they met mine, and she hastened to make her exit from the soulless conversation she was trapped in. Luckily, before she could beeline my way, a few of Cal's cronies blocked her path.

"Well," Mehrdad grinned as he clinked his glass to mine once more, "I have some business to attend to."

"During your own party?"

"You know what they say. No rest for the—"

I wasn't sure if he'd said "weary" or "wicked" as he pushed off through the low hum of the crowd. Honestly, either could have been true. I was certain it took a lot of work to pull off a weekend like this—even if its reputation thus far had far exceeded the reality—but the tilt of his lips also foretold the wickedest of witches behind closed doors. I sighed contentedly as I sipped down the last of my glass and asked the bartender for one more.

"You are the infamous Darragh Cullen."

I thanked the bartender and closed my eyes before I turned around. Despite the trio of Stooges in the elevator, I'd gotten used to folks telling me who I was as a statement rather than asking if it was me. Still, my notoriety was beginning to place me in the cauldron. But that was better than the oven, I supposed.

"And you're the king of the *leiprea-ceann*," I quipped.

Cal had traded his crushed red velvet suit for a thin black leather tailcoat, fitted perfectly to the slimness of his frame, adorned with gold stitching in a winged baroque pattern. A silken black shirt beneath the coat hugged his pale skin, straining just slightly enough at the buttons to imply the vulnerability—and thus, easy removability—of his clothing; and the fit of his slacks left little to the imagination when the light struck the dark fabric just right. The embroidery of his boots matched that of his jacket perfectly. It was obvious the entire ensemble was bespoke.

"Fantastic," he mused. "I'm so glad we know who we're dealing with. Now that those pleasantries are out of the way, I wondered if I might have this dance."

My eyes jutted past his shoulders to the empty dance floor, the neon sign that was my face proclaiming my reluctance. Though that had nothing to do with Cal. He was definitely sexy. Well, that or the recent advent of Spring had spurred my sex drive to full throttle. Or maybe both. But I had enough eyes on me already. Becoming a spectacle on the dance floor was not going to help.

"First rule of business," Cal purred, slipping my cocktail from my hand and passing it to one of the floating waitstaff. "The more they talk about you, the more successful you know you are."

My skin bristled at the sharpness of his aura as he pulled me through the crowd, and he quickly reeled it back with a questioning look in his eye. It felt like metal grinding on metal, like a painting of a picture of a landscape that couldn't quite replicate the real thing. Like a caterpillar attempting to cocoon within a beehive.

I wondered if my own felt as aberrant to him. As unknown yet alluring in its gruffness. I imagined the irritation making him want to drop my hand and run, but it didn't stop him from luring me forward.

"I—uh… I don't know much about dancing," I admitted, tracking the asynchronistic beat of the jazz musicians as we moved. "Unless I'm in a harness and the DJ sticks to four-four time signatures or 80s tunes."

"You certainly know how to paint a picture," Cal grinned, his lips growing thin as they stretched high into his cheekbones. "There'll be plenty of time for that later."

Our shoes tapped the smooth varnish of the wood, and, as if on cue, the jazz band cut to a slowly rendered waltz, clipping out a regal time signature as Cal pulled his body against mine. Tight. Even without looking, I could feel the eyes of the other attendees turn to us. Their soft murmur of business speak faded into the hum of the clarinet's lowest register, and I found my steps through the thrust of Cal's hips on mine.

It felt magical.

Even though, as a witch, I'd been surrounded by magic my entire life—and practicing my own since I was an early teen—the movement of our bodies inside the air conditioned humidity of New Orleans evoked the surrealist fantasies I'd grown to love from my rom-coms and romance novels. I was beginning to understand the true power of the BOG Witch Convention and Gala. It wasn't so much the wheelings and dealings that thickened the wallets and bank accounts of those present. It was the chance—after eons of secrecy—to exist, all of us witches, all of us in one place, none of us having to hide who we truly were. We were together and vocal and unapologetic. And that was a headier intoxication than all the Spring Breakers had on Bourbon Street.

"You're making quite the impression for your first time out,"

Cal whispered as we step-slid-stepped in a triangular formation.

"Just following your lead," I blushed, fumbling a bit but quickly catching up. "Or at least trying to."

"I don't mean your dancing," Cal chuckled. "That's—well, it is what it is. I'm addressing the rumors that both Mehrdad Yaisien and the Council appear to be courting you heavily to their sides. Not to mention the fawning eyes Calendula Hawthorn makes whenever she closes her mouth long enough to peer in your direction."

"Apparently, Cal Juventus likes me too," I mused. "I'm sure this dance will get the toad's tongues popping."

"Like I said. You've got to keep them talking."

Cal smiled as his arms moved from my hips to my hand, and he spun me out and back into his embrace. Our bodies heaved together, his skin cooling me as the sharpness of his clean-shaven cheek brushed against my stubble. The waltz was coming easier now, my legs moving like the practiced motions of a spell I'd learned once and repeated until it was second-nature. I was surprised by how much I was enjoying myself, even with all the corners of eyes still trained in our direction.

"Mehrdad is just being nice to the new guy," I insisted. "The Council paid for a room I haven't used, and I've not heard from them since. And I've known Dula since before she was the big wig she is now. I think she had a crush on my uncle."

"So enticing others is a family trait?" Cal purred.

I slipped my arm around the small of his back, relishing in the fine feel of his coat's soft leather, and dipped him back in a move that felt like it belonged more within a tango than the dance I was trying to perform. His eyes were wide and joyful as he floated his torso back toward mine. My breath caught shallow in my throat as he positioned his face before me, moving so close I could feel his own brush my lips.

"We will meet again, Darragh Cullen," he whispered, releasing me with the last beat of the song and grinning as he stepped away.

I stood shocked for a moment, catching my breath as he departed. But at least our excursion had given permission for the dance floor to fill in a bit, so I didn't appear all alone.

"The second rule of business," Cal growled as he disappeared into the crowd. "Always leave them wanting more."

"It's good to know you're light on your feet, Darragh Cullen. Yet another attribute which makes you a fine candidate for the Council."

My eyes rolled so hard they practically turned my head for me, but the expression on the witch's face proclaimed his flattery wasn't exactly a lie.

"I hope you've found the room to your liking," he continued. "The Yarrow Tooth Suite is simply one of the many perks one can receive through membership in our little enclave."

His suit was new—well-pressed and finely tailored—and the top hat he still wore matched it perfectly. I summoned my most charming smile as I peered upward to meet his amber eyes, taking a moment on the trek up to nod to his two anchored companions.

"I actually haven't seen the room yet," I admitted, keeping my grin as sharp as his own. "Though I'm sure it's beautiful."

His placid expression flushed a bit as he took in my words, and I appreciated the falter in his pomp and circumstance. There was a real witch underneath the airs he put on, so much so that even that little break was almost endearing.

"Is that so?" he asked, quickly catching my appreciation of the real within him and relaxing his demeanor slightly to meet mine. "We assumed from the room service charges you'd had quite the feast."

Oh, Amy. I was glad that whatever she was running from—or towards—had not prevented her from taking full advantage of my offering. Even if it was just for one night, the vibrant girl I'd met on the sidewalk deserved a little taste of the finer things. Besides, it also imparted the message quite clearly that I couldn't be bought, regardless of how much cash they tried to flaunt.

"Seeing how I had made my own arrangements prior to learning of your gift, I offered the room up to a friend," I sighed. "Non-witch. Nice young woman. Just for tonight. I assume that's not a problem for the Council."

The tall man's entourage shared worried glances, but his expression remained perfectly calm.

"No problem at all," he assured me, then, relaxing his body even further to prevent the strain in my neck from looking up to him from becoming too uncomfortable, leaned in to add, "It seems we've gotten off on the wrong foot, Darragh. I warned the other members of the Council you did not seem the type to be swayed by money. So, please. Allow me the chance to start fresh. I am Osmund Linnegard."

Thin and long, his fingers extended toward me, but at least the calluses on his palms were proof he did his own planting when I shook his hand. Even though I ran a magic supply shop, I had trouble respecting any witch who didn't at least grow some of their own spelling ingredients. It took getting our hands dirty to retain our connections to the earth, to the source of our magics. That despite the auspicious persona Osmund put on, he still had the tell-tale markings of the hand trowel's handle went a long way in my book. Perhaps I'd misjudged the organization.

"Charmed, I'm sure, Mister Cullen," Osmond's male lackey chimed in. "Maybe now you will listen to reason in joining our conglomerate."

Or perhaps not. Though even Osmund seemed annoyed by the aggressive eagerness of the witch. I closed my mouth, tilting my head to the side as I took each of the Council members in. Dressed to the nines, their clothing was just as bespoke but altogether more modern and stylish than Osmund's. The male witch—the one who'd spoken—was cute in an *if-I-didn't-know-any-better* sort of way. His brown hair, shorn short on the sides and slicked back against his crown, teetered somewhere between sand and ash, and the thinness of his nose and lips fit his narrow face perfectly. A sharp Adam's apple bobbed just above his bowtie as he swallowed hard at Osmond's glare. His finely manicured fingernails looked to me as if they'd never twisted a potion, let alone met the soil, but I couldn't know for sure unless I shook his hand. Folks of his stature—witch and human alike—often used glamours to disguise the more "common" crafts. And he kept his hands rested securely in the folds of his crossed arms.

The female witch had a softer smile and a knowing gleam in her cinnamon eyes. The jumbo twists in her deep brown hair looked both elegant and casual as they swept back from the roundness of her face and lips. She held herself with grace, her voluptuous curves both a beacon and a promise to every witch who looked her way. The amusement in her eyes told me she'd been where I stood not too long before.

"Do forgive Carter," she laughed, the New Orleans in her accent doing little to hide the way a Haitian lilt had mixed to a Creole roux. "His excitement for the Council is unmatched, though he forgets sometimes to turn it off. And yet it's that same impetuous nature that made him a leader in the field of green energy initiatives."

I smiled. At least if Carter wasn't working with the earth to craft his spells, he was working with the earth to make our impact on her better.

"And you are?" I asked, taking her hand in mine.

"She goes by Lady Z," Carter moaned, his voice softer now as it became evident whose tact created the best inroad with their potential new recruit. "Won't even tell us her full name."

"Names have power," she purred as she looked me in the eye.

For a brief moment, I thought she could see the Fae in my past. It didn't help that she was repeating one of their favorite phrases. But the moment passed, and the gleam returned to her eyes.

"We shan't take more your time, Darragh," Osmund interjected, nodding to dismiss Lady Z and Carter before returning his gaze to me. "It is a party, after all. Though I do hope you will enjoy the Yarrow Tooth Suite at some point this weekend. And, if you're so inclined, give us the opportunity to explain exactly what it is the Council has to offer."

And what it is I have to offer the Council, I thought, but I kept my expression bright.

"Shall we say tomorrow?" Osmund asked, tilting his head with such excitement I was surprised when his top hat did not fall off. "Noon? We can meet in the Lobby and travel wherever you'd like as we chat."

I supposed it wouldn't hurt to hear what they had to say and was about to say as much out loud, but it didn't matter. Osmund and his crew had already disappeared into the crowd, knowing full well I had the curiosity of a black-toed cat.

The witching hour of 3AM had come and gone, and—though I could tell several of the revelers had made it their intent to keep the festival churning until the first rays of the new day pierced the panes of the high arched windows lining the banquet hall—weary witches were beginning to trickle out toward smaller covens or sleep. I'd not seen Mehrdad, Cal, or any of the Council members again after our initial encounters, but Dula kept me company with tales of my uncle's past when she wasn't slipping off to the arms of this witch or that for a dance. I didn't have the heart to tell her, now that I was an adult, I'd heard most of Uncle Gardner's stories before, even though a few of the details had been more blurred in his recollection than in hers. But the company was nice. As the night wore on, I could see her becoming more and more like the frizzy-haired spell caster I remembered from the sales floor at HEX, and that that piece of her persona was ecstatic to have purchase in her life once more.

I didn't want to disturb Amy, and judging by the yawns I was suppressing, I wasn't going to be awake before she set off on whatever adventure she'd determined for herself, so I decided to slip a note under the door to wish her well. My intuition told me she needed more folks on her side. And, though it wasn't much, a comfortable bed and the idea of someone cheering from her corner went a long way.

The twenty-second floor was lush yet more subdued than the lower levels of the hotel which only served to make it altogether more elegant. As all the rooms were vast suites, the hallway lined the exterior wall of the building, giving guests a remarkable view of the French Quarter rooflines from the other side of Canal Street. Gas lamp sconces punctuated the gilded wall coverings, adding a warm and no doubt magicked light between the large bay window groupings with floral chaise lounges. Tables of fresh fruit and produce, juices and iced champagne, breads and fresh herbs dotted the pathway to make the corridor itself a fine and welcoming place to stay. I couldn't even imagine what the suites were like.

Scanning the signage for the Yarrow Tooth, I almost didn't notice Amy, legs pulled beneath her on a fainting couch, head pressed against the window as she took one last look at the beauty of the city before the riverboat took her away. I couldn't blame her. New Orleans truly was a magical place, even for those who didn't have magic in their blood.

"Couldn't sleep?" I asked, keeping my voice low as the chime of the Canal Street streetcar called the patrons of Decatur Street to or from their slumbers, depending on which side of the bottle they were looking at.

But Amy didn't answer.

Amy didn't move.

A chill washed through me even as the warmth of my power pulsed to find her aura, returning to me empty and still. Throat dry, I fished my cell phone from my pocket to dial the front desk, then waited in muted silence.

Even the brightness of a Friday night in New Orleans was darkened as it pushed in waves of disjointed revelry through the windows. I knew better than to touch the body, standing back to take in the posed placidity as if her death was the culmination of some great work of art. There were no signs of struggle, yet everything felt wrong. The pallor of her skin ached against the lamplight around her, begging for a heat which would not come. Her limbs were thin—thinner than I remembered them being when I'd met her on the street—and her neck stretched long as it craned to prop her head on the window.

I shivered as I studied her reflection in the glass. Wide eyes peered steadily into the void as it welcomed her into darkness. Her mouth hung hollow and limp, a whisper of terror still perched like a ghost on the tip of her tongue.

I briefly considered phoning Uncle Gardner. It was nearing 5am in New Orleans, so he and his husband Bill would be ready for their Key West EST six o'clock wakeup soon. Although the MAW had long since pulled any know how on communing with the dead from witchly circulation—to the point where only hacks and liars tended to claim the power—as a Seer, Uncle Gardner may have been able to give me some insight as to what happened. But he generally needed a connection to the subject, and my brief encounter with the living soul of the dead would not have been enough of a conduit. And Learco wouldn't have access to the MAW's archive rooms until at least Monday, assuming he got his job back, so finding a "lost" communing rite was off the spelling table.

It didn't matter anyway. The elevator dinged to announce the arrival of the hotel staff, breaking the silence with rapid movement and anger. I stood helpless as Mister Landry and his staff attempted control, caring less about the death than about the trouble it could cause the hotel. I was quiet as the hotel manager attempted two phone calls through his frustrations, barely able to offer more than a weak yet insistent response when he finally spoke to me.

He was not impressed.

"I said we do not need you here, Mister Cullen," he growled, shooing me toward the exit.

I stood my ground as hotel employees milled about the elevator bay and stairwells to prevent any onlookers who happened to the floor. My eyes were locked on the yawning receptionist—Kara, wasn't it?—as she donned nylon gloves to check the pulse in Amy's neck. Two puncture wounds shone dark against her pale skin as Kara moved Amy's hair back to get at the jugular. They told a story none of us wanted to hear, explaining the paleness and the eeriness in two consecutive periods.

"I said leave, Mister Cullen."

"She was here as my guest," I insisted.

"Yes," the hotel manager growled. "And now, because of you, we have a dead human body and may soon have the cloven hooves of the local police department traipsing through our distinguished halls. That is, should the organization decide to turn to them in place of the MAW. Both of which could prove disadvantageous for our business."

I didn't know what was worse for the man: that a guest was dead or that the guest was what he had deemed a vagabond unworthy of these halls. I squinted as I cocked my head to match his eyes, my power fuming in a fury behind my irises. It was rare for me to get so angry, but his disregard for life incensed me.

"Look," he continued, his voice and demeanor suddenly shifting to one of compassion. "She was a street urchin junkie. If not for you, she would have perished in some alleyway all the same. You gave her a night of beauty. You should rest easy in that knowledge."

My brow furrowed at his sudden change of tact until I turned to see Mehrdad approaching us. The witch was all business, even in his robe and sweatpants, even with the obvious sleep still heavy on his deep brown eyes. The door to the suite at the far end of the hallway was still closing behind him as he stomped forward with a grumpy purpose, but I was glad he was there. Finally, someone could understand the situation before the hotel staff tried to sweep it all under the rug..

"Mister Landry," he said softly, nodding to the manager before turning his eyes to me. "Darragh, if you could come with me."

CHAPTER 5

I planted my palms firmly against the grass. Manicured and curated as it was, I could still feel the natural systems teeming beneath the soil; the aching of the roots to spread, the insects pupating, the call of the river against the soil from so many yards away. All of it was connected still beneath the concrete and the asphalt, beneath the padding feet of the tourists or the pawing hooves of the horses lined up along the street just beyond the gates, ready to take folks out to look at all that was man-made and beautiful and resting just above all that was eternal and cyclical and gorgeous in its own right.

Amy. She would never feel those calls again. Never succumb to all that was natural on her path through all that was built. All the magic that was the world—magic she didn't even need to be a witch to experience—was now lost to her.

I had no idea why I was taking her death so hard. Maybe it was the lack of sleep, the four large coffees, or the utter lack of consideration any of the hotel staff had paid to her corpse. Even Mehrdad, for all his forced empathy for me, had seemed to have already washed his hands of the young girl simply because she was human. After he'd arrived at the crime scene, he'd accompanied me down to the lobby and stood there nonchalantly, heaving in the filtered light of the rising sun, as I'd tried unsuccessfully to convince him there was more at play than some runaway overdosing on whatever was hip and available. There was more to Amy than that.

Or maybe all my time spent glancing over my shoulders for Faeries and MAW agents was really getting to me.

The sun had been awake for two hours now, and the glow that bounced from the river lit up the stone of the buildings with an emphatic joy. I swallowed hard, breathing deeply to center myself, and pulled my palms from the earth. I needed sleep, but I'd already cycled through fatigue to second wind to caffeine high. At least the buzz in my ears was subsiding thanks to the moments I'd spent with the earth. Or maybe I was just too far gone to notice it.

The truth was, I had stayed awake expecting my phone to ring at any minute. I was sure Mehrdad would reach out—having finally heard all I'd told him through the haze of his grogginess— to tell me Amy's death would be fully investigated. Or that the late night assumptions I'd made had been unfounded, and the actual cause of her demise had been something much more mundane. But Mehrdad hadn't called. And whatever closure I was seeking wouldn't come.

I pulled myself to my feet, shaking a bit as my legs settled beneath me, and wiped the remnants of grass from my ass as a familiar voice called my name.

"What are you doing here?" Chester asked, grinning wildly from the sidewalk by the gate of the Square. "I figured you'd be sound asleep after your wild night of dancing."

I shrugged at his quip, relaxing a little as a smirk crossed my lips, and I shook my head.

"Just out seeing the sites," I smiled. There was no use

bringing him into the drama of the night before. Especially since, apparently, the Crow's Court and the BOG Witches were already so quick to forget it. "I thought I might find something cool at the Art Market."

Chester nodded, shifting the large wicker basket he carried under one arm as he checked his watch.

"Still a bit early for the folks to set up here in the Square, but I'm sure they'll get here soon," he said. "Meantime, it's the first Farmer's Market of the season down on the Riverwalk. If you feel like checking it out."

I hesitated as a yawn overtook my body, shivering the whole of me in an attempt to push the sleep from setting in.

"Or my moped's over on Madison," he added, tilting his head backwards in the direction of the street. "This early, I can usually find a free parking spot for her. I can give you a lift back to the house if you want to hit the sheets."

"Nah," I said as I joined him on the sidewalk. "We can check out the Market first. I'm still shaking the night from my system anyway."

"Must've been one hell of a time," Chester laughed.

"Something like that. Can we grab a coffee first?"

So what if I'd had four? One more would keep me upright, and the line at Cafe du Monde didn't seem too long. I went with an iced latte while Chester got his chicory-laden brew black, no sugar with a flirty joke about keeping his abs tight.

Walking felt good, and I sighed as the tension released from my muscles. Although I could still feel the death—and the surreal circumstances I was sure surrounded it—gnawing at the back of my mind, fretting wouldn't lead to real answers. Plus, it felt good to be in Chester's company. He had the same calming effect on me as Learco did, and—despite his brighter features—the same seductive smile as Cernun. I matched pace with him as we turned left at St. Peter to cross Decatur, breathing in the rich, loamy air as we descended toward the waterfront.

"I usually get a booth here myself," Chester grinned as we rounded toward the walking path. "But Spring just hit, so the first Market of the season is more for the ramp and strawberry growers. Still, you can sometimes find great stuff. And it's just nice to smell all that green again."

There was a reason why, once upon a time, so many witch families had moved to agriculture or distilling. That connection with the soil, with the plants and their energy, with the green of it all—whether by growing and farming or by foraging and brewing—kept us connected with the source of our magics and allowed us to practice in the open without being caught. Farmer Sinclair could grow the biggest gourds in the county, and everyone would smile at his green thumb. Brewmaster Carter could infuse the best damn beer this side of the Mississippi, and no one would laugh at her pointed hat. Often, it had become a point of pride.

On this literal side of the Mississippi, flannel and overall-clad growers were laying out baskets of fresh-cut herbs, trays of oysters in ice, and tins of crawfish climbing over one another with the little pincers raised in protest. I figured there was bound to be a witch or two amongst the purveyors, but it also filled me with joy and hope to see so many humans who, like Chester, truly appreciated all that the earth could give. *It's all about life,* I reminded myself. *And death,* my brain quickly added, goading myself mentally as only I could do. *The two are together in the natural cycle.*

I supposed I was right, even if that lingering buzz in my brain was fixed to the thought that Amy's death was unnatural. Even if my mind's eye was locked on the tiny marks along her neck; the bloodless paleness of her limbs; the ever-repeating, ever-louder call of "vampire!"

As far as I knew, vampires weren't real. But then again, a year ago, I would have said the same thing about the Fae-folk. Just over four years ago, witches were the stuff of legend too, at least as far as the human world was concerned.

"You got quite the battle raging there in your mind, huh?" Chester noted, more amusement than concern in his eyes as we paused to survey the offerings before us. "That eternal war between sun and sleep getting to you?"

"I guess I am a little tired," I lied. Well, half-lied. "But I think the Market will do me some good."

At the very least, I thought, *I might meet some magically-inclined folks who'd have their ladles in the cauldrons of the local lore.* I was hoping that would be enough to sate my foreboding. Though I knew what I heard had the potential to make it worse.

"So you're kind of famous, huh?"

The Farmer's Market was a bust. Sure, there were plenty of witch-run stalls—Kathy's Cove had particularly robust strawberries—but once their recognition fawning had faded and Chester had wandered off to the next booth, any questions I had about other creatures who may have gone bump in the night were met with laughter or blank stares. Most of the witches thought I was yanking their broom handles, calling back to my own sudden spell that got caught on camera and revealed us to the planet with a tongue-in-cheek wink. Other's thought I'd fallen off the broom altogether. Hell, maybe I had.

"Infamous might be the better word," I replied to Chester's question as I helped him strap his haul of berries and greens to the front of his bike. "I, uh… I'm kinda the guy who exposed us all to the world."

"You're the dude from the video!" Chester exclaimed as if he'd just realized it, though something told me he'd already known. "I remember when that came out. It made a lot of waves. Well, not around here really, but in the world at large. 'Round here, we all kind of grew up knowing about the witch down the way, you know. Fuck, I mean, voodoo and ghosts and zombies and vampires and séances are all pretty standard practice in these parts. But it was kind of cool seeing the rest of the world catch on."

"Zombies and vampires?" I asked, raising my eyebrows as I took the spare helmet from his hands and adjusted the strap to fit my chin.

Chester shrugged as he donned his own.

"Never met any personally," he said. "I mean, caught a few zombies leaving Bourbon in the early light of day, but not the kind we're talking about. Still, I'm thinking there's a lot to this world we don't know, right?"

I could see his thoughts trail off to Félicité and his quest for his own magic to win her. If there was more out there than we realized, that could keep his hope alive even if it had morphed beyond a means to get the girl.

"Lici said her family had a history of fighting vamps, anyway," he continued. "Told me she'd never seen one, but all the know-how was in her family's Book of Shadows."

"Seriously?" I asked.

I was trying to sound incredulous and respectful simultaneously, but what came out of my mouth accomplished neither. Still, Chester just shrugged once more as he straddled his moped and motioned for me to climb on behind him.

"I mean," I corrected as I took my seat and wrapped my arms around his chest to hold on, "I'd love to see that Book. I enjoy reading the histories passed down through different families."

Chester cranked the bike and pushed us off toward Decatur, weaving through the crowds of cars and carriages and pedestrians as if he was the only one on the road.

"I think her older sister got it," he yelled over his shoulder as the cool breeze of travel rushed past us. "I'd bet money she keeps it at the museum."

My brow furrowed with my question, but Chester's quick swerve to miss a tourist knocked the words from my lips.

Concern clouded Chester's eyes as he idled in the drop off lane in front of the hotel, the low hum of his moped agitating the valet nearby but him paying the witch no mind.

"You sure you don't want me to wait for you?" he asked. "You're kind of looking like you're at death's door."

He didn't know how right he was, but I was certain it was the fatigue he was reading on my features and not my ever-present worry over Amy's death. Still, I'd promised Osmund Linnegard I'd meet him at noon, and I was a witch of my word. Besides, I thought, I could potentially use the meeting as a means of gathering some information on what had happened.

But I *did* need sleep. And I certainly wasn't ready to use that damn suite.

"You need to get your Market haul back to the house," I insisted. "But if you're in the area in an hour or so, I wouldn't turn down a ride."

The air conditioned chill as I entered sent a shiver across

my skin, and I stifled my shake with a quick glance around the lobby. Osmund, Carter, and Lady Z stood in congress near the concierge desk, smiling as they saw me walking towards them. Carter and Lady Z idled respectfully as Osmund approached me with his hand extended.

"Good to see you, Darragh," he beamed. "And precisely on time. Though I see you're in last night's ensemble. I suppose that means the suite has still gone unused by you, but you no doubt had one hell of a night."

I blushed as I looked to the Moirai ensemble still draped across my body, whispering a quick spell—*galghlan*—to quickly steam away the wrinkles the fabric had picked up from the lawn of Jackson Square.

"Impressive," Osmund noted, true appreciation in his voice. "And yet another reason why I believe you to be perfect for the Council."

"I still don't even know what the Council is," I admitted.

Or why a simple anti-wrinkle spell would be impressive, I thought. But, I supposed, flattery was high on the list of their recruitment tactics.

"That would be why you're here," Osmund spoke, nodding his head to signal action from Carter and Lady Z. "It's quite obvious to me you are not one for the hard sell. But perhaps you'll indulge us in a drink at the hotel bar? Or maybe lunch?"

My stomach growled audibly at the mention of food, not satiated by the coffee and the few ripe berries of my morning stroll through the Farmer's Market. Plus, if the conversation went sideways, I could always pay for my own meal and leave. No quid pro quo required. Besides, if the Council knew anything about what had happened to Amy, a few drinks could help loosen their lips.

"I've really only got an hour in my schedule," I sighed.

"Seminars?"

"Sleep."

Osmund's laugh was cheerful, even though it verged a little on rehearsed.

I eyed Lady Z and Carter negotiating a table with the host stationed at the far end of the lobby as I followed Osmund across the marble floor to the stepped entryway to the Crow's Cove. As we arrived, the maître d' urged us to follow him in with a placid yet polite expression, but I could tell he was perturbed. The space was obviously closed, utilizing the hours between the lunch rush and dinner service for a much needed break and reset, yet somehow the Council had spelled the locks from the doors. Money was often a more powerful magic than any of the stuff that swirled within us. Or, at least, I had to assume it was the offer of a generous tip that had given us access and not sanctimonious threats. Otherwise these definitely were not the type of witches I wanted to be acquainted with.

The restaurant was long and narrow, with intimate, well-spaced tables settled along the windowed exterior and a long, dimly-lit bar cascading the interior wall. The bartender, elbow-deep in slices of fresh citrus looked puzzled as we passed, but gave me a sympathetic nod and shrug as I mouthed "I'm sorry." We were sat at a table far from the entrance, and the maître d' stepped away as the bartender appeared by our table. He introduced himself, smiled as graciously as he could manage, then whispered *incendo* to ignite the candle resting between the already stationed water glasses and silverware setups. I rarely heard witches use Latin in their incantations anymore—the power urging it on was thought to be as dead as the language, and most practitioners who spoke it had discovered their power without the help of a family line or Book of Shadows—though it did the trick just fine.

"May I get y'all started on something to drink?" Simon, the

bartender, asked as he passed menus around the table. "I'm afraid the specials for the evening are not ready at the moment, though the kitchen can supply you with our standards."

"I believe a round of Old Fashioneds are in order," Osmund called, and I smirked at yet another BOG Witch knowing more about me than I did about them.

Carter opened his mouth to protest, but quickly resided at Osmund's glare. I busied myself with the menu, attempting to find something that wouldn't burden the cooks too much at this off time of day, as the trio ordered their meals. My po' boy and fries were a far cry from the panéed rabbit, bouillabaisse, and coq a vin chosen by the rest of the table, but I felt good about it.

"An extra grand is in it for you and the chef should you make it speedy and allow us our privacy," Osmund announced as Simon tucked the pen back into the pocket of his apron, and I couldn't help but scoff.

"So purchasing people is a regular practice of the Council, I assume," I sniped as Simon scurried away.

"And you would deny that poor witch the gratuity he deserves?" Carter snapped back. "For Fae's sake, he did his spell in Latin."

"Now, now, boys," Lady Z scolded. "Do we need to separate you two?"

"I apologize for my bluntness, Darragh," Carter quickly demurred. "Green energies, despite the aid they give to the natural world, despite the purchasing power it requires to get them started, are not exactly a place where money is appreciated. The circles I run in—the Council aside, of course—do not tend to look kindly upon those of means, even when those means are helping them. Which, I assure you, Darragh, is what the Council is attempting to do. I don't think you understand precisely what is at stake."

"How could he?" Lady Z asked.

"Oh, I believe he does," Osmund said, leaning in to settle down his companions. "That's why he's here, after all. He understands something is amiss. Even if he is unsure of what it is, instinct and curiosity have brought him to our table."

Like a black cat drawn to a Faerie ring, I thought. I just hoped the toadstools they were feeding me wouldn't be rife with poison. Still, there was a chance their "something amiss" had ties to Amy's and who knew how many other's deaths. Of course, it was Linnegard who'd commanded the hotel staff to keep her murder in house. That didn't bode well for them.

My eyes squinted as I bit my tongue, searching the remarkably calm faces of my companions as Simon distributed the quartet of Old Fashioneds to our seats with a promise that our meals would be right out.

"Let us toast," Osmund called, lifting his glass as I timidly wrapped my fingers around mine. "To the possibilities of coming together for the greater good of magical creatures everywhere."

I was still confused as I tapped my glass to his. If Osmund and his crew thought that covering up the death and possible murder of a young woman fell into the "greater good" category, we certainly had differing definitions of the words. But he was right: curiosity kept me grounded in my seat. And my intrigue made him smile.

"You seem to appreciate a straight forward approach, Darragh," Osmund continued as he licked his lips of the whisky flavor from his sip. "As such, I'll be blunt. Those with magicks are under attack. Dark forces are at work against us, making strides to supplant our power with their own. Do you know of what I speak?"

Now we were getting somewhere. Even if I had no desire to join the Council, if they knew something—*anything*—about what had happened to Amy, perhaps it was best to lay all my cards out on the table. I leaned forward, checking behind me to ensure Simon wasn't approaching before I scanned the faces of the Council's recruitment force.

"Vampires," I said bluntly.

Lady Z's eyes went wide as Carter's expression descended into a strange mix of anger and worry. Osmund, for his part, simply laughed.

"I had heard you were funny," he hissed. "But this is no laughing matter. Magically-inclined creatures, all of us, have faced centuries of backlash and brutality. Some of it stems from misunderstandings, as with regimes and organizations like the Catholic Church and their Crusades or today's Defend Mankind From Magic. And yet, there is also danger brewing from within our ranks. Deals penned into spell books within the Business Owners Gathering; Magics sealed and buried by the Moral Authority. Power stripped from us by those chosen to protect and serve. You, of all creatures, must understand the dark times which lie ahead."

"The attempts to police and control us have grown ten-fold since we were outed in the public eye," Lady Z added. "As you, Darragh Cullen, are the face of that outing, we can think of no better witch to be the face of our mission to regain and retain what is rightfully ours."

I slumped against the back of my chair, lips pursing as I took in their words. Mehrdad's analysis of the Council had been correct: it was all just a power grab. And what better way to grab power than to convince folks others were out to take it from them?

"You seem disappointed," Carter huffed, folding his hands on the table before him to naturally lift his shoulders and make himself appear taller as he stared me down. "Yet you have had your own run ins with the MAW and the DMFM. You have experienced firsthand how they have attempted to stifle your magic."

That was true. But as much disdain as I help for both organizations, I could never be convinced that a Machiavellian transfer of power from one group to another would solve the problem. Hell, even before my time in the Fae Realm—before traversing the magical barriers they had constructed to define some sense of safety from one another and the alienation and fear those barricades had created—I'd believed in a much more egalitarian approach. The Council's research should have told them that instead of just my go to drink.

"How is the Council any better than the MAW?" I blurted. "Particularly after what you did to Amy"

Lady Z's eyes darkened as they shot from me to Osmund, and she hid her lips behind the rim of her glass. The combination of whisky and bitters, glowing from the sunlight passing through the window at her back, matched her irises perfectly.

"Who?" Osmund asked, his anger at being rebuffed overtaking his usual calm. "Oh, that silly vagabond you allowed to sully your room. Whatever would you think we did to that miserable child?"

"She died last night. In this hotel. And you commanded the staff to cover it up."

Osmund licked his lips as he cocked his head to look at me, taking a deep breath to regain his composure.

"It was a calculated risk," he said, dropping his voice to a near purr as he attempted to reel me back in. "That young woman had no family, no steady place of residence. There is no one who will come looking for her. And we will see to it that her remains are respected and lain to rest. But. Were her death to become public knowledge—her death which occurred within the walls of a magic-owned hotel during a magic-exclusive event—the DMFM would use that knowledge as evidence of our misdeeds. It would be all the ammunition they needed to convince hundreds if not millions of new followers to their way of thinking."

Though his voice was low and had fallen back into his usual, practiced clip, I could still hear the anger that urged the syllables forward. I hated it, but I understood the truth in his words. Still, that was no reason for someone, even in death, to simply disappear. Especially if she had been murdered. But maybe Osmund truly didn't know anything supernatural had occurred there. Maybe he actually believed she had died by her own hand. That or he was damn good at hiding the truth behind his stolid veneer.

Lady Z, though, was not as good at keeping it together. She didn't have the cool, casual demeanor of a seasoned Council member yet. And I already knew it was a countenance I never wanted to possess. Her eyes rushed around the room, the worry lines in her forehead becoming more evident as she caught my stare. But Osmund wasn't about to entertain her emotions.

"It was also a risk we took for you," he said, settling back into his chair with the confidence of having something over me. "Do not think for one moment the circumstances around her appearance in this hotel would remain secret were her demise to get out. Was it not you, Darragh Cullen, who invited her into our midst? The MAW and the DMFM already hate you—perhaps more than you hate them. Your involvement in that girl's demise would not go unnoticed or unanswered."

Osmund leaned back to give Simon access to the place settings as he approached with our plates, but this time he did not stop speaking, ensuring I saw his knowledge as some sort of the power he was so desperately grasping towards.

"If, as you insinuate, she did not die naturally, her final hours, her blood-drained body are on you. You could renew your position as the poster child for their movements, for their policing and their persecution. Or you could join us."

Simon, for his part, was doing his best to place our meals and slip away as quickly as possible, but Osmund's palm gripped his forearm as he started to leave, holding the bartender in place as the Council leader continued to stare me down.

"Your choice is simple: the feared and detested Wicked Witch of the East or the powerful and protected newest member of the Council. I believe we've given you enough to consider. Boy," he said turning finally to the trembling bartender, "please wrap up Mister Cullen's food in a travel container." Then, to me, he added: "Feel free to utilize the room we've so graciously provided you to mull it over. After all, there's no use crying over baseborn swill. Or denying the charms we creatures of power require."

I was shaken to my core as I rose from the table, breathing deep to calm myself as I followed Simon to the bar, thanked him for my food, then slipped back into the lobby and outside. I wanted to get as far away from the Council as I could, and was grateful to see Chester's smiling face atop his waiting moped, asking if I needed a ride.

My head swam with the threats and implications Osmund had thrown at me. But what really stuck out—the thing my mind attached to as the wavering fear around his words subsided in the smell of Chester's thin leather jacket and the rush of wind on my face—was not the Council's deliberate separation of an "us" versus a "them." It was the vocabulary Osmund had used to describe that "us."

I didn't think I'd heard him say the word "witch" once. He'd called us "magically-inclined" or "creatures of power." I was certain he knew more than he was letting on, that his decision to hide Amy's death had not been to service me. And his language, while it didn't scream "vampire" did not deny their existence.

My head spun as we turned off of Magazine Street and did not stop until my face met the unfamiliar pillow in my rented bedroom.

Sleep would not come easily although my body craved it desperately. The foreign bed, the strange sheets, and the memory of Amy's body waged war against my internal clock, stifling every sigh that threatened to lull me into slumber. The red numbers of the alarm clock blurred across my slitted eyes until the tonality of blood, of mystical creatures watching me from the edges of some darkness filled the whole of my vision. When my eyes did close, exsanguinated features haunted me.

I did manage some sleep though—I must have—and before I knew it, dusk had descended upon the city. The first stars of an ethereal night called me to rise.

My feet were uneasy as I shifted to a seated position on the mattress, dangling them from the side and reaching my toes to find purchase on the floor. It took a moment for my eyes to adjust to the incongruity of the bedroom. First, the pale background of the throw pillows I'd tossed to the chair waiting in the corner appeared like billboards calling silly catch-phrases about my craft to me before the side tables made their edges clear and I could manage my way toward the light switch. The brightness was jarring as I flipped it on, and I quickly shielded my eyes before turning it off again. *Better to feel my way through the dark*, I decided subconsciously, as if something deep within me was guiding my movements. I slipped into a pair of grey sweatpants I'd left draped over the foot of the bed before I slipped from the room.

Chester was all smiles in his *Thyme For A Kitchen Witch* apron as I jostled through the doorway.

"The creature of the night awakes," he caroled as he spun his spoon through the bubbling pot on the stove. "I figured you might be hungry after sleeping all day. Have a seat; have a seat."

"All day?" I asked as I pulled out one of the chairs at the breakfast table and poured my body atop the woven wicker seat. "I feel like I just laid down."

"You were dead to the world," he laughed, adjusting the heat on the burner and moving to retrieve a bowl from one of the upper cabinets. He obviously knew his way around the kitchen well, and I wondered how many other guests he'd cooked for.

"It's real sweet of you," I said, smiling as he pressed the button on the coffee maker and the lively smell of brewing beans began to waft my way, "but you didn't have to cook for me again."

Chester shrugged.

"I like cooking," he said, still smiling as if his lips were stuck that way. It was almost unnerving, the way his grin never faltered. I shook my head and wiped the last bits of sleep from the corners of my eyes.

"Besides," he continued, "maybe you could let the owners know how much I did for you. Could be a nice amenity to add to the OccultList listing, right? I feel like a lot of witches would appreciate a human concierge to tend to their needs when they stay here."

I wasn't sure if he was joking, but I laughed anyway.

"Here you go!" he said, placing a bowl in front of me and widening his eyes. "It's black broth. Spartan warriors used to eat it, and I have a feeling you've got quite the battle ahead."

He spun quickly on his heels and doddered around the room as I stared into the plate before me. Thick chunks of red meat swam within a still boiling crimson sauce. My face flushed and then paled as I breathed in the heavy scent of iron. I knew I couldn't eat it, but I didn't want to be rude.

"This is really sweet," I lied, "but they're feeding us at the convention. You could put it in the fridge for later."

"Aww." Chester's words sounded like a frown and yet he continued to beam. "That's okay. Black broth doesn't really keep. All the blood starts to clot. But I can make a fresh batch later. Why don't we get you to that hotel?"

I was at the Crow's Court before I knew it. I wasn't even sure how I'd made it upstairs—I must have been more sleep deprived than I realized—but there I was, standing in the ballroom on the tenth floor, waiting for the party to begin. Although I'd slept the day away, I'd still managed to arrive early.

Decorated for the second night's party, the ballroom was draped in black as if the color were a suit it could wear. New Orleans stood at attention just beyond the window panes, a city turned martyr as it became a safe haven for all of the darkness the rest of the world was too inadequate to hold. I could feel it emanating off the rooftops, billowing out from the courtyard gardens of the Quarter, and wafting the scent of Jessamine and Fern as if it could carry the guise of "natural" if it just tried hard enough. It was spellbinding in the way it wove through the arteries of the land, lifting like music on the march.

The main doors leapt open behind me, and I spun in place. My breath caught in my throat. There were not a bevy of handsome, well-dressed witches making their way into the room. Instead, it was the darkness, creeping in from the streets to billow around me like shadows in my mind's eye. Swirling, the black took the form of ghouls—of Balor or Aiden or pitch-clad MAW agents—slinking in the silence of an elaborate dance I didn't know the steps to, yet one they insisted I join. They spun my body, taking turns jostling me like a marionette, bending the arms and legs of my voodoo doll until my jilted steps syncopated with their own. I tried to fight, tried to quell the sensations rippling across my body like external magic struggling to siphon my own, but it was no use. My form bent and pulled with theirs, with all the demons of my past, until our movements merged into one.

A song I'd never heard before yet recognized deep within my core hummed in time with our movements. Primal and new and whole and unfinished, I wasn't certain if we were lurching to its melody or if the song itself was created by the positions our bodies took as we ambled through the ritual. A low, moaning wail startled me, arcing to join the melée of our dance. It took me far too long to realize it was coming from me.

Balor—one of the Balors; there were no many of them— steeled his fiery eye on mine and smirked as Aiden's hands found purchase on my stomach. Two faceless MAW agents—faceless save for the red irises burning where their eyes should be—clasped strong, ethereal fingers around my arms, holding me akimbo even as they pushed and pulled my limbs in time with the rhythm. Aiden's fingers burned against my clothing, straight through to my flesh, as he coaxed the wild magic within me to action. Verdant and vigorous, it swelled inside me, sparking across my skin as it reached toward the darkness swirling around me, as it pulled me to become a part of it.

"That which is missing contains the element of the whole," Balor groaned.

"That which flowed like rivers must be made once more to roar," Aiden purred.

"To the darkness!" Balor called. "To the night!"

The lament in my throat swelled to a howl as my power shot from me, igniting the demons around me as their jaws gaped to expose their fangs. Sharpened, opalescent daggers in a sea of black, their bared growls grew and merged until the darkness was erased by their rust-specked white, until their maws were so large they threatened to swallow me whole.

CHAPTER 6

I awoke with the sunset, the nocturnal call of the city beckoning me from my agitated state of dreaming with a swift and sudden thump. I wasn't sure what my vision was trying to tell me exactly, but I knew I needed to pay attention. Some witches—like my Uncle Gardner—were incredibly gifted seers, able to quickly decipher codes or outright see what was to come in every blink of their eyes. Other witches never got a notion of the past or future save for what they'd been told. I was somewhere in between. My dreams had a way of showing me things I'd only realize as real in retrospect. Still, in learning to pay attention to them, I was beginning to catch on faster. Whatever the hell was happening in New Orleans, I just hoped I'd figure it out before anyone else died.

I knew the demons my mind had conjured were simply placeholders for whatever evil was truly at work. And though I imagined—or maybe hoped—the idea of vampires was a stretch, my dream did tell me where to start looking: the BOG Witch Convention. I knew the setting wasn't a mistake. Hell, maybe the vampires weren't either. Just because I'd never seen one didn't mean they weren't out there somewhere. A year prior, I'd have said the same thing about the Fae. And now I knew their reality all too well.

I attempted to shake the low-crawling fear from my mind as I pulled myself from the sheets. My phone screen showed a couple texts from Learco and Cernun, both wishing me well and telling me things were fine in Atlanta, that they hoped I was having fun. It was comforting to hear from them. What would have been more comforting was having them by my side. I considered calling them for a brief moment. But the minute they heard the worry in my voice, the moment I'd told them about what was going on, they'd hop the next flight out of Hartsfield to Armstrong. I couldn't risk putting them in danger—again. At least not until I knew more.

I used a warming spell to reheat the jambalaya Chester had left plated in the fridge for me, and rolled my eyes at the green that lit up on the Magic in Monitoring device plugged in next to the stove where a microwave or toaster would normally be.

"Thanks for keeping that little charm on your approved list, Moral Authority," I grumbled aloud, though I was sure—or at least I hoped—the MIM/MAW program didn't actually allow them to listen in. "Fae forbid a witch overheats his leftovers."

I ate slowly, letting the rice soak up the grump that had settled into my belly, resigning myself to some level of external cheer before I headed back to the Crow's Court. If I was planning to investigate Amy's death from inside the organization, I needed my suspicion buried as deep within me as possible. I'd learned as much from Learco. His dedication to reworking the Moral Authority of Witches' practice from within had required as much nuance as knowhow. Of course, his association with me had all but destroyed that work, but I was certain come Monday that would be rectified. Too, outright asking had not gone over too well with the Council, and threats and recriminations would get me nowhere.

The night sky had taken on an onyx so pure even the refracted lights of the city paled against it by the time I'd finished eating, showered, and slipped out the front door. I prayed my gratitude toward the New Moon in a quick, silent ritual as I waited on the sidewalk for my Broomer to arrive.

Growing up on the farm, my mother had insisted on lavish ceremonies twice a month to honor the lunar cycles, culminating on both the Full and New Moon events. My father and I had joined her in whatever field was laying fallow that season, dancing and chanting and pulling power from the sky through to the revitalizing land. There was food and chocolate, candles and oracle cards, intention and reverence. Now, most months, only the intention and reverence were left, but I still made it a point to honor the moon in her cycle.

I closed my eyes, grinning as the moon's whisper replied to my call, the dark reset of her journey spilling through the atmosphere to displace my fear with calm.

You've got this, she told me. *Whatever this is, you've faced—and survived—a hell of a lot worse.*

"Not by choice," I reminded her. "The facing, that is. Not the surviving."

And she laughed, the faint joy of her still sounding through me as I poured myself into the backseat of the car.

"Uh, excuse me, Mister Cullen."

The young witch who'd checked me in for the conference leapt up from her seat as I attempted to breeze past her into the ballroom. All business and clipboards, she motioned for me to join her at her table.

My brow furrowed as I staggered her way, glancing down at my ensemble to make sure I was appropriately dressed. It may not have been the Moirai outfit I'd worn the night before—or the amazing green suit Learco had given me to wear the final evening—but I still thought I looked pretty sharp, if a little poor compared to the suits and gowns parading passed us. I was gearing up to complain that nothing on my invitation had mentioned a dress code when she smiled sourly at me.

"You failed to attend any of your seminars or presentations today," she barked, eyebrows raised as if she'd asked me a question.

"I was told the classes were just a formality," I stuttered in time with the clicking of her pencil eraser as she tapped it swiftly against her clipboard.

"By whom?"

"Mehrdad," I winced. I didn't like playing the I-know-your-boss card, especially when someone was just trying to do their job, but her disdain toward me was starting to feel a bit pointed.

"Mister Yaisin was mistaken," she growled, clearly not impressed by my attempt to fly over her head. "While, as founder, he does have the ability to grant that luxury to some members— members who've been with us and supported us for years—first time attendees to the Business Owner's Gathering of Witches are required to attend all events. It's necessitated by our bylaws in order to maintain our tax status. I'm afraid your failure to do so means I cannot grant you admission to this evening's festivities."

My lips pursed into a semi-frown as I considered her words. So much for my casual investigation. The young witch mistook my grimace for sadness.

"I truly am sorry, Mister Cullen," she said, her voice softer now yet with the same stern cadence she'd used to admonish me.

"Darragh," I insisted.

"Darragh," she nodded. "Layla."

I took her hand cautiously when she offered it. Her fingers were stiff and her palm was cold as we shook, the deep red of her nails sharp against my wrist. A resigned breath slipped her lips as she pulled her hand back to her clipboard, her face grim as she returned her eyes to mine.

"You have three courses scheduled for tomorrow afternoon, and two others on Monday prior to the closing ball," she winced. "Should you attend them all, start to finish, not even a moment late, you can go to the masquerade. Though, were I you, I'd just return to Atlanta now. If you have no intentions of taking the convention seriously and are simply here for the parties, you have nothing to offer our organization."

Her swift return to her clipped phrasing startled me, and the question in my eyes was met with a stoic glare. I shrugged off the snickers of the patrons still entering as Layla widened her eyes and turned away from me, nodding toward the elevator bay as she retook her seat at the "welcome" table.

I leaned back against the hum of the elevator wall as the attendant pressed the button and cranked his lever to take me upwards, only the slightest agitation evident after having guided me all the way down to the lobby first. It had taken the ten floor descent for me to resolve to stay. Just because I couldn't get into the ballroom didn't mean I couldn't still investigate. Whatever killed Amy had done so on the twenty-second floor, and I still had a key to the room.

"Sorry for the double-back," I grimaced, hoping to gain some points with the second shift since it hadn't gone so well with the daytime attendees.

"It's my job, sir," the attendant huffed gruffly. "At least until two. Then you're on your own until the day shift comes at six."

I guessed I wasn't fairing any better with the night crew. Joking that I thought I could handle hitting a button didn't help.

I froze for a moment in the hallway, startled by the total inconsequence of the scene. Less than twenty-four hours prior, a young woman's body had been found, a supposed investigation had unfolded, but the hotel staff had reset the space as if nothing had ever even happened. It was somehow more unnerving than Amy's body had been, the way the living so quickly replaced what was true with what they wished there to be.

If there were any clues to be found, they'd be inside a vacuum cleaner bag in some hotel staff closet or whisked away by the sanitation spell they'd no doubt performed once the body had been carried away. Still, even with the whitewashing of the hall, I figured it was worth seeing if any trace energy was left behind. Psychic energies were not exactly my specialty, but with enough connection, I thought I may have been able to pick something up. Plus, I had no idea what my newfound wild magic was capable of. Maybe now that I was beginning to understand it—to look back on my past and figure out how it had been there all along—I'd be able to pull more than I'd once thought I could.

I approached the sofa more timidly than I wanted, the determination in my gut staggered by the fear in my mind. My desire to figure things out—to not allow Amy to be overlooked— ricocheted against the steadfast barriers the safety of not knowing had built. The last thing I wanted to do was open another can of worms in my life, especially when I was certain they weren't the spring-loaded fake snakes of a child's magician's kit but would be just as impossible to shove back behind the lid all the same. Once I understood what had happened to Amy, there was no turning back. But I also understood the young woman I had met on the street, the sweet girl who'd needed one night of extravagance—of not looking over her shoulder—to stifle the agony of whatever it was she was running away from, deserved someone in her corner, even if it was too late for her to know.

I pulled my cell phone from my pocket, disabling the WiFi and the cellular signal to prevent any distractions as I tried to concentrate. Too, the lack of invisible rays would make my circle stronger in the event I needed to conjure a quick mode of protection against anyone who happened by and didn't like what I was trying to do. Fuck, I hoped I wouldn't need to cast a circle.

I slipped slowly around the far edge of the fainting couch and lingered for a too-long moment with my back to the sofa in the narrow expanse of the bay between glass and cushion. It truly was a glorious view. The French Quarter spread before me, a reveled enclave of history and modernity: revered, historic architecture housing the best tomorrow had to offer; the luminescence of oil lamps shining warmly beside the LEDs and neons; the throngs of people who knew the earth marching alongside those who knew the asphalt, all of whom loved the night. Even the river to my right, winding like a serpent to reach the delta, housed the rambunctious reckoning of gamblers throwing back dice and bourbon on the decks of majestic riverboats. The city was so alive, so beautiful. I really hoped I'd get the chance to explore its offerings. Especially since right behind me was death.

I reminded myself to breathe as I sat, pulling myself into the closest approximation my limbs could make of the position I'd discovered Amy's body in. Fuck. The way she was sitting alone should have told me something was wrong. But as uncomfortable as I was, I swallowed hard to center myself, closed my eyes, and tapped into the swirl of green power already quickening inside of me.

It would have been easier with a little yarrow to guide my journey or maybe some rue to ward off whatever evil was lurking in the darkness, but a good old-fashioned divination would work with just my magic. As long as I guided it correctly. Of course, there was no telling what I'd actually see. If the death had been traumatic enough—when was death ever not traumatic?—or if the connection a witch had to the life that was lost was strong enough, a powerful imprint could lead to a vision that offered answers. If the connection was faint, I'd at most get a jumble of disconnected sights burned through a flurry of emotions.

Still, I had to believe I'd get something, especially if I triggered the wild magic inside of me. Hell, even some humans got divinations from time to time. Not every ghost sighting was had by witch-kind after all. Of course, we witches knew the "ghosts" were simply manifest memories so strong they reverberated through time. And while all of me hoped Amy's passing hadn't been brutal enough to trigger that, a part of me wished for answers.

Clearing my mind of all my fears and suspicions so they wouldn't force falsities into what I saw wasn't an easy task, but I allowed my breath to leave me blank as I centered in on Amy's last moments, hoping to catch a glimpse of what she had seen.

"No son of mine is gonna be seen making fancy eyes at no boy!"

The bellowing voice was gruff, stained with grease and tobacco, and sent a shiver down my spine before I even opened my eyes. His face was as red as his words, pinched and beleaguered as he huffed from the shadowed doorway of a bedroom lined with posters of young female pop stars or bare-chested superheroes in power poses. A trash can by a desk was overflowing with crumpled pages torn from notebooks, and a set of unused dumbbells sat discarded in the corner of the carpeted floor.

It was a bedroom I knew all-too-well from my own queer coming-of-age. Of course, my experience had been different— happier, more accepting. Most magical folks were able to see beyond what society "expected" to allow for a broader spectrum of existence. Maybe it came hand-in-hand with our enlightened connection to all that was natural. Wherever my magic had taken me, this was not a pleasant memory.

"Well, I've got good news for you, Dad," Amy cried, her voice feeling like it was coming from my own chest with determined resignation, as if everything that had been bubbling inside of her was pouring out whether she liked it or not. "I'm not your son. I'm your daughter."

My eyes shifted, and I caught sight of myself—errr, Amy—in the mirror perched atop her dresser. She was young, fourteen at most, but despite their tearful red, I could still see the girl-who'd-seen-too-much-already in her eyes. Her hair was shorter, choppy, and a dirtier blonde; and her neck craned with the poor posture of pubescence, but it was definitely her.

Shit. My spell had taken me too far back. And seeing this made me hate her death even more.

"Get out!" Amy's father spat. But now the vitriol was gone, replaced by a cruel dismissal that cratered every pump of her heart. "Now."

Amy closed her eyes.

When they opened again, there was a body, just not the one I'd been searching for. Not hers.

The corpse looked peaceful though, prone as if she were sleeping, arms crossed over her chest, eyes closed and mouth slightly ajar. I—or maybe it was Amy—kept expecting her to snore, to jerk herself awake with the sudden noise, to, at any moment, fight off the hands of Hades and sit up on the bed with a laugh. But that wouldn't happen. Both Amy and I knew the truth.

Amy's eyes were sore, bloodshot and dry from all the saline that had passed through them. It made it difficult to see, but I could still make out the contents on the bedside table: three plastic, compact-shaped containers I knew were stolen birth control pills; a few strips of clear patches; two vials of estradiol valerate with a syringe; and a stack of final notices.

Amy slipped the medications into her purse, then leaned in to kiss the body on the forehead.

"Thank you for taking care of me, Mama Nadine," she coughed, the words heavy on her parched throat as she adjusted the lace where Nadine's wig had come unglued.

My own eyes felt as dry as Amy's despite the tears that welled within them, threatening to pull me from the vision. She'd endured so much in such a short amount of time. I felt the wild magic surge within my gut, spurred onward by the swirl of rage and sorrow of being so close to Amy's memories. Except they weren't her emotions; they were my own. The intensity of her past was breaking my hold on the spell. I could feel it beginning to slip away as the hazy outlines of the Crow's Court corridor began to insert themselves into the edges of Amy's past.

And yet, the untamed power within me pushed forth, hurrying me toward the end, as if it was one with my thoughts. It was unlike anything I'd ever felt before, and I'd felt a lot of magic in my time. My breath fell ragged as the deep of my power yelled for my focus. It was right. Whatever was happening to my magic was later's discovery. My intent lay with Amy.

As the vision picked up speed, I picked up understanding. No matter how quick the flash, I saw it all with crystal clarity. It felt as if I were looking straight into the flaw inside the quartz tower point, allowing its scattered prism to point me through all of her past. I saw thumbs on roadsides and knew she would get into an old red sedan that would take her as far west as it was going, then a pale blue minivan would take her "as far as Gulfport," then a little black two-door with a driver whose brown hair was so greasy it looked black inside the too-tinted windows. I knew she would tell him "no" once, assertively when his hand slipped off the gearshift and onto her knee. I felt my own fingernails twitch with the sensation of the driver's skin when she scratched the back of his hand when it "accidentally" slipped again. My chest burned with her hopelessness when he left her ten miles from the nearest gas station on the side of the road. My lips curled with her smile at a group of no more than seventeen-year-olds on their way to the Crescent City to see if their fake IDs would work or if Louisiana still had those Under 21 laws on the books. I saw her first glimpse of New Orleans as the SUV made its way across the High Rise over Lake Pontchartrain; experienced the renewed sense of place and magic the city lit within her.

The vision was moving even faster now, one sight blurring into the next as I tried to keep it all straight in my head. We were nearing the end. We were nearing answers.

I saw her meet me on the sidewalk; felt the shame mixed with encouragement as she listened to the front desk's insistence she was unworthy while I stood up for her. I felt her excitement crash as she spun into my hotel room and fell to the bed for a long-awaited, comfortable sleep; saw the darkness as she closed her eyes.

In the blackness, the hazy edges of the corridor were becoming solid. I was losing my grip on the vision.

I heard a faint knocking. Shit. Someone was trying to draw me out of my trance. I willed it onward, gasping as the wild within me zapped my eyelids open.

There *was* knocking. At Amy's hotel room door!

It was too dark to see anything as she opened it. My eyes struggled to adapt to the black. I felt Amy's shock, her pain as she was pulled from the room, and then… nothing. An absence swallowed the pain, and yet the numbness was nearly worse. I felt her wooziness as the blood left her body, the quickness of her life slowing so rapidly it began to stand still. It was still too dark to see anything. A spell was definitely at work.

I felt Amy's body forced into place on the fainting couch, and adjusted my own body to better match the position my memory had slightly altered. As I sank my own limbs into place, my vision began to surge. The orange flames of the oil lamps along the hall flickered into the edges of my sight. I was weak. Amy was dying. But as the spirit left her body, the spell that was upon her left too.

My eyes—Amy's eyes—fluttered as the last bit of strength left her. The ding of the elevator reaching the floor chimed far away. Amy's eyes—my eyes—ached toward the noise just in time to see the figure disappear behind the door.

The knocking was back though—louder now—closer. But it didn't matter. My eyelids were so tired. I just wanted to close them, to shut down, to find peace.

"Darragh? Are you okay?"

I gasped as I pulled to, shaking the remnants of my trance away as my own life sucked back inside of me.

Shit. I'd never experienced such an intense vision before. Was this what seers like Uncle Gardner felt every time he used those aspects of his power? It was no wonder he didn't break out the skill too often.

A rough breath escaped my throat as I opened my eyes to

find Mehrdad standing over me, a worried expression clouding his features as he knocked his knuckles against the window to try to summon me from the beyond. When he saw me come to, his woe slipped into an apprehensive smile.

"Too much to drink at the party?" he laughed.

I shook my head. The somersault of emotions I'd experienced still ran ramshackle in my mind, and I had to force my own thoughts to take control.

"I wasn't allowed at the party," I smiled, the sound of my own voice helping to ground me to the present. "So no drinks for this witch."

Mehrdad frowned, then rolled his eyes as understanding flashed through them.

"That Layla really is a stickler for the rules, huh?" he laughed. "I'll have a talk with her. You are a special guest, after all. The regular 'first-timer' protocol need not apply."

"Thanks," I grinned, stretching as I stood to guide my body back into itself. Mehrdad caught my arm as I stumbled, and my smile matched his as our eyes met. "Thanks," I repeated.

His fingers fell from my tricep as I pulled my face away from his. Fae dammit, he was sexy. And though a part of me wanted to tell him what I'd just seen, I didn't want to drag him into things until I had a better grip on what was happening.

I blushed again, then nodded as I turned to make my way to the Yarrow Tooth Suite door.

"So, uh. If it wasn't the booze, what knocked you out like that?" he called. His arms were crossed over his chest, and the worry was back on his eyebrows.

"I tried a seeing trance," I admitted. "They're not really my strong suit, but I wanted to see if I could figure out anything that happened to Amy."

"And?"

I shook my head. Mehrdad frowned as he crossed to place his hands on my shoulders.

"Darragh," he sighed. "I know you feel responsible for letting her use your room, but the truth is, if it hadn't happened here, it would have happened regardless. At least you gave her a comfortable bed and a beautiful view for her last few hours. But her overdose was not your fault."

The BOG Witches and the Council, even if they were on opposing sides, had settled on the same narrative regarding Amy's death. Even though I knew it wasn't the truth—hell, any witch with eyes could see that—I had a hard time believing a vast conspiracy was taking hold. Besides, if I needed to investigate, I'd get a lot more details from those who didn't believe I was searching for answers.

"Look," he continued, his face brightening as if the empty sentiment he'd given me was enough to change my mind. "The party downstairs is kind of drying out. I'm having a few select friends over to my room for a more… intimate affair."

My eyes squinted as I tilted my head, and he laughed.

"No, not like that. At least not yet," he purred. "Just some drinks and conversation."

As if on cue, the elevator door dinged and Mehrdad's guests poured out. So it really wasn't a pick up line. *At least not yet.* I found myself blushing again as I shook my head. The spell had taken a lot out of me. And I needed time to process it.

I was about to formally decline his invitation as the guests swarmed around us.

The men and women milled about the hallways with the mix of disinterest and attention appropriate for their imagined stations. These were the people so far above it all, they were able to look down on everything that happened around them. I imagined I'd be able to get some real information out of them if I pulled the right tarot cards from the deck.

But what really quenched it was seeing Lady Z move to flank Mehrdad's smirk.

What was one of the recruiters for the Council doing amongst this lot? I was certain that was what each of them would label as a Conflict of Interest in their personnel files.

Beneath the luxury of her hair, she wore the same blank gasp I'd seen in Amy's memory, the same cold steel in her eyes as she'd had while standing just beyond the closing elevator door watching Amy's life slip finally away.

CHAPTER 7

I felt like a detective from Doyle or Christie or Poe. Except I didn't have a doctor companion or a bushy French mustache. But Dupin's ability to get into the literal mind of the murderer, to read the thoughts of those around him did have *witchcraft* written all over it, which was no surprise given Edgar Allan's supposed lineage. One thing was certain though: I was going to need every bit of the calm, collected, and casual demeanor each of those characters possessed if I had any hope of getting to the bottom of the cause of Amy's demise. Especially since I had deposited myself directly into the center of the hornet's nest.

I gave a quick smile when Lady Z caught me glancing at her from across the expanse of Mehrdad's exquisite living room. Now that my vision had settled into memory and I was able to distinguish my own thoughts from the intertwined emotions of the spell, I was positive it was her face I had seen as the life slipped from Amy's body. At best, she—or the Council—was somehow involved. At worst, given both collectives' inclination to sweep the whole thing under the cauldron, the entire Gathering was culpable. And here I was, chumming up to them.

"Tell me, Darragh. How are you finding the fête?" The man

who spoke had a narrow face and a nasal quality to his voice that seemed more trained than natural. But it could have been the alcohol that was flowing as freely from Mehrdad's ensuite bar as it had been at the party downstairs. "What I wouldn't give to see it all again with the eyes of a first-timer."

"It's definitely been an interesting experience, Wulfric—"

"Ric is fine."

"Ric," I continued, nodding to commit the shortened version of his name to memory as I carefully chose my words. I could feel Mehrdad and Lady Z watching me even as they continued their own conversations around the room, Mehrdad warning me not to say anything; Lady Z checking if I would. "Most everyone I've met has been incredibly nice and welcoming. Even though I still feel a little out of my league in comparison to everyone else here."

Mehrdad and Lady Z both sighed away from our conversation as Ric guffawed and clasped his palm around my knee.

"I felt exactly the same during my first Gala," he chuckled. "What was it? Five years ago now? Back before *you* allowed us to do things like this out in the open. One acclimates quickly. A casual change in cadence boosts a hell of a lot of confidence. Before you know it, you fit right in."

"Still," I insisted, "you all have multinational empires. I run a single supply shop that I inherited from my uncle. I mean, I do alright, but… What do you do again?"

The blush on Ric's face looked as practiced as his cadence.

"I facilitate the mobile transport of the magically-inclined in all fifty states as well as twenty-three countries."

"He means he owns Broomer," Marguerite cooed, smiling seductively from the other side of the olive in her martini coup.

"Says the witch CEO of over ten thousand Brew coffee locations," Ric poked back.

Marguerite leaned forward with a glimmer in her eye and a

smirk on her lips as she perched her glass gingerly on the edge of the coffee table. Damn. Even their fun seemed choreographed. Every tilt of their head, every cross of their legs was blocked like they were in a play. Or, I guess, we were in a play. I just needed to gear my lines toward garnering information without making it obvious I was going off script.

"See?" I laughed as I attempted to stay in the scene. "Compared to y'all, I'm the mold on a Dead Man's Toe."

"Come now," Ric insisted, leaning forward to clasp my knee once again. "It's your first Gala, and you've already found your way into Mehrdad's afterparties. You've got Cal Juventus courting you heavily. We all saw that little number on the dance floor last night."

"I heard the Council is wooing him too," Marguerite giggled as she popped her eyebrows at Ric. "Paid for his room even. Just down the hall."

It was working! I wasn't much for bragging or for being the center of attention—except for when it came to certain bedroom rituals with Cernun and Learco—but I'd heard the whispers of the other BOG Witches already so I knew a little demure quip would get the conversation steered toward the Council. My eyes caught the quick twitch on Lady Z's face at the sub-organization's name, but she only turned her ear in our direction. It didn't matter though. Her presence couldn't stop the tongues from wagging. And if she interrupted to stop the conversation, my suspicions would be confirmed.

Despite Osmund's total disregard for Amy's death, or maybe because of it, I was certain the Council had something to do with what happened to her. The room she was in belonged to them, after all. Not to mention the group's apparent aversion to those "non-magical." Even without seeing Lady Z slinking away in Amy's final memory, my misgivings were already scattered around them like Fae dust.

The subtle clearing of Mehrdad's throat as he crossed to our enclave refocused me to the conversation.

"A room that as of yet has gone unused," Mehrdad smirked. "Darragh does not seem to be one so easily impressed by the Council's antics."

"Then perhaps I could coax you as well," Marguerite smiled. "Your connection to Learco Clarke could definitely help reduce the cost of the spells on our MAW-sanctioned warming cups."

"Not to mention the bonuses a burst of the Kyteler fortune could yield if your Cernun were to become an investor," Ric purred.

Of course it was my boyfriends who'd sparked the interest of the group. But neither of them owned a business. Damn. In a world that was all about connections, it shouldn't have surprised me. Plus, the lustful undertones in Mehrdad's stare assured me I had plenty to offer on my own.

Still, there was something about his insistence on making sure they knew my room had not been used which irked me. I supposed he didn't want word of Amy's death to spread and cause a panic amongst the revelers. I decided I could come back to that later. Being a detective was not as easy as those authors had made it seem, especially when the very thing being investigated was being obscured and concealed.

And I certainly didn't want to become the witch who screamed vampire. That had not gone over well with Osmund.

My best bet was to play along in hopes the pieces would fall into place.

"It sounds like my boyfriends are the witches who should have been invited and wooed," I huffed.

"Where you go, they follow," Ric smirked. "Or so we've been told."

I nodded and tried to make myself blush in the same way Ric had. The showmanship of it all was actually kind of addictive.

"What's the deal with the Council anyway?" I asked, leaning forward conspiratorially like my mother used to do when her book club devolved into gossip. I raised my eyebrows and averted my eyes slightly, just in time to catch Lady Z's face pale. "I heard someone call them 'the Collectors.'"

Mehrdad laughed as he took a seat in the chair next to Marguerite. His smirk told me he knew what I was doing, but he seemed satisfied I wouldn't reveal anything about the murder. Lady Z's face had barely regained its color as she moved to stand behind the seating arrangement with her arms crossed over her chest. She wasn't subtle, but I wasn't about to out her as a plant. Plus, I assumed I'd get more information on the Council's true nature from her facial expressions than I would from whatever rumors Ric and Marguerite had to impart.

"I've told you already of the coup they attempted with the Gala," Mehrdad sighed. "Since then, they've been hellbent on growing their membership in order to try again. Hence the Collector moniker."

Lady Z's face was placid, but the slight twitch at the corner of her lip said there was more to the story than Mehrdad was saying or knew.

"That's one reason," Marguerite chirped, finishing off her cocktail and reaching for the bottle of gin on the side table to refill her glass.

"Don't be crass," Ric warned, winking widely to acknowledge his enjoyment of the Brew CEO's bluntness.

"The truth is never crass," she shot back. "Besides, as a woman, I clawed for my position with straightforward direction, not by making notches on my bedposts."

"Are you insinuating their nickname is about sexual

conquests?" I asked as Lady Z stifled a giggle.

"No. Not at all. I'm flat out saying it." Marguerite's lips pursed as she wrapped them around the edge of her glass, swallowing the floral mixture of juniper and evergreen without portraying a hint of the alcohol it contained on her cheeks. Her shoulders shrugged as she leaned back in her chair. "We witches, we all know, are highly sexual beings. It's in our nature. It's in the magic that swirls in our guts the moment our bodies begin to twitch and moan their way into adulthood. And yet, we do not use that sex for power. The Council does. In their attempts to collect more meat for their stores, they pervert the sacred potency of our bodies."

"Sounds like someone's upset they weren't invited to the orgy," Ric poked.

"Did someone say 'orgy?'"

Cal's voice startled us all as he spoke. He grinned his lascivious smile, licking his lips as if he were hungry from the open doorway. A calm spread over most of the guests as he invited himself in, but I could see Lady Z stiffen.

"Good," Cal continued as he crossed to us. "I was hoping I hadn't missed it already."

"Oh, Cal," Marguerite purred, standing to kiss him gingerly on each cheek, their hands clasped between them as their faces parted. "If only I had all the parts you were looking for."

"You know your parts work wonders," he purred, kissing her ferociously before his eyes found me. "As for the other equipment required, I imagine this room to be rife with volunteers."

"Here, here," Ric cheered, leaning back against the couch and loosing his tie for the first time all evening.

He had the same lustful glint in his eye as Mehrdad now held in his, the same longing that crowded the eyes of all the guests as they ended their disparate conversations to feather the edges of our grouping.

This was the real reason for the afterparty. The irony in calling out the Council for similar practices seemed lost on the group as Cal's arrival—the intense vibration of his aura—called the crowd to order. The blunt ferocity of it still grated against mine, pulsing the way the gravel of my childhood dirt roads had scraped across my knees. Though, that pain, in and of itself, was beginning to feel… good. I wondered if his aura felt that way against everyone's or if it was just mine. I wondered if the pain was intentional. It neared the edges of a power play, like a challenge, like a lure.

A part of me wanted to take the bait. I could think of worse ways to spend the night than with an entourage of sexy witches, scratching their brooms toward a sweaty, spent morning light. I felt the push of aura after aura enter the room, making the entirety of the suite heavy and thick with promise. All those auras at once was euphoric, undulating across every scrap of cloth-bare skin as the heat quickened our pulses.

Well, everyone's except for Lady Z's. Her eyes rolled as she pulled away from the conversion, quickly making her way toward the door.

Her exit was all I needed to break the spell on myself. I winced sincerely, standing with a forced frown.

"Maybe next time," I sighed. "As a first-timer, I have classes I must attend tomorrow. We wouldn't want anyone to lose their tax write offs, now would we?"

"Keep talking fiscal responsibility," Ric cooed, reaching out to run his hand across my ass.

His shirt was fully unbuttoned now, pushed to either side of his torso as his loosened but still bound tie hung like a rope across his surprisingly toned chest. His nipples were garnets in the sea of white-blond fur which covered his pecs, and a well-rendered tattoo of his namesake wolf clawed its way out from his shoulder. The bulge in his tailored slacks promised more surprises as he peered up at me with a seductive smile.

"Yes, Darragh," Mehrdad moaned as first his jacket and then his button-up slipped from his slim shoulders to pile by his feet on the floor. "I'll speak with Layla first thing tomorrow. Please. Stay."

Damn it! He was even sexier than I'd imagined. Not that I'd spent a good deal of time on picturing what he looked like under his expensive suits since I'd met him at that opening reception. Of course, I hadn't.

His svelte torso was packed with tense muscles aching beneath the tight expanse of his tan skin. The blackness of the hair that slipped from his naval behind the hemline of his pants was nearly as dark as Cernun's, and the nimble way his tongue excited his lips was almost as seductive. My eyes traced the tendons in his neck down to the flex in his biceps as his hands moved to work the buckle on his belt.

Fuck. They were really going to make it hard—quite literally—to leave.

"Perhaps Darragh would prefer a boy's night," Marguerite moaned, leaning into Cal's lips as he pushed her bra strap from her shoulder and worked his way across her neck. "The ladies and I can simply watch if you'd prefer."

"No, please," I insisted. "Y'all should enjoy yourselves. I'll… um… Tomorrow then."

I stumbled over my words as I worked my way through the shed clothing to the door. I could tell Mehrdad was disappointed—I was a bit, too—but by the way he was looking at Ric as he rounded the coffee table, I knew he was going to be okay. The guttural groans escaping from the witches' throats were singing loudly as I made my way into the hallway, but vanished, alongside the push of their auras, as soon as I closed the door. Those rooms really were soundproofed.

I sighed as I spun, collecting my thoughts as I freed myself from the fantasy that had overtaken my system, coming to just in time to see Lady Z step into the elevator car. My feet started moving before I could even call her name, and I arrived at the closing doors just in time to see the look on her face as the reflective gold shut to replace her worry with mine. It was the exact same expression I'd seen in Amy's death memory.

Shit. I needed to question her. And now that her eyes told me she knew I knew, I needed to move fast, before I had a chance to become a target.

Privacy concerns or decorative choices had left the Floor Call signs off the elevators on the Suite floors, but my ears told me the gears were pulling the car upwards toward the roof. How was that for old fashioned detective work? Still, there was no time to congratulate myself, and I couldn't wait for the elevator to return. My boyfriends would have told me to slow down, but I knew I was onto something, and I hoped my wild magic would keep me safe.

"I'll find out what happened to you," I whispered to Amy's ghost as I made my way toward the stairwell.

The warmth of Spring had yet to overtake the night, even in the swamp of New Orleans, as I pushed into the open air twenty-four stories above the city. The far-away sounds of merrymakers and music hung to the night like pin-paper stars. It was a magic unto itself, the way the soul of a city—of the nature it was built upon—could carry on in revelry even as horror unfolded high above. They were the true creatures of the night; those paying reverence to the freedoms and beauties offered by the darkened skies, in the pull of the moon, not whomever—or whatever—had caused this.

Grotesque in their simplicity, the bodies were posed in a seated embrace, their limbs just awkward enough in their stretch and turn to immediately show any onlooker something was amiss. The woman's eyes were closed, her head tilted sharply at the chin to meet the man's shoulder. It had happened by force and after death, the twist disconnected from the congenial flow of neck and shoulders as her body morphed to the unnatural coercion of shape. Even her hands, folded neatly across her lap, appeared out of place and small, two fingers on her right hand lifted and crooked like the chelicerae of a spider ready to pounce. Her right leg, bent clumsily at the knee, pushed just slightly too far outward and planted against the rooftop decking in order to keep the pose stable. The whole of her settled against her companion as if to make the two small specs of blood, the only remnants of it anywhere near her body, as evident to the blackened moon as possible, like whomever had done this was challenging the sky.

The man's left arm angled sharply back and then forward at the elbow, the bend resting atop the corner of a planter before returning to cup the woman's shoulder. His eyes were open though, and his head tilted back from the woman's forehead, mouth agape as if waiting for a breath to return or escape, caught in the liminal space of eternity. His punctures were hidden by the frizzed brown flow of the woman's hair, but I was sure they were there.

Cautiously, I tapped into the agitated sea of magic swirling in my gut, hoping the same disruptive beat of my heart, the drumming bolts of my pulse in my ears, would equalize the growing fear that zizzed through my body. Whoever had killed this couple, whatever had murdered Amy, was staying close to the Gathering. And they seemed to enjoy posing the bodies like dolls meant for ritual. Maybe now Mehrdad would take me seriously when I told him something was afoot. I just wished it hadn't required more death for him to believe me.

I stepped forward carefully, crossing the rooftop garden and terrace to get a closer look, making certain I did not disturb anything that could become a clue. My breath burned as it held in my chest, my lungs taking it upon themselves to pay homage to the stillness of the crime scene. Every step felt like an eternity against the forever of the couple's state. Every twitch of my muscles felt so cold and casual against the stillness.

I didn't recognize either of the corpses, and while I certainly had not memorized the faces of every BOG Witch attendee, something told me these two had been human before their demise. The pallor of their skin—a perfect match to the Brunia buds Learco loved to include when he bought me flowers—was a near-transparent silver blue, and the expressions on their faces announced "sleep" moreso than "death." Or at least they would have if the man's hollow eyes hadn't been wide open, if their bodies hadn't been exsanguinated.

There was nothing of note about their clothing—no rips, no dishevelment, no drops of blood. There were no signs of struggle; no obvious clues waiting to be found on or around the bench where they were staged. There were no glowing eyes watching the scene from the shadows, and if Lady Z had made it all the way to the rooftop, she had departed before I'd arrived. I couldn't imagine that she would have had time to drain the pair and set the scene before I'd hoofed it up the stairs. No. The notion of vampires was seeming more real by the minute.

I closed my eyes as I stood before them, breathing deep the pre-dawn air to center myself to the task at hand. Although imprinting on Amy's death had taken a lot out of me, I hoped my connection to the air element this high above the earth would make it easier. It also couldn't hurt that the bodies were still here. Even if I had no idea who they were, no meeting of their living souls to draw from, perhaps the wild magic within me would be able to give me at least a glimpse of what happened to them. And a glimpse was better than the nothing I had to go on.

I let my magic sizzle within me, careful to keep it contained beneath my skin as my mind—and only my mind—reached out towards their pasts. If the MAW showed up, and now that there were three deaths connected to a witch event they likely would, I wanted no trace of my spell sign near the crime scene. Leland Hyde was still looking for any reason to flame me at the stake, and even if spell signatures wouldn't hold up in the MAW's kangaroo court, it wasn't worth the risk. Besides, I needed my magic to bolster my sight, not theirs.

I steeled my nerves for what I was about to receive, asked the new moon for her guidance, and pushed my thoughts backwards through the undulation of time to find… nothing. Only blackness stared back at me. Although seeing spells had never boiled my cauldron, this felt different. It did not hold the fizzle of a spell refusing to work. No, I could still sense my magic coursing through to action. My power just couldn't break through. It was as if something—some dark and powerful force—was blocking my spell.

I sighed as the power subsided within me, exhaling the tension that had begun to pound against my temples. Shit. There was nothing else I could get from the scene. So much for my master detective fantasies. It was time to bring in the authorities. And though I didn't believe the human-manned police were the right agency to deal with this, perhaps they'd take these deaths more seriously than the witches below me seemed to. At any rate, these were human deaths—however mystical they seemed—and the human world had their own type of MAW to handle these things.

But I'd let Mehrdad make that call.

"Hey, uh… It's Darragh," I called quietly after a gentle knock on the door went unanswered. I had to assume whatever spell was placed to keep the suites at the Crow's Court soundproofed from the inside out also allowed voices to carry from the outside in. But maybe they were too wrapped up in the magic of their orgy to hear my calls. I felt bad interrupting what had looked like one hell of a good time, but I knew the leader of the BOG Witch Gala would want to know.

I was about to turn to go when the door swung open. Mehrdad, sweaty and erect and without a hint of modesty, stood snarling with a wildfire in his eyes.

"It pleases me you've decided to return," he growled.

"Oh, uh…"

I stumbled over my words as my eyes couldn't help but take him in. Moisture turned his tan skin golden against the dim lamplight of the hallway, accenting the compact curves of his muscles which thumped with the moaning chorus behind him. His cock throbbed in the air between us, excited by my vision caressing the shaft as if my hands were clutching it. And by the Fae, I wanted to. But that wasn't why I was here.

"Could I talk to you? In private. For a moment," I stuttered, pulling myself together and my irises back to his.

His smile widened as he licked his lips.

"Need a little one on one time before you're ready to join the party?" he purred.

"That's not what this is about."

The seriousness of my stature struck him, and Mehrdad nodded, snapping quickly out of his role as seducer and into the duty of leader. He pawed the wall beside him to produce a red and white silken robe, wrapping it around himself as he stepped out to join me in the hallway. I sighed as he covered his frame, and once more as I watched the power of his erection subside beneath the cloth, but it was for the best. As much as I'd enjoyed the view, the scene on the roof was more important.

"What is it, Darragh?" he asked, concern replacing lust as he closed the door behind him and placed his hand on my shoulder. "You look rattled to the bone."

"There are two more bodies," I said, trying to sound secure even as my voice wavered. "Drained of blood, just as Amy's was. I wanted to tell you first. Before I called the cops."

"Where are they?" Mehrdad asked.

I assumed he'd want to put on more clothing, but he was already barreling toward the elevator.

"Roof," I said, falling into step behind him.

His finger hovered above the elevator call button before he thought better of it. It was only a few flights after all. We could make it up before the car even made it back to our floor. I nodded in agreement as I followed him to the stairs.

"And they were right here? You're sure?"

"Yes!" I insisted. "No more than ten minutes ago."

Mehrdad frowned as he inspected the region around the

rooftop bench, clutching the lapels of his robe tightly as his eyes darted around the empty area.

"Could it have just been a couple?" he asked. "As in a living couple enjoying some alone time in the garden?"

My mind flashed to the image of the bodies: the way their limbs twisted, the giant stare in the open eyes on the man. There was no way they were alive. Plus, I'd spent so much time right in front of them, ogling them, tripping through the blackness of whatever had blocked my spell for a good fifteen minutes. And there were the puncture wounds—just like Amy's—adorning their necks.

Of course, I hadn't actually touched them. So maybe the woman truly was asleep. Maybe the man's frozen expression was more to do with my morbid curiosity and a strange witch approaching them in the middle of the night. Shit.

"They were human," I insisted. "And you've bought out the entire hotel for the BOG Witches."

"Yes, but humans do tend to find their way inside," he countered. "As you well know know."

The circus performance of my facial expressions brought a sympathy to Mehrdad's eyes.

"That young woman you let stay in your room," he sighed, crossing to me and cupping his hand on my trembling bicep, "her death has you shaken. I believe that you believe what you think was here. But you're seeing Faerie circles where there's only toadstools."

I nodded, clutching his hand with my own and emitting a sorrowful sigh. I was certain of what I'd seen, but whatever was at work here was also covering its tracks. And if I wanted to get to the bottom of it, the fewer witches I put in harm's way, the better.

"Maybe you're right," I lied. "I haven't slept well since last night. My mind is playing tricks on me. Sorry I interrupted your… festivities."

"Interrupt any time you'd like." The mischievous grin Mehrdad had worn when he'd answered the door returned to his face. "Or better yet, join in."

I chuckled as his hand dropped from my arm and he made his way toward the elevator bay.

"What were you doing on the roof anyway?" he asked as we waited for the car to arrive.

"Just came up to commune with the moon."

It was another lie, but whatever suspicions I had about Lady Z were best kept under my pointed hat, at least until they were confirmed. I wasn't about to start a witch hunt amongst a hotel of witches. Besides, her presence near both murder scenes after the fact proved as little as her dual alliances with Mehrdad's crew and the Council. I decided I needed to speak with her directly—and with a strong protection amulet or two—before I made any accusations.

"Well," Mehrdad was saying, "as much I'd love to take you back to my room, I think it's probably best for you to get some sleep in your own. That way, tomorrow evening can become—"

He stopped short as the elevator door dinged open, and I turned to take in what had dropped his jaw.

There was Lady Z. Her skin was gray, her head slumped to the side, and her body poured against the gilded corner of the lift. The unmistakable punctures I'd witnessed on the other three bodies adorned her neck like a calling card, like a warning.

Mehrdad swallowed hard as he looked from her body to me, coming to his senses quickly as he reached out to stop the closing doors.

"It appears there may be more to your story than I thought," he sighed, a distraught tinge to his voice as his business-mind attempted to compartmentalize what was happening. "Perhaps we should talk in your room."

CHAPTER 8

My own footsteps pounded against my eardrums. Quick and purposeful, they beelined from the green and yellow damask settee that was nearly too uncomfortable to sit on to the fine walnut writing desk that had never seen a drop of ink. If I hadn't been so distracted—sent to my room like a child being scolded while Mehrdad dealt with the aftermath of Lady Z's body—I may have been able to take the time to appreciate how truly beautiful the Yarrow Tooth Suite was. Its lively greens and floral golds were perfectly suited to my power, and though the ornate expanse of it verged on ostentatious in its folksy garb, its knowing hand fell just short of the kitsch found in my OccultList BnB. The Council had obviously chosen the suite for me with purpose, and their extensive knowledge of the inner workings of my life and power left me even more ill at ease.

Well, that and the fact that I didn't like being sidelined by Mehrdad when I was the one who'd suspected something was amiss in the first place. His offer to "talk" in my room had turned to placations as his own feet remained planted in the hallway and the door closed gently between us. But he'd been correct in stating I'd be better off were my name not involved when the MAW inevitably showed, which, considering there was now a witches death to contend with, they inevitably would.

I resigned that my pacing just wasn't working as the beat of my own steps quickened the heady pulse of blood in my veins. I tried to occupy myself with the fabled Gala agenda that was finally in my hands, hoping it would distract me until Mehrdad returned. I had missed three classes already, but it appeared I had a course in Copyrighting History and a lecture on MAW-Approved Monetization Methods in store for the following day. Er… later that same morning judging by the glinting light beginning to peek around the edges of the embroidered drapes. But while the promise of "claiming ownership over and pursuing claims to" ancient and universal methods of magic or sidestepping Moral Authority mandates seemed, at best, kind of shitty—well, the first one anyway—the real issue I had with the BOG Witch Gala was the four deaths already haunting the halls. Between that and the fact that room service—or maybe the Council itself—had already cleared any sign Amy had ever been in the room, I was beginning to regret my decision to accept their invitation altogether.

Of course, there was still the possibility that the deaths had nothing to do with the witches present for the convention.

Could vampires truly be real? Could they be responsible for what was happening?

A year ago, I would have laughed at the very notion. Vampires were mythological creatures created to feed the nightmares of humans and witches alike, to make us fear the darkness, to keep our paths straight and narrow. But a year ago, I would've said the same about the Fae, and I'd had firsthand experience—of both the terrifying and the titillating type—that they were as real as I was. Hell, four years ago, most of humankind believed witches to be the stuff of fable before my errant spell had shattered that whole magic mirror.

I tossed the schedule back to the desktop as I closed my eyes, reluctantly willing the sight of Lady Z's body back to the front of my mind. Though her face had held the peacefulness of sleep within the horror of death, the scene had been so different from Amy's or the unknown couple on the rooftop. All three of them had been posed meticulously, left with a state of care, in tranquil positions that would have confused any passerby who didn't look too closely. Lady Z, though, was slumped against the corner of the elevator car, legs splayed wide before her, head craned and fallen as if the killer had run out of time. The puncture wounds along the neck were exposed instead of hidden. In my mind, the wounds were more jagged this time, less precise. But that could have just been my memory attempting to make sense of the horror of it all.

My yelp at the knock on the door made me happy for the soundproofing spells on the suites, and I squinted through the peephole before I let Mehrdad enter. He'd replaced the silken robe with a finely tailored suit, and I marveled at his composure amidst all that was happening.

"Moral Authority agents are arriving later today to investigate," he said as he stomped into the room, and I closed the door behind him. "For now, Lady Z's corpse is resting in the hotel's basement cold storage. The local police have agreed it is a witch matter alone."

"Did they not make the connection to Amy's very human death?" I asked. My voice was louder and harsher than I'd intended, and I attempted to calm it as I continued. "And what about the two bodies I found on the roof?"

Mehrdad winced at my anger, holding up his hand to calm me before crossing with sure steps to the bar to pour us each two fingers of whisky.

"The police searched the public areas of the hotel, but no

other bodies were discovered," he said as he handed me a glass.

"I'm sure this hotel has cameras," I insisted.

"At the request of the Gala, the cameras are disabled during our tenure. As we've chartered the whole of the Crow's Court for the duration of our convention, we felt it the best practice to prevent any unforeseen leaks of information that may come through the hotel's human staff."

"Great," I huffed. "So a serial killer is targeting guests of the hotel, and we've got nothing to go on."

"We have you," Mehrdad replied calmly, taking a seat on the armchair and gesturing for me to join him on the couch as my anger magicked its way quickly to confusion.

I downed the whisky he'd poured for me and made my way back to the bar instead of sitting across from the BOG Witch king. Damn, that spiced caramel flavor was smooth, and I had a feeling I was going to need more for whatever he was about to say. It was obvious these folks thought there was more to me than met the eye. And though I did have wild magic within me, a fact I could not tell another soul, it did not equip me with any grandiose skills.

"There are rumors," Mehrdad began when I finally took a seat and stared at him expectantly, "circulating the witch-world like bubbled cauldron gossip, that you, Darragh Cullen, possess a great deal more power than your average spell caster. Yes, we all witnessed your spell to save your boyfriend, yet that could be explained away, as you have insisted, as adrenaline. And still, the word on the wind is that it was you who discovered the identity of and stopped those Gowdie's from stealing witchly artifacts. It was you who put an end to the murders of another witch serial slayer."

My face fell as he spoke. Both of those things were true, but it had been a group effort with Learco and Cernun by my side. Too, both my own and Cernun's names had been kept out of the official reports to keep us safe and give the MAW full credit. That

Mehrdad knew I'd been involved was troubling. Though it didn't surprise me that he would have moles inside the Moral Authority.

"I just run a magic shop," I finally sighed, letting go of figuring out the how he knew which rampaged through my thoughts and bringing myself back to the present.

"Perhaps," he shrugged, sipping his own drink and smirking at me from beyond the rim of the glass. "But how many magic shop owners can say they faced one of the Fomóraiġ and won?"

I furrowed my brow as I watched him, hoping it read as confusion and not concern. My face was not usually great at hiding my emotions, but I couldn't let on that the Fae were real. It helped that I couldn't fathom how in the hell he'd known about my confrontations with Balor. That definitely helped to sell the bewilderment.

"Relax," he laughed, "I'm not planning to broadcast that little tidbit to the world."

The musicality of his chuckle felt strange and jarring against the atmosphere of the room, cold and sharp against everything that was going on. Whether I admitted it or not, he had chosen to believe it, and nothing I said would change his mind.

"As witches," he continued, "we both know there is more to this world than what is easily seen before us. And I believe that is what we are facing here. Your encounter with the Dark Fae may indeed prove handy."

Now it was easy to wear my incredulousness.

"You think Faeries are responsible for Amy's death?" I asked. "You think some sprites left Lady Z in the elevator?"

"Not at all," he insisted, finishing his drink and leaning forward to look me in the eye. "And yet, I do believe the culprit to be something else long deemed not of this world."

I twisted my mouth to match my brow as I looked at him expectantly. An almost gleeful spark raged behind the conspiratorial look in his eyes, and I swallowed hard to wet my throat against his flame. His eyes darted across my features, studying me once again to decide if he believed I was trustworthy, I was ready. Finally, he sat back and stated one simple word:

"Vampires."

"You sound groggy," Cernun laughed.

"Those BOG Witch parties keeping you roaring 'til the early morning light?" Learco added.

Although a three-way call was not exactly the *ménage à trios* I wanted with my boyfriends, it was damn good to hear their voices. I had managed to get a little bit of sleep, but Mehrdad's lecture on vampire lore—and his insistence that part of the Council's "Collector" moniker was due to them recruiting creatures beyond our understanding—had worn on for hours as he tried to bring me up to speed with what he knew. Or thought he knew. I supposed I should have grateful to be trusted, but it actually felt like he was unburdening himself by placing all his weight on my shoulders.

"Something like that," I stuttered.

Although I wanted to tell them everything, I knew they'd drop their lives to come to my side, and I didn't want to place them in any more danger than I already had during our time together. Besides, I wasn't even sure I believed Mehrdad when it came to the fanged fiends supposedly lurking the shadows of the Crow's Court.

"What's going on?" Cernun asked, his cheerfulness dropping to concern as he read the worry in my voice.

"Uh," I stalled, reeling in my thoughts until I convinced myself their opinions, their help, and their love were why I'd called in the first place. "There've been some deaths."

I could feel the tension, as real as my own breath, through the phone line as my lovers fell to my level. I heard Cernun tell Stacey to man the floor as he excused himself into the backroom while Learco switched into the investigator mode he'd honed so well during his tenure at the MAW.

"How many?" Learco asked when Cernun let us know he was in a place to speak freely.

"Four. Amy, the young woman I let stay in my suite; an unknown couple I discovered on the rooftop; and a fellow witch called Lady Z discovered early this morning. All here in the Crow's Court."

"Could they be coincidences?" Cernun asked, hope barely clinging to the edges of his words. "Or do you think Balor is back in the mix?"

"It's not Balor," I sighed. As much as I never wanted to see the Dark Fae leader again, a part of me thought he'd be much easier to face. The monster I knew and all that. "But they're not coincidences. Every body was completely drained of blood."

"Fuck!"

Cernun's growl nearly drowned out Learco's "interesting" as his mind began to work the case.

"Mehrdad is convinced the deaths are the results of vampires," I continued. "But we all know they aren't real, right?"

"I wouldn't be so sure," Learco hummed. His voice was distant as he pushed mentally through his recollection of MAW matters. "The Moral Authority has collected extensive lore of other supernatural creatures beyond just we witches. And though none of the data has been verified, the humans would have said the same about us a few short years ago."

"And we'd've said the same of the Fae too," Cernun added.

Great. I'd hoped their responses would have usurped my own thought processes, not verify them. Maybe I really was facing vampires. Whatever was killing folks, I had a feeling they wouldn't be as sexy and seductive as Anne Rice penned them. Or as primed for ensouled redemptive arcs as the creatures presented in teen soap operas were.

"Madison left this morning to visit their parents for the first time since the whole feline fiasco, and I gave Verne the week off to go to Florida for Spring Break," Cernun huffed. "I'll cover Stacey's salary for the next few days myself, but I need to close the store to come out there."

"I'm coming too," Learco insisted. "I'll start looking at flights."

"No!" I insisted. As much as I wanted them by my side, I'd never be able to live with myself if I put them in more danger. I could hear Balor's warning that I was destined to get them killed ringing through my ears as they tried to persuade me otherwise. I needed to keep them as far away from New Orleans as I could.

"What I mean is," I continued, slowing my speech to a calm, collected realism, "HEX is the only real magic shop in the city. Folks need access, especially at the start of Spring." It was a shit excuse, but it was the only one I had. "And Learco, your meeting with Leland Hyde to get your job back is tomorrow. I can't be the reason you miss that." At least that was a better reason. Still, I could hear their teeth grinding as they considered my response.

"Look," I finally sighed. "I'm still not convinced we're dealing with creatures of the night here. Something steeped in darkness, sure. Like a Pu-erh left in the pot too long. But until I know for sure, I'd feel better if you two were far away."

They both began to protest, but I cut them off.

"If it gets hairy—or fang-y—I'll open a portal to get my ass out. Or get your asses here. I promise."

"Fine," Cernun sighed reluctantly. "We know you can handle yourself. But if you get turned into some fair-skinned creature who bathes nude in the light of the moon and uses the cover of night to hide all his depraved activities…. You know, it kind of sounds like I'm just describing who you already are."

I laughed at his joke, comforted by his confidence in me as I steeled myself for what was to come. And at least now, if I turned up bloodless and cold, my lovers would know where to start looking for my killer. That was something, right?

"Be careful," Learco warned, snapping me back to the present.

"I will," I promised. "Besides, since the fourth victim was a witch, MAW agents will be slinking through every corner of this hotel by noon."

"That's not exactly comforting," the former head of the Southeastern Division replied.

He was right. When Leland Hyde wasn't busy trying to get me to sign up for their ranks, he was trying to have me jailed or flamed. Having a bunch of his guys storming the castle didn't exactly add the layer of protection for me it should have.

Learco and Cernun made me vow to be cautious once more before they were willing to hang up the phone, and I crashed back against the mattress in my Council-provided suite. I felt better having spoken to them, though they probably felt worse knowing I was in danger. But we'd faced our fair share of danger before, and we'd always come out on top. If a vampire was truly stalking the halls of the Crow's Court, I had plenty of daylight ahead of me to make a plan to stop them come sunset.

I just needed things to start making sense in my head. My mind was a flurry of "what if"s and "but then"s.

Mehrdad had been pretty certain the Council was involved

somehow. It made sense. The first victim had been in a Council provided room. This room. But how did the rooftop couple fit in? How had another two non-witches even gotten into the building when the BOG Witches had rented out the entirety of the hotel? And then there was Lady Z. Why had the vampires jumped from human prey to witches? And, if the Council was truly involved, why set their creature loose on a Council recruiter? Though she had been at Mehrdad's party. Maybe the Council assumed she was playing both sides and wanted to sever any loose ends. But what would the point even be for the Council to play with a vampire like he was their own personal assassin?

None of it made any sense. And yet, the facts were all there, waiting for me to arrange them in the right order. I truly could have used some of Dupin's "ratiocination" to bring it all together.

Frustrated, I clicked on the television, hidden discretely behind a gilded frame with a carefully selected recreation of one of Goya's Black Paintings, to divert my brain from the spiral of the past two days. I still had a few hours before my afternoon seminars—I definitely had to attend those now if I wanted to get any investigating done at the after hours rituals—and I didn't want to spend the morning diving down a rabbit hole. The Crow's Court home screen, advertising the amenities within and the sights outside, showcased New Orleans as a city of light, of magic, and of jazz. Riverboats rocked along the wide waters of the river; tourists paraded down Bourbon Street with oversized drinks and smiles; clarinets bounced in time with saxophones as their players marched through the streets; and even the guided tours offered of the cemeteries seemed joyful and historic. Still, one attraction did catch my eye, and I committed its address to memory as I hopped into the shower to wash off the misery of the previous night.

The sunlight felt cleansing as it fell upon my face, and I was happy to be out of the shadow of the hotel. As a witch, I'd always held a deep appreciation for the dichotomy of dark and light, the balance of night and day, but the horrors of the past two moons had left me craving the unadulterated brightness of the sun. There was something about the chaos of the radiance, bouncing off every shiny surface, glowing on the skin of the tourists, sparkling through the mica flecks of the asphalt that gave me peace as I let my brain rationalize the possibilities of a vampiric presence. Not that I was fully ready to believe in such thing, but it was the only lead I had.

I half expected to find Chester's little moped idling as I took a left onto Dumaine Street, and, for a moment, I fantasized about hopping on the back, wrapping my arms around the dense muscles of his chest, and riding with him back to the Irish Channel to spend the rest of my trip nestled in the garden at my OccultList BnB while letting the BOG Witches deal with whatever terrors they had unleashed upon themselves. But that wasn't in my nature. And whatever unnatural force was fighting for a foothold at the hotel, I wouldn't be able to turn away until I'd done my part in stopping it.

If I hadn't been searching for it, I would have passed right by the Voodoo History Museum. Two sets of storm shutter doors, painted a rich, deep black, opened to a tiny vestibule and storefront setting the museum slightly back from the sidewalk. A chalked fleur-de-lis, embellished with runic-styled symbols, had nearly disappeared beneath the footsteps of the tourists on the sidewalk, yet the faint scent of yucca, vervain, and orange peel mixed into the chalk drew my attention. All three were purification and protection plants, and the placement of the image made it so that any patron had to pass over the spell to enter. I made a mental note to implement something similar once I got back to HEX—*if*

I made it back—even as I wondered if the wild magic I now knew coursed within me would trigger any alarm bells as I passed.

The museum itself was small—not at all like the Magical Artifacts & Antiquities Museum back in Atlanta with its vast halls and carefully curated exhibits. But where MA'AM kept its treasures behind glass, the New Orleans Historic Voodoo Museum displayed them openly and with an overabundant bravado, making use of every square inch of space in the waste not want not mentality that was inherent to actual magical practice. A few of the items were dead—replicas or recreations set to give the viewer a taste, an inside look at the rituals of power, at the tools we used to guide our will—but I could feel the residual energies of so much historical magic surging through the space. It was nearly as overwhelming as the display, and I wondered if the fleur-de-lis served double duty in keeping some of that power in..

I dug through my pockets for cash to pay homage to the Fae— er, Orishas as the island-descended practitioners, included Learco, called them—and dropped a ten dollar bill into the offering plate spelled and resting on the front counter. I knew the Fae didn't give two shits about the money, but I also knew the proprietors had to keep the doors open somehow. Spaces like this were important points of preservation for witch history. Even a glance around told me the owners of this museum were doing more for witch-kind than all the business owners at that gala down the road combined.

I moved slowly as I made my way around the room, taking the time to view and appreciate each item. It was all so different than the witchcraft I'd grown up with but also strikingly similar. The dolls, made of cloth and hair, were not so far off from the poppets I remembered my grandmother twisting from the corn husks she'd gathered after we shucked the haul for dinner. The stone pottery used to collect herbs and burn incense and my cast iron cauldrons could have come from the same set. But the biggest difference was the use of animals.

Sure, the practice I'd grown up with had our "eye of newt" and our "dead man's toe," but those were creepy code words for the mustard seed or mushrooms our ancestors had used to keep their potion ingredients secret and stir up a little shock and awe from the townsfolk. But this museum was filled with bones. Skulls of cattle or crocodiles or humans rested on altars and adorned the tops of statues. Chicken bones, sharpened to points, were implanted as teeth inside masks. Femurs were etched like wands with symbols I had never seen.

I felt my heart quicken as my mind considered the implications. If animal parts were not off-limits in their magic, was it such a stretch to believe blood to also be a crucial ingredient? Shit! I tried to play it cool as I inched my way toward the door, worried I'd just walked into a vampire's lair of a trap. I'd have to find out the information I wanted some other way. Maybe I could convince Chester to reach out to his long lost girlfriend Félicité. He'd said she'd spoken to him of her ancestors fighting vampires and zombies. That had to be safer than this.

"Leaving so soon, mortal?"

The voice echoed through the small room just as my toes reached the threshold, sending shivers down my spine as the words wove through the lower octaves of an island lilt. A part of me wanted to run, to push out into the sunlight and disappear into the droves of pedestrians until I was beyond the reach of whatever was lurking in that room. But the wild magic in my gut sizzled to stop me and urged me to turn around.

As soon as I did, I wished I hadn't listened.

My breath caught heavy in my throat, turning quickly into an apple core meant to suffocate me with my eye-found knowledge. My jaw dropped open as my eyes scanned the impossible.

Before me, eyes down and mouth twisted into a seductively

evil smirk was someone who could not possibly be there. Someone whose dead body I'd seen with my own two eyes. Her name escaped my throat in a whispered question as my faculties began to return.

"Lady Z?"

CHAPTER 9

"Oh. You're not a tourist," the woman who looked exactly like a very not dead Lady Z smiled. "You can, um… drop the magic. I'm not a threat."

My eyes dropped to the sparks of green radiating from my palms. I hadn't even realized the power had slipped them, and the spell—whatever it was—was like nothing I knew, nothing I'd seen before. A calming breath filled my lungs and coaxed the magic back within me, and I exhaled slowly as I brought my eyes back to the museum's proprietor.

She looked so much like Lady Z. The same cinnamon eyes sparkled with curiosity above the same knowing grin. And, as she dropped the hood of her cloak, I saw the same deep brown hair twisted into a messy yet elegant braid. This woman's hair, though, was woven through with sun-kissed blonde streaks, and the dimples in her cheek were slightly more pronounced. Still, the resemblance was uncanny.

"I'm sorry," I said when I finally found my voice. "You startled me."

"I should be the one apologizing," the woman laughed as she shrugged off her robes to reveal an understated jeans and t-shirt combo beneath. "Most of the people who come in here are human tourists primed for the dark mumbo jumbo of a show. The sigil out front usually lets us know if the patron holds magic."

"I, uh… I must've passed too quickly," I lied. I was certain my awakened wild magic had something to do with me slipping through the magic detection spell buried beneath their fleur-de-lis, but that was an issue for another time. There were far more pressing matters at hand. "You look so much like…."

"You must know my sister, Zamiah. Or 'Lady Z' as she's taken to calling herself."

The woman said the moniker with all the grandiose snark of a little sister jabbing the ribs of her sibling as she rolled her eyes and reached beneath a counter to pull out a moka pot and two ceramic cups. She poured a steaming black liquid and dropped in four dark sugar cubes before offering me a glass.

"The witch is eight years older than me, and yet somehow we could pass for twins. I keep asking what Orisha she sold her soul to, so I can make the same deal, but she swears Yemaya would make me pay for her to take it."

She took a quick sip of her coffee and smiled as she topped it off, barely pausing her words to swallow down the rich, earthy-scented brew.

"My name's Félicité. Or 'Lady F,' I suppose. And you are?"

She was certainly more talkative than her sister was. Or ever would be again. And my heart sank as I realized she had not been told of Lady Z's fate.

"Darragh Cullen," I gulped, fighting with my features not to plummet into the despair I was feeling before I could deliver the news in a calm, rational manner.

"Darragh Cullen," Félicité repeated, punctuating every syllable like her tongue was savoring the words. "Zamiah was definitely excited to meet you. I suppose, since you're here, she's had a chance to tell you of our mission?"

"She…" I started, crossing the few steps to the counter and placing my coffee down as I tilted my head in the sympathetic manner I'd seen actor after actor do on those dramatic medical tv shows when they had to deliver bad news. "We did not get the opportunity to speak much."

Félicité's brow furrowed at my expression, then softened as understanding swept across her face.

"Shit," she said simply, her face paling as she set down her cup. Her eyes unfocused as they reached into the distance.

Sorrow swept through me, edged in the wonder of how she could have known what I was about to tell her with so few words escaping my throat. I was still trying to determine how I was going to explain what had happened, how much information I could readily offer, and what exactly true condolences looked like in a situation like this when a bold shadow thickened the air from the doorway. My confusion compounded yet Félicité's softened as we faced the newcomer.

"They got Zamiah," she whispered.

My throat dried, my eyes welled, and Chester rushed to embrace his old flame.

The back room of the museum was smaller than the front, but it was the death of Lady Z which hung heavy on the air, making the cramped quarters seem impossibly stunted. I sat across from Chester on a wooden chair at a cloth-draped table designed for rune and tarot readings while Félicité shuttered and locked up the front. He winced as he watched me, pulling awkwardly at the ruffles along the cushion of the seat as his mouth fought to find any words of explanation. None he could conjure were deemed right.

"I'm so sorry, Lici," he said, leaping to his feet as Félicité entered. His arms raised slightly to embrace her again, but he dropped them as she pushed past him to the third chair at the table.

"She knew the risks," she said solemnly, swallowing hard before she turned to look at me. "I suppose you're here to talk about vampires."

"I… Yeah," I stuttered as my eyes darted between Félicité and Chester. "But I feel like I'm a few pages behind on this story. Plus, right now, shouldn't you be more focused on your sister?"

"Ironically, I am," Félicité winced. "I guess I'd better start at the beginning."

She sighed as she reached beneath the table to pull out yet another tray of saucers and ceramic teacups, but this time an unopened bottle of rum replaced the stovetop espresso maker. She nodded as Chester reached to open it and downed a full glass before she continued with her story.

"My sister wasn't at the BOG Witch convention by accident," she said, pausing only briefly to swallow another sip of the fermented sugar cane before continuing. "Our family has a little bit of a history in fighting against the darkness, and, well, when word spread through the underground that vampiric actions had started happening around the Gala, she worked hard to jockey herself into the fold so she could investigate."

Although Chester had never actually said it, if the implied family history around Félicité and her sister were to be believed— if they were truly descendants of the great Marie Laveau herself— then 'a little bit of a history' was very much an understatement.

Still, it explained how Félicité had been so quick with her understanding when it came to her sister's demise. Particularly since Lady Z had been there trying to root out the demons. It also explained why she was playing both sides with the two most powerful groups at the function. And why she was the last thing Amy had seen as she died. Shit. And here I'd been suspecting her when I should have been protecting her. Not that I could have been expected to fare any better than a self-proclaimed vampire hunter.

"When we found out you'd been invited this year," Félicité continued, "Zamiah went into overdrive endearing herself to both Mister Yaisien and the Council. She wasn't sure which faction you'd pick, but knew they'd both attempt to court you. And, well, having the guy who exposed magic through one hell of a display of power on our side in this fight, well… that could have changed everything."

"I really was meant to be out of town," Chester added. "But once we found out you were staying in the main house in front of my place instead of at the hotel, Lici asked me to stick around to help guide you toward the sisters."

"So you thought you'd just seduce me so I'd be more willing to help your girlfriend?" I growled, though it wasn't the time to be upset. I was on their side. I just didn't appreciate the subterfuge.

"Hey, that's bi erasure," Chester huffed, the gleam in his eyes telling me he was sorry and that everything I'd imagined, he had too. "I hadn't intended to seduce you. That was just a bonus."

"Plus, Ches and I are just friends," Félicité insisted. "I'm married to a great man and have two beautiful, if often insolent, children. Zamiah never married. That's why she volunteered to be the witch on the inside. Even knowing the risks…. Whe— Where is my sister's body?"

My face fell as the gravity of the moment recaptured me, and

I bit my lip before I answered.

"She's being kept in the hotel's cold storage," I winced. "The Moral Authority is en route to investigate her death, if they're not already there, alongside its connection to three other bodies. All human. All drained completely of blood. I'm sure they'll send an agent to officially inform you soon."

Félicité nodded, taking another swig—this time straight from the bottle—of the rich dark rum before offering the neck of the bottle to refill mine and then Chester's cups.

"I'll, uh, stick to the black stuff," Chester smiled and poured another cup from the moka pot, waving off Lady F's offer of sugar as she shrugged and recapped the bottle of rum.

"Those creatures rarely go after us witches. My guess is there's something in the blood that don't sit quite right in their stomachs," she sighed, something akin to pride coating the skin of her words. "Zamiah must've gotten really close to something. Cheers to that."

Awkwardly, I clinked the rim of my glass against hers, then allowed the sweet density of the drink to bolster my confidence before my eyes returned to the wild look in her own. I could tell there was more grief for the loss of her sister than she was letting show, but, like every good witch, she had buried it behind the task at hand. She would cry later, after the danger had been dealt with. I supposed it helped that we were all taught from an early age that death was a natural part of life, that it was a mere step in the cyclical turn of the world, of its renewal. And though that rarely made the absence any easier to hold, the understanding did seem to bolster us through the worst of it. For Félicité, completing her sister's mission was the best way—the *only* way—to process her sorrow, and I wanted nothing more than to help.

"I'm sorry," I said, "I'm still having trouble wrapping my head around the idea that vampires actually exist."

"Oh, they do," she assured me, though the look on her face said she was reassuring herself too. "The trouble is pushing through all the legends to get onto some kernel of the truth."

I nodded. Our own witch history was rife with disparity between lore and fact. In fairness, some of that was perpetuated by us, like the old tales of familiars we once used to hide our Fae-magic transformations into animals. Hell, even that had been ret-conned by the earliest form of the Moral Authority long ago to hide that Faeries were real so that the bulk of witch-kind alive today believed familiars were fables sprung from our proclivity to love the company of cats and dogs and birds and reptiles. Other incongruence formed naturally through oral traditions in storytelling: like how an earth witch's use of medicinal plants—the old word for which was *wort*—got retold and retold until the leaves on our noses became warts and turned our skin green. There was safety in befuddlement. There was hiding in the uncertainty. If everyone out there was looking for black pointed hats and grass-tinted skin, we could slip by unnoticed. It made sense that other more than human creatures would embrace a little mystery, either of their own devices or by not correcting the extravagant tales formed when witnesses couldn't understand what they'd seen.

"Are there any similarities in the different stories we could start with?" I suggested. "Threads that sort of weave through them all? In everything I've read or seen—which, granted, has not been strictly *educational* as it were—the vampires are always... incredibly sexy. Like leading man material sexy."

Chester's eyes darted from mine to the resolve in his friend's, picking up quickly on her need for focus, and quipped, "Are you looking to bed them or slay them? Plus, every witch I've ever met has been one hell of a looker, but the Old Wive's Tales depicted you all as gnarled hags."

That was true. And yet another tale we perpetuated ourselves for our safety.

"So you're thinking they're more German Expressionist than Teen Flick Thriller?"

"Or perhaps the truth idles somewhere in between," Félicité offered. "Also, not to add more suspects to the board, but there is another possibility. Have you ever heard of the Rougarou? You saw an effigy of one in the main room."

I thought back through the organized abundance of the museum until I held firm to the image of the man's body, wrapped in denim and plaid, and topped with the head of a wolf.

"I took that for more of a werewolf than a vampire," I admitted. "And, well, I've seen the bodies. They aren't mauled. The incisions in the necks are precise; the blood is gone; and their expressions, for the most part, are peaceful. It doesn't exactly read animal."

"Yes, but even Dracula could turn into a bat or a wolf," Chester acknowledged, wincing as he considered the robust possibilities of what we were dealing with.

It was a lot. And if these creatures had somehow been able to hide themselves, for the most part anyway, from our magics, I wasn't sure my own power could do anything to stop them.

"The Rougarou doesn't maul his victims," Félicité explained, reciting the words as if she were dictating from a textbook, which she probably was. Despite the florid language of our ancestors, each generation's hold on their family's Book of Shadows attempted to distill the past's lessons down to the facts, even while adding more ornate descriptions of our own. "Like the Chupacabra or the Greek Striges, the Rougarou may have a fierce visage, yet is sustained by the drinking of blood, not the ingestion of flesh. Too, according to my family's lore at least, the Rougarou can shift. Yes, like a werewolf, but perhaps more accurately like Chester's Dracula analogy. He can blend while in his human form, perhaps even walk in the day. But his other form is for feeding. So the old tales of him living in the darker recesses of the swamp, picking off wayward fisherman and hunters and runaways may not be entirely true. That, or he's changed his hunting grounds."

But maybe not his modus operandi, I thought. Amy had been a runaway. I now knew that for sure from my vision. And no one had been able to identify the couple I'd found on the rooftop. Of course, no one but me had seen their bodies. But no one had come looking for them either, which probably meant they were tourists visiting the city together, and it would be a while before anyone realized they were missing. The only outlier was Lady Z, but if she was investigating the vampire—or the Rougarou—her death was probably self-preservation.

It wasn't a lot to go on, but it was a name. And names held power. At the very least, the whispers of the word could bring it out of hiding. Hopefully not with its fangs barreling toward my neck.

"Zamiah believed the Rougarou had moved in from the swamp and was implanting himself amongst the BOG witches," she continued. "Either to have them cover up his killings to avoid any bad press or to pin the deaths on us in order to keep his existence hidden. That's why she'd worked so hard to implant herself within the organization. She was hoping to root him out."

We took a solemn moment, and another shot, as we paid homage to Lady Z's sacrifice. I wished she had spoken to me, had clued me into what was going on, but between Mehrdad and the Council's courting—and not knowing where the Rougarou hid— she was still figuring out if she could trust me. I hid my wince and the accompanying fear behind my shot glass as I swallowed hard.

"But you and your family," Chester said, an earnest excitement filling his voice as he tried to push away his own worry, "you've fought vampires and zombies before. You're like the Creole version of Van Helsing for these parts." When Félicité's confusion crashed against his words, he added, "At least that's what you told me in high school."

Recollection slapped her memory, and she laughed.

"I told you that so I would sound cooler than I was. I wanted you to like me."

"I already did," he promised, and I smiled at how even the memory of love—of real love—could be so strong even as time slipped away. Maybe that was another reason death was easier for us witches to understand. We loved, and we loved hard. And that love ensnared itself to memories that kept that feeling ever-present, even when the recipient was lost.

"In truth," Félicité admitted, "neither of us has ever seen a vampire, be it sexy seducer, Nosferatu, or Rougarou. Hell, it's been hundreds of years since any real identifiable vampiric activity has been recorded. I mean, it was just in the last year or so that we even saw the signs. But once we did, once we compared them to our books, it was unmistakable."

So the vampire activity had only just begun. But if the eternal creature existed, there would have been signs long before, no matter how well he kept them hidden, particularly for those like Ladies Z and F who knew what to look for.

Shit. One question burned in my brain, and I had a feeling I was not going to like the answer.

"When exactly did the signs start turning up?" I asked, holding my breath even though I already knew what she was going to say.

"Late June of last year," Félicité said. "Just after the Midsummer Solstice."

Fuck. I hated to be right. I bit my lip as my mind flashed back to the blood-letting, power-grabbing spell of my former protégé, Aiden Gowdie. The ritual which had brought Learco into my life and solidified his relationship with me and Cernun, but it had also opened the cracks to allow pieces of Balor, parts of Fae-magic into our world. And the Rougarou certainly sounded Fae. Or at least of Fae power origin. But even beyond that, even if tales of the Rougarou were exaggerated or meant to be parables, even if we were facing the blood sucking fiends I was more used to imagining, if Fae magic was involved, it was going to get even messier before it got better. The Fae's unpredictable nature added another uncertainty to a situation I already knew too little about.

Félicité's brow furrowed as she watched the terror rampage its way across my features.

"There is some good news though," she said, though even she didn't sound convinced. "I mean, whether the Rougarou is real or we are facing some sexy undead creature of darkness, the means of stopping them are fairly universal. They don't like garlic. And though the Church would call the liquid 'Holy Water,' I do have a recipe for a potion my ancestors swear by. And of course, there's always the good, old fashioned…"

"Stake through the heart," Chester finished for her. "In fairness, I feel like that would kill pretty much anything."

He had a point. On both counts. A spear through the heart had made quick work of Balor, at least for now, and he was a Dark Fae leader. But it would also do in anyone sitting at that table too. We'd have to be certain of the vampire's identity before we went all slayer on him.

"Zamiah's theory was that the Rougarou could only be slain while in his transmogrified state," Félicité sighed, once again reading my expression correctly. "But that's also his most violent form."

"So no pressure or anything," Chester quipped.

"Look," Félicité said, reaching across the table and cupping her hand over mine. "I don't know what sort of vampire is out there or even what sort of creature we're looking for. But I do know, just from feeling your aura, that you can handle this, Darragh Cullen. I felt it before you even came to New Orleans. That's sort of my gift. It's not exactly foresight like some practitioners have, but it's a feeling. Like a guide. Or an oracle. That's why my sister was seeking you out. And that's why I know you are the only witch I trust at that convention."

My mind churned with possibilities as I clung tightly to Chester on the back of his moped. Unfortunately, they weren't the types of possibilities I typically preferred to ruminate on. It meant a lot that Félicité entrusted me with her family's lore, even if it left me with a larger list of enigmatic spooks to look for. But her addition of a Rougarou killer to the already vague vampiric mythos didn't worry me nearly as much as the suspect she didn't know she'd revealed. The possibility that the Fae—or that Fae magic—was somehow involved terrified me. But the timeline was just too aligned to be a coincidence. And it meant the killings wouldn't cease at the end of the BOG Witch Convention unless someone who knew what they were truly dealing with stopped them. And since we did not want to MAW discovering the Fae were real, that someone had to be me.

Fuck.

Although maybe I could leave it to the leader of the BOG Witches to deal with. Mehrdad had somehow known about the Fae, even if I had done an adequate job of seeming confused and shocked by his recounting of my own history to hide my association with them. He hadn't made the connection between the Fae and the deaths, but maybe that was all conjecture on my part anyway. Witches loved rumors nearly as much as we loved puns. Still, having set up shop decades before in New Orleans—plus, him being so quick to use the V-word—perhaps he had more of a handle on things than I could, making him the right witch for the job.

But could I ever just leave knowing the danger I was turning my back on? I knew I couldn't. And if the dormant wild magic within me was what had sparked the cracks to make Aiden's Fae-summoning spell work, then I couldn't help but feel responsible for every strand of power it had awakened within our world. So maybe the active wild magic that now swirled with the power I had always known was exactly what it would take to end the carnage.

"Why'd we stop?" I asked, yelling over the engine as Chester's idling stance at the corner of Camp and Canal broke me from my mental breakdown turned pep talk. I was already twenty minutes late to my first seminar, and even though Mehrdad had promised to speak with Layla, I didn't want any trouble—or the appearance of preferential treatment—when I ambled out to the party to investigate later that night.

Chester's chest tensed, and even though I couldn't see his face, I could feel the worry emanating through his helmet as he nodded toward the Crow's Court. My eyes followed, expecting to see the unnerving presence of black-clad MAW agents combing the sidewalk as they made their never-truly-subtle "covert" presence known. Instead, I was met with the slack-jawed, angry-eyed dawdling of the DMFM.

"I was wondering when they were going to show up," I huffed.

Wherever witches gathered, Defend Mankind From Magic was not far behind. The hate group founded by Cernun's adoptive parents and led by his brothers was the only organization I knew who embraced the fairytales of witch lore more than us witches did. Their makeshift posterboard signs were scribbled with Bible versus or protestations that we were Satan's offspring, and a few of their rallies had turned violent as they carried out their modern day witch hunts. But, for the most part, the protesters were just noisy bigots directing the media's attention away from the real work of the DMFM as lobbyist throughout every level of government, fighting to control the magically-inclined as second-class citizens.

"I'll be fine," I assured Chester. "They're like stray dogs when they're hungry. Their bark is much bigger than their bite. And they're way more afraid of me than I should be of them. Besides. There's what? Seven of them? I've taken on more than that at a house party."

I was hoping the joke would lighten Chester's mood, but his concern still lingered. And though I didn't need protecting, it did feel nice to be looked out for.

"Look. See? They're not going to be a problem."

We watched as a combat-clad MAW agent pushed his way from the hotel lobby, yelling for the crowd to disperse. He was met with fistfuls of salt and buckets of water—because those morons truly believed everything they saw in the movies—but it was the swinging of the signs with their solid wood or metal posts that caught both me and the agent off guard.

Magic sparked in the agent's palm but quickly resided as he retreated closer to the building. The MAW had rules against using magic on mortals, except for extreme circumstances, and even its agents were not above sanctions. Besides, the camera phones at the ready proved the group was trying to goad a witch into using their power to add more fuel to their fires. We did burn so much easier once the flames got big, afterall.

"Is that Darragh Cullen?!?"

I heard my name before I even registered where it was coming from and dropped the visor on my helmet quickly as the protesters turned toward me. As the boyfriend of the DMFM's main target and as the witch who'd made us all known in the first place, my photo had been circulated in more hate group newsletters than in all my high school yearbooks combined.

"Nope," Chester said. "I'm taking you to the house. Hold on."

I gasped as he turned the wrong way down Camp, holding my breath as he wove against oncoming traffic until he righted our route on Common. I was surprised at how fast his little moped could go when pushed, and he refused to let up on the throttle until we were back in the Irish Channel.

CHAPTER 10

I let go of a breath I didn't know I was holding as the moped slowed to a stop in front of my OccultList BnB, shivering slightly—from the situation or the journey?—as I released my tightened grip on Chester's waist. Now that the Crow's Court was crawling with MAW agents and DMFManiacs, both sects of whom would rather see me flamed at the stake than merely existing, it was going to be a lot harder to make my way back into the hotel to continue my investigation. Add in the vampire lurking within the gas-lamp lit halls, and I was happier than ever that I'd snagged an offsite point of residence during my stay. Not to mention, Chester's aid and company was a near-adequate stand in for my coven—complete with its own sexual tension—as my boyfriends dealt with their own shit back in Atlanta.

Or so I thought.

Learco stood with a smirking grin on the front porch of the house, rocking chair still swaying behind him and his go to travel bag slumped beside the front door. His skin looked exquisite in the early afternoon brightness, dappled with humidity and glowing against the salmon-painted siding behind him. His bantu knots, still pressed a bit from the plane ride, were freshly tied after our excursion to the Fae Realm giving highlight to the sharpness of his cheekbones and the appearance of a well-deserved crown.

I fumbled with my helmet as I pushed it into Chester's hands and leapt the few brick steps to the porch to pull him into my arms. His lips, chewed with worry, were rough on mine, and his tongue still tasted of the coffee and cashews of his travel. The rush of our auras mingling—his fast yet calculated; mine pulsating and wild—relaxed me as much as it excited me, and I pulled him closer into our kiss. Damn, it felt good to have him in my arms.

"What the hell are you doing here?" I growled when our lips finally parted, feigning anger despite the curve of my mouth letting him know I was ecstatic to see him.

"Sight-seeing mostly," he purred. "I hear the train set up at the Botanical Garden is not to be missed."

Cernun was rubbing off on him, and I squinted my eyes at the joke he'd used to hide the obvious worry in his.

"You didn't think I was going to let you face a vampire in the Voodoo City all on your own, did you?" he continued. "You really can't take all the best villains."

"But you've got your meeting with Leland tomorrow," I insisted, touched by his willingness to give up his career for me. Though, it wasn't exactly the first time he'd made that choice, this was the closest it had ever actually come.

"I joined the MAW to do something good for witch-kind," he smiled, wincing slightly as his resolve pushed through, "not to police our own. This is something good for witch-kind. My meeting with Leland Hyde can wait."

I kissed him again as my fingers fumbled through the code on the door's lock, grateful as Chester stepped up to actually unlock it and grabbed Learco's bag as he let us inside. My lips didn't leave my lover's until I'd pulled him to the overstuffed couch. Chester cleared his throat from the hallway.

"I'll, uh, leave you two to get reacquainted," he said, pantomiming his exit with a wide-eyed nod.

Learco pursed his lips with mischievous intent, raising his eyebrows as he looked from me to Chester and back again. My own brows raised in answer, and Learco laughed.

"Don't feel obligated to leave. The choice is yours," he called, grinning as he pinned my shoulders down and his lips returned to mine.

Feeling his weight atop me, his aura mingling with mine, cleared my mind briefly—well, not too briefly—of the horrors of the past few days. He shivered as my fingers slipped beneath the hem of his shirt, relishing the taut feel of his abs beneath the tight, high-end fabric he preferred to be clad in before I moved to work the buttons for better purchase. He swept his lips from mine, giving me a brief chance to catch my breath before his tongue began to work the space where my neck met my ear, and it caught once more in my throat. But my fingers still managed to do their job, and I pushed the shirt back over his shoulders—first one and then the other arm for balance—as I freed his rich, dark skin to meet the early humidity of the air.

My eyes shot open as his teeth found contact with my neck, moaning gratefully as my head tilted back to give him a better angle. When my eyes focused, they locked on Chester. He had found his way back into the room and stood timidly watching us from a few feet away, his bottom lip curled under the bite of his jaw. His eyebrows lifted when he caught me looking, and his lips curled upward as he pulled his t-shirt over his head and dropped it to the floor.

My chin brushed the side of Learco's head, and he turned to take in the view of Chester's pale, muscular torso with a wicked appreciation. As Chester stepped forward, I took the momentary freedom of movement to remove my own shirt and toss it to the neighboring chair. Learco growled as his lips returned to mine, his rumble intensifying as first Chester's hands and then Chester's mouth met his shoulder. He worked his way down the tight bicep of Learco's right arm as my boyfriend moved his mouth to my right shoulder, allowing Chester's lips to meet mine. They were soft and tasted of a pickled spice that was at once exotic and right at home amidst the air of New Orleans. On instinct, my aura pushed to envelop him before I pulled it back.

Witches had to be extremely careful with aura play when it came to humans. A little pulse here and there was fine, but the power, the sensuality, and the ecstasy inherent in a witch's innermost soul was enough to push most humans over the edge, leaving them bound like addicts to the feeling. Even if the MAW had not forbidden the practice of pushing that far centuries ago, I still would have refused to perform it.

"It's okay," Chester groaned as he sensed my reticence pull from him. "Not to brag, but I've had plenty of practice."

"I'm sure you have," Learco chuckled as he pulled himself up to his knees and pushed his lips against Chester's.

My tongue wet my own lips as I took a moment to appreciate the beauty of their kiss, of their bodies aching to connect skin to skin above me, before I reached to free the growing bulges pressing on the fabric of their pants. With the button undone, Learco slipped from the couch to stand and let his slacks fall to the floor. His ass clenched, tightening to accentuate the round firmness of his cheeks, as my tongue traced the small of his back to the jut of his hip, then slipped from his skin to leave the cool wisp of wanting more.

I poured myself to the soft shag of the rug, planting my knees to either side of the men as I untied the laces of their shoes then shifted the tight denim of Chester's jeans down below his hips. Both men's cocks danced the air before my eyes, rigid with excitement and the exuberance of freedom. I cupped my hands to the small of each man's back, pressing them to one another until their erections met and throbbed against their stomachs. Learco's hand dropped to run through the reddish mop of my hair, curved the back of my head, and pulled me forward as they shifted sideways for me to taste them. I pulled them slowly into my mouth, first Learco then Chester and then back to my boyfriend, as they each clawed at my shoulders and groaned.

Their taste was exquisite, and, as I fumbled with my jeans, a thrust of Learco's magic sent me backward to the floor. I smiled as both men kicked off their shoes, shed their pants like cloaks no longer needed for the ritual, then dropped to join me. Hands whipped against my skin, massaging, tugging, and pushing until what was left of my clothing had been discarded and we were clad only in each other. We heaved as the sunlight of the early afternoon pulsed through the windows to light our way through each movement, a conductor for the symphony of our sex.

Chester's ability to keep up amidst two witches proved he truly did have the experience he'd claimed, and a soft, barely-there thrust of his aura proclaimed he either had some distant power in his bloodline or else he'd found a way to tap into the inherent magic of all living things. Either way, the hunger in his eyes as he took first me and then Learco into him was intoxicating. It made me wish Cernun was with us. Though, in fairness, the recounting of the story—the recreation of the activity with him—would be just as hot once we returned to Atlanta.

I sent a tendril of my aura to twine Chester's body, grinning as he leaned his head back, a gentle gasp escaping his throat. The gold of Learco's aura joined the green of mine, wrapping around him like the soft glow of dawn. The magic undulated as we tested the edges of Chester's will, careful not to push too far. The restraint, in and of itself, was highly erotic as the hunger in

Chester's eyes begged for more, and we worked in tandem to send him over the edge.

Chester came first, howling as his ejaculation shook through the whole of his body, and signaling Learco and I to make use of the broad expanse of his pecs as we finished the rites. Our bodies pulsed in a jumble on the floor, quaking as we slowed back to the equilibrium of day. As our breaths and our hearts returned to normal… As the terror which had prompted Learco's journey set back in.

"I'll, uh, go get cleaned up," Chester purred, clearing his throat as he pulled himself up and cupped his arms across the dripping trails of his midsection. "You mind if I use the shower?"

Learco waited until we heard the water shift on before turning to me, the lust in his eyes replaced with pragmatic concern.

"What the hell is going on?" he asked.

I winced as I reached for my jeans, sighing when I tossed my boyfriend his shirt and watched him slip back into it.

"Exactly what I told you on the phone: Four bodies," I replied, wincing as the stillness of the words escaped my throat. "Well, two if you ask the witches over at the hotel. Amy, the young human I let commandeer the room the Council got for me, and Lady Z, a witch from the Council. But, before their corpses disappeared, I found two other humans posed like marionettes on the rooftop. All of them drained of blood. All of them with two tiny puncture wounds along their jugulars."

"Hence the 'vampire' of it all," Learco nodded, buttoning his pants before sitting in one of the recliners opposite the couch.

His face clouded as he waited for me to say more, eyes darting through the folders of his mind as they accessed the years of information he'd gathered as both an agent and then a leader of the MAW. In most circumstances, he held that knowledge fairly close to his his tarot deck, even when it came to me and Cernun.

The near-constant battle between love and duty he displayed was part of what made me adore him, even during the times I was left in the dark. In that New Orleans living room though, the expressions were different. He wasn't a MAW agent, at least for the time being, and I could tell he was testing the work-around for merit in his head.

"Here's the thing though," I said, leaning forward and giving him an out before he revealed more than he was prepared to. "I don't think I buy it. I know before we actually met the Fae, I imagined them as parables, as personifications of elemental notions elevated to gods. And so, maybe I'm doing that here. But the Fae were trapped in their world, wholly apart from ours, for centuries. That on its own explains the surprise of their being. So if vampires were right here, living amongst us for so long, how were they able to stay hidden?"

"You mean like witch-kind did?" Learco smirked, raising his eyebrows as I frowned and leaned back against the over-plush couch.

He had me there. Places like New Orleans and Salem aside, we had managed to keep our craft the stuff of story for the most part. If vampires were real, the same could be said of them. And there were certainly places around the world that brokered in vampire lore.

But the real thing amusing Learco was our reversed roles in the conversation. I was typically the witch to go extravagant, ready to believe in the magic—light or dark—of what surrounded us. Learco, on the other hand, tended to take a more pragmatic approach, relying on sight and sound within the scope of known and practiced power to see through the subterfuge of those doing wrong. The about-faced dance we were performing was actually funny. And it warmed me to know just how much we were influencing one another.

"The deaths are all happening at the BOG Witch Gathering, all inside the hotel," I countered. "Before we burn the straw men, we have to consider that someone at the Crow's Court is responsible."

"Fair enough. And perhaps you are right. But you've also taught me that we would be remiss to not consider all possibilities. For instance, it may be possible that the reintroduction of Fae magic—of your own wild magic—into our realm awakened creatures whose powers and abilities have lain dormant since the Fae's departure from our plain."

Shit. I'd thought that too, briefly, but I hadn't wanted to accept it and have another thing that was my fault. Our best theory was that it was the underlayer of wild magic within me—the bit of my power which came through wholly from the source of whatever had given both the Fae and witch-kind our abilities—that had enabled Aiden's blood spell to summon the Fae back to our world to actually work. It was the wild within me that had enabled mounds of chaos from Balor, from Changelings, and from Fae only knew what else. If my blood had also awakened vampirism, I didn't want to know what else I could inadvertently release upon the world.

"If that were the case, it would not be your fault, Darragh," Learco assured me, a worried gleam in his eye as he read my face to perfection. "But the locale of the murders, having them all centered upon the BOG Witch Convention, could very well mean that you are actually the intended prey. If the wild brought forth these creatures, they would no doubt be in search of its source."

I frowned, not because I was a potential target—I was used to that—but because it really didn't free me, in my mind at least, from culpability in Amy, Lady Z, and the others' deaths.

"It is also utterly possible that this isn't related to you in the least," Learco continued. "As much as Leland Hyde may think all roads lead back to Darragh Cullen. Vampire lore has existed for nearly as long as our lore has. We must also consider the possibility that they are real."

"That's what Lici said. Chester's witch ex-girlfriend who runs the Voodoo Museum in the Quarter," I explained to Learco's confused look. "She told me about the local legend of the Rougarou."

"Ah, yes. Back home we had the Lougaroo or the Soucouyant. All shape shifting, blood pedaling creatures of darkness. They appeared as wolves or bats or fireballs to frighten children into doing their chores." Learco rose and began to pace the floor the way he would when his mind was fast at work. "This is exactly why Leland Hyde, when he's not trying to kill you, is trying to recruit you. You've got an innate sensibility. The MAW has evidence that these legends were created to hide dark witches and their use of blood magic. They allowed the myths to perpetuate, even as they sought the very witches culpable, to hide the darker sides of our histories. And, despite all evidence presented, you saw through it and centered on the witches at the Crow's Court."

"Well, I mean, a part of me still believes it could be vampires."

"Don't worry. This is not a sales pitch. Hell, I'm not even sure I want my own position back with them. I know you can handle yourself, and I still hopped on a plane instead of keeping my appointment to watch Hyde grovel tomorrow."

"Yeah, we're going to need to talk about that," I huffed. "I feel the love, but I don't want you sacrificing yourself for me. Because I love you too."

Two quick swipes of Learco's hand waved away my anxiety, and I smiled as I saw the casual confidence he usually carried return to his form.

"That will all work out," he assured me. "But you come first. And Cernun. Your mission is my mission."

His lips were warm as I stood to kiss him, wrapping my arms around his shoulders and relishing in the closeness of his skin. Even though I worried I was putting him in the danger Balor had foretold, it felt good to have him near.

"I will say this though," Learco said as we parted and we heard the water in the shower shut off. "While I do agree we should center our focus on the BOG Witch attendees, the MAW also possesses quite a bit of evidence that magical creatures beyond witches do live in our world. We would be remiss to rule out the more lingering ideas of vampires and their ways outright. If nothing else, whomever is behind this is emulating them. So in either case, vampire or witch, that lore may tell us how to find and combat them."

"So it's back to the Crow's Court then?" Chester asked, appearing in the doorway with nothing but a pair of briefs and the drape of his towel as he dried his hair. "Those protesters recognized you. How do you plan to get in?"

Learco's brow furrowed as he turned his gaze from Chester's frame back to me.

"Oh, yeah," I huffed. "The MAW's arrival to investigate Lady Z's death alongside a twenty-four floor convocation of witches brought the DMFM to our doorstep."

"I could try to distract them," Chester offered. "A water balloon and a couple yelled words in Latin go a long way in pulling a bigot's attention."

"Thanks for the offer," I chuckled, "but you shouldn't be any more involved than you already are. Being seen with me has a tendency to place folks in the line of fire of both the Defend Mankind maniacs and the Moral Authority. Let me make a call."

Chester looked a bit dejected as I pulled up Mehrdad's number on my cell, and Learco crossed to cup his shoulder as the call connected.

"After our time this afternoon," Learco laughed, "you should fully understand that Darragh can always find the backdoor."

The other BOG Witches, those not fortunate enough to snag rooms at the illustrious hotel, could come and go as they pleased through the lobby, albeit with a bit of heckling from the DMFM protesters out front. In truth, they had their signs and their vitriol, but they were probably more scared of the magic we held than they were loud in their yelling. Learco and I, on the other hand, had faces Cernun's adopted brother's had sent out as public enemies number one. We'd need to find a different way in.

Layla greeted us at the delivery door near the rear side of the Crow's Court. Or, perhaps *greeted* was too kind a word. The sour look on her face as she ushered us inside and slammed the door seemed permanently etched into her skin. The screen on the hotel staff time clock just inside the door gave me a clue to the reason.

"I know I'm late," I offered. "I'm sorry."

"Mister Yaisen has already spoken to me," she growled, "and exempted you from the ordinary regulations."

"But I really do want to attend my seminars."

Okay, so that was a lie, but Learco had insisted that following the rules—or at least not standing out any more than I already had—was the best way to keep me safe if some creature of the night was truly hunting the wild magic within me. Plus, it would give him time to get as much intel from the MAW agents on site who may have been more reluctant to speak with me around. Assuming his dismissal had not yet filtered down through the rank and file anyway.

Although it had made me even later, we'd forgone a Broomer to the hotel so I could give Learco a rundown of my major players list in the relative privacy of too-many-ears-to-actually-listen on our walk through the CBD. I'd told him of Mehrdad and Cal, the smarmy hotel manager and his crew of awe-filled and awful workers, but the folks I kept getting stuck on were those within the Council. I'd only officially met three of its members—and one of them was now a victim—but I was starting to wonder if their Collector moniker meant more than the rumors swirling around. Besides, having a vampire in your crew of "magical creatures" was exactly the type of feather Osmund wanted for his hat.

Layla eyed me suspiciously for a moment before she nodded, pulling her card from her lanyard to scan for the arrival of the back of house freight elevator.

"You'd do best to hurry then," she said. "Eighth floor; Lily of the Moon meeting room."

"That's settled then," Learco said, turning on the bright smile he used for work that I knew as fake, but most others fell straw over broom for. "Do you mind telling me—Layla, was it?—where I may find my agents?"

I smirked as the doors began to close on Layla stumbling over her words, barely squeaking for "Mister Clarke" to follow her as the stainless steel mirrored back my reflection. I was certain Learco would be able to use his status—as long as folks still assumed he was the director of the Southeast Division of the MAW—to get the inside scoop on how things were going. I just hoped my classes would yield more than *Clever Ways to Hex my Customers* or *Making Cross Dividends Work For* me.

"Seminars were a bust," I called, pushing through the door of the Yarrow Tooth Suite and hoping Learco had fared better than I had. "Unless you think understanding Cybersecurity in the Age of Hexes and Hacks will get us anywhere."

With as many suspicions as I had around the Council, it still felt strange to be in the room, but I was grateful Learco and I had a private home base inside the Crow's Court to discuss our separate segments of the investigation. Or perhaps *private* was too strong a word.

"Yet another reason I believe the Council to be the future of the organization, Darragh."

Osmund smiled at me from his perch opposite Learco at the kitchenette table. His ever-present top hat rested upside down on the polished hard oak as if it were waiting for a rabbit to hop out. A sea of file folders—reds mostly, but a few green and tan—were shuffled about the surface, brimming with papers but closed tight to prying eyes, and I smiled at Learco's makeshift interrogation room. He truly was in his element amidst the trappings of his former position, nearly as much as he was with the botanical tools of our shared craft. But the covert documents, the casual court of knowledge as power, went a lot further with folks like Osmund Linnegard than Belladonna or Rue.

"Mehrdad is out of touch with what truly matters to those magical creatures he gathers here," Osmund continued, this time speaking as much for Learco as he was for me. "That is why the Council was formed. To advocate for those of us not solely at the top. Much, I may add, in the same way the Moral Authority of Witches rooted itself in our history."

My face flushed as I held back my laughter at a billionaire attempting to position himself as an underdog, and yet that wasn't nearly as funny as his attempt to posit the MAW as an egalitarian force. At least to me anyway. But it did prove one thing: word had not spread regarding Leland's impetuous dismissal of Learco. We could definitely use that to our advantage.

"Darragh," Learco said, startling me a bit with the stiffness his voice took on when he'd slipped into his MAW agent role, "do you mind giving us a moment to wrap up here?"

"Why should he leave?" Osmund interjected. "After all, this is an informal conversation, is it not, Mister Clarke? Besides which, we are in *his* suite, paid for by myself and my colleagues as it were. It would appear we all have just as much right to be here as the other. Not to mention, this is the space the poor girl who was killed had utilized just prior to her demise."

My brow furrowed at his statement, but a quick glance from Learco kept my lips closed. That Osmund believed their "conversation" was centered on Amy meant he either was unaware of Lady Z's murder or was damn good at hiding it behind his assumption that we didn't know. I neededsome certainty.

"Lady Z…" I started.

"I can assure you the fine Lady had no part in that human's death," Osmund interrupted once more. The way he said *human* made my skin scrawl. "She may have been on this floor, but as a new member of the BOG Witches and a prospective member of the Council, she was merely doing her due diligence to fully realize her station. Yes, I admit we had her spying on Yaisen, but I do not believe that form of espionage is illegal under any MAW edicts. That said, whatever she discovered at Mehrdad's after party last night—the event I believe you yourself were at, Darragh—must have spooked her. I have not heard a peep from her all day."

Well, you wouldn't have, I thought as I studied his face, attempting to find something true beneath the smug contempt he was wearing. Learco, though, was a lot more practiced for the situation.

"Do you believe something amiss has occurred?" he asked, the casual concern in his question almost shocking since I knew he knew the truth.

"All I can say is this," Osmund purred, turning on the charm as he switched his gaze from me to my boyfriend. "While I appreciate the presence of the MAW to deter the DMFM protesters outside from setting foot within our Gathering, perhaps your time would be better spent looking into Mehrdad Yaisen and his accomplices rather than tracking details surrounding the death of some human vagabond who wandered into our midst. If he did discover Lady Z's duplicity, I fear what he would do. Even to one of our own."

Learco nodded as Osmund swiped his hat from the table, twirling it to his crown and rising from his chair. He shook each of our hands firmly, promising to come straight to Learco if any new information arose before showing himself out of the suite.

"He makes it hard to get a word in edgewise," I huffed as the door pulled to.

"It's a way of staying ahead of the conversation," Learco nodded as he rose to give me a hug and a quick peck on the cheek. "It's a means of control. He feeds us the information he wants us to consider before any questions can be delivered. And most of that info points a finger somewhere else."

"My mother always said when you point your broom handle at someone, the bristles will sweep your own toes."

"Perhaps," Learco sighed. "But I do believe he is unaware of Zamiah's murder. Otherwise, he'd be using it as a platform to topple Mehrdad."

"Or he knows and wants you to levy the first accusation," I offered. "It keeps his hands clean, so to speak."

"That is definitely a possibility," Learco acknowledged, the look in his eye telling me he was holding something back.

Perhaps his standard MAW-mode was sinking into him again as he donned his old duds.

"Still, even if it was pointed, it looks like you got a lot of information today," I smiled, pressing forward to reach for the bevy of folders on the table. I peeled open the one closest to me to find all the sheets blank.

"Appearances," Learco shrugged, a sly smile slipping across his lips. "Layla let me borrow some office supplies to make my questions seem more official."

"Oh," I sighed, slipping into the chair Osmund had vacated. "Looks like we both had a bust."

"Not entirely."

Learco cleared his throat as he walked to peer out the window. His eyes were distant as he took in the rise and fall of the Mississippi through the glass.

"There are no bodies," he finally said.

"You mean they've taken them from the hotel?" I asked, concern closing my features as I watched Learco's fingers tap rapidly against his thigh.

"No. The MAW never took possession. In fact, they believe they are here in response to the DMFM. But Amy and Zamiah's bodies, both supposedly moved to the walk-in cold storage within the hotel, are nowhere to be found."

Learco's face was worried as he turned from the window to face me once again, and I bit my lip as I took in his words.

"Couple that with the two corpses you discovered on the rooftop that also disappeared," he continued, "and all the evidence begins to point down a particular path."

"Dead bodies don't just get up and walk away," I protested.

"They do if they're undead," Learco stated bluntly, not a hint of disbelief edging his voice. "They do if they're vampires."

CHAPTER 11

"Are you sure you have to do this?" Learco asked, a worried crinkle in his eyelids as he kept his voice low within the crowded gates.

"I don't like it any more than you do," I huffed, wincing against the late afternoon heat.

It was true. The idea of using my wild magic to reach across the planes to The Mórrígan was far from pleasant, but with four exsanguinated bodies now mysteriously vanished, I needed to know if we were dealing with the Fomóraiġ. At the very least, it could give me some peace of mind. I had faced the Fae thrice before and survived. And were we facing something else entirely, perhaps the Fae Queen could direct us where to look.

Concern still heavy on his words, Learco asked, "Would you not rather do this back at the house?"

His eyes darted to the sideways glances of the passing tour guides and tourists before landing back on mine as I shrugged.

"The OccultList BnB has the MAW's Magic In Monitoring system, and I don't trust that it doesn't extend to the backyard," I sighed. "The last thing we need is for Leland Hyde to have another reason to lock me up or keep you from getting your job back. And I don't really trust the Crow's Court either. Besides, the only outdoor space there is the rooftop, and that empty blackness, while dissipating, is still there."

Learco still didn't look convinced, and his uncertainty was dissolving my resolve.

"Look," I pleaded. "I know it's not ideal. But, if nothing else, it takes a potential bad guy off our list of possible suspects."

"Or it opens the door to add a separate villain and disaster to contend with."

"The spell won't be that powerful," I assured him. "It won't open a door, just a means of conversation. If we can rule out the Fae with certainty, we're one step closer to figuring this out."

Learco grumbled as he pulled me forward through the tourists, eyes quick to take in the entirety of the scene as he guided me toward an empty pathway.

"Why are you so resistant to believing this could be the work of vampires?" he asked, his voice hushed as he kept his eyes trained on mine.

"Why are you so certain it is?" I countered.

It was strange, this bit of role-reversal we were both facing. In most cases, it was my inclination to believe the unbelievable while Learco kept me grounded in the face of facts.

"Look," I continued, lowering my voice further into empathy as I took in the struggle on his face. "I like my vampires in books and movies. And I'm trying to learn from you, to keep this centered in the known and observable. To not go in half-cocked. Watching you, learning from you during our time together…. You're so strong, so sure. Such an inspiration to me. I'm trying to follow your example."

Learco winced as his eyes darted quickly from mine and his hands dropped from my shoulders.

"Well, let's hope we get some answers quickly," he nodded,

peering past the mausoleums as the final patrons trickled out of sight. "I called in a favor with the Archdiocese to get us in here without a tour guide, and that's typically the kind of thing that ticks up the ladder to Leland's lap."

I swallowed hard, gratitude filling my eyes as Learco once again placed his love for me over his personal ambitions. Not that his leadership within the MAW was actually an ambition. But it was his job—his livelihood—and he had been working diligently from within to change some of the more misanthropic elements of the organization. As repugnant as I found the Moral Authority, I didn't want him to change himself, to let go of everything he'd worked toward, for me.

"Don't worry," he smiled, sensing my anguish as I peered up at him. "I just used my name. Never said it was a MAW mission. Though it won't stop him from trying, this holds no smoke for Leland to scream fire."

Now I was worried that I'd unnecessarily chosen a difficult space to perform the spell. Yet something inside of me had led me here. I knew it needed to be outdoors, that it needed to be away from the MAW's watchful eye and further still from its clutches, and New Orleans offered a bevy of magically infused places. But in guiding a new and wild magic to a strange and foreign land, St. Louis Cemetery Number 1—tomb-side to the great Marie Laveau—had seemed the obvious choice. For over a century, folks—magical and nonmagical alike—had flocked here, etching crosses into the stone, leaving offerings of baked goods, asking questions, and paying homage to the historical relevance of her power. The constant barrage of people was what had led to the need for special permission to be here without a tour guide in the first place. Still, something in me told me this was the place to perform my ritual. And if what Chester had told me was true, if Lici and Zamiah really were her descendants, perhaps the remnants of her magic would want answers for the death of her however many greats granddaughter.

"Okay," Learco said, turning back to me as I heard the sound of the metal gates closing in the distance. "The last tour group is out. We've got thirty minutes. We best get to it. What can I do?"

"Keep me grounded," I said, slipping my hand into his as he sat in front of me.

"Always," he smiled. "Even if I do adore your flights of fancy."

My chuckle felt good as it eased the tension I hadn't realized I'd been holding within my chest, and I sighed as my breath equalized with the light humidity of the air around me. I would have preferred to have a bit of Rowan with me, but the Resurrection Ferns growing nearby as well as the bit of Winged Elm leaves I'd scavenged on our walk over from the Crow's Court would have to do. Besides, though the Traveler's Tree had a special connection to the Faerie Realm, I only wanted to open up a phone line, not a direct flight.

"Here goes," I sighed, tapping into my magic as I always had, then pushing through to find the wild that swelled beneath.

It was nearly the same principle used in Fae magic—the one I'd picked up from studying The Mórrígan's own spell casting— in which the threads that made up the universe were shifted, or snipped, or realigned toward the final destination of the spell. It gave them the power of portals, within reason, and of transmogrification, and Fae knew what else. But I was a witch, not a faerie—no matter what the kids on my childhood playground had said—and though the wild magic I now knew I held allowed me to practice their craft, I was going for something else entirely. I wasn't looking to shift the worlds to my will, I wanted to bring them together.

Grabbing hold to the wild, I carefully tugged a strand of its bright green manifestation forward, twisting it around the kelly green of the magic I'd grown so used to. I trembled as the powers twined. A surge of energy pulsed through me as the craft that had always been within me met and merged with newfound discovery. Its vibration grew stronger with each new twist until I had mentally braided my magics together, and I smiled. That was one powerful landline. Holding it within me, my eyes met Learco's, and he nodded to urge me forward.

"Uh, hello?" I mumbled, even in my mind, as I used the united magic I held to open a connection.

It was dark for a moment as the dull dial tone of the ether reverberated through my brain. I focused on the green of my power. It was, after all, so close to the hue of her eyes. Perhaps it would help me reach her.

Darragh Cullen, she huffed, the musicality of her voice sounding through my eardrums in equal parts surprise and annoyance. *If any witch could find a way to enter my head from the other realm, it would be you. To what do I owe this disturbance?*

It had worked! And—at least for now—there were no unexpected outcomes. Just a simple line of communication. No cracks; no entryways; no paths for the Fae to fuck up my life any more than they already had.

"Hi, uh… The Mórrígan," I said, doing my best to sound reverent while displaying the power I knew it would take to earn her respect. It always felt strange using the "The" while addressing her, but she insisted it was a part of her moniker. "Thanks for taking my call."

As if you gave me a choice.

The connection was stronger now, growing from a voice line to one visual, and I could see the exasperated look she was attempting to shield on her features. She was just as beautiful as I remembered her to be. Her eyes, the deep emerald of a grandmother's brooch, sparkled with a radiance nearly as blinding as the feathered iridescence of her raven black hair. The high arching cheekbones above her dahlia lips highlighted the pursed smirk she held there and made the paleness of her skin glow. Maybe that was the cost of the spell. Impressing The Mórrígan was not an easy task, and each time I had, she'd taken a renewed interest in me. Catching the eye of any Fae was risky, but particularly so when it came to the leaders of the Tuath Dé or the Fomóraiġ.

Well, she moaned, her eyes studying the edges of my spell while attempting to figure out its method, *get on with it. I am quite the busy Queen, after all.*

"I thought you'd be relishing in your new lands now that Balor is gone," I quipped, hoping a gentle reminder of what my coven and I had done for her only a few days before would warm her up to my cause.

Her laughter, musical and grinding all at once as if the gears of the gramophone wanted to get in on the record's action, sent a breeze across the nape of my neck.

My simple summer child, she purred. *The defeat of Balor—which I orchestrated—occurred two, no three years ago. Or did you forget the disparities of time betwixt our realms? His death, as it were, created what you would call a vacuum. And, as I imparted to one of your kind long ago, nature abhors a vacuum. I have graciously stepped in to fill that void, though not without undue hardship and stress on my behalf.*

Time in the Fae Realm truly did spin differently, stretching or slowing in discordant measure to our own. For all I knew, I could reach back out in two years on Earth and find her just finishing up the current conversation we were attempting. It was nearly as confusing as whatever the hell was happening at the Crow's Court.

Though I must admit, she said, throwing me a bone as the falter on my face began to send waves through the connection of my spell, *the items you gathered for me have made my wrest at control easier. As such, I suppose I can hear you out.*

I knew she was more interested in keeping my spell up so she could figure out its working than hearing what I had to say, but as she held up a shield with the opalescent glow of the *Ollphéist* scale twined around the edges with the red feathers of the *murúch cochaillín draíchta*, I was just as enchanted. The shield transformed into a spear then to a dagger before settling into the form of a pendant that she hung from her neck. She had used the fortitude of the scale combined with the transformative powers of the merfolk's hat to create an impenetrable weapon which could take any form. And though I wasn't much for weapons, I was just as interested as she was in figuring out the method behind the magic.

"Ask her," Learco urged, snapping me out of my trance and back to the task at hand.

Do I hear Learco Clarke? The Mórrígan sang. *I suppose that means Cernun Kyteler is also nearby. Have you finally come to your senses and now require a Fae fourth to your ensemble? I could be swayed. Cernunnos had fantastic things to speak of you, Darragh Cullen, once he bent the knee to me.*

I hadn't realized the spell was broadcasting my thoughts and The Mórrígan's replies aloud, at least in the immediate vicinity. I was glad Learco had used his connections to clear the cemetery now. The spell would have taken an explanation neither of us were prepared to give.

Learco concealed his laughter as he rolled his eyes at the Fae Queen's proclamation, but it was enough to snap me back to reality. And maybe into a little bit of fantasy about my time in the Fae forest with the Great Horned King. But those were tales for a different time.

"People," I said, "human and witch, are dying."

Your kind die everyday. How is this of my concern?

"They are dying unnaturally," I insisted. "I am trying to ascertain how."

And your first thought is that it must be me or my kin, she howled, her voice buzzing through the ether in admonishment. *Just like a witch to blame all their issues on my kind. I believed you to be different, Darragh Cullen. Perhaps I was mistaken.*

"I'm not blaming," I replied quickly as I felt her pull away from our connection. "I'm just looking for answers from someone who may know more than I do. And you have more knowledge than anyone I've ever met."

It wasn't exactly true, but flattery went a hell of a long way with the Fae, even when it was obvious.

When you speak the truth, whether you believe it or not is irrelevant, The Mórrígan beamed. *So ask your questions, Darragh Cullen. But understand what the favor of my answer means.*

Shit. Maybe this wasn't such a good idea. The currency of the Fae-folk always resided in the quid pro quo, and their claiming of their quo always bit a witch in the ass. And not in a good way. Still, I needed to know.

"What do you know about vampires?" I asked.

The bemused expression on The Mórrígan's face was quickly replaced by amused tranquility. There was something near sympathy as she peered into my eyes before speaking.

I can see why you came to me, she sighed. *When faced with immortal beings who have utilized their centuries of existence to perfect the art of passionate love-making, it is only natural for a witch's mind to wander toward the Fae.*

"So they're real," I stated, my face falling as I caught Learco's grimace from the other side of my spell.

Yes, The Mórrígan proclaimed. *No. Perhaps. You, as a witch, know full well that there is more to our realms than that which we know or understand. Throughout the centuries during which our realms were united, creatures and occurrences existed that seemed beyond the wealths of knowledge either of our races had encountered before. The same must still be true.*

"But you've never met one?" I asked, lifting my chin as I realized her "vast knowledge" was as reliant upon tale and fable as my own. Damn. I should've known answers wouldn't come so easily, particularly when involving the Fae.

One must assume the light of my kind to be too great for such creatures of darkness, The Mórrígan responded. *So, no, Darragh Cullen. I can not confirm the existence of vampires for you. But nor can I deny it. And yet, such knowledge is not the true reason for your contact.*

"It isn't?"

You want to know if you are the reason this is happening, she said. *If your wild magic is to blame for whatever so-called evil is surfacing.*

My breath clung to my throat as I squinted through the haze of my vision, realizing—finally—that as we had been speaking, the edges of the spell had become clearer, more concrete. Double damn. The Mórrígan had figured out the workings of my spell and bolstered it from her end, reaffirming the connection and potentially giving her access to my mind.

Relax. I'm not reading your thoughts, she assured me, which really didn't help. *Your face, Darragh Cullen, has a tendency to broadcast louder than your words. So what I will tell you is this: your spark of wild magic ignited in a space before time or reality were formed. It is primal, and with that primality comes the potential for other primordial developments. Not all will be good. Not all will be bad. And, 'less you conduct the spell, none of them are your fault.*

That didn't make me feel any better, and I winced as Learco tapped his watch to signify the end of our uninterrupted time inside the cemetery.

"I don't even know how to use the wild."

It came out as more of a whine than I'd intended, and The Mórrígan rolled her eyes.

You witches are such a conundrum, she sang. *You know that the power is within you, and yet you continue to view it, to use it, as some external thing.*

You see it as merely a connection instead of what it truly encompasses. You will learn to use that spark when you've silenced the external and moved to look within. There is much for you to learn, much you can accomplish when you use the wild as it was meant to flow as opposed to letting it bolster the currents of your witch magic. But that, as well as the way of the vampire, is not something I can teach you.

I nodded. Three years may have passed in her realm, but I was only a few days into even knowing about the wild—or the spark from which Fae and witch magic flowed.

I could hear the crowds gathering beyond the cemetery gates, the agitated tourists and the put-off tour guides attempting to quell them with promises of only "a few moments more."

"Thank you, The Mórrígan," I sighed. "I won't take any more of your time."

I will leave you with this then, Darragh, she intoned, a smooth combination of love and pity on her breath as she stated only my first name. *While I cannot confirm nor deny the existence of vampires, I can give assurance that the Fae are not involved. We trade in power, not in something as frivolous as blood. So, as you are hunting your demons, look to those who would deem fluid and not the spark as the source. I wish you well, Darragh Cullen, in facing your dangers. And not simply because should you live, when our paths cross again, I may lay claim to the favor you now owe me.*

I allowed the braid to unravel, and the spell dissolved as I hunched over myself in my seated position. It had taken more energy than I'd realized to keep that connection going, even with the addition of The Mórrígan's power. I felt Learco's hand tussle through the hair on the back of my head as I heard the gates of the cemetery push open, and tourists once again hobbled inside.

I left the volume on mute as I absently scrolled through the channels on the large flatscreen in my hotel room, splayed akimbo on the decidedly not comfortable cushions of the couch as I attempted to regain the strength my spell—coupled with our vigorous early-afternoon delight and the overall lack of sleep the past few nights—had taken from me. Even though I'd insisted to Learco I was fine as we left the cemetery, I'd actually been grateful for the locked doors and the mourning shroud hung outside the Voodoo History Museum sending us on back to the hotel. Not that I was happy for Félicité's sorrow or Zamiah's death, but I needed rest in spite of the drive within me to fight to figure out what the Fae was going on. At least now I knew the Fae, and, by proxy, myself were not involved. That had to count for something.

The truth was, I was more worried about Learco than I was about myself. He'd led us the long way around to get to the still-undiscovered-by-the-DMFM backdoor of the hotel. He was adamant in the presence of an unknown immortal race that survived on blood living within our midst. And though his clothes were his own, they lacked the stiff, pressed quality he generally presented with as he grabbed them straight from his knapsack before pulling them on.

The Learco of even one week prior would have marched headstrong through the midst of the Defend Mankind Maniacs with warning in his irises and a casual dismissal on his lips. He'd have been the one convincing me to quit my flights of fancy and focus on the more mundane and known magics of our universe. And he'd have never misaligned the buttons I'd had to help him with on his shirt after our romp on the living room floor. His aura, though, had proven it was him and not another Changeling attempting purchase through our forms.

And yet I could hear the rising excitement on his voice as it carried in from the other room. Though his words were not as measured as they usually were, all of the love and directness which made Learco who he was was still there as he talked Cernun through what was going on.

Maybe it's just jet lag, I told myself, craning my neck to find a more comfortable position against the brocade fabric of the sofa. *A portal from the Fae Realm followed by a few hours in the air is a lot of miles for any witch to undertake in so short a time.*

"Cernun sends his love," Learco chimed as he slipped from the bedroom and slid his cell phone into his pocket. "And he made me promise we'd both make it back to Atlanta without becoming enthralled to any creatures of the night."

"Where's the fun in that?" I quipped, pulling myself into a more alert seated position but still not rising from the couch.

Learco chuckled as he sat beside me, perched on the edge of the cushion with his knees bent at the ready beneath him.

"Next steps," he started, trying on the cadence I was more accustomed to when he went into work mode. "As word of my temporary dismissal has not reached the halls of the Crow's Court, I would like to speak with the manager—Landry, you said his name is—to acquire access to the room listings for the guests as well as the hotel's security system. If we are dealing with a vampire who is targeting the BOG Witch attendees, determining how they are coming and going will help us identify the creature."

"That won't work," I frowned, doing my best to look compassionate as my lover's brow furrowed. "Landry's a bit of an ass. And Mehrdad told me they have the cameras shut off for the duration of the convention in order to... keep our activities private. Besides, all the lore suggests the fanged ones can't be caught on camera."

"I see," Learco sighed, but his expression remained undeterred. "Then perhaps I can convince Landry to reinstate the cameras, at least in the lobby, for the evening. Particularly with our boyfriend's brother's cronies amassing outside. Then you and I can begin to question the hotel staff to determine if they've seen anything or if they're aware of any areas within the building in which someone untoward could operate undisturbed. Too, I believe it would behoove us to have another chat with Linnegard. His proclivity to describe all non-humans as 'creatures' in his speech strikes me as odd. Unless he is aware of more than we witches. And perhaps Cal Juventus should be questioned as well. His knowledge of the Fae-folk leads one to believe he may have knowledge of other species as well."

Learco had a point. Osmund's odd way of speaking had certainly unsettled me. And there was the strangeness of Cal's aura as it grated against my own to contend with. But none of that necessarily meant they weren't witches—or that they were vampires hiding in plain sight. Was it possible that an entire coven of vampires—they called their groups "covens" as well, at least according to the fictional books I'd read and the shows I loved—had infiltrated the BOG Witch Convention? Vamps loved a nocturnal dalliance as much as we did—also according to the lore—and a 3AM rager lead to many a skipped sunrises. And that was without even mentioning the penchant for black the majority of my fellow attendees had. Plus Lady Z had infiltrated the Gala amidst rumors the convention was rife with vampyric activity, even in previous years. But Mehrdad hadn't mentioned anything, even after we found her body. Did that mean he was in on it too? And yet, there had been no news stories about famous and rich witches going missing at these events. That would have surely come to light. So was it just humans who happened in— like when I'd invited Amy—who'd been drained and disposed of with no one the wiser? Had I inadvertently ordered lunch for the monsters? Had they figured out Zamiah was investigating and that's why they jumped to witch blood? Did that mean Learco and I were next?

Ugh. I had more questions than I'd started with and fewer answers than a tongue-twisted sphinx as the days dragged onwards. Plus the hungry growl in my stomach. At least the unknown had somehow jostled my energy back to near-full throttle to match the near-manic approach Learco was taking as he attempted to suss out reason.

"Maybe we go a little more covert in our operation," I suggested, my mind flush with the image of Zamiah's drained body slumped against the wall of the elevator. "I mean, we're not exactly undercover at this point, but there's no sense in flashing a neon 'bite me' sign over our necks. We can question Osmund and Cal at the party tonight. Get them dancing. Get them chatting. Maybe a little bit of wet-works...."

"Wet-works is murder," Learco laughed.

"Oh," I blushed, happy to see the humor on his face replacing the rapid-fire stoning of his attempt at control. "I thought it was alcohol. Getting their lips wet to loosen them. Loose lips sinking ships, and all that. Real spy stuff."

Learco shook his head as he kissed me softly. Even though he knew I was lying, my lame attempt at a joke had brought him back into himself.

"Spy stuff it is," he said as he pulled his lips from mine. "In the meantime, let's get you some food. Your stomach's loud enough to scare off any vampires hiding within a two mile radius. Then we'll never get the bottom of this."

CHAPTER 12

The few MAW agents in the back corridors—taking a break while their compatriots paced the hotel lobby in a casual show of strength against the advancement of the Defend Mankind From Magic maniacs marching their own show of force outside—pulled themselves to quick attention as Learco and I made our way through to the backdoor. My boyfriend nodded respectfully to each and every black-clad operative we passed, his expression as blank as theirs but his eyes alight with acknowledgment. It was a kind gesture, one the other higher ups within the Moral Authority would never deign to do—not the ones I'd met anyway—and was a large part of what made Learco so good for the MAW. He was sincere in his want to realign their values, to posit them for witch-kind instead of above us. But centuries old organizations had a tendency to cling to the "old ways" making change come slowly. Still, Learco was a start.

"Maybe when we find the vampire," I joked as we slipped onto the side street at the rear of the Crow's Court and crossed the asphalt before heading southwest toward the Garden District, "we can convince him to scare Leland into giving you your job back. I mean, we don't have to slay him right away."

"Leland or the vampire?" Learco jostled back. "I told you, I'm not worried about my position. Leland acted without authorization, and while it technically stands, no paperwork has been filed, and we both know the MAW loves their paperwork. There's zero need for worry."

He was lying. Even if I had not grown to know him so well—to love him so well—throughout our time together, I would have been able to sense the anxiety he was trying to subdue within himself. Plus, he was missing his scheduled meeting with Leland to be in New Orleans helping me. That coupled with his Changeling-induced disappearance from Salem—which we couldn't tell the MAW about without revealing that the Fae were real—and Leland Hyde's incomplete-but-said-with-gusto version of events would hold a lot more credence in his "unreliable employee" report on Learco. Of course, if he managed to capture a vampire....

"Is that why you're here?" I asked, keeping my face light and my voice low as we wound our way through the CBD. "To make sure Leland remembers just how valuable you are once you catch the bloodsucker terrorizing the BOG Witches?"

Learco stopped dead in his tracks, a look of sour astonishment on his face as he sized me up.

"I'm here because I love you," he said, "despite—or maybe partially because of—all the messes you tend to find yourself in."

My lips pursed into a semi-frown as I nodded and took his hand. Of course he was the type to always put others above himself. And that wasn't simply relegated to his family, born or chosen. True, those inclinations got a little complicated when it came to the MAW, particularly when the oath he'd sworn to the organization came in conflict with the silent one he'd given me and Cernun, but I'd never once doubted the witch would be there for me if I needed him. It was wrong of me to imply otherwise.

"Still, catching the bad guy wouldn't hurt my standing," he smiled, letting me off the hook as he squeezed my hand, pulling me onwards toward the slowly setting sun.

"*Bonswa, Mesye* Clarke; *Mesye* Cullen. We got your table right this way."

Learco hadn't even spoken as we approached the man, lounging idly atop a short series of stone steps in his finery, rubbing the tips of his fingers through the nearby rosemary shrub to release an aromatic wave of clean and green into the dimming sky. There had been something quite perfect about the sight: the way the black sheen of his tuxedo folded against the whitewashed concrete; his seeming disregard for the "station" of his wardrobe amidst his closeness to the earth; the glow of the Edison bulbs on the porch behind him so bright they subdued the rest of the world—all of it was so anachronistic and yet so timely, so ethereal and yet so perfectly situated to New Orleans. It was certainly the type of witch-owned establishment Learco's MAW connections made available. For a moment, I felt just as I had when he'd invited me to The Dove and Crow back in Atlanta, except this time I wasn't worried Learco was trying to flame me at the stake.

As we passed through the curtain created by the lights, I grinned at the liveliness of the courtyard restaurant within. Zydeco music pulsed from one side of the peristyle, filling the air with a soulfully elevated rhythm. Drinks flowed and patrons laughed, dancing between courses and spinning the waitstaff to join with their amusement. Some were dressed in elegant gowns or suits though others seemed just at home in their patchwork shorts and flip flops. So maybe it was not like The Dove and Crow at all. There was definitely magic at work to keep the sound and the revelry of the open air restaurant contained. I had a feeling that was less for keeping the display hidden and more for the tranquility of the nearby Garden District homes. Plus the speakeasy feel really spoke to the city.

A perfume of roast and spice clung to the notes pushed from the accordion and rubboard, held up by the base notes of earth and ozone which gave the unmarked establishment its name: Petrichor. And even though I was still hungry, the pleasant aroma of dry earth quenched filled me immediately with a sense of satiated solace. The magic here was geared toward merriment—the ritualized fulfillment of it—and sang of connection and home.

"This is one of my favorite restaurants in the States," Learco smiled as we found our table and thanked the host for the menus he'd passed us. "The reserved table may be the only thing I'd really miss from my position with the MAW."

His eyes were distant as he peered throughout the space, but I could tell from the quiver in his skin, the one dancing atop the sharpness of his cheekbones, he was not thinking about his position but rather than comforts of his island upbringing.

"The peristyle," he said when his eyes returned to mine, "is where all the public facing ritual occurs. And over there's the entrance to the *hounfor*—the altar room. Which, for a restaurant, is the kitchen. That's one of the things about Yoruba-based traditions, we never lost our flare or our pride in public spectacle. We put our magic out there for all to see. Maybe that's part of what, when you so publicly pushed that spell to save Cernun, attracted me immediately to you."

I grinned as my hand reached for his across the soft, smooth tablecloth. It was nice to see this side of him, nicer still to hear him reminisce about his youth. For all he'd done to try to change the Moral Authority from within, it had also done its share of changing him. It had made him much more reserved in his show of power—at least when it came to the magic that swirled within him and not the perceived power of position—during his time as the head of the Southeastern Division; and that was directly due to the MAW's attempts at utmost secrecy, even in the wake of our modern revelation.

In truth, I could kind of understand that aspect of their "authority." European traditions had once had our Altars to Athena, our Stonehenge, our Dowth, and our Faerie Rings, but countless crusades and witch hunts had deemed those relics of a past hysteria as we hid our ways for safety. That fear had clouded a large part of my relationship to my power, even as my family and I had always fully embraced it within the privacy of our closed quarters. To listen to Learco's memories of the peristyle near his family's home in the Caribbean Sea, to hear his unabashed joy in the allowance of being fully free, fully himself in his magic—a feeling that had long ricocheted within me as well—made me feel even closer to the man who shared my bed.

He was still beaming when the waiter returned with my Old Fashioned and a glass of rich, red wine for my lover.

"Any questions about our offerings?" the server asked, bopping to the music as if torn between a desire to serve and a need to dance.

"We haven't even had a chance to look over the menu," Learco admitted. "Too caught up in the reverie this place incites."

"It do, indeed," the server grinned. "How 'bout we let the chef cook you up something special, and the two of you can free yourselves in the atmosphere? *Mange Iwa* or *mange sec*?"

"*Mange Iwa*," Learco replied, and I furrowed my brow in question as our waiter bopped away.

"Food for the gods," he explained. "Which often meant animal sacrifice. *Mange sec* is a dry offering, so, for here, vegetarian food."

"Gotcha," I laughed. "My family would just leave butter out hoping the Brownies would help with the household chores. Judging by the offerings at the Wayward Inn back in the Fae Realm, I can't say we were too far off. But certainly not nearly as fancy as your traditions."

"Fancy-schmancy," Learco howled. "It was all about the party. The sacrifice was given to the gods, but it was to remind us of our place in nature, of the natural cycle of things. And every witch—those with the big houses and the fancy labels inside their lapels or those with the straw roofs and worn out slacks—was inherently a part of that cycle and, thus, welcomed at the party. I mean, just look around."

I let my eyes spin the impromptu dance floor which had sprung up between the tables, soaking in the joy on everyone's face and failing to see any disparity between the red-bottomed heels or the rope-knotted sandals. I knew things were not always as easy or as simple as they were in recollection, but it was nice to see Learco nestled into comfort after the struggles of the past few days.

"Do you wanna dance?" I asked, taking a chug of my Old Fashioned to bolster my rhythm as I extended my hand once more across the table. "I'm sure we've got some time before our food is ready."

Learco smirked as he rose from his chair, licking his lips while I downed another gulp of liquid courage and stood to join him. I closed my eyes to let the music seep inside of me, trying to remember the casual ease with which Cal had led me on the dance floor what seemed like years ago. If I could waltz with him, I could certainly manage a mambo with my lover. Or some approximation thereof.

When I opened my eyes, Learco's arms flailed as his feet twisted and rose to the elevated beat. I watched each flourish in awe, attempting to swing my limbs in a similar manner, and Learco winked.

"Don't worry so much about control," he whispered, leaning in close and taking my hands in his, pulling me to his chest and then pushing me back. "The steps don't matter as much as the music. Just let it flow through you."

I nodded and kissed his cheek as he released me.

Dance like no one's watching, I reminded myself as the rhythm began to pulse in my bones. I felt my heart rate elevate to match it, feeling my chest pump with each drum beat as I began to move.

"There you go," Learco assured me.

"I finally feel like I'm in New Orleans," I called back.

"What?" he asked, swinging his arms around me as our torsos grinded to the beat. "You mean the inner halls of a fancy hotel don't have that Creole lilt?"

I laughed, feeling myself free for the first time in way too long as the weight lifted from my chest and I began to move more broadly.

"Looks like we found our horse tonight!" our waiter exclaimed as he brought two fresh glasses to our table. "You feel that *Ogan-Sig-Wedo.* And your meal will be out shortly."

"Does he mean I'm graceful or that I'm clomping around wearing metal shoes?" I asked as the man departed, and Learco paused for another sip of his Malbec.

"A 'horse' is someone who's been possessed by an Iwa. As if they're being ridden," Learco explained. "In this case, the deity of music. It's a good thing."

Well, that was something. Emboldened, I pulled my lover closer to me. My feet kept time as the music sank to a lowered tempo blues, and I pulled in the intoxicating musk of my lover.

"It's a shame Cernun isn't here," Learco hummed. "He would love this."

"Yeah," I agreed. "But I prefer to keep him—as I had preferred to keep *you*—as far away from those bloodsuckers at the Crow's Court as possible."

"You mean the potential vampires? Or the business folk thirsty for a drop of that Kyteler fortune?"

"Both," I chuckled. For a moment I considered confessing Balor's warning to him—that I would be the one to bring death to my coven—but I didn't want to spoil such a magical moment.

Besides, something else was about to.

"Holy shit," I gasped.

Across the peristyle, half hidden by the shadow of one of the columns, I saw her. Her face was pale, her lips slightly ajar, and an intense hunger mixed with desire inside her eyes as she stared me down from across the restaurant. Her hair flowed free of its braid and waved seductively atop her bare shoulders to touch the hem of an exquisite, skin tight gown. It's darkened velvet dripped like blood from her frame in the wafting light of the Edison bulbs. My feet stopped moving as I stared.

"That's Lady Z," I whispered. "Zamiah."

Learco turned as I blinked, but she was gone.

A worried expression cascaded down my face, but I shook it off as I watched the waiter approach with our entrees.

"Two chef's specials," he smiled. "Here we got a Gulf-caught Redfish Courtbullion for you, *Meyse* Clarke. And the chef thought a breaded and deep-fried Pork Boudin with fresh greens and riced potatoes might appeal to your Irish sensibilities, *Meyse* Cullen. *Bon appetite.*"

It looked delicious, paired perfectly to our palettes thanks to the MAW's extensive research on the both of us, and I tried not to seem distraught as I returned to my chair and nodded along with

Learco's compliments.

My eyes scanned the crowd as the waiter departed, darting beyond the bobbing hips and fork-holding hands for any sign of that maroon velvet dress, that ravenous glare. I was so sure it had been her. Her eyes had locked on mine, as if she had sought me out. Like she was following me. Hunting me. I could feel the cold air that followed her beneath my own clothing, pricking my skin as it traced a path across my spine.

"Perhaps it was Félicité," Learco offered, concern fresh in his own eyes as he tried to calm me. "You did say the sisters looked quite a bit alike."

I sighed as I nodded once more, steeling my face and bringing my eyes back to the meal set before us. It did make more sense for it to be Lici, but if that were true, why had she not just crossed the floor to say hello?

"Regardless, you need to eat," Learco said. "That spell earlier took a lot out of you. And you can't fight vampires on an empty stomach. I'm sure that's somewhere in all the lore."

I smiled a weak smile but agreed as I pulled the cloth napkin from beneath my silverware and spread it over my lap. It did smell amazing. And the hunger in my belly was growling nearly as much as the yearning I'd seen in Zamiah's eyes.

"Maybe my mind is playing tricks on me," I conceded as I took the first bite of my meal.

It was exquisite and reminded me a lot of my grandmother's blood sausage breakfast patties she'd make for me when I was visiting. Or rather, my mother's take on the recipe, after she infused the spices of the rich peppers and herbs she grew in her kitchen garden. I could also taste what Chester had referred to as the Holy Trinity in the mix—that celery, onion, and green bell pepper mixture that was quintessential to all Southern Louisiana cooking. Each flavor held its own, bright and sweet, as it mixed into a spell of overall flavor. Cooking was a lot like magic in that way, all the disparate yet connected elements coming together to make a whole. I could understand how the kitchen was like an altar. Plus, a great meal with the right ingredients could definitely produce a trance-like state.

Learco seemed to be enjoying his dinner as much as I was, and I scattered my discomfort as I took in the hazy grin he held between his bites.

"How is it?" I asked.

"Delectable," he purred, and I did not even grimace when he used his fork to pop one of the redfish eyeballs into his mouth.

As much as I was enjoying the meal—and the time with my boyfriend—I couldn't help but feel the unease of being watched nestle its way between my shoulder blades. I tried to ignore it, to stay present int he ritual of the supper, but my vision continued to wander.

Glimpses of Zamiah's face plagued me from every corner, and yet she was gone before I could even voice her presence to Learco. Our eyes met each time I saw her, and I felt the intensity of her ache burn into my chest. Too, there was amusement there, like it was a game for her, as if the act of stalking her prey was nearly as satiating as dipping her fangs into its neck.

Or maybe my mind was confusing my concern with the revelry of the environment, twisting them together to force me to remember my focus.

"Just how was everything?" our waiter asked as he effortlessly slipped our finished plates from their settings and balanced them in the crook of his left arm. "Will you be having anything else?"

"Just the check," Learco smiled.

The waiter pouted appropriately—a brief puffed lip at his sorrow we wouldn't be staying to dance through dessert—then turned to walk away before I stopped him.

"Um… can I ask…? The sisters who own the Voodoo Museum. Are they here tonight?"

I thought it best not to mention Lady Z's death. I wasn't sure what the family had said about it nor how far that word had traveled.

"Sisters?" the waiter replied, himself confused for a moment before he shrugged it off. "The family who own that, they are regulars. But they take the week around the Equinox to travel and do their rites back there in the French countryside. Shame that means the Museum is closed. It's small, but it packs a wallop."

Learco made small talk with the Broomer driver as I huddled against the window, ear pressed to the receiver as Chester's cell phone trilled somewhere in the distance. The "text if it's important" of his voicemail message was followed by a robotic voice telling me the user's mailbox was full before the line disconnected. I grumbled as I pulled my phone from my cheek.

"He's not answering."

"Do we need to change our destination?" Learco asked, eyebrows raised as he turned his head to face me but stayed leaning forward between the driver's side and the front passenger seat.

"No," I huffed. "We need to get back to the hotel before the party. Besides, he's a friend of theirs. Even if the sisters were pretending to be people they aren't, I don't think Chester's in any real danger from them."

What I couldn't wrap my head around, though, was *why* they

were pretending to be someone different. In fairness, Zamiah had opted for mysterious versus an outright lie in her infiltration of the BOG Witch Convention. Though her presence in and of itself had been a bit of a ruse. And it'd gotten her killed. Did Félicité think she needed the sway of the Museum, of a grand witch heritage, to pull me to her side? That may have been the case if she thought I was just another BOG Witch obsessed with status. Whatever the reason, those answers would have to wait until we discovered who—vampire or otherwise—was behind the deaths at the Crow's Court.

Give me a call when you get a minute, I texted Chester as we slipped from St. Charles around the Harmony Circle and down to Camp Street to take us back to the hotel. I felt my muscles tense as we turned onto Canal, heading toward the river, toward the hotel. There were only two night's left of the BOG Witch Convention, and I wanted to end whatever the hell was happening before anyone else died.

"You're going to want to take a right when we hit Magazine," Learco told the driver as we slowed our way through the throngs of tourists beginning to make their way toward the French Quarter for the evening. "We're going for the back entrance these days."

"Hold that thought," I called, directing Learco's attention to the flashing blue lights swirling before the hotel. "Maybe we should get out here."

Shit. I hoped things hadn't gotten out of hand between the MAW and the DMFM. The last thing we needed on top of everything else was the New Orleans Police Department attempting to quell a disturbance between a sect of militant witches and militarized humans, even if the latter were bigots.

As we moved closer, I could tell the protesters were more afraid and shocked than angry. Tears streamed down some faces, and their homemade signs were discarded around their feet. Several of them looked as if they wanted to run, to get as far away as possible from the hotel, and yet that human inclination to watch the accident head-on, to rubberneck past the wreck kept their feet planted and their heads craned above the wall of police cars.

In fairness, I supposed Learco and I were doing the same as we made our way toward the scene.

The police officers, for their part, appeared just as confused and disoriented as the DMFMers. But they held the line as a few MAW agents circled the pavement a couple of paces beyond the entrance to the Crow's Court, the four of them attempting a recreation spell that kept fizzling out. I could feel the same black emptiness I'd felt on the rooftop in the wake of their endeavored spell, the same dull thud of nothingness it created.

"She must have jumped!" I heard a witness calling, comforting her friend who was sobbing silently against her shoulder.

"Is she a witch or a human?" another asked.

"I bet a witch sacrificed her in some dark arts ritual," someone else called. "Ain't no way she jumped and stayed that intact."

"Why would they kill one of their own?" another said. "Ain't nobody but witches inside the whole of that hotel."

"Coulda been a cleaning lady."

"That look like a maid's uniform to you?"

"Coulda been a call girl."

The voices went on and on as we neared, the time between whatever had occurred and a factual statement from someone of authority edging forward a tale to fit the preferred narrative of those nearby. Most of that would wash away by morning, though whatever had happened would remain.

I breathed slowly, pulling calm into my lungs as I attempted to assuage my fears of another vampire strike. Particularly one so public. It didn't match the M.O. of the killer we'd been dealing with until now though. But a police officer's spoken thoughts confirmed my fears:

"Why is there no blood?" she asked, tears as thick as the fear on her face.

CHAPTER 13

"I suppose there's no keeping this quiet anymore," Mehrdad sighed, and I groaned from my chair inside the lobby.

She may not have been the nicest of witches, but Kara certainly hadn't deserved to die. Mehrdad's lack of reverence for the demise of the receptionist who'd handled his Gala for the past however-many-years irked me, no matter how rude she had been to me personally. Still, he was also right. The camera crews now lined up outside to cover the *Death at the Crow's Court* certainly put a spotlight on the situation. Luckily, the body had been covered before any of the television stations arrived. And though Learco was doing a great job at his impromptu press conference on behalf of the Moral Authority of Witches, I could hear the Defend Mankind Maniacs yelling "Demon sacrifice!" even through the thick-paned glass of the hotel. The very public display of Kara's body—hell, the involvement of the NOPD too—put not just the BOG Witches but the whole of witch-kind under scrutiny.

"What the flying Faerie fuck are you playing at, Yaisien?"

The anger on Osmund's words echoed from the marble of the gilded lobby, and Mehrdad and I spun to watch him barreling towards us from the elevator bay. His face was red, darkening the hue and reflecting from the sheen of his top hat as he stomped forward.

"In addition to that human girl I graciously helped you with," he continued, stopping before us but failing to lower the volume of his tone, "I now hear there are at least three additional bodies found at the Crow's Court, including one of my prospective Council members. And now, amidst all this death and secrecy, the lovely Kara—a cherished employee of this exquisite hotel— has thrown herself from the rooftop. In protest, no doubt, of the treatment the hotel staff receive under your leadership of the Business Owners Gathering of Witches."

"It is rather gauche, Mister Linnegard, to attempt to use the death of one of our own in order to usurp me."

Mehrdad, for his part, was calm in his reply, but the intensity of his words were as thick on the air as the fury of Osmund's. Even with their pronounced height difference, their eyes met in a glinting stand-off beneath the suddenly razor lights of the news crews beyond the glass.

"It is not I who misled the entirety of the Gathering in willful ignorance," Osmund snarled. "You have denied this ceremonial coven and, by extension, the poor workers of the Crow's Court itself the ability to protect themselves from whatever evil has been unleashed upon this property. Such a slight shall not go unanswered by the Council, nor, I dare say, the Gathering at large."

Mehrdad huffed, turning his head to let Osmund win the staring contest and yet one-upping him in a casual disregard. Pity and promise plagued his eyes as he looked at me, silently requesting I take his "side" in all that was happening, before he tried once more to defuse the situation through obfuscation.

"I would think, Mister Linnegard," Mehrdad hummed, licking the syllables of the Council leader's name like a cat cleaning its tail, "an organization such as yours, what with your besetting adherence to the dominance of—as you say—'magical beings,' should have much more cause to be alarmed here. Three of the supposed victims, whose deaths come hard to prove in the lack of corpses, were human after all. It is not the BOG Witches who detest humankind but your little upstart at rebellion. Too, the one witch who died was, of your own admission, a prospective member of your little group. One who happened to be a turncoat judging by her participation in my after-hours soirée. Darragh, here, as well as several other upstanding members of our community can attest to her presence. One should be wary of pointing broom handles, Osmund, when the spell craft is not on one's side."

Osmund stumbled in place, stuttering over words like "set up" and "preposterous" as he found his back in the proverbial corner Mehrdad had pushed him toward. I squinted as my eyes darted between the men, attempting to make out any sign of guilt or confession in their faces. I had thought every word Mehrdad had spoken. Okay, maybe not in such precise language, but the Council did seem awfully suspicious given their tact of elevation through subjugation. Still, it was equally possible the vampire's victims had been chosen as a matter of convenience, and the inherent hatred in the Council made the coincidence into convincing evidence. Or maybe it was Mehrdad and the BOG Witches themselves who'd learned to control the vamp, and they were in fact attempting to set up the Council to wrest back control. Mehrdad's sharp-tongued negotiation of the facts certainly seemed to point that way. Even moreso when he tossed Osmund a bone.

"Yet none of that unpleasantness," he continued, "should have anything to do with the suicide of a troubled young witch, so dazzled by and jealous of the extravagances we live, she deemed fit to take her own life from the rooftop of her workplace."

"It was not suicide."

At the sound of Learco's voice, a wave of reassurance washed through me to cut the tension of the room. Things were dire, true, and only getting worse, but I felt better knowing he was near.

"The victim was drained of her blood prior to being dropped to the sidewalk. Too, as evidenced by the impact damage to her body, she was not thrown from the roof, but rather a lower floor of the hotel. I'd say one no higher than the fifth."

Learco crossed to stand between Osmund and Mehrdad, giving me a soft nod as two MAW agents carried Kara's limp body across the marble floor and two others stationed themselves against the exits.

"This is officially a Moral Authority matter," he said, "and as such I will be taking command."

Fuck, it was sexy to watch him take control. I bit my lip to keep the trembling smile I was forming from crashing against the seriousness of the situation.

"I will work with the New Orleans Police Department if necessary, but the MAW shall take precedent in all proceedings. Agents are now posted at each entrance and exit, MAW internally, PD externally, and no persons shall be allowed to enter or exit the hotel until these murders have been resolved."

It was a risk, Learco taking charge like that, but he was technically still director, no matter what Leland said. I also had a feeling it placed a big target on both of our backs—er… necks— as the vampire would no doubt want to hinder being discovered. But maybe that was exactly what we needed to draw them out.

"You cannot trap us here like criminals," Osmund spat. "Especially if, as you say, there is a killer amongst us."

"I can, and I have," Learco assured him, the power in his voice greater than any of the forced strength I'd heard from Osmund or Mehrdad or anyone else at the convention since I'd arrived. It was remarkable to witness the two witches who'd never been told "no"—except by each other—succumb to my lover so quickly. Though Learco didn't seem the least bit fazed by it. It put why he'd been so amused and astounded by my denial of his invitation to join the MAW during our first meeting in a whole new light.

"So what do we do?" Mehrdad asked. "Remain in our rooms until you've completed your investigation?"

"Carry on as normal," Learco instructed. "Have your little party. Dance, drink, and let me do my work without the killer knowing I'm searching for them. It should be quite simple to ignore this victim's death. After all, you've done it thrice—four times when considering the couple Darragh found on the roof top—before."

"Fae damned, that was hot," I growled, pulling Learco to me by his belt buckle as we poured ourselves into my suite and bolted the door.

His lips tasted of clove and cinnamon, even in the spicy air of New Orleans, and my cock strained against the zipper of my pants. His own pulsed the fabric to meet mine, and I sent a tiny tendril of my aura out to envelop us in our passion. The sensation intensified as sparks of his gold magic twirled my green, and I guided us, lips still pressed firmly together, to the sofa. Roaring, I forced his ass to the cushions and smiled as my knees met the couch to straddle him.

It wasn't the power he'd displayed over the witches downstairs that had my libido revving, but my boyfriend's stalwart desire to make things right—or at least as "right" as they could be—as he brought foul-players to answer. His position in the MAW made that easier, but I knew whatever happened, that aspect of his personality would not waiver.

"We've got a little bit of time before we need to continue the investigation, right?" I purred, working my hands down the buttons of his shirt to expose the ebony skin beneath. "At least an hour before the party anyway."

"We really should go over what we know. Come up with a plan," Learco gasped, the fight between duty and spoiling the moment thick on his breathy words.

My fingers stalled a moment as a fake pout puffed my lips, but I shrugged as I unfastened the clasp which revealed the first of his eight-pack abs.

"We have to get undressed to get dressed," I countered. "Besides, the way you handled those guys down there—the news crews; Cernun's brother's lackeys; the NOPD; and the two most powerful witches at the Gathering—I've no doubt you've got this. *We've* got this."

The aching anticipation in Learco's skin fell, crashing his body against the sofa as the lust in his eyes was replaced with sorrow. My own desire left me just as quickly to make room for a sudden burst of compassion, and I settled lightly on his thighs.

"Did I say something wrong?" I asked.

"No," he assured me. "It's just…. That down there, that was only possible because they believe I'm still the Director of the MAW. It wasn't me; it was my station. And if Leland has his way…."

There it was: the pain behind the false bravado he'd displayed since Leland Hyde had sliced the athamé over his career. I'd caught a bit of it behind the shock of seeing all his worldly possessions, boxed up and moved from his Buckhead high rise condo to Cernun's Grant Park home when we'd returned from the Faerie Realm. It had hidden itself within the wrinkles of his typically finely-pressed clothes. Hell, even though I knew his joining me in New Orleans was for the most part because he loved me, a portion of it—hidden like the latent fire ingredients in a water-based spell—was probably an attempt at avoiding the inevitable. If he did not meet with Leland, the finality of his firing could be delayed.

I slipped from his lap to sit beside him but kept his fingers firmly intwined in mine.

"That down there," I said, borrowing his words to drive my point home, "that was you. Feeling the MAW behind you may have given you the confidence. But that force, that desire, it's all inside of you. Are you worried Leland will see the press conference and use it against you?"

"No. It was local news. He'll see it eventually, but by then this should all be behind us. Still, if he does see it before we talk, he could try to use it against me. Say I'm abusing my power or something. At the very least, say my claiming control of the scene while on a suspension is evidence of a dereliction of duty on my part."

"And that could turn your supposedly 'in the bag' meeting on its heels?" I asked, trying to sound sympathetic but fearing I sounded incredulous.

"My sources could very well just be telling me what I want to hear," he moaned. "Leland wields an awful lot of influence there. And not just stateside."

I frowned as I squeezed his hand, hurt myself by the pain in his eyes.

"Would it be so bad if you weren't hampered by the Moral Authority of Witches?" I asked.

Learco sighed as he pulled his fingers from mine, shifting his body to look me directly in my eyes.

"I know you hate the MAW," he said. "But they were my chance to do something good. To change things for the better for all of witch-kind."

"Doing good within an evil organization is still tinged with evil," I countered. "A dark magic spell for the sake of something great is still coated in the blood of its sacrifice."

I was trying to make things better, to offer a bit of perspective, of hope, but as Learco huffed and pushed himself from the sofa, I knew I'd said the wrong thing. His eyes were hot as he turned to look down at me, and I bit my lip in empathy.

"Not all of us have the privilege of being a radical," he snapped, even as he kept his words tempered. "Some of us must work within the system created to oppress us in order to find some level of freedom. In hopes that we can send that freedom out to others."

"I'm a gay witch from the South," I said. "It's not 'privilege' that lets me see through the pain and the misery that organization has caused."

Learco's chuckle was startling as he shook his head and walked away from me. He paused at the suite's bar and poured a hefty shot of dark rum into a rocks glass, downing it with a gasping wheeze before he spoke again.

"You're a white man who inherited a business and housing from his family. You can afford to stand on some moral high ground against the Moral Authority because, when the shit hits the fan, it's not you they're coming after. I figured that'd be evident by the big nothing which occurred when you saved Cernun."

"You mean aside from them trying to recruit me and control me," I replied, standing to join him in a shot of whiskey to counter his rum. "They let what I did stand because, as evidenced by this entire event, there was big money to be made by revealing ourselves to the world."

"They let what you did stand because I asked them to."

My face dropped as I took in Learco's words. I'd always assumed my spell had just been taken for what it was once the immediate public reaction had been one of wonder instead of hatred. Well, that coupled with the evident opportunities that arose from coming out of the broom closet. I'd had no idea Learco had played a part in what kept me from the MAW's stake.

"I was Leland's assistant at that point," he explained. "Based out of Salem and working my way up through the ranks. I convinced him that a spell like that spoke of power. I convinced him to wait and see what the public outcry contained. And three years later, I was given my position in Atlanta. In part to keep an eye on you. In part to recruit you. I just didn't know I was going to fall in love."

The shock on my face was replaced with care as I reached out to touch his hand. He squeezed mine, then pulled away as he paced the room.

"Look. I know my family back on those islands is, on paper, more well-off than yours. I know I've had experiences and opportunities in this life you've only dreamed of. But, every time the clock strikes three, I am still a black man. Often that's all people see. My rank, even within the MAW, is viewed as 'in spite of' by some and 'because of' by others. There's still so much that has to be done. You may rally against people—against me— for not being progressive enough. For not working to topple the system that has governed us into submission. For attempting to work within those structures to change it at its core. But it's all I have. I have to work within those structures in order to stay safe. To keep witches who look like me safe. So they can see that witches who look like me belong and should be, no, *must* be a part of the conversation. I have to be a part of the system because that's where my power lies."

I bit my lip as I took in my boyfriend's words, breathing slowly as I concentrated on the depth of sorrow and obligation beneath them. He was trembling as he spoke, and I stopped his pacing to embrace him.

"You're right," I sighed. "So let's solve this shit, catch the bad guy, and portal you back to Atlanta so you don't miss your meeting with Leland tomorrow. That passion you just displayed should be enough to convince him. And bagging a vampire couldn't hurt."

Still shaken by his own admission, Learco settled himself into the staid, business-first demeanor that had kept him safe for all those years. He winced slightly at the amount of emotion he'd shown, and I nodded my support. He wasn't one to get worked up often, even with me and Cernun, and I hoped he understood he would never need to rely on that defense mechanism he'd built when it came to us or our love. The soft kiss he placed on my cheek told me he was at least starting to.

"Okay," he said. "So what do we know?"

"I feel like the list of what we don't know is much more robust," I sighed, sliding back to the bar to top up our respective rocks glasses. "We can't even confirm if vampires are real or not."

"So let's focus on what we do know as true," Learco smiled, taking a sip of his rum and raising his eyebrows at me to start.

"Okay. We know there have been at least five victims. Amy and the couple on the rooftop were human. Then Zamiah, and now the receptionist, Kara. Both witches."

"So we know the killer is elevating," Learco said. "If we want to place it in Osmund Linnegard's terms."

Learco pulled the tablet of Crow's Court branded stationary from the coffee table and jotted his notes as we spoke, creating his own case file in lieu of having the MAW's extensive background and research at his fingertips.

"Which does give a lot of credence to Mehrdad's accusation

that it could be a Council plot to posit the BOG Witch leadership as incapable," I offered. "Starting with humans and then moving to witches when the humans didn't get the response he wanted does seem like something Osmund would do."

"Perhaps," Learco agreed. "Though we can't rule out Linnegard's cry that it was a set up to quell their uprising. So that's five victims and two somewhat solid suspects."

"There's also Cal Juventus," I offered. "You'll meet him tonight at the dance. He knows about the Fae, and a sort of coldness follows him. Plus his aura feels different—like a cheese grater—against mine. Which brings us back to the 'vampire' of it all."

"Alongside the disappearance of the bodies, and you seeing Zamiah tonight at the restaurant," Learco gulped. "That does speak to the undead rising. But again, that's conjecture. We should keep it in mind, but stick to the facts."

I couldn't help but smile. Learco was sounding more and more like himself. But through my happiness at his return, I kicked myself mentally for not recognizing the true anguish he was going through at the potential loss of his job, for letting my own disdain of the MAW cloud my impression of what he needed and wanted in those moments. I promised myself I'd be better in the future. Focusing on this case was a start.

"The killer wants to be caught," I said, and Learco cocked his head in question.

I squinted as I thought through each scene, realizing they were not the site of the murders but the site of discovery.

"Amy," I continued, "was posed in the open hallway near my room. Yes, like she was sleeping, but out in the open where anyone passing by could have found her. The couple on the roof: you should have seen them! Limbs twisted and placed like they were creatures in a surrealist painting. Zamiah was less posed, but there was less time. And she was still in the elevator, just waiting for those doors to open on whatever floor the lift was called to after the attendants called it quits for the night."

"And now Kara who was dropped into the most public place of all," Learco finished. "You're right. It may not be an invitation to be caught, but it's definitely an invitation to be found. They want credit for what they've done. They want the world to know."

"It'd be a hell of a way for vampires to come out of hiding," I winced. "A show of dominance over humans and well-off witches in one fell swoop."

Learco's brow furrowed as he looked over his notes. His fastidious handwriting was small but easily legible, even from across the room.

"Perhaps it's not about being found out, but about finding the right victim," Learco offered. "There's a meticulousness here, more a searching than a feeding."

I watched the cogs turn in Learco's mind as he tried to make some sense of everything that had happened, as he attempted to deign motive to make the pieces fall into place.

"Which, unfortunately, brings us back to the 'me' of it all," I said. "The Mórrígan claimed I'm not responsible for the actions of others, but it could still be the awakening of my wild that whatever is doing this is looking for."

It was a frightening thought, one now that we'd both acknowledge, but a notion neither of us wanted to dwell in.

"We also cannot forget the sisters," Learco sighed, giving me an out from my worry and jotting their names down but not placing them under his list of potential suspects. "Though one was a victim, she was supposedly here to investigate something which had not yet occurred."

"Maybe she was a seer?"

"Potentially. That still does not explain their subterfuge in claiming to own the Museum. Or the haunting of Zamiah you experienced, whether she was really there or your magic, in that way it does, was attempting to tell you something. I've learned it always best to pay attention to your sights."

I smirked as I thought back to the vision of Lady Z while we dined at Petrichor. She had all the hallmarks of every great seductress vamp I'd seen on film or read about in books, except for the visible fangs. Maybe my magic was trying to tell me something. It felt good that Learco was so keen to take it to heart.

"Have you heard from Chester yet?" Learco asked, breaking my reverie as my hand fished through my pocket.

In all the drama that occurred as we arrived back at the hotel, I hadn't even thought to check my phone. Still, the screen notifications were empty.

"I'm sure he's fine," my boyfriend answered the worried crease on my face. "We did have a… rambunctious afternoon. Not many humans could keep up with two witches and their auras. He most likely went to bed early to sleep it off."

He was probably right. Yet there was an uneasy feeling in my gut. Well, another one anyway, to pile on top of the other rocks which had formed there since I'd first arrived at the BOG Witch Convention.

Learco crossed the room and placed his palm against my cheek, attempting to massage away the worry that was pooling there.

"Would you look at that?" he purred. "We made it through me finally being honest—with myself and with you—about my true feelings surrounding the MAW. *And* we got through our case prep with over twenty minutes to spare."

His lips met mine as his fingers cupped the hem of my shirt and lifted it upwards. The hotel air conditioning bristled on my newly exposed skin, but the chill was quickly replaced by the warming pulse of my lover's aura. I grinned as our lips parted, and Learco finished the job I'd begun of unbuttoning his shirt. As he let it fall to the floor behind him, I licked my lips at the sight.

His dark, pert nipples begged for my tongue to find them—or maybe it was my tongue begging for them—and I followed his lead in shedding my clothing across the living room floor of the Yarrow Tooth Suite. He grinned as he reached the bathroom, turning away from me for the first time to shift the shower on. I seized the opportunity to clutch the muscled orbs of his ass in my hands, dropping to my knees to kiss his skin.

He inhaled deeply as my teeth grazed the small of his back in a nibble and shifted to lean further forward, bracing his hands on the porcelain of the tub. My tongue found his hole in quick, lingering bursts, and he moaned in appreciation. I buried my face in him as the water heated, and the steam from the shower began to mist around us like our own auras clinging to the air.

Turning, Learco's hand clutched my chin to guide my lips back to his, and I shivered as our cocks, hard and throbbing in anticipation, pressed between us, rolling back and forth across our skin with each shift of our hips.

"The party starts in fifteen minutes now," he gasped between kisses, and I growled as I bit his lip.

"We can be fashionably late," I assured him. "Besides. All the real power players here will be."

CHAPTER 14

As expected, the fourth floor ballroom was charmed to the rafters for the penultimate party of the BOG Witch Convention. They'd returned the festivities to the same space they'd used for our welcome as workers and spell casters were deployed to the tenth floor to prepare for tomorrow night's Masquerade Ball. It sort of felt like coming home as we stepped off the elevator, and a ping inside me hoped the feeling meant an end to the murders and a fresh start on our last day in New Orleans with no vampires or blood-letting in sight.

Learco looked exquisite in the tux one of his agents had managed to procure for him, and I smoothed out the creases in the one they'd also grabbed for me. *Moving up from detective to spy*, I thought as I caught my reflection in the window glass. The bright lights of the French Quarter across the way glistened on my skin, and I grinned as Learco clutched my hand.

"You look wonderful," he whispered to my ear, and my smile broadened.

"Afterglow will do that to me," I told him, and we did our best to stifle our evident arousal as we joined the line of guests moving toward the entrance.

"Mister Clarke, Darragh," Layla said in a monotone as we reached the entryway and her ever-present clipboard.

"I attended all my classes today, teach," I promised her. "Raised my hand before I spoke and everything."

I was nearly knocked backward by the purse in her lips and the amusement in her eyes.

"I'm well aware," she smirked. "Welcome."

As she slipped to the side to allow us to pass, she reached to tug my elbow and whispered "we need to talk later" into my ear. The expectant look in her eyes spoke of urgency, and I nodded respectfully, wondering what I'd done wrong this time. I had no clue why Mehrdad's assistant had set her evil eye upon me, but I was grateful that my boyfriend's presence had—at least in this instance—kept it somewhat subdued in front of the other guests.

Learco's eyes widened as he entered the room, and I smiled as the grandiosity of it all settled upon him. Floral bouquets, this time in golds and whites and blues, floated through the air. The goldenrod petals looked like constellations against the darkness of the ceiling, and I couldn't help but think the magnolia blossoms were clouds in a Van Gogh swirling of the sky. The band was stationed atop the platform where Mehrdad had offered his welcome speech, and their fingers themselves seemed spelled as they flourished across the bodies of their clarinets and saxophones, malleted their xylophones, and danced across accordion keys. The smaller yet still grand room did not have a designated dance floor, yet the witches in attendance were already moving—even just forty minutes into the event—in whirling circles amongst the scattered high top tables and evenly placed mobile bars.

"They really go all out for these things," Learco smiled. "We're lucky if someone brings a working mp3 player to our MAW events."

"That's because the MAW funnels all its donations toward

incarceration instead of celebration," I smirked, then quickly added, "Sorry."

"No, you're correct. It does." Learco's voice was soothing as he clasped my hand in comfort. "Just because I still want my job, that does not mean I expect you to give up any of the fire and vitriol you've amassed for the less desirable aspects of the organization."

A slight blushed rosed my cheeks, and I nodded. Learco truly was one spectacular witch. I was lucky to have him as a lover. And a friend.

"So where should we start?" I asked, guiding us both beyond the spectacle of the space and to the task at hand. "Should we divide and conquer? I take Mehrdad and you take Osmund. Trap 'em in a corner 'til they talk? Rough up a few of their henchmen in the backrooms until they squeal?"

Learco laughed at my joke, and the heads of the other guests which had turned and started mumbling upon our arrival seemed put at ease by the musicality. With as public as Kara's death was, the presence of the head of the Southeastern Division of the MAW told everyone an investigation was underway. But I was sure most of the attendees thought it was just about the receptionist. As much as both men vying for control wanted to use the deaths to their advantages, I was certain neither of them had let the gossip slide further than a small circle, and that was an advantage for us. Learco's chuckle had signaled he was here for play instead of work, and that would put the other revelers at ease, keep the drinks flowing, and—hopefully—the tongues wagging.

"I hope it doesn't come to that," my boyfriend smiled. "Though I am interested in having a conversation with Cal Juventus. Is he here?"

"Not yet," I said as my eyes scanned the crowd for the flamboyant witch. "Trust me. You'll know when he arrives. He likes to stand out."

As I continued to watch the room, Dula's earnest stare met mine, and she padded her way towards us with a smile.

"Prepare yourself," I whispered as I nodded toward her advance. "She's a talker. But she's sweet. Used to be a regular at HEX before her glow up."

Dula's grin broadened as she stomped through the crowd. Her flowing black dress, hemmed in golden thread just above the ankles of her thin suede ankle boots, shifted its hard creases with each step she took; and her knee-length cardigan, sewn through with gold and white floral embroidery, billowed behind her like a cape. She really had the High Witch fashion trend down, but I appreciated that I could still see a bit of the hippie witch she'd once been in the styling.

"I see my old pal Darragh here finally convinced one of his handsome men to join him at our little fête," she said, extending her hand, palm down, toward Learco. "Calendula Hawthorn. But you can call me Dula. Darragh used to know me as Serena, back when I knew his uncle as Big G."

"Charmed," Learco purred, laying his charisma on thick as he gently took Dula's fingers in his and let his lips brush her knuckles. "Learco Clarke."

"Of course I know who you are," she mused before turning to me to add. "He's a spicy one. Good on you. Any chance your other lover with his Kyteler good looks might grace us with his enormous presence too?"

I laughed as I shook my head, shrugging my shoulders as her expectant stare remained on me.

"Cernun's looking after HEX while we're here," I said. "Can't cut the Atlanta magic community off from their supplies."

"Shame," she said, scrunching her lips as much as the smoothing spell she'd placed on her face would allow. "What I wouldn't give to see you three hunks all together in one place."

Her eyebrows hopped twice on her forehead before she turned back to Learco. "Darragh tell you I used to have a thing with his uncle? Well, I would have, back when I was younger. If he hadn't been gay and hadn't met Bill. But I was a different witch back then. Full of flower power and burning bras and free love and…."

"I hear your retreats provide a certain type of 'flower power' of their own," Learco interjected, cutting off her wildly spiraling excursion down memory lane with a finesse I wished I could master. "The Calendula Hawthorn Healing Centers have created quite the buzz nationwide."

"Cast the spells you're good at," Dula beamed. "It's mostly humans who come to stay with me. But I do offer discounts to witches who need a little R&R in the mountains. Deeper discounts for throuples."

"We'll have to look into that," Learco promised, cupping her hand in his once more and patting her wrist to signify the conversation was over.

Of course, Dula didn't take the hint.

"Well, you just let me know what weeks you have in mind so I can make sure I'm there," she said. "Hot springs are clothing optional, you know. And there is nothing on this earth compares to a fresh jaunt through the woods in late Spring when the moonlight filters glimpses through all the fresh new leaves and the real animals of this world all come out to play. I tell you: it's quite the sight to behold."

Learco hid the clearing of his throat in a chuckle as he pulled his hand back from hers, eyes darting toward mine for assistance. His usual charms didn't affect the woman in the least, at least not in the way he'd intended them. But I had warned him before.

"Did y'all hear about that poor receptionist Kara?" she asked, leaning closer and lowering her voice to a conspiratorial stage whisper. "Of course you did. That's probably why you're here,

Learco. Anyway. Word in the salt is that it may have all happened in this very room. That she went over that balcony right over there."

My eyes darted to the open balcony where Mehrdad had taken me on my first day, after rescuing me from another never-ending conversation with Dula. The floor arrangement made sense in terms of her body's impact, or rather lack of a high fall impact, against the concrete. I couldn't quite remember where the balcony was situated in terms of the first floor lobby, but, if I ever freed myself from this conversation, it'd be worth checking out.

"Of course, they're also saying it may not have been suicide," Dula continued, and my eyes shot back to her as her own widened and she zipped her mouth shut.

She seemed to relish in our eagerness as she raised her shoulders and sighed, giving us a look that was equal parts *I've said too much* and *Don't you want to hear more*. I felt silly asking the witch to speak again, as if it were an invitation to carry on forever, but Learco took the bait.

"What is it people are saying?"

"Well," Dula huffed, glee frolicking on her voice even as she spoke of the *poor receptionist*'s death. "There are some who say they saw Kara right before it happened, and she didn't seem the least bit depressed. Not even as dour as usual, according to… I'll keep the names redacted for the save of preserving the innocent. But I even heard claim she was laughing—can you imagine that?!? Kara laughing!—as her shift ended and she wandered into the stairwell with a young man who had been chatting her up."

My heart pounded in my chest. Could the lead we'd been looking for actually fall out of Dula's busy lips? I tried to keep my external cool as I glanced at Learco and he urged me forward.

"What time was this?" I asked, smiling sweetly.

Dula, for her part, seemed ecstatic that someone was finally asking her to continue speaking. She nearly hummed as she bobbed before us, bristling with conspiritorial energy

"Kara got off at seven, so must have been seven ten, seven fifteen," she smiled. "And she jumped—if you believe she jumped—right after ten. You ask me, three hours is plenty of time for some hanky-panky and some heartbreak. Maybe she broke that young man's heart, and he forced her over the ledge. Or maybe he broke hers, and she made the leap on her own. Or maybe the sex got a little out of hand—she did seem the type to like it rough, all close-lipped like she was. But that's not speaking ill of the dead. There's nothing wrong with whatever gets you off. Anyway, maybe things got rough and… Kersplat."

Dula seemed pleased with herself—or perhaps caught in the erotic revelry of her tale—as she slapped her hands to close the space between us and punctuate her story. It was all hearsay and conjecture, true, but it was the closest thing we had to a lead. And even a discarded tarot deck was bound to get a few cards right in the spread.

"Do you know who the man was?" Learco asked, leaning forward as if every word she had to say, even her off-color asides, were the most important thing he'd ever heard.

Dula blushed a bit and fanned herself with her hand, then pouted as her face fell.

"No," she admitted. "I didn't see the young man. Those who did only saw him from behind. Slender and blond and moneyed, they said. Which, in fairness, describes a third of the men here."

As if on cue, the king of the slender, blond, and moneyed men at the Gathering made his grand entrance. A thin smile stretched his face as Cal greeted his entourage. Once again, his bespoke suit and matching shoes paired perfectly with the decor. He bowed with an exaggerated flourish, then pointed toward the band, whom he had no doubt paid before hand, and they immediately started in on a jaunty, high energy jazz number even though they had been mid-song just before.

His feet pulsed in a contemporary tap as he pointed toward his shoes and began to swish through the crowd at an elevated pace, spinning those whose hands met his and kissing their cheeks as he twirled them from his path. Even Dula closed her mouth to watch him move, joining in the thunderous applause as he finished and bowed once more.

"I take it that's Cal," Learco whispered, and I nodded as Dula turned back to us with a broad smile.

"I see your dance partner moves much better on his own," she winked at me. "Anyway. I should stop commandeering all your time. You two sexy young things should be conversing with witches your own age. And preferred gender. But you can't blame an old hag for wanting to watch. You get your third one out here, and you just may have the whole Gathering following your every move."

"I'm not sure I've ever met a hornier witch," Learco laughed as Dula wandered back into the crowd and we made our way toward the nearest bar. "Which is saying something for our lot. Especially since I'm dating you."

I smirked at his joke, feigning indigence with an eye roll as we moved.

"I'll have to do something to reclaim my title," I said. "After we've taken care of the vampire currently stalking this place."

"I like the promises you make," Learco purred back, and I

found myself blushing at the amused look on the bartender's face as he took our orders: my usual Old Fashioned and a French 75 for my boyfriend.

"It's Simon, right?" I asked as he topped the champagne in Learco's flute. "I'm so sorry about Kara."

Simon shrugged as he turned to dash the Angostura bitters into my rocks glass then reached for the nearest bottle of rye.

"She was kind of a bitch. Thinking she was better than everyone else," he blurted, then quickly added, "I mean, I didn't want her to kill herself."

I nodded sympathetically at his wince and assured him I understood what he'd meant.

"We heard she had a gentleman caller right before her death," Learco pressed, making the question sound casual as if he were in on all the employee gossip. "Was she dating anyone that you knew of?"

Simon shrugged once more as he stirred my drink and passed it over to me.

"The hotel has a strict policy against fraternization, between employees and also with guests," Simon said. "Mister Landry barely allows us to talk about where we like to go for dinner outside this place, much less who we're dating."

"Sounds like an exciting work environment," I said.

"It has its perks."

Using our bodies as cover, Simon downed a swig of the most expensive tequila the bar had stocked and smiled. I chuckled as I slipped a twenty into his tip jar and thanked him for the cocktails. There was something I admired about the young man. That his Latin incantations meant he'd grown up in a family who had lost their traditional lore yet he'd still found a way to make his magic work was admirable. Plus, he'd managed to keep his edge despite the *get-in-line* directives of working at a place like the Crow's Court.

That, in and of itself, showed a level of strength I appreciated.

"Were you planning to introduce me to your date, Darragh Cullen? I suppose this means your dance card is full for the evening."

Sipping my Old Fashioned, I turned swiftly to face the expectant smile on Cal's face. He hovered just behind us at the bar, his cronies all tasked with keeping the other witches away.

"I was waiting for your meet and greet with your fans to settle," I assured him. "Besides, after my showing our last time out, I didn't think you'd want to attempt another waltz with me. You put on quite the show all on your own."

"Nothing sells the shoes better than a quick romp across the dance floor," he chuckled, clicking the heels of his brocade boots together as he pointed to their craftsmanship. "Except perhaps the illicit image of a pair discarded by the bed."

"Cal Juventus, this is my boyfriend, Learco Clarke."

"Pleasure," he said, taking Learco's hand in his and pulling both of us away from the bar so that Simon could continue his service. "Of course, I knew who you were immediately. Yet introductions are only proper."

"I've heard a story or two about you as well, Mister Juventus," Learco smiled. "I even have a few pairs of your shoes on the rack in my closet back home."

"I see," Cal smiled, taking the adoration appropriately as he looked down to the quickly-bought, off-the-rack dress shoes the MAW agents had gotten us on Lower Decatur. "Shame you aren't wearing them tonight. I'll have to send you a new pair or two. You're an eleven?"

"And a half," Learco confirmed, and Cal smiled seductively.

"Hey now," I huffed. "No one offered me any fancy shoes."

Cal laughed at my joke as he reached to clutch my bicep. A quick brush and then retraction of his aura grated on mine, but he barely let the sensation show on his face.

"Your tens are being cobbled as we speak, Darragh," he promised. "Green with hints of blue and gold. To match the suit Mister Clarke here had tailored for you."

The shocked expression and raised eyebrows on both our faces pleased the witch.

"I have eyes an ears everywhere," he smiled. "Particularly in the world of fashion. Your shoes will be delivered to your suite tomorrow evening. I do hope you'll see them fit to wear at the Masquerade."

"I'd be honored," I assured him. "Especially if they can make me move like you."

"No promises," Cal smirked. "That would require magic the MAW does not allow."

The music shifted once more, and I caught sight of Osmund through the crowd as the witches ended one dance to begin another. His face burned red, Carter hot in his ear as the Council leader's expression continued to sour. We needed to know what they were talking about. And we'd have a better shot if it was just me asking. Maybe. Besides, there was still something off about Cal, and Learco needed the chance to feel it for himself.

"You know, Learco here is much lighter on his feet than I am," I smiled. "Perhaps he'd be able to keep up with you."

"And now it is I who would be honored," Cal said, extending his hand with a bow.

Learco raised his eyebrows to me as he took Cal's hand, and I jutted my chin in Osmund's direction. Understanding swept his face, and I mouthed "feel his aura" to my boyfriend as I excused myself to tackle my own leg of the investigation.

I kept my eyes locked on Osmund's top hat as I made my way across the ballroom, feeling like a double agent in my tux as I prepped my messaging. It would be much easier to talk now that the Council knew of all the deaths that had occurred—or *publicly* knew anyway. I still wasn't convinced his show of discovery in the lobby earlier that night had not been a ruse. Still, neither he nor Mehrdad had mentioned the vampire of it all in that setting. But I figured, with the right questions—alongside Learco's more adept yet subvert interrogation of Cal—we were bound to catch some leads before the witching hour sent folks off to their various rooms or after parties. I decided I could lean into Osmund's "magical creatures" vernacular as the perfect segue.

"He only needs two more to turn before...."

Osmund shushed Carter as he watched me slink within earshot and spread a practiced smile across his lips.

"Are you here as Yaisien's gofer or a prospective member of the type of leadership this organization truly requires?" Osmund grumbled, the pleasantries in his voice from our first meeting long buried in an inflection that told me he thought he knew the answer already. Then, glancing beyond me to the show Learco and Cal were putting on, he added, "Or perhaps this is a fishing expedition for the MAW."

My lips curled in on my teeth in an apprehensive smile as I shrugged.

"I really don't know," I replied honestly—for the most part—as I stepped in closer. "Can it be all three?"

Carter's glare felt like a spell in and of itself, but the magic dissipated as Osmund shoved his empty glass into his chest and he fell into subservience as he grasped it.

"Looks like Darragh could use another as well," Osmund instructed, and Carter grabbed my rocks glass before slipping off toward the bar.

For a moment, the witch was silent as he sized me up, then he sighed as he let his eyes wander the crowd.

"It seems Mehrdad was too much of a coward to show his face at his own event," he muttered before settling his wincing stare back on me.

"I imagine he's busy coordinating with the Crow's Court management regarding Kara's death. As the witch in charge should."

I knew I was goading him, and his expression said he did too, but I needed to throw him a little off-balance if I had any chance of wresting any truth from his chest. The double-speak and the wheeling-and-dealing of the business minded acumen of nearly all the BOG Witch attendees had gotten old. Hell, it'd been beyond me from the start. I craved a true conversation that wasn't rooted in power plays like they were the peatiest of soils.

"Showmanship in the face of a random suicide does not a leader make," Osmund snarled. "It's posturing for the sake of posterity. A true leader—"

"Uses death to threaten other witches to follow him?" I interrupted, and Osmund blinked rapidly as he remembered our conversation at the Crow's Nest.

"Not my finest moment," he succumbed. "And yet. There is a war on magical beings being wrought on all fronts. Behind closed doors at the Capitol. In ones and zeros on the internet. Even right below us as camera crews soak in every vitriolic word spewed by the Defend Mankind From Magic protesters lined up outside, all so angry that our kind would dare to convene beneath one roof. The amount of money in this room—and Darragh, I assure you that in a world we let become overrun by humans and capitalism as we hid in the shadows, money is where any true power lies—could be utilized to free us all. Instead, under the leadership of Mehrdad Yaisien, we wear pins which promote derogatory stereotypes of our kind; we forego spells for kitschy throw pillows with words that mean nothing; we bow to politics instead of assuming our rightful place as stewards of this world."

My hand instinctively found the BOG Witch pin on my lapel, moving over the gnarled witch fingers emblazoned there as I thought of the overabundance of non-witch "witch" paraphernalia littered throughout my OccultList BnB. Osmund had a point—about some things at least. But where he saw submission, I saw pushes toward acceptance. Even if I thought the marketing was cheesy, it still felt amazing to see myself, my history (of a sort anyway) represented in the world. And we witches certainly loved our puns, even if the ones which stuck for public consumption weren't always the cleverest.

"Kara's death was not a suicide," I said, pulling the conversation back toward the tract I needed it on. I had purposefully avoided planting seeds of fear—particularly when I knew they'd be used for fight—in my investigation. But we only had one day left of the convention, and I needed that garden to grow. "Learco told you her blood was drained from her body before she met that sidewalk. The same was true of Amy when I found her. Passing them off as suicide may work best in your vendetta against Mehrdad, particularly when you are obsessed with upholding 'magical creatures' as some greater than force, but insistence on a proven lie places you no better than those humans you think so little of. There have been five deaths at this convention, all with the same M.O. And every single one of them reeks of nonhuman cause."

Osmund's face was calm, his eyes squinting only slightly as he studied me. I watched him with the same intensity.

"Tell me, Osmund," I continued, borrowing a bit of the staid bravado I'd witnessed Learco practice to many times, "what magical beings are you so hell-bent on protecting?"

My eyes met his with ferocity, and even though I was looking upward toward his towering frame, the gritted tremble in my cheek made me feel twice as tall. I had called him out. I just needed to wait to see if he would open the coffin.

"Tell me, Darragh," he finally countered, "what is it you are insinuating?"

It felt like a game of chicken except this time I knew the one who spoke first might not actually lose. A single word, spoken into being like a spell, could alter the entire course of the night with whatever reaction it could elicit. And it was high time it was spoken aloud.

I kept my voice low but audible, fighting any question that still lingered on my larynx to present it as total fact. I refused to blink lest I miss his immediate response as I spoke:

"Vampires."

CHAPTER 15

I hadn't expected that.

Osmund's laughter was louder than the music as Learco and Cal ended their dance and the attendees' heads turned from the show to our hubbub. It cascaded through the air, and even Carter looked surprised as he wove through the suddenly still bodies, carefully balancing three drinks in two hands. Osmund was still chuckling as Carter reached our high top and distributed the cocktails.

"Is that what Yaisien is playing at now?" Osmund howled, pulling his Sloe Gin Fizz to his lips to try to stifle the amusement which still lingered on his tongue. "He's so desperate to retain control, he's turning to folklore and fear-mongering to keep his constituents on his side."

"Witches were once the stuff of fear and folktales too," I reminded him, doing my best to keep my voice low and direct as the band started back on their standards and a moaning rendition of "I Put A Spell On You" sent the onlookers back to their movements.

"To all who weren't magical," Osmund corrected me. "*We* still knew we existed. And, save for those few poor bloodlines too frightened by the brutality of the human world, we kept our magic and our power alive in secret. To state so bluntly and absurdly that a mythical race of vampires are stalking the halls of this hotel, draining the life of their victims…. Well, it reeks of exactly the type of subterfuge a witch like Mahrdad Yaisien would utilize to meet his needs. I had not taken you for one so gullible, Darragh Cullen."

"I did," Carter interjected, cutting me with the ice of his glare. "Next thing we know, he'll be insisting the Fae folk are more than bedtime stories our parents told us to make us do our chores."

"But," I stammered, still holding tight to the end of the thread that the Council somehow knew what was going on and were incredibly adept at hiding it, even as I felt the entirety of the tapestry unravelling, "you shushed Carter when he was talking about turning two others…."

"Into vampires?!?"

Osmund's guffaw nearly brought all the room's attention back to us, and I hid my blush behind the rim of my rocks glass. The sparkling scent of orange expression mixed with the headiness of the whisky to calm me, and I winced as the humility of my accusations sank in. At least we'd be able to cross the Council off our list of suspects.

"Just as we have," Carter explained, "Yaisien has been working to turn members of our collective back to his side. Three have jumped ship since the gossip spread of their confrontation in the lobby earlier tonight. And two more make a coven."

I nodded.

"You know," Osmund said, his words still ringing with amusement, "I actually have to thank you, Darragh, for showing me you are not Council material after all. Had I know you to be so influenced by flights of fancy, we would have foregone the suite and simply promised you the chance to play fetch with a werewolf or go skinny dipping with the Loch Ness Monster. If this is all

Mehrdad has to work with, you may assure him the Council is ready and able to call his bluff."

I tried to appear appropriately humbled as the Council members marched away, looking back every few steps as their laughter reignited, and I downed my drink.

"Sounds like you had quite the conversation," Learco smiled, humming as he slid in beside me and placed a new Old Fashioned beside my half-finished one.

"I pulled out the garlic and the crucifix, but the Council wouldn't bite," I shrugged. "How'd it go with Cal?"

"Uncertain," Learco smiled, sipping his drink and attempting to look as casual as possible for the prying eyes of the gathering as he filled me in. "He knows—or perhaps *believes* is the better word—the Fae are real. Yet I'm still not sure if that means he believes in vampires. Or is one. Though I felt what you meant about his aura. And he seemed equally as perplexed by mine."

I was a bit disappointed I hadn't gotten to watch Learco and Cal cut a rug. There was something strangely alluring about the witch, even aside from the peacocking of his outfits and his ostentatious personality. That our auras rubbed like burning sand on melting ice was unfortunate—and something I'd never felt before—but auras weren't required for the more physical of attractions.

"You need to focus," Learco teased, reading the wandering of my mind like a romance novel on my face. "The last thing we need is you attempting to bed a potential vampire tonight."

"Really?" I joked back. "Could be a great way to get him on his back and, um, stake him."

"Already working to win that title back from Dula, huh?"

Learco rolled his eyes as he kissed the edge of my lips with his smile. He looked so dashing in his tux. It was all I could do to not imagine him out of it.

"Alright," I sighed. "So where does this leave us?"

"You ruled the Council out," Learco said, his eyes soft as he reviewed his mental files. "But Cal is still in play. There's something off there, even if it's not to do with the case."

"I was hoping for the chance to get some answers from Mehrdad tonight," I said. "But he hasn't even shown for his own party." A terrible thought filled my head as I scanned over the crowd. "What if he's off sucking the blood from some other poor victim while we're all here? Every death except Kara's happened during or just after one of these parties."

"I have agents posted on every other floor, and we are here on the fourth," Learco assured me. "The publicity surrounding Kara's death means he's probably elbow deep in lawyers and public relations emails right now. If anything happens in this hotel, by or to Mehrdad, we'll know."

I breathed a sigh of relief even as the anguish inside me continued to build.

"There's still the possibility that it could be any of the hundreds of folks here," I huffed, finishing the Old Fashioned Carter had brought me and starting on the fresh one from my boyfriend. "I've been focusing on Mehrdad and the Council and even Cal, but haven't looked into any of the other witches here. What if I've had us on a wild goose chase this whole time?"

Learco smiled as he rested his hand on top of mine, his eyes pleading for me to calm.

"You focused on the people with eyes and ears everywhere," he said. "Even if they weren't responsible, you knew they'd know something. It's exactly what I would have done had I been here from the start. And it's exactly why the Moral Authority is convinced you'd be a good agent."

"You don't even have your job back for sure, and you're still trying to recruit me?"

"I'm not," Learco laughed. "I know and understand your stance. Though, pulling you into the fold would go a long way toward getting me back in Leland's good graces."

"Fuck Leland," I pouted, but I couldn't help but snicker at the joke. "Even if I could be convinced to join the MAW, I could never work with Leland Hyde. Not after what he did to Samara."

"What did he do to Samara?"

The confusion on Learco's face made me gulp as I thought back to the last time I'd seen his former assistant. In all the excitement of the Faerie Realm, of getting home and getting our lives back—plus getting our Ostara on before I flew out to New Orleans—I'd not had the chance to tell him about the interrogation Leland had put me through. And even though Samara had worked with Aiden to try to kill us both, she had not deserved whatever Leland had put her through. The once strong witch had been a shell of her former self with absolutely zero recognition, of others or even who she was, in her eyes. It had been downright chilling. Whether or not it was sanctioned by the MAW—I had a feeling it was since Leland tended to be the arbiter of those things—I knew it wasn't something Learco would have approved of for the witch who'd served beside him for so long.

"Layla!" I nearly shouted, and the confusion on my lover's face doubled. "I will fill you in on Samara, I promise. But, right now, if I can't interrogate Mehrdad, his assistant is probably the next best witch. And she did tell me we needed to talk as we arrived."

"You're right," Learco agreed. "One thing at a time. Right now, we're vampire hunters. We can deal with the MAW shit once that's all done."

Though her welcome duties had ended, Layla had not strayed too far from the entrance to the ballroom. It's grand wooden doors were closed and spelled, no doubt, to keep the lively entertainment from seeping through the hotel hallways—even though we were the only guests staying there—but the balcony was wide open, allowing the music to filter into the 2AM air and mix with the revelry of the city. Not to mention increase the ire of the protesters below.

"They're saying this is where she went over," she said as she felt us approaching her from behind.

She was leaning against the railing, peering down at the smattering of DMFMers still congregated on the sidewalk below, an empty coup glass dangling gingerly from her hands. Her ever-present clipboard had been tossed to a nearby table. The balcony was empty save for her. And now us.

"None of the other guests will come out here," she said. "They don't want to spoil their fun with thoughts of some lowly witch's death."

When Layla turned to face us, there were tears brimming the bottoms of her mascara'd eyes, but she gave us a half-hearted smile as she tilted her head.

"Kara was sort of a bitch, even when you got to know her," she laughed. It was one of those sad laughs, like the memories were getting away from her. "But she did not deserve what happened to her. And Mehrdad…."

Her voice trailed off. Learco stepped in to gently remove the empty glass from her hands.

"You worked together for a long time," he said. "I imagine planning this event year after year takes far longer than the four days the crowds descend upon the halls. Too, Mister Yaisien and Mister Landry do not seem to be the heavy-lifting type. I would think the two of you worked together quite a bit."

"We did," Layla nodded.

It was sweet, hearing him comfort her. And also a key example of why he was so much better as a MAW agent than I would ever be. With her trailing off on Mehrdad's name, I had to bite my tongue to prevent myself from pressuring her to continue.

"So you must have known about the new guy she was seeing," he cooed.

There it was. He was smooth. Maybe a brief stint with the Moral Authority wouldn't be so bad. I could learn all their suave interrogation techniques, get Leland off my back, and help save my boyfriend's job in one grand gesture. One agonizing flourish where I sold my soul to a fiercer bloodsucker than what we were facing.

Nope. I couldn't even fantasize about it.

"Kara did mention there was someone," Layla shrugged, "but she refused to tell me who it was. She only said things had the potential of becoming incredibly messy if anyone found out. That was sort of what I wanted to talk to you about, Darragh."

My brow furrowed as I took a step closer. Learco and I flanked the young woman as she looked around to ensure no other ears were listening.

"I know you probably thought I was being really rude," she started, apology thick on her words as her lips quivered and her eyes met mine. "It's just…. I've been Mehrdad's assistant for a long time. He has a tendency to use people. I don't know if it's intentional, but…. Well, he finds a new toy every year and just sort of… bleeds them dry."

My eyes snapped to Learco's at her phrasing, and I cleared the sudden lump in thy throat before I could speak.

"You don't think Mehrdad was Kara's new love interest, do you?" I asked, attempting the same casual cool Learco had mastered.

"No!" Layla exclaimed, then tensed as her face fell. "I don't know. Maybe. But I do know he'd set his sights on you for this Gala. That's why I was being such a stickler. I was trying to keep you away from him. The courage you showed in saving that witch all those years ago, the magic you revealed that allowed us all to be ourselves…. I just didn't want my boss to pull his usual tricks on you."

It was kind of sweet, Layla's looking out for me like that. And I was certainly relieved she hadn't simply hated me for some reason. Still, the picture she'd painted of Mehrdad didn't seem to coincide with the witch I'd met.

"When you say Mehrdad 'bleeds them dry,'" I started, letting my words trail off as Layla scrunched her face.

"I mean most of his 'special invitees' aren't invited back the next year," she huffed. "Fuck. Half of them don't even make it to the Masquerade Ball before they've checked out early from the convention and disappeared without a word."

Damn. Things really weren't looking good for Mehrdad. Especially if this wasn't the first year guests had "mysteriously vanished." But had he really created the entire organization and grown the BOG Witch Convention and Gala to such an extraordinary size to make for easy hunting? I had to admit, it would be an ingenious way of hiding in plain sight. If one or two folks "left early" every year, particularly with so many attendees, the disappearances would be easy to overlook. Plus, if he'd gone for human targets as well—like with Amy and that couple on the roof—well, a city full of witches was one hell of a scapegoat when the bodies started piling up.

Shit. A part of me had thought something was off, but I truly hadn't expected it to be this. I needed to know what had happened on the balcony. I needed to see for myself if Mehrdad was the man who'd lured Kara to her death.

My fingers gripped the railing as I inhaled deeply, pulling the cool air into my diaphragm to balance myself with the night. I closed my eyes and reached for the power in my gut, twining the greens together as I pulled. That was coming more naturally now. My wild magic was rising to meet the power I'd always known on impulse. It made me feel stronger. And a little dizzy.

On my exhale I sent my intentions out to pull a vision, even just a glimpse, of the early evening comings and goings on the balcony. But there was nothing.

The same blackness, the same empty void I'd experienced on the roof, stared back at me.

"You're not going to see anything," Layla sighed as my shoulders slumped. "Seeing is kind of my specialty, and I don't get anything but black. It's like a counter spell was put out here so that whatever happened got erased."

That didn't look good for Mehrdad either, especially since he was the only one who knew I'd traveled the scene of Amy's death. That every subsequent body had worn a shroud of darkness definitely meant someone hadn't been happy with me looking into things.

"Where is Mehrdad tonight?" I asked, releasing the metal railing and turning back to face Layla. "He doesn't seem the type to miss his own party."

Layla shrugged.

"He waffled between excuses of needing to meet with Landry to 'make things right' for Kara's family and having a headache," she said, "but he promised he'd make an appearance before the clock struck three."

Or maybe he's out looking for another blood donor from the party strays, I thought.

Dammit. If we'd spent our time chasing tails at the party while the vampire amongst us sought another victim, I would not be able to stop myself from staking first and asking questions later. Even Learco was distressed. Despite the calm exterior he maintained, I could read the worry in his eyes as they told me we needed to find the head BOG Witch. Fast.

We had about eight minutes before the Witching Hour hit and the entire ballroom began to empty into the hallway to wait for the elevators to carry them off into the night. We needed to leave before the crowd kept us planted in their dust.

"Thanks for looking out for me," I told Layla as she stared sorrowfully at the railing once more. "Learco and I will find out what really happened to Kara. I promise."

The huffing sigh behind her nod told me she didn't really believe me, but she appreciated the effort all the same.

"We're going to slip out before everyone else here gets the same idea," I continued. "Maybe stick to the crowds tonight. Or keep a group with you in your room. You shouldn't be alone."

It was an effort to keep her safe on two fronts: from the vampire and from the grief that was welling in her eyes. Her wincing smile said she understood, at least about the latter.

"I'll, um, get the doors for you," she said as she pulled herself together and began to head back inside. "They're kind of tricky if you aren't used to them."

My eyes met Learco's as he took my hand, and we followed Layla with purpose. Maybe the process of elimination we'd taken hadn't been such a bad thing. And though nothing was certain yet, we knew exactly where we needed to go. Plus, thanks to his assistant, we had the right questions to bring to Mehrdad.

The party-goers inside were still dancing and drinking, but the bodies were closer together, the clothing more disheveled as their energies pulsed with the anticipation of the after-events being formed and distinguished as the band moved into their closing number. The lust in the room was palpable, breathing in time with the auras mixing in the air. It would have been a heady experience. It was certainly one I hated to turn away from.

Layla grunted as her fingers worked the floor bolt, releasing the trigger that freed each of the ornately carved wooden doors to swing open. As she slid them into place, her eyes glanced out to the hallway and she froze. Her face paled. And then, low at first, as if the sound itself was afraid, a wailing scream escaped her throat.

The band stopped. The crowd sobered and looked toward the noise. Learco dropped my hand as he rushed to the young witch's side. His eyes took in the scene beyond the doorway, and he turned swiftly to hold his hands up toward the approaching gathering.

"Everyone stay back," he commanded.

I rushed forward to clutch Layla's shoulders and give Learco the opportunity to settle into his authority over the group.

In my mind, there was another body, perhaps even Mehrdad standing over it. Fangs bared. Lips still moistened with blood. It would be a horrible thing to witness for Layla, much less for everyone else in the room.

But what waited in the hallway was so much worse.

The stakes were makeshift, even a little sloppy where the posts were nailed to the bases, but they did their jobs. There were three of them, staggered six feet apart, each one framed in the bay windows overlooking Canal Street. The wood was old, gray and splintered by time and sun-damage, giving the structures a sense of being cobbled together despite their inherent intentionality. Each base was slightly different. I couldn't tell if subsequent creations had learned lessons in stability from the previous or if it was simply due to whatever scraps of wood were left available. Still, they sang with one simple message: *I'm here! Catch me if you can!*

A cold chill shivered down my spine as I entered the hallway with Learco. Layla had collected herself somewhat and was doing her best to keep the witches in the ballroom at bay, though an aghast fear was also doing the job. Still, I could hear the muttered cries and whimpers as another witch got close enough to see then turned away.

"I'm assuming these are the vanished corpses," Learco said, keeping a circled perimeter as he studied the scene.

"Amy. And the couple from the roof," I confirmed. "Zamiah isn't here."

Learco nodded, tapping a quick message into his cell phone before turning his attention back to the corpses bound to their stakes.

"So just the humans," he noted.

I shuddered at the implied significance of that, at the memory of Lady Z haunting me—stalking me—at the restaurant only hours before.

Amy looked somewhat peaceful, hanging there upright, her hands bound behind her to keep her high on the post, her feet strapped with leather to the base. Her head was tilted slightly forward, and her soft blonde hair hung against her cheeks, parted in such a way to make the puncture wounds on her neck all the more evident. She was wearing the same clothing I'd found her in, but it was more disheveled now, pressed and wrinkled as it hung from her limp frame.

The same was true of her companions. Their grotesque,

impressionist howls had subsided as rigor mortis passed, and the odd angles of their limbs now twisted to hold them upright against their own posts.

"I demand to see what the hell is going on out there!"

"Sir, please stay back and let the Moral Authority do its work."

The anguish in Layla's voice was hard to listen to as she tried to keep Osmund's bluster in line. The crowd was growing restless. It would not be contained much longer, especially as more and more witches peeked through the doorways and the horrid descriptions traveled from lip to ear throughout the room.

I felt something close to relief as the elevator dinged and the four agents Learco had texted pushed their way into the hall. Well, as much relief as I could feel while staring at three corpses and with MAW agents who weren't my boyfriend around.

I nodded as Learco moved to brief his agents, and turned my back on the scene to help Layla in her mission.

"That's the girl you let stay in your room, isn't it, Darragh?" Dula asked as I re-entered the ballroom. "Who are the other two? Are they attendees? Is anyone missing from the gathering?"

"They're all tied to stakes," another witch cried. "It's got to be a message from the Defend Mankind From Magic protesters out front!"

"It's a death threat, is what it is!"

"We never should have come out of the broom closet!"

"It's all *that* witch's fault!"

The crowd was scared and angry, and it appeared I was the closest punching bag. I was starting to understand first-hand how the witch hunts of old had taken place. I needed to calm them, yet every time I opened my mouth another accusation was bellowed. Then I heard Cal's voice break through the violence building in the room.

"My fellow witches," he cooed, and I watched in wonder as

the space around him cleared and every eye turned to meet his. "We do ourselves no favors in turning on our own. Whatever 'message' is intended by the display is not Darragh's fault, nor is it his doing. If fear is the response it was meant to incite, we do a disservice to all our kind by allowing ourselves to feel it."

It was eerie watching him speak. I'd imagined his appeal amongst the BOG Witches to be his fame and fortune, but there was definitely something else at play. They clung to his every syllable, growing more and more entranced as if they were spellbound as he continued. A faint, burning sensation pressed against my aura, and I knew Cal had sent his out. But all the other attendees seemed enamored with the feeling.

I couldn't name a single witch who possessed magic like that.

He kept his calming smile, but squinted his eyes at me when he felt my resistance push back on his.

The elevator chimed once more, and I spun to see Mehrdad rush from the lift. He looked rough, with bags under his eyes and wrinkled clothing barely hanging from his body. His five o'clock shadow had rounded midnight, and his hair was disheveled atop his head.

"What the fuck?" he shouted after a brief pause to take in the scene. "Get them out of here!"

The command was to Learco's agents, but the BOG Witch leader rushed forward on his own, throwing himself at the dead man's body and attempting to untie his hands. An exasperated fury filled his eyes as he worked, and Cal's spell broke as more and more attendees jockeyed to watch the show.

"Mister Yaisien, please step back," Learco commanded, his voice rich and full as he stepped forward to stop the man. "My agents will see to the removal of the bodies."

But something else was wrong. I felt it before I could see anything, a gnawing feeling in my stomach, like my wild magic was urging me to action.

Without thinking I rushed back into the hallways, grabbing my boyfriend's arm to stop him as the first fire lit. It ignited so quickly, taking form as if it were a thought at the base of the stake and rising to consume the whole of the man's body in an instant. I barely had time to gasp before the woman and then Amy were engulfed as well.

Mehrdad howled as he leapt back from the pyre, his own clothing aflame as the fire licked his skin ferociously. The nearest agent to him tackled him to the floor, rolling his body to put out the fire as the hotel's suppression system activated to send jets of water down on us all.

The flames did not seem to mind. They sizzled as each drop met their edges, burning brighter as the corpses and the stakes were consumed.

CHAPTER 16

"Try to get some sleep," Learco told me as he stood anxiously by the door of the Yarrow Tooth Suite.

"I don't think I can," I admitted. "Not after that. Besides, the vampire's still out there, and he seems more than angry. I can't let you investigate alone."

"I will have agents with me at all times," he assured me. "And I'll be in that bed with you before you wake up. I promise."

His lips still tasted of ash as he kissed me, and I could smell the faint aroma of smoke on his clothing as our bodies pressed together.

It'd been quite the endeavor, carrying Mehrdad's body down to the waiting paramedics—witches, thankfully, working at New Orleans Med—before funneling the rest of the crowd to their rooms for the night. With Learco's lockdown in effect, it had taken some maneuvering to find space for all the witches who'd chosen to stay outside of the Crow's Court, but we'd managed. And even though that scene had frightened them, most agreed there was strength in numbers. *And* solace in sex.

The exit had been slow as we tried to keep what was left of the crime scene in the wide hallway intact. But between the magicked flames and the gallons of water dumped on them to put them out,

I doubted much evidence would be there to rifle through. Still, it wasn't so much the what-was-there but the how-it-got-there that had Learco's investigative mind churning.

"All I'm doing is talking with my agents and the hotel's security," he promised. "No daring missions without you. It won't take long."

His kiss lingered on the air as I closed the door and turned to face the empty room. I was glad he was here, even if I hadn't wanted to put him in danger. And his MAW credentials—as hazy as they were on our end—would definitely garner him a lot more access and information without me tagging along.

The hotel's Hibiscus and Lemongrass Wash—courtesy of Dula's C.H.H.C. Botanicals line—was pleasant, but I missed the earthier, muskier scents of my usual soap and made a mental note to sneak out of the Crow's Court to retrieve my belongings from my OccultList BnB. I'd need the suit and mask Learco and Cernun had gifted me for the Masquerade Ball anyway—if we all survived to close out the event—and it'd be a good opportunity to check on Chester. The memory of Zamiah vamping about the outskirts of Petrichor still worried me, particularly given her witch-form knowledge of the man. And yet, as I positioned myself beneath the rainfall shower head to allow the suds to rinse from my body, and even more frightening thought occurred.

The bodies—Amy's and the couple's—were the only human victims we knew of before they were burnt to a crisp before our eyes. The witch corpses—Zamiah's and now Kara's, before she met the sidewalk and was carted off by the local coroner—were not among those destroyed. Did it take witch blood to make a vampire turn? Had the one stalking the convention figured that out? The thought potentially placed Chester out of harm's way, but it put one hell of a target on every attendee's neck.

Freshly showered, my skin was rid of the odor of smoke and

burning flesh, and I zipped the tux I'd been wearing into a garment bag to try to mitigate the aroma there. No spell I knew worked to stop the smell, and I had to remind myself that magical fires could not be fought with magic. They had to burn themselves out. The same was true for the remnants they left behind. The magic of the fires certainly lended credence to the idea that it took one with witch lineage to become a vampire. It explained the shapeshifting and the thrall in too. But damn, I hoped I wasn't right.

I used my hand to wipe the steam from the mirror and tussled my wet hair with my fingertips as I studied my reflection. Wet, it had more curl than when it dried, and I scrunched it a bit to exaggerate what was naturally there.

At least, I thought, now we could pull Mehrdad from our suspects list. The burns he'd received while trying to pull down the bodies had been painful and intense, and I doubted he'd have taken them willingly, even in an effort to throw us from his trail. Too, the fact that Osmund and his cronies had been inside the ballroom all night, plotting and scheming their takedown and takeover of the BOG Witch convention, erased any lingering doubts I had in removing them from the list as well. Which meant, aside from everyone else I hadn't met yet, left me with a list of one: Cal Juventus.

He'd been the last to arrive, making his grand entrance well after Layla had closed the doors. Had he used that time to set his stage and then danced the night away while he relished in what was to come?

In truth, I couldn't really buy him as a vampire, even with his elaborate dress and fair skin. But there was the way my wild magic magic seemed to churn whenever he was nearby. And the effect his aura seemed to have on everyone around him—except for me and Learco anyway. Still, my instinct told me it wasn't him, even as my brain insisted I study all the options.

Whatever the case, we had one more day—and one more night—to find the being responsible for the murders and bring justice to those who were lost. One more day before the throngs of attendees scattered to every corner of the globe and the trail went as cold as the ashes MAW agents were sweeping and bagging in the fourth floor hallway.

I pulled myself beneath the lush, goose down comforter of the bed and stared into the blackness of the room. The morning sun was fast approaching, but there was still plenty of time for things to go bump.

A thunderous banging on the door woke me just before dawn. The last vestiges of night, holding strong in the sky as the sun lingered just below the horizon, whispered to me in the form of fading starlight. I stumbled in the darkness, feeling for the light switch that wouldn't work as my toes gripped at the rough carpet of the floor. At least I managed to find the robe hanging from the hook on the back of the bedroom door. I slipped it over my shoulders as I sidestepped the coffee table, then slid the security lock from the hotel suite door.

Cal's knocking fist dropped to his side, and his newly formed smile glistened in the fiery gas lamps as their light poured from the hallway into my room.

"Did I wake you?" he purred as if he hadn't spend the last five minutes pounding on my door. "Aren't you going to invite me in?"

"What time is it?" I asked, wincing as my eyes adjusted.

"We are mere moments before the light crests the eastern

horizon," Cal smiled, glancing over his shoulder to the large windows overlooking Canal Street and the eerie quiet it held before its pavement worked overtime to hold up the soles of strangers, "making now the perfect time to sink our teeth into the possibilities of tomorrow. Aren't you going to invite me in?"

My fingers swam against the door, pulling time from the wood as I used it to keep my sleepy body steady, subconsciously ensuring at least two fingers and my thumb on the other side held it firmly ajar.

Cal's grin was wicked and curious, naive and knowing in its promise. His crimson track suit, adorned with golden, paisley embroidery, had never seen the inside of the gym—let alone the man wearing it sweat—and yet it clung to the the thin musculature of his frame to accent the hard curve of his pecs, the jut of his nipples, the bulge of his cock. The white-blond of his hair was wild as it danced in the lamplight, and he licked his lips as he watched me watch him.

"I now understand why our auras do not align," he cooed, making the rift sound sexy, like it was a challenge we were meant to overcome. "You have tasted what I have yet to penetrate. You must invite me in. Show me where to push. So that I may taste that which I have longed for. That which resides now in you."

As he spoke, my focus shifted to the scene unfolding beyond his shoulder. The hallway was a hotbed of predawn activity. Bodies rose from shadows, like birds chasing the morsels the cool of the night had left as offerings, swarming through the dim light in the choreographed chaos of the natural order. Or maybe unnatural.

Osmund and Carter stood frozen, captivated by the alluring and slinking movements of Zamiah as she preened before them, her sister Félicité joining her in a sultry dance. Dula and Ric and Marguerite and Layla followed Kara as her enlivened corpse sauntered through the space, stretching her limbs to realign them to her shape. And Mehrdad, still beautiful even with the puckered burns he'd received, waited patiently in the center of the corridor as Chester led Learco and Cernun through the mess and to his feet.

Cal's smile held but had turned desperate when my eyes shifted back to him against my will.

"Our time is nearly up," he wailed. "We must meet the world as it was meant to be. As it once was. When gods moved amongst us all. When we were beings of the eternal. Aren't you going to invite me in?"

I jolted upright, really this time, to find a silhouette framed in the light from the bathroom door.

"It's just me," Learco said, and my eyes adjusted to take in his comforting smile as my breath reentered my lungs. "Did you have one of your visions."

"I don't know," I groaned. "I think my brain is just trying to make sense of all the things that don't seem to add up here. How'd your night go? Did you find the clue that makes everything fall into place?"

"Not as such," he sighed, tossing his tie to join the tux jacket he'd draped over the back of a chair then moving to unbutton his shirt. "The elevators were not used. And though there were a few grace periods, none of my agents nor the security guards heard anyone on the stairs. It could be that a magic beyond that which we know was used to get the bodies to that hallway. The hotel's Magic In Monitoring system was never activated. But that would have taken calling and consulting with Leland to get any real info from anyway. But if the vampire's magic was that powerful, strong enough to transport three human bodies, then why would they have needed to use an accelerant to keep the fires burning? Why would the three have ignited in succession instead of all at once? I have a feeling the corpses and their stakes were being held in a storage room on the fourth floor itself."

"And when Layla closed the doors to keep the music contained, the culprit went to work."

"Exactly. There are two staging rooms just outside the ballroom with enough space to make that happen. But according to Landry, his staff was in and out of both of them until mere hours before the event to grab tables and tablecloths and cutlery for the evening."

My mouth scrunched as I considered Learco's assessment, pulling myself from beneath the comforter to help him finish his buttons and push the soft white of his starched shirt over the tight broadness of his shoulders.

"So we are looking for a vampire who has the knowledge of a hotel employee when it comes to the schedule and the layout of the Crow's Court," I summarized, "alongside a seemingly innate comprehension of the BOG Witch events schedules and the underlying political power plays which rock its inner circles. One with both physical strength and magic, who can move amongst us without being noticed since there is always someone out and about, all while they both stay hidden and work hard to make their presence known and obvious too every witch here."

"Yep," Learco chuckled as he unbuckled his belt. "Which essentially boils it down to a bubble in a cauldron."

I dropped to my knees before him as I helped to shift the fabric of his slacks below the curve of his hips. Just because we were in the throes of trying to figure things out didn't mean a little bit of sexy foreplay was off the table. Besides, the distraction as our blood energized within our veins could actually help us unlock whatever secret we were searching for.

"What if it's not one vampire?" I asked as he lifted his foot and I slid first one pant leg and then the other from his body, followed by the thin black silk of his socks. "What if it's really an entire team? What do they call their groups? 'Covens,' right?"

I scoffed at the irony of the word as I rose from the floor, taking the time to admire the taut tension of his eight-pack abs as my eyes rose to meet his.

"It is possible it's a coven," he continued, sighing and shaking his head as he attempted to rid it of his worry. "In one way or the other. But we can think about this in the morning. Right now that bed is inviting us both in."

The morning sky roared as the heat of Spring clashed against the departing Winter, pulling the water of the Gulf into the sky to fall back upon the city in torrents. Lightning broke the air as if the firmament needed to display the ubiquity of her own magic, to show whatever powerful creatures dwelled below her that the connection between the elements would remain alive and well even after we had passed. The heat of it all, the power of its majesty, made the bed feel like a cloud, and I nestled further beneath the sheets to watch it through the window.

"The first storm of Spring is always my favorite," I whispered when I heard Learco stir beside me. "It's one of the things I love most about the south."

"Even when it's a portent of the day ahead?" he asked, wrapping his arm around my side as he snuggled in behind me and laid his cheek against mine to watch the show with me.

"Especially when it's a portent of the day ahead," I smiled. "That rain out there, it's washing away all that was to leave the answers bare. It's making sure all those seeds we planted on Ostara, all that good will we imbued them with, will germinate and grow."

"That's a lovely thought. I wish I had your optimism."

I could feel the tensions in Learco's chest as he pressed himself against my back, and I glanced over to the bedside alarm clock.

"Shit," I gasped as the digital display ticked to 7:45. "Your meeting with Leland is supposed to start in fifteen minutes. And you are here with me."

"I'm exactly where I'm supposed to be," he sighed, but I could hear his unease.

Despite his insistence that his reinstatement meeting was merely a formality, I knew Learco had wanted to be there, if only to put the whole thing behind him. Besides, it wasn't often a witch like Leland Hyde was put in his place. And though Leland wasn't the type to grovel, he was epitome of someone who'd use Learco's no-show status to his advantage.

"I'm glad you're here too," I said, shifting to face him as the rain outside intensified. "But maybe you can teleconference or something. To at least hear Leland tuck his broom between his legs."

Learco winced as he pushed himself from the mattress and moved to push the draperies further from the window.

"He'll only ask where I am," he explained. "And the last thing we need is him showing up to run ramshackle over the Crow's Court. We have one day left to stop whoever is behind all this, and we don't need Leland tossing his stomach around our investigation."

"Fair," I nodded.

Leland wasn't exactly adept at nuance. He'd never really had to be. As the MAW's resident witch hunter general, he'd made it his mantra to blunder through with force, bully out a confession, and leave all the real questions for the folks who needed to make the pieces of the puzzle fit to support his case after the fact. Hell, he'd even tossed me in a cell a week prior because he believed I'd magicked up a few hundred daffodils. And even though that wasn't illegal by Moral Authority standards, he'd used my supposed show of power as an excuse to show his own.

"Still," I added, " it would be kind of funny to hear his nasal New England accent pronounce 'vampire.'"

Learco chuckled as he slipped into one of the plush gray robes—not white like in my dream—and pulled the laminated menu from the drawer of the bedside table, closing it gently before changing the subject.

"What are you thinking for breakfast?" he asked. "Room service or venturing out into the rain?"

"Aren't we on lockdown?"

"The hotel is, yes," he confirmed. "We don't have to be. Though I'm sure I can find some ropes if that's what you'd prefer."

"Now who's challenging Dula for the title?" I laughed.

My phone buzzed aggressively as I began to pull myself from the luxury of the bed, and I furrowed my brow as I reached for it on the charger. Cernun's sexy smirk peered back at me from the screen, but, given the time, I knew it wouldn't be a sexy call.

"Hey, babe," I said as I pushed the button to accept and held the phone out in front of me. "You're on speaker. Got me and Learco both."

"Have you seen the news?"

The anger on his voice was pulsating, and I could almost see him gritting his teeth as he scrunched his lips between words. Learco darted to the living quarters as I grabbed the other robe and followed, assuring Cernun we were fine—so far—as Learco fought with the remote to switch it from the Crow's Court's in house offerings channel to the national news. I held my breath as the TV stalled between channels, anticipation churning in my chest even though I already knew what was coming.

There was only one thing in this world that could make my partner so agitated.

Sure enough, as the stark definition of the live stream clicked into focus, Jason, Cernun's adoptive brother and the mouthpiece for his family's Defend Mankind From Magic group, spat his vitriol into a sea of pointed microphones with a smarmy, trying-too-hard-to-appear-innocent-and-dejected look on his face. A blue, airport-purchased poncho hid the bald spot of his thinning, mousy hair, and I could tell from the wrinkles in the cheap suit beneath the plastic that he'd caught a red eye from Albuquerque to be camera-ready first thing this morning. He'd positioned himself in front of his protesters, all scrunched together under umbrellas to make their numbers seem greater, and I could see Landry fuming through the windows of the Crow's Court lobby behind them.

"Turn it up?" I asked, and Learco adjusted the volume before sitting on the edge of a couch cushion.

"These vile, reprehensible creatures have gathered here in mass," Jason huffed, his words gathering speed as he fought for the repeated soundbite every station would carry like a sinful preacher telling his sheep they needed to repent, "turning on one of their own! Her body was dropped before us right here on this very sidewalk. A horrific sight. A warning that we are next. And there are reports they burned three others of their own in the late hours of the night! My team witnessed the fires through the fourth floor window with their own eyes. This scourge upon the population of a fine, Godly city such as New Orleans shall not go unanswered...."

Learco switched the television to mute to stop the spew of violence, and I shuddered as I held my phone between us.

"It's gotten picked up by nearly every station," Cernun huffed through the speaker.

Jason's mouth was still moving as the camera briefly cut away to the reporter before archival footage of Learco's impromptu statement from the previous night was shown. He cringed as his face filled the screen.

"Guess Leland knows why I was unable to make our meeting this morning," he sighed. "I imagine he'll be on the next flight here."

"I will be too," Cernun said. "Whatever the fuck is happening in New Orleans, I don't want y'all facing it alone."

"The trouble is," Learco countered, "we don't have a clue as to what is really going on."

"All we know is," I added, "whoever or whatever is behind this likes making a show of it. It's like he's playing a game with us."

"All the more reason..." Cernun started.

"For you to stay right where you are," Learco finished. "We both love you, and we'd both love to see you. But we've got today and tonight to put an end to this, and then we'll be home. I've got agents on site, and Darragh and I will stay out of harm's way until we bring this killer to heel. I promise."

"Fine," Cernun groaned. "I'd probably end up in a cell for knocking Jason in that sycophantic mouth of his anyway."

"I could handle that for you, if you'd like," I joked.

I'd only met Jason once before, right after his minions sent my shop up in flames, but his holier-than-thou attitude would have been enough to warrant a hard slap if I wasn't such a pacifist.

Even if he hadn't just attempted to destroy my livelihood. Even if he hadn't spent the last few decades hellbent on torturing Cernun and all those like him. That he was right downstairs preaching his hatred made the power in my gut churn, and I had to remind myself of the witch's mantra: *And it harm none.*

"No. He'll get his three-fold," Cernun assured me. "You boys be careful out there. I love you both."

"To the stars and back," I said, echoing his usual response before I ended the call.

Learco, still frozen on the edge of the couch, blinked his eyes slowly before hitting the power button and tossing the remote to the coffee table before him. Though his façade was calm, I could tell his mind was aflutter with the ricocheting if/thens surrounding his job. Not that he was trying to hide anything, but Learco running an inquest with MAW resources while he was on Leland's shitlist had the potentiality of becoming messy if Leland decided to make a fuss. And, with what little I knew of the man, he would.

I wished there was something—anything—I could say to help the situation, but before I could even form the correct words of comfort, my boyfriend shifted his own mindset back to that which he could control: the investigation.

"I need to get dressed and get downstairs," he said, standing suddenly and bending to realign the remote control beside the coffee table decor where he'd tossed it askew. "I'll try to get on top of the public relations fiasco the reporters and the DMFM are creating outside. Last night's lockdown is still in effect so no one should be coming or going from the Crow's Court until this matter is settled. But I can still send an agent over to your OccultList BnB to grab our things so we have something other than yesterday's garments to wear."

He paused at the bedroom doorway as he peered at the

discarded tuxedo and the wrinkled button-up and slacks he'd work the day before. He whispered "*dan jade*" to smooth out the wrinkles on the more casual outfit, then turned back to me.

"Shower while I'm out, and I'll hopefully have clothes for us both when you're done," he smiled, attempting to show me—as well as himself—that everything was under control. "Then we can tackle those storage rooms on the fourth floor. My agents went over everything last night, but maybe you—and your wild magic—could find something they missed."

I nodded. Even though I expected to be met with the same blank darkness that had accompanied every crime scene since I'd found Amy, at least it was a place to start. And even if my wild magic garnered no leads, perhaps my eyes would.

The buzz of my phone still in my hand startled me, but a faint sense of relief washed through me as I read the text message on the screen.

Sorry I missed your call last night, Chester wrote. *I was a bit wiped after our amazing afternoon and passed out early. What did you want to talk about? Y'all ready for round two?*

I was glad he was safe—and still horny for that matter. Though I wasn't sure I'd really seen Zamiah at the restaurant, her appearance had felt like an omen, and his connection to the sisters made me concerned he'd become collateral damage. Now that I knew he was still alive and kicking, it gave me another thought. Unfortunately, it wasn't the sexy kind. The sisters had recruited him to their plan, and even if Zamiah hadn't been turned into a vampire, perhaps they—or he—knew more than they were letting on. The fact that they'd pretended to be witches they weren't to get me on their side certainly said they had more secrets. I wondered what exactly Chester knew.

"Hey, babe," I called to the other room as Learco perched on the side of the bed to lace up his shoes. "Hold off on sending an agent for our stuff. Chester just reached out. I think I can get him to swing by with our bags."

CHAPTER 17

Slowly and as quietly as possible, I pushed the Yarrow Tooth Suite's coffee table across the room to nestle awkwardly beside the dinette table and chairs before settling myself in the center of the floral rug. I didn't think I'd need the full six feet expanse for my circle, but I figured it was better to be safe than sorry, especially when attempting such a new spell. Or at least new to me. Its reliance on the wild within me made me certain the magic had been around for much longer than any of us, but I'd only performed it twice before.

Learco had offered to ensure his agents knew to admit Chester when he showed up with our bags, but between the storm, the DMFM, and all the reporters piled up outside, I didn't want to risk him—or me—needing to answer questions as to why a human was able to break the barricade of the MAW's lockdown. Plus, now that I knew the hotel's Magic In Monitoring system wasn't active and Learco had told me the OccultList BnB's wouldn't extend beyond the house's outer walls, I wanted to try. Besides, I was sure our sweaty stint of mingling auras and my knowledge of both the backyard of the BnB and my suite at the hotel would allow me to get a solid lock on him and pull him through. At least that's what the loudest voice in my head was telling me as it attempted to silence the ever-present worry which questioned what would happen to Chester if I failed. Would I splice him in two? Would he re-materialize within a wall or end up lost between the threads of the universe for eternity? Would I leave a piece of him behind?

I pulled my breath into the depths of my lungs, exhaling out the fears in a swift, steady push. I'd seen The Mórrígan pull objects and people—including myself!—through space so many times I was beginning to think she used the entirety of the Fae Realm like a backpack to sort through for what she needed. Plus the excited tingle of the wild magic within me showed it was aching to be used. I just needed to trust in myself to make it work, and that wasn't so different than the magic I was used to.

Chester texted me that he'd grabbed my and Learco's things and was waiting under the awning of his ADU home, and I tossed my phone beyond the six foot perimeter so the cellular reception wouldn't disrupt my circle. Even if it wouldn't normally be such a big deal, I couldn't risk any outside interference. I also didn't want to chance anything going wrong with the portal which was why I was forming a circle in the first place. The twice prior I'd pushed myself—alongside Learco, Cernun, and Madison—through the spacial plain, I'd used only my wild magic. Now though, I felt it best to combine the protective rites of the power I was more accustomed to with that which swelled within me. If nothing else, it gave me a sense of control.

Even though the wild was rollicking inside my gut, I pulled on the darker green of my witch magic to cast the circle first. Thankfully, the kitchen cabinets of the suite had been stocked with the basics—basil for the air of the East; ginger for the fire of the South; lavender for the water of the West; vetivert for the earth of the North; and the room's namesake yarrow for Spirit— and they all seemed relatively fresh in their dried repose. I didn't have my small, cast-iron cauldrons though. Or the wooden inlaid pentagram Uncle Gardner had fitted to my living room floor at home. But I could make do. Besides, a circle set to a pentacle, as strong as it was, was attuned to a witch's magic. A circle set to the corners, calling all elements to their cardinal directions and centering the spirit of the casting witch at the core, was more aligned with nature. When attempting to move someone through the physical space of it, I figured that type of circle would be a better place to start.

A few quick thoughts in rapid succession ignited the dried ingredients I'd placed in ceramic tea cups at the four corners. Each flame quickly extinguished to release a thin plume of white smoke and the sultry scents of their respective plants into the air. The yarrow, resting in my cupped palms, would be trickier, but I had to have faith. I held its image in my mind's eye as I pulled the excited bright green of my wild to twine within the kelly green of my witch magic, sending it to coat the skin of my hands to protect them from the quick flame. As the yarrow extinguished, the pleasant smell of pine and earth and leather filled my nostrils, and I felt the circle set.

I kept my eyes closed as I brought my vision to the fabric of what was and what would be. It was beautiful. All the threads which connected the earth, woven through like roots, like strands of light, like drops of water stretched to form a whole even as they showed themselves to me in the individuality of their nature. I concentrated on Chester, on the feel of his unique aura, as I allowed the wild magic within me to push through the threads, shifting them ever so slightly this way or that, careful to not allow them to break as they strained to allow an opening.

I saw him before he saw me, huddled under the thin overhang of his shed-turned-house with my and Learco's bags as he attempted to stay dry in the storm. His eyes widened as I appeared before him, and I tried to keep my expression casual and calm as I held out my hand for him to follow me back through to the Crow's Court, even though the wild—and my heart—were raging.

It was a heady experience, using wild magic, and when combined and woven with my witch power, it sent every cell in my body to vibrate. It was akin to a feeling of true connection, the kind I'd experienced only a few times before—first with Cernun, then with Learco, and threefold with them both. I made a mental note to test the edges of our aura play with my wild the next time we were all together. Not only would it be a safe way of experimenting with my newfound magic, I wanted the two of them to have a chance to feel even a fraction of what I was feeling.

Chester's breath was heavy as we rematerialized in the living room of my suite, and I realized he'd been holding the air in his lungs as we made our journey through the ether. A quick thought of thankfulness brought down my circle, and I smiled as my guest dropped the bags to the rug.

"How did you…?" he asked, squinting his eyes as he looked at me and cocking his head in a way I hadn't seen him do before. "I've been around magic my whole life, and I've never seen any witch do anything like that."

His words were breathy and slow, but I could hear the quickness of his pulse beneath them. It had to be a lot for a human, even one accustomed to magic, and I shrugged as the wonder in his eyes rounded off to a quick flash of suspicion. I'd shown him the power because I felt I could trust him, but I wasn't ready to tell him—or anyone else for that matter, aside from those who already knew—where it came from just yet.

"Every family's Book of Shadows is different," I said. "Plus the MAW has a lot of really old spells in their libraries."

It wasn't a lie exactly. The words themselves were true. It just wasn't a direct answer of his question.

"Thanks for collecting our things."

"No problem," he said, shaking his head to break his gaze and peering down to the bags at his feet. "You want me to put them in the bedroom?"

"Oh, I can get them," I assured him. "You just have a seat."

His body looked awkward, standing in the center of the witchy hotel room, and I gestured toward the sofa behind him. The travel through the portal must have been harder on his human body than I'd anticipated, but I was sure a smooth cup of tea or a rich cup of coffee would settle his nerves.

I filled the lower chamber of the moka pot with grounds and placed it on the electric coil of the stovetop to boil. The aroma was delicious as it mixed with the lingering of my spell, and I dug through the cabinets for two demitasse cups and saucers, hoping I hadn't sullied all the china while casting my spell.

"This place is really snazzy, huh?" Chester asked, crossing his legs as he turned to rest his arm on the back of the couch.

"Sure is," I joked, pouring our coffees and making sure the stove was off. "But it didn't come equipped with a resident hotty waiting shirtless in the backyard."

I expected Chester to blush as I'd seen him do time and time again, but his gaze stayed firm on me as I rounded the kitchen island to deliver our drinks.

"Some amenities are just meant to be," he purred.

He slurped his coffee with an exaggerated purse to his lips, cooling the thick brown liquid with his breath as it coated his tongue.

"A place like this got any sugar?" he asked, dropping his cup and scraping the roof of his mouth with his tongue.

"Uh... Yeah."

My brow furrowed as I went back to the kitchen to grab the canister of raw sugar from the counter. He dumped four heaping spoonfuls into his glass and stirred, taking another sip with a smile.

"Looks like you called and hung up three times last night before your 'we need to talk' text. Guess you really needed your bags, huh?"

His voice was still slow and practiced, as if the words were having a hard time coming out. I winced a little as I watched him try out pose after pose, repositioning his body in an attempt to get comfortable. I guessed the trip—or our tryst—had been more exhausting than I'd realized.

"I actually wanted to chat with you about the sisters," I said, thinking it best to dive right in so he could get some rest.

"What about them?"

He learned forward with a renewed interest, his elbow slipping from his knee before settling back to balance his eager face.

"You said you grew up with them, right?" I asked, hoping the conversation would help to center him back within himself.

"Yep. Back in Butte la Rose," he smiled. "I was sweet on Lici for a long, long time."

"And they're related to Marie Laveau?"

His lips pursed with laughter and he squinted his eyes as he cocked his head toward me again, hands raising in surrender as if he'd been caught.

"Everyone around here with any witch in their veins is related to her somehow. At least that's what they say anyway," he explained. "The woman had fifteen children. And, as a midwife, she oversaw the births of countless others. There's a little bit of her magic in almost everyone 'round these parts."

I nodded. In fairness, it wasn't much different from the witches I knew who swore their lineage traced back to Salem or Stonehenge.

"But they don't actually run the museum?" I asked.

"How'd you find that out?" The suspicion on Chester's face was replaced with resolve, and he shrugged. "Not as such. But the part of the family that does is always gone this time of year. And a family business is family business, no matter how distant the blood, right?"

His words were picking up in speed—his gestures too—but it seemed to be taking a lot out of him. As the final lilt of his question left his lips, he slumped over himself. He braced his palms against his knees, barely lifting his head as he looked at me in… pain.

"Darragh, I…."

His voice sounded finally like his own, and he buried his face in his hands for a moment before popping back up with a lascivious smile.

"I have to say, after feeling the power of your spell, I'm even more interested in exploring you further. What do you say we test out this body, and I get to experience what your aura feels like?"

Something was definitely wrong. Even with the disorientation of the portal spell, Chester wouldn't have forgotten the afternoon he shared with Learco and me. I was about to press forward when a loud knocking startled us both.

I answered the door to find Cal smiling in the hallway, a beautiful pair of finely cobbled wool and leather boots held forward in his hands like a crown.

"Your shoes are ready, sir," he beamed. "I wanted to deliver them personally, particularly after all that nastiness in the corridor last night. Aren't you going to invite me in?"

I stuttered as the memory of my dream echoed into my present, and I felt the wild magic slip upwards within me as I found my words.

"I'm sorry," I said. "They're just so beautiful. I was caught off guard."

"Of course you were," Cal spoke, arrogance and appreciation

in equal measure on his voice before he switched to his more practical business-mode. "You and I have much to discuss. I believe I know now why our auras are so disjointed. You taste of what I've longed for. Invite me in so we can discuss this all."

"Now's not really a good time," I said.

I was trying to keep my words—my voice—cordial, but the intensity of Cal's were really beginning to freak me out. At first, I'd been more concerned about whatever the fuck was going on with Chester, about protecting whomever had knocked from whatever he'd succumbed to in his trip through the ether as I tried to figure out where my spell had gone wrong and right it. Now, it seemed I had monsters on both sides of the door.

"Come now, Darragh," Cal insisted, taking a step closer to the threshold but not daring to cross it. "I know your secret. And I would like for you to know mine."

A clearing throat from behind me broke the intense stare Cal had locked me in, and he handed me the boots as he pushed the door further into the suite. I turned to follow his gaze to find Chester standing shirtless before the couch, licking his lips as his eyebrows arched and his fingers worked the buckle of his belt.

"I apologize," Cal said suddenly, backing away with a slight bow as he returned his eyes to mine. "I did not realize you had company. We… We can discuss this all later. Please, wear the shoes tonight to the ball. And I shall have your… other lover's shoes delivered before nightfall."

Cal was at the elevator bay before I'd even managed to close the door, and I shivered as I turned back toward Chester. The persistence of the witch would have been enough to frighten me, the similarities to my dream aside, and I was somewhat grateful that Chester had scared him away. But Chester was an entire other issue. He definitely wasn't acting like himself, and I had a feeling it was more than just the trip through the threads of the universe that was shaking him.

I placed the shoes Cal had given me on the floor then turned to face the man, keeping a casual smile on my face as he re-buckled his belt and swiped his shirt from the arm of the sofa.

"Are you feeling okay?" I asked, making sure the door was locked before I crossed back toward the center of the living room.

"What do you mean?" Chester asked, the innocence on his words jarring as he stretched the fabric of his t-shirt across one hand like a rag then reached into his back pocket to produce a small amber bottle in the other.

"The changes in your speech aside," I said, pulling my magic—both the witch and the wild—to the ready as I took another step forward, "you don't take sugar in your coffee."

He grinned a half grin, stretching one cheek outward as his eyes squinted and an expression that was altogether foreign clouded his features.

"Well," he said, "you can't blame a witch for trying."

In one swift motion, he'd bit the cork from the bottle and dumped its contents onto his shirt. I didn't even have time to react before he'd shoved the fabric across my face, covering my nose and mouth. I could not even summon a spell before it all went black.

I came to in what looked like a forgotten catering kitchen, the smell of chloroform still clinging to my nostrils. It was sweet— almost pleasant—but I was glad its effects were wearing off, and I huffed a strong breath outwards to try to push any residuals of the manmade potion away. Ropes bore tightly into my wrists and around my ankles, and I had an overwhelming sense of *déjà vu* as I struggled against the chair I was sat in.

Wire racks of aluminum warming trays and stands alongside a bevy of nicer chafing dishes were stacked against the walls near a few discarded boxes of expired gel fuel. There were three stacks of warming ovens; a dish, hand, and mop sink; and two long and polished prep tables. Two industrial refrigerators hummed against the furthest wall. The room was surprisingly clean, though it looked like it hadn't been used in years. But at least I knew I was still inside the Crow's Court.

Catering kitchens were commonplace for human hotels, particularly the ones with extravagant ballrooms that liked to host weddings and conferences. But for witches, a simple thought could keep the meals warm for a fraction of the cost, so many of those rooms had been left discarded once our power was revealed and we'd established centers and businesses for ourselves. At least until a remodel could figure out better uses for the space. It would actually make a great spelling kitchen, and I made a mental note to tell Landry of the possible amenity for his guests. If I made it out of whatever I'd gotten myself into alive.

I craned my neck to peer behind me and found Chester slumped in another chair near the doors which had once been used for the staff to access whatever meeting space we were adjacent to. Still shirtless, his chin balanced against his shoulder and his arms hung limply at his sides. It was shallow, but his chest was moving, so I knew he was still alive. Whatever had taken hold of him—had taken me!—was gone, and had thought little enough of him to leave him behind unbound.

I needed to get us both out of there, but I swooned when I reached to tap my magic. The dissociative dizziness I'd attributed to the chloroform was something else entirely. Whoever had trapped me had cut me off from my power. I realized the scratchy poke at my wrist was from the mixture of wormwood, mugwort, and vetivert stalks braided into the bonds of the ropes. Separate, each of the plants were a powerful ingredient in witchcraft. Combined and with the right incantation, they could prevent even the best of witches from accessing their magic. Even the wild within me was affected, and I looked down to find a chalked circle drawn around my chair with symbols that looked a lot like the Fae writing I'd seen during my time in their Realm.

Dread flashed through my brain. Perhaps The Mórrígan had lied to me, and the Fae truly were behind the misdeeds going on at the hotel. That or she didn't have quite the control over her denizens as she believed. Or maybe Balor was back! He was the only thing I'd ever seen possess another's body before, and Chester had definitely been possessed. My dreams had warned me of him, and even The Mórrígan wasn't certain his death would stick. The Fae could die a thousand deaths and would still return unless the exact circumstances of their prophesied demise were met.

Shit. I really didn't want to have another Fae battle in a hotel filled with witches and MAW agents. But at least I knew I could beat him. His hubris had been his downfall time and again, no matter how powerful he was.

I gripped the seat of my chair as much as the ropes would allow, shifting my weight through my torso to try to shift my position. If I could break the chalk line of the circle, there was a strong chance I could pull a tendril of my wild into being. At least that was my theory. Although the wild magic had always been inside me, it had lain dormant until my time in the Fae Realm summoned it into my awareness. Now that I knew it was there, and was beginning to learn how it differed from the witch power I'd always known, I didn't think the dampening spells would work on it if I broke the chain of the Faerie circle.

Of course, the theory was hard to test. No matter how I shifted my weight, I couldn't get the legs to budge more than half an inch in any direction. Even when I tried rocking, the chair's balance made it impossible to tip.

"Chester?" I called lowly, hoping if I could rouse him, it would actually be him.

My throat was still scratchy from the anesthetic, and I swallowed hard to wet my windpipe before calling his name again. He groaned, but he didn't come to. Yet, as his head wobbled to rest on his other shoulder, the sight of the two fresh puncture wounds on his neck sent another fear shivering through me.

Maybe it wasn't the Fae after all, but the vampires we'd assumed were wreaking havoc. I wasn't sure which was worse. I'd dealt with the Fae before. I knew their ways. And I knew I could best them. Vampires, though, were creatures entirely new. To me anyway.

It made sense they would have an understanding of both witch and Fae magics if, as the lore suggested, they had been around for as long as they had. As immortal creatures, if that part of their story was true, it was possible the being stalking the Crow's Court had once been friendly with The Mórrígan or Balor, had learned their ways, and was now using them against me.

It also explained the strange way Chester had been acting. Every story, every movie, every TV show I'd watched concerning vampires had always included some Renfield-like element of thrall—a hypnotic state the vampire could leave an emissary in to do their bidding in the daylight hours. Someone had definitely taken over Chester, but whoever it had been had called themself a witch. Hadn't they? Maybe that was just to throw me off.

Ugh. My head ached from the thoughts coupled with the residual effects of the chloroform. Not to mention the tingling ache which swelled within me the longer I was cut off from my power.

"Hello?"

The slow scrape of the hallway door on tile pulled my attention to the other entrance, and my heart pounded as Dula stuck her curious face into the room. She winced when she saw me, a sadness in her eyes as she took only three small steps into the space, stopping with her hands wringing at her waist.

"Dula!" I yelled, louder than I'd expected. "I need you to untie these ropes. That man over there has been hurt. I need to help him."

Her eyes brimmed with wetness as she looked to Chester and then back to me, a quivering resolve in her cheek as she sighed.

"Oh, Darragh," she gulped, a single tear cascading from the edge of her eye to the bright red of her lip. "I'm so sorry."

CHAPTER 18

"What do you mean you're sorry?"

The question came out as more of a demand, and Dula cringed at the mixture of surprise and anger in my words. She held her stance close to the doorway, eyes darting from my fury to Chester's limp body and back again. Her lips quivered as she took in the scene of her doing, and my mind struggled to make sense of it all.

Was she really the vampire I'd been looking for? The change in her appearance—hell, even her new name—should have been a dead giveaway, and I wasn't even looking in her direction. I shuddered as I considered the newfound aggression in her demeanor, so disparate from the moon child, hippie witch who'd once danced the aisles of HEX for her lavender and rose quartz. I bit my lip at the memory of her telling me the main offerings at her resorts were late night, moonbeam baths! How could I have been so blind?

"I didn't have a choice," she spat, explanation veering into vindication on her lips as her eyebrows raised to widen her eyes. "You have to believe me when I say I was over a barrel."

My laughter was both nervous and unconvinced, and I used

the mounting frenzy within me to try once more at shifting my chair. The push of the metal legs on tile echoed through the room, and Dula turned swiftly to close the door to the outer hall.

"Please don't make this harder than it already is," she commanded.

I bit my lip as I tried to breathe through the rising intensity pushing from my core. At least it was overcoming the dizziness I felt from being disconnected from my power. The air washed to clear my head as I refocused. My body and my magic were bound, but I still had my brain.

"How long have you been a vampire?" I asked.

Dula's laugh bounced through the wire racks, shaking the aluminum trays and rattling the lids of the chafing dishes like something from an old movie where the darkness shifts to technicolor and the villain gets her due.

"Didn't your uncle teach you any better than that?" she asked, still holding her belly as the last remnants of her amusement settled into a departing giggle. "Vampires are not real. But blood magic is."

My heart sank at her words, at the resolve that fell over her expression. Blood magic was the darkest of witchcraft. For centuries, the MAW had done its best to eradicate any traces of those spells from our books, even the Books of Shadows which were passed down by families through the years. But some spells had made it through. And they were never, ever good.

"Is that what these symbols are for?" I asked, nodding to the chalk outlines adorning the circle on the floor around me. If I could figure out where the spell was heading, perhaps I could determine a way out of it.

"I suppose," Dula shrugged, finding herself—or some darker version of herself—as she pulled a chunk of salt-infused chalk from her pocket and began her stride toward me. "They're not my runes, whatever they are. But they're the last thing he's making me do before I'm free."

Dula tossed her flowing cardigan to the prep table and fished a slip of paper from the pocket to study. At a glimpse, I thought I recognized the handwriting, but I couldn't quite place it. Then, she bunched the excess fabric of her skirt in one hand between her knee as she knelt to etch another circle adjacent to mine, carefully recreating the Fae lettering as she worked.

"Just so you know," she hummed, not daring to look me in the eye as she continued to scratch the chalk along the tile, "he promised me you wouldn't be killed by the spell. You'll lose a little blood, but you won't die."

I scoffed at the ache beneath her rationalized nonchalance. Both were out of place as her free limbs set the circle and she moved to chalk another. My wrists and ankles burned against my bonds as I twisted my joints in vain.

"I guess the same couldn't be said about Amy," I growled. "Or those humans from the rooftop we all saw burnt to ash. Or Zamiah or Kara."

The determination on her face faltered for a brief moment before she poured herself back into her work.

"The spell needs blood, human and witch," she gulped. "And the humans were transients no one would miss."

"Someone will miss them," I insisted. "*I* will miss them."

Dula's expression wavered as she looked at my face, and I wondered if she'd caught a glimpse of my Uncle Gardner, the witch she once claimed as a friend, in me. We didn't look much alike in the present, but I'd seen pictures of him from his heyday that could have been me with a different haircut and some mod-style clothes.

"What happened to the witch who used to pal around with my uncle?" I asked, drawing on every ounce of sympathy I could still hold for the woman to lay on the guilt. "You were friends once, weren't you? Hell, before you left to start your new life, I thought we were friends too."

"That witch grew up," she huffed. "You know, I was fine for a long time being the kooky old woman down the street, hanging my crystals from my window panes and watching all the kids too scared to ring my doorbell for candy every Halloween. But then you revealed who you were. You showed your power, and suddenly they weren't just rumors of the wicked witch in that house at the corner. I was real. Life was real, and a lot more complicated. I had to work hard to change that narrative. To be someone folks would respect instead of someone they would hate. You are what happened to that witch, Darragh."

A heavy sigh poured from my chest. I'd known not every witch had had the warmest reception when I'd revealed magic to the human world, but time and fascination had healed a lot of the wounds. And most witches were grateful to be out of hiding, despite organizations like the DMFM yelling their slurs out front.

"You don't need to feel sorry for me," she chuckled, suddenly cheerful again as she regained her composure. "I like who I am now. All that money buys a hell of a lot of crystals. And all those housewives who used to say hateful things to one another about me now throw their credit cards into my palms while thinking a moonlight bath is going to get rid of their baby weight or make their husbands stop sticking their dicks in their secretaries."

She finished drawing and stood to check her work against the sketch on her paper, nodding with satisfaction, then sighing as she looked once more to me. For a brief moment, I saw what almost looked like regret cloud her features before she shook it off in the remembrance of her own worries and extortion.

"He was surprised when you arrived without your boyfriends," she said. "Particularly when I'd worked so hard to get you on the list. Said you never traveled anywhere without them. He needed death to get the MAW here so that Learco would come. He needs you in danger so that Cernun will. The Cullen, the Clarke, and the Kyteler. Your bloodlines activate the spell."

Shit. Here I was again, the family lines of my coven placing the three of us in danger. At least I knew who the other two circles were for. And with Cernun safely in Atlanta, there was plenty of time for me to get out of it.

"Who is he?" I asked, the answer already ringing in my head. "What does he have on you?"

Dula set the third circle in a whimpering bust of purple light before she sidestepped it to grab her cardigan and stash the chalk and paper.

"I'm not allowed to tell you," she said as she slipped back into the coat and wrapped it tightly over her waist. "But his father once helped me bypass a lot of red tape and zoning to get my Blue Ridge Healing Center going. He has all the documentation, all the backroom handshakes and illegal spells that greased the way. It would destroy everything I built if that came out. And he said he's not going to kill you!"—This time she said it truly for only herself.—"He just needs a little bit of your coven's blood."

I decided to save my breath and my vocal cords when Dula locked the door behind her. I imagined the room had the same sound-barrier protection spell as the rest of the hotel when the doors were closed. Besides, if Aiden Goldfinch-Gowdie had been on campus since day one, blackmailing the witches present into submission as he carried out round two of his plan to reignite his family's magic using my coven's blood, I couldn't be certain how far his reach had extended. It was entirely possible no one under the hotel's roof aside from Learco had been immune to his... charms.

As a lawyer and a state legislator in Georgia, Aiden's father Adrian had amassed quite a bit of political power for himself. There were deals made and favors owed, restrictions lifted and sanctions sidestepped all because of him. For a gathering of witches more immersed in the power of their businesses and bank accounts than the actual magic swirling inside of them, that sort of thing went an awfully long way. With Adrian dead thanks to his son's first attempt at wresting back the magic that had died within them, I assumed whatever dossiers he had kept as collateral for his practices had fallen to Aiden.

Aiden was a desperate man, and desperation was a perfect bedfellow for no-holds-barred evil.

Fuck. I really needed to be better at interpreting my visions. My dreams had warned me he was involved, and I'd written it off as my fears using the demons of my past as placeholders. If I got out of this alive—*when* I got out of this alive—I'd be better at paying attention.

The truth was, knowing I was trapped in yet another ruse courtesy of my former protégé did make me feel a bit better. I'd made it through the first one mostly intact, save for a nasty cut and some wounded pride, and it had brought Cernun and I closer and Learco into our lives. He needed us alive for the spell from his Grimoire to work. He needed the blood to *actually* flow. And though he had me in his grip, and Learco was in the building, Cernun was over four hundred miles away. He'd failed already, despite the damage he'd amassed.

At least, I hoped so.

This spell was different than the last judging by the preliminary efforts he'd put into place. The individual circles, the Fae writing, and the buckets of blood he'd collected spoke to an entirely different ritual than the one he'd attempted before. He'd obviously spent his time in hiding researching and honing the darker sides of witchcraft, and, if it hadn't been so foul, I may have taken some gratification in the effort of my former student.

"How's it hanging, Teach?"

I turned slowly to face him as he sauntered through the swinging double doors that led to the adjacent meeting space. I refused to give him the gratification of a startled, swift movement, of angry words. My external calmness, even though I was raging inside, could be enough to throw him off his game.

He looked horrible. Decades instead of months had burrowed their way into his features. His blond hair, shaggy and loose now instead of perfectly coifed into a tailored side part, hung limply atop his head. There was a hollowness to his eyes I'd only ever seen in people who'd seen far too much or known way too little, and his lips now curled over his teeth instead of revealing them when he smiled. He had a few new scars too, connecting the faint freckles on his cheeks, pitting the life line of his palm. He'd had a hard time going since he'd attempted this the last time before having to flee Atlanta with a patricide warrant on his tail.

I almost felt sorry for him, and that pity was an emotion I was not afraid to let my ever-expressive face show. He scoffed when he saw it, then marched over to pull himself atop the prep table, slamming his hands down beside him to make the metal ring.

"Certainly not your fancy white ash spelling table back at HEX," he said, pulling his legs under him to sit cross-legged and leaning toward me like we were old friends, "but it'll definitely do in a pinch, don't you think? Plus it's a lot easier to wipe down steel. I think the blood would probably stain the wood."

"Thoughtful," I spat.

"I try to be," he smiled. "Of course, I was just going to leave you in here to suffer in your thoughts until your fuck buddies arrived, but good ol' Calendula Hawthorne showed up early to do her part, and I figured that'd get your mind working overdrive. So why don't we chat to keep you occupied?"

"Why would I want to talk to you?"

"You're cut off from your magic by mugwort and wormwood," Aiden chuckled. "And those ropes are spellbound so there's no slipping free. What else do you have to do?"

"How 'bout you get him some medical attention, and then we can have any conversation you want?"

Aiden's eyes followed mine to Chester's slumped frame before he turned back toward me with an exaggerated pout.

"Aww. Poor, dumb Chester," he whined in mimicked sorrow— potentially the only kind he truly knew. "Don't worry. He's not in any pain. He really can't feel anything at all. The blood loss though, that'll keep him passed out for a while. At least until I need him again. See, the new ritual I found requires a sacrifice. In addition to the living blood of my favorite trio of butt fuckers."

I didn't like the sound of that. But Aiden did seem primed to talk, and if I had more information, I might be able to figure out an escape.

"I can already tell you this spell isn't going to work," I said, relaxing as best I could as I released the tension in my shoulders and leaned back into the chair. If I could take on the demeanor of his former boss and teacher, he might just listen to me. If nothing else, I hoped I was able to poke some pinpricks of doubt into his plan. "These circles? That scribbled language? It's as made up as the Fae-folk. You can't pull power from a magic that does not exist."

In our realm, I added silently. Although a part of me feared the quickened wild within me was enough of a bridge for the Fae-based spell to spark.

"I don't need the Fae to exist," Aiden shrugged. "Wasn't it you who told me the names we gave them were just shorthand for the elemental pairings we wanted to call? The shorthand's still there regardless. Languages change; the spell remains the same."

I frowned. I *had* told him that, and, for a long time, it's what I'd believed to be true. Quite honestly, for a long time, it was. The Fae weren't around, and though stories of them persisted, those tales had morphed to align themselves with the ways we witches understood nature. We'd kept them in our spells as a means of reconciling the past, the anecdotes of our ancestors, with all that we knew and understood.

Long ago, when the Fae world and ours were entwined, when passage between the two realms was possible for those with any form of magic within them, the Fae had offered bargains to witches to bolster our spells. But every single one of those bargains had required a higher and higher cost until the earliest incarnation of the MAW had formed to expel the Fae to their own plane while severing the ties that connected our worlds.

I still wasn't sure if they'd truly known what they were doing, if they understood the consequences or had simply weighed the loss of magicks as a better price than the Fae-folk's deals, but they'd spent the next few hundred years eradicating any trace of Fae-spellwork from our witch's libraries. We could nevermore transmogrify into our animal selves to feel the freedom of the moon on our basest instincts. Travel by portal was no longer an option, even with the aide of the Rowan Tree. The direct animal communication we had known was replaced with an innate understanding versus actual words. The Moral Authority had worked all that to their advantage though, claiming a deterioration of power through the lines. They'd used it to prove out why they were so important, why their structure and their guidance would keep us steady and safe.

So maybe they *had* known what they were doing. Or, like Aiden, had simply tried to shift the course to their advantage.

"You're really okay with all this?" I asked, trying to appeal to any slip of humanity left within him. "All this death? All this murder? Just to reignite a power that will punish you for all the things you've done."

As his mentor, I'd hammered the Rule of Three through all of my teachings. Witches believed—well, the good ones did anyway—that every bit of magic we sent out into the world would come back to us threefold. It was intended to keep our magic true, to prevent a spell of love from becoming a spell of possession, to ensure our thoughts were in the giving and not the gaining. It helped us to understand the balance of the natural world and not try to mold it to our wants and desires beyond that which was willing to bend. Hell, maintaining the Witching Hour for high energy spells at 3AM was a not-so-subtle nod to the rule. But, I supposed, 3PM would work just as well, and judging by the growling in my stomach, we were just rounding noon. I had to work fast.

"You think you're so pious, don't you?" Aiden growled, leaning forward to grab my chin in his hand and examine my eyes. "You have used your magic to fuck and to fight and not for some holy venture. Without thinking, you performed a spell that revealed witch-kind to the whole of the world for some guy you'd just met. And all because you wanted to get your dick wet. So don't come at me with any of your Rule of Three nonsense. Besides. I am setting nature right. I'm restoring the balance of power to my bloodline."

I shifted as he leapt from the table, but kept my eyes on him as he crossed the room to fondle Chester's head, waving it around like a puppet only he could control.

"You know, Chester here," he continued, "once had the magic in his bloodline too. His family squandered it, gave it away for a simpler life of trawling the bottoms of swamps and basins for sea-born insects rich people like to eat. My family—the Gowdies—it was taken from us. Thinned out by witches like you, like those fuckers in the Moral Authority, who needed to feel more powerful by stripping the magic from others. That's what makes Chester the perfect sacrifice for the ritual. The three who have it, the three who never could, the one who found the path, and the one who gave it all away. Poetic, right? You always told me there was poetry in magic."

My brow furrowed as he released Chester's face, and I sucked in a quick breath as my friend's body slumped deeper into his chair. I'd felt Chester's aura, so I knew he wasn't a witch. But even the fact that he could push it outward meant, once upon a time, some form of power had been there. But how had Aiden discovered it?

"Bet you're wondering how I knew," Aiden laughed. "Your face really does telegraph every single stupid thought that migrates through your brain, doesn't it? Once I got Dula to invite you to this event, I knew I was going to need someone local to help me with the more… unsavory bits. After last time, I knew you'd refuse to use your magic to ignite the spell, so a powered witch was called for. Turns out, there's an awful lot of witches who don't like you. Even more who feel they deserve more power than nature granted to them. That's when I met Lici. I believe you know her as Lady F. A poor, eighth-line witch from what should have been a prominent family barely able to feed her kids with the money she was bringing in reading tarot cards on Frenchman Street. She told me all about Chester, how he'd pined for her like a love-lost puppy, and how she'd felt his aura back when they were kids. How he'd do whatever she asked of him, and how someone like you would be just his type. I knew you wouldn't be able to resist. I mean, look at him. I'm straight, but I woulda left his shirt off even if it hadn't been covered in chloroform. Kudos to you, though. Whatever you did to the boy made him extra receptive to Lici's aura-thrall. I've never seen a witch able to take over a human quite like that before."

Shit. Our afternoon delight had been intense, and I'd known that too strong of an aura push with humans could leave them susceptible to fawning, but Chester had been able to handle more than any human I'd ever met. I wondered if the wild that now coated my aura had met the power that once resided in his blood and triggered it somehow. It was my fault he was in that chair, and all the more reason I had to rescue him.

"Félicité let you kill her sister?" I asked, pulling his attention away from his captive and back to me.

Aiden laughed his horrible laugh once more—he was really laying into the whole super-villain thing—as he came back to me and patted my head like a child.

"Zamiah's not dead," he said. "Did you even bother to check for a pulse?"

I hadn't, but I could have sworn Mehrdad had. The whole night was so insane, I hadn't been thinking straight.

"She knew you were onto her, so we had to think fast," Aiden grinned. "Some makeup and a few fake pokes really look great under an elevator's awful lighting, huh? Plus it gave us a chance to fuck with you some more while you and Learco were out enjoying a night on the town instead of getting your other boyfriend here to help you clean up this mess."

So I *had* seen Zamiah stalking the edges of Petrichor. I cringed at the memory of her watching me, slinking between the columns, playing me the whole time.

"The whole vampire thing was a stroke of genius, if I do say so myself," Aiden continued. "I got the blood I needed and created a mystery for you to solve in one fell swoop. I knew it'd get Learco here fairly quickly. It's just a shame I had to elevate things with Kara to try to get Cernun to show. She was a sweet girl. I mean, kind of a bitch, but dynamite in the sack, which I'm sure you can appreciate. And the little fire show last night was just a bonus to amp up your fear plus get rid of the bodies."

"That still wasn't enough to get Cernun here," I sighed. "He's not coming. This is over before you even start."

Aiden surprised me as his face suddenly crumbled, his eyes wincing as he feigned despair. But the "whatever shall I do"s he wailed proved he wasn't as good of an actor as he thought he was. The smarmy conceit that lived just below the surface of his skin was too prevalent to hide.

"I'd bet you being missing is enough to get him on the next flight. Especially with the state we left your room in. Hell, he might even use some of that Kyteler money my daddy helped him find to book a private jet."

"Guess you've thought of everything."

I'd wanted it to sound concerning, like I knew something he didn't, like I still had secrets up my sleeve he wasn't ready for, but we both knew that was a lie. Aiden had planned it all out in much greater detail than he had before. He was a defunct witch with nothing else to lose, and that, coupled with time, had made him all the more dangerous.

"I really have," he spat, gliding toward the doorway with a satisfied look dripping from his features. "Now you just sit tight and wait for the magic to start."

Aiden had it all figured out. I couldn't believe I had been gullible enough to fall into another of his traps. He'd used his knowledge of me, knowledge I'd given him freely when I'd believed him to be my friend, to orchestrate everything from my invitation to my capture. He'd compensated for every curveball I'd unknowingly thrown him: killing Amy when I'd given her my room to keep me in the hotel; using Chester through Félicité to keep an eye on me at my OccultList BnB; raising the stakes of his game to bring my lovers to my side.

Still, there was one thing he did not know about: the wild magic I now had within me.

Of course, I couldn't access it thanks to the Fae writing on the floor. Plus there was a good chance it was the wild magic itself that would allow the old ritual he'd found to work in the first place. But it was still a—pun-intended—wild card, and I could use that to my advantage. I just needed to figure out how.

CHAPTER 19

Learco was unconscious as Zamiah and Félicité carried him through the door. Well, Zamiah carried—or rather, dragged—him, her grip tight beneath his armpits as his shoes skipped and scudded along the floor. Félicité led the way, barking orders to *watch out for that corner* or *get a move on* as they entered. Although she was the younger sister, it was easy to tell which of the two witches was in charge.

I held my breath as they heaved him against the prep table, pulling a chair into the circle adjacent mine to my left, and pushing him upright into its seat. There was redness around his nostrils, and I knew he'd been chloroformed as I had. A part of me was grateful for that, all things considered, and I swallowed hard as I diverted my eyes to Chester's blood-drained body. Zamiah winced as she followed my gaze, a look akin to sorrow or pity in her eyes, before her sister snapped for her attention.

"Well?" she huffed.

Zamiah apologized as she pulled four slips of rope from her bag and went to work on knotting my boyfriend's limbs to the legs and back of the chair. I studied the knots as she worked, until Félicité clapped two inches from my nose to retrain my attention.

She smiled as she leaned back against the prep table, her lips peeling like apples over her teeth.

"'Having the guy who exposed magic through one hell of a display of power,'" she said, mimicking the sweet, adoring cadence she'd used to butter me up when I'd met her at the Museum, "'that could have changed everything.' Your susceptibility to flattery aside, turns out you *will* change everything."

The mockery was all over her face, and I shifted my weight in my chair as I squinted my eyes.

"Why are you helping Aiden Gowdie?" I asked. "You know he doesn't care about you, right?"

"And I could give a crow's tail feather about him," she shrugged. "But right now, our priorities align, so we make friends where we can. The thing that witches like you never realize, Darragh Cullen, the thing our relatives don't seem to understand, is that there is a massive power disparity when it comes to our craft. So we're taking what we should have been given. This is about equity, pure and simple. Miah, how long does it take to flick a simple binding spell?"

Her misuse or misunderstanding of the word *equity* aside, the irony of her invocation of its principles as she ordered her sister around nearly made me laugh. I probably would have if I wasn't tied to a chair, my boyfriend knocked out beside me, and my new friend nearing death's door in the far corner.

Zamiah huffed as she rose, the ache in pressing her knees against the tile obvious. She whispered her spell, and I quivered as the faint orange glow of her magic set my lover's bonds. She looked to her sister for approval, but there was no acknowledgment—let alone appreciation—on her face.

"Go check on Chester for me, will ya?" Lady F said instead, pretending to be asking this time at least. "We can't have him dying before it's time, right?"

The heartlessness in her sister placed the timid fear I'd noticed in Zamiah, poking out from beneath the cool demeanor she'd put on while she was undercover, in a whole new light. I wondered if any of this had been her will. In the end though, we were the company we kept, and I was seriously beginning to despise the folks around me. At least those who were conscious.

The others, though, Learco and Chester, did not deserve any part in this.

"Chester was really easy to thrall," Félicité bragged when she caught my glance in his direction. "I've been laying that trap since we were children. I almost had him eating bugs, you know, to lay into the whole vampire thing, but I thought it may be overkill."

She and Aiden truly were two of a kind. I was sort of happy they'd found one another. Almost. Each of them deserved a taste of themselves in their lives. And if I laid my tarot cards right, they would get it. I just had to figure out the correct meaning behind the layout.

"Thing is, though," she continued, pulling her face close to mine and lowering her voice so her sister wouldn't hear, "while I was in there, I saw something mighty interesting. How did you do it?"

Shit! I'd figured out he was possessed, but I hadn't even considered that someone else was riding his body when I'd used my wild magic to portal Chester into the Crow's Court. For someone as power hungry as Félicité—or Aiden—knowledge of that magic would lead to horrors. I decided to play dumb.

"How did I do what?"

Félicité smacked her lips as she smirked at me, moving even closer to my face until her large brown eyes were all I could see.

"Don't worry," she purred. "I haven't told Aiden or anyone else what you can do. And it can stay that way. We might even be able to make a little deal to help you out of this mess. *If* you teach me how to do it. Think about it while we collect your other lover from the airport."

She rose to a standing position and snapped her sister to her side, smiling at me with a wicked glint in her eyes.

"You know, Darragh. I wanted to send you on a wild goose chase to find the thirteen objects that would confuse the Rougarou," she laughed. "Aiden convinced me to settle for three."

Her face turned dark as her eyes darted from me to Learco and back.

"Two down," she smirked as he pushed her sister from the room.

Learco groaned as he came too, struggling briefly to clutch his head before he realized he was bound. His eyelids fluttered as he took in the harsh, industrial lighting of the room. I watched his pupils dilate and took heart that he was okay. Well, as okay as he could be while tied to a chair inside a dark magic circle as we waited through the preamble of whatever insidious spell our captors had in store. But he didn't seem afraid, and a faint smile perked his lips as his head turned to settle his eyes on me.

"I really have to stop getting knocked out and waking up bound to a chair next to you, Darragh Cullen," he growled. "Aiden Gowdie?"

"Aiden Gowdie," I confirmed. "Working with Dula, Zamiah, and Félicité."

"So not a vampire."

"Well, he is a bloodsucker. But not a vampire."

"You seem surprisingly calm."

"Only because you're here."

"Sweet. Is that Chester?"

"Yeah," I gulped, my feigned good mood halting as we both turned to take in his limp body, realigned in his chair by Zamiah before they had departed. "Apparently, he's the appetizer, and we're the main course."

"Great," he sighed, clocking the third circle to my right and adding, "I suppose that's for Cernun."

"Yeah. The sisters are on their way to pick him up at the airport."

"I must have been out longer than I thought," Learco grimaced, craning his neck to quell the throbbing from the remnants of the chloroform's grasp as best he could. "After I found the room and you gone, I didn't even call my agents first. I called him, and he insisted…."

"I get it," I interrupted. "I mean, Aiden's spell won't work without him here, but we've got a better chance of getting out of it if we're all together."

Learco nodded, squeezing his eyelids tight as the pain from his welt woke up a few minutes after he did and settled in. The deep sigh which seized his chest, though, was one of resolve, and it bolstered me in my own perseverance. We'd been through a lot together, and Fae knew there was a lot more to come. *If* we survived.

"I don't recognize these runes," he said, studying the floor around us as his brain flipped through his studies in the MAW's abundant archive rooms.

"I'm pretty sure they're Fae," I explained. "Another throwback from the great Gowdie Grimoire."

The hope that sparked his eyes was quickly replaced by understanding. In any other situation, since the Fae were exiled to their own world, spells which incorporated Fae magic would not work. But, just as it had during Aiden's first attempt, the wild magic within me had provided a crack through the realms. And now that my time in their world had pulled it from its dormant state, I was worried the effects would be even greater.

"Any chance you picked some Fae-speak up while we were there last week?"

I frowned. Every Fae we'd encountered had spoken one of two languages: English or sex. And though I'd noticed a few symbols carved into trees or printed on the Wayward Inn's menus, they'd quickly transitioned into the languages I spoke. I was sure the *murúch*'s song and Cernunnos' orgy had occurred in their native tongue. Whatever the realm held to enable translation and communication had been powerful. A spell like that would have certainly been useful to know.

Not that I could have performed it. I was cut off from the magic inside of me, unable to connect the sparks within to the elements without which made the power work.

That was something Aiden and Félicité didn't seem to understand. It wasn't the amount of innate ability inside that made someone a good witch, it was their capacity to connect that power to the natural flow of the world, to ask and to guide, to be as delicate as they were forceful which presented as truly powerful magic. Aiden and the sisters could take a piece of us—or try, at least—and it wouldn't make their spells any brighter. Or so I hoped.

Learco was right though: the key to getting out of the magic was in translating what the symbols meant. Figuring out how a spell worked was the fastest way to produce a counter-spell. But I doubted even Aiden knew what the lettering meant.

"Any other ideas?" I asked, despair coating the hope in my voice.

"We wait," Learco shrugged. "Aiden's ambitious but an amateur. His recklessness makes him sloppy. No matter how well he thinks he's planned this, he will fuck up and give us our window. We just have to be ready to take it."

"And potentially leap the fuck out of it," I nodded, but I wasn't so sure. But then, neither was Learco. Aiden had spent months planning, the patience I'd always attempted to distill into him finally making itself known. Still, it helped to hear the words. They were somewhat soothing, a lull in the rollercoaster that dipped and swirled erratically through my head.

Cernun entered the ballroom with his hands held high, a talisman around his neck glowing faintly as it restrained his magic. But at least he was upright and controlling his own two legs. His wild, sable hair—the blackest black I had ever seen—rose like dark flames above the ice of his blue eyes, and the warmth of his smile when he saw Learco and me—bound but intact—made my heart flutter so much the dizziness in being cut off from my magic amplified. The vivid colors of his tattoos shone as they peeked from the collar of his shirt, and I wanted nothing more than to get lost in their stories. I hated he'd been trapped, but Fae-damn it was great to see him. The knife against his back, however, was not so welcome a surprise, and I tried not to let my face show fear as Félicité urged him onward with its blade.

"Hey, fellas," he smirked as the witch guided him to the circle, her sister quick behind her with an additional chair for his part in the ceremony. "Having fun at the convention?"

"It's been a welcomed distraction from the usual," Learco shrugged, playing along with Cernun's nonchalance. "But the magic on display has been utterly subpar."

"Not to mention the witches performing it," I added.

It was all a bluff, the confidence we pretended, but I could see it was getting under Félicité's skin. Her teeth gritted as she forced Cernun to sit, switching the blade of her athamé from the center of his back to his throat as Zamiah went to work on his binding knots. I was a little worried about pushing them too far, but they needed our blood for the spell so I doubted they would spill it too soon. Besides, we had the opportunity to drive a wedge between them and the guy who was leading the charge. That or, as a long shot, get some actual knowledge regarding what was about to happen.

"Can you believe these two are playing Fachan to an unpowered witch?" I asked.

The sisters wouldn't know what the word meant, but the sentiment was enough to cause their faces to pale in anger. Plus, it let Cernun know we were dealing with Fae magic and a different leader altogether. He nodded as he got it and raised his eyebrows sympathetically at the woman still holding him at knifepoint.

"Aiden Gowdie?" he asked. "Didn't he end up killing his daddy the last time he tried this?"

It was working. The quiver in Félicité's lip showed we were giving them new information, and it didn't sit well with the ideas she'd created from Aiden's smooth-talking ways.

"Sure did," Learco confirmed. "Well, before using his accomplice to raise him from the dead and then killing his zombie dad too."

Zamiah froze in her kneeling position on the floor, her palms resting a few inches away from completing Cernun's final knot. Félicité's nostrils flared, and I worried the shaking in her hand would cause a nick on Cernun's throat, but she broke from fear to anger quickly.

"Shut up," she commanded us before dropping her eyes to her sister. "Ain't you finished yet?"

Zamiah gulped as she went back to work, but I only grew bolder now that the athamé wasn't trained on my boyfriend's jugular.

"Don't you want to know who you're bathing in blood with?" I asked. "Shouldn't you be prepared for when his spell fizzles out, and he decides to turn on you? I mean, look at these runes! I don't think the lyrics to 'Twinkle Twinkle Little Star' are going to summon forth much power."

In the intensity of Félicité's frozen glare, I worried I had overplayed my hand until Zamiah's "I told you we should have vetted the spell" told me they knew just as much as I did. Damn. I wouldn't be able to garner any real information from them. And though it was fun to play the brave witch, staring skyward as the townsfolk carried torches to his stake, the ire we were raising couldn't cause any stumbles if there were no missteps to be made. Still, it was enough to instill doubt, and doubt could go a long way in disrupting a spell. Plus, with the witch knowing what I could do when I had access to all the parts of my magic, the courage may have actually read as true.

Félicité turned her stare from me to her sister before ordering her out of the room, her own legs turning to march behind her as she attempted to regain her countenance, hoping that would retain her upper hand.

"You know," Learco huffed, twisting the knife deeper than she had threatened to as she paused in her exit, "I really had hope we were dealing with actual vampires. Discovering another magical species would have been so much more interesting than battling incompetent witches."

I could feel the spite emanating off of her as Félicité slammed the door, leaving the three of us—and Chester—alone. We held our breaths as the collective bravado we'd put on dissipated and the rush of fear and anxiety reset our bones in sporadic nervous chuckles.

"Here we are again," Cernun sighed as the laughter subsided, trying hard to keep the confidence present in his voice. "I just wish I could have kissed you both before they tied me up."

My face fell immediately. Every ounce of composure I'd been attempting rushed to well in my eyes, clinging to the salt like life rafts even as my lashes threatened waterfalls.

"Balor was right," I moaned, softening it to a whisper as I focused on the light glinting off the stainless steel prep table in front of me. I couldn't bear to look either of my lovers in the eye even though their faces were all I wanted to see. I didn't deserve them, their empathy. I was the reason they were in the mess they were in. "He told me I'd be the death of you."

Learco's laughter was genuine this time, and it startled me as Cernun joined in.

"The weight of the world is not on your shoulders, Darragh," Learco promised as the burst of his cackle subsided. "Don't forget, I was a field agent with the Moral Authority for years—decades—before I met you. I've been in hairier situations than this. None of which were your doing, no matter what some desperate Faerie told you."

"I left home at fifteen," Cernun added. "A witch who didn't understand his power, moving from town to town, hopping trains and sleeping in bus stations as I tried to figure it all out. You can't possibly think I've only known trouble since I fell in love with you."

The words were sweet, and though I understood them, I couldn't let go of the guilt. *I'd* brought Aiden into our lives, and this was twice now he'd tried to wrest power from our blood. It was *my* wild magic that had broken the divide between our world and the Fae Realm, that had allowed their frightful mischief and outright destruction to strike as it attempted to claw its way through. Hell, it was *me* saving Cernun so impetuously and publicly that had given actual rise to the DMFM, proved their fringe conspiracy theories were real, shown his adoptive family where he was, and placed a target on every single one of our backs. Whatever trouble they had faced in the past, *I* was the reason for the mess we were in now.

"I'll tell you one thing though," Cernun continued, snapping me from my downward spiral and back to the woe of the moment, "that Aiden boy sure does have a lot of gall. Attempting this with a hotel full of witches and MAW agents on the inside, not to mention those maniacs readying their pitchforks on the outside."

His words sparked something within me, some glimmer of something I was meant to know. I just couldn't place it.

"He does have a flare for the dramatic," Learco agreed. "I mean, his first attempt was inside the atrium of the Georgia State Capitol building. I'm guessing there are remnants of those grandiose gestures, all that smoke and mirror showmanship somewhere in his Gowdie blood. What do you think, Darragh?"

I wanted to answer, to get in one last conversation with my boyfriends before everything went to shit, but I couldn't. My mind was racing. Cernun's words had reminded me of something that was just outside my reach, something I was supposed to understand... or figure out... or come to terms with. It was something about myself that had the potential of freeing us. Or at least show me the way.

I gritted my teeth, but nothing came.

The scratch of the metal of Learco's chair legs on the tile brought me back to the present, and I shook my head to recenter my focus.

"How the hell did she tie these ropes so tight?" he huffed.

His wrists struggled against the knots, and I could see his leg muscles straining through his slacks.

"They're magicked on top of the knots," I sighed. "I watched her set yours before you woke up. Her fingers worked whatever trawler knots she learned back in Butte La Rose, and then she set them with her faint orange glow."

"She didn't set Cernun's," Learco said, brow furrowed.

"What?"

"She didn't set Cernun's," Learco repeated.

My eyes lit up as we both turned to our lover. I guessed our cajoling hadn't been simply to get under their skin. It had distracted both sisters enough to forget a crucial detail. Of course, the wormwood, vetivert, and mugwort were still there—alongside the amulet they'd forgotten to remove from his neck—to cut Cernun off from his magic, but at least the knots were not locked with a magical key. That was something. That was hope.

Cernun's sheepish grin slipped into a pained wince as the veins of his forearms pulsed in their struggle.

"They're still tied pretty damn well," he growled.

I was sure it didn't help that the double whammy of the bonds and the amulet was no doubt making him dizzy. Witches always felt off when cut from their power, but the two sources of severance together were no doubt sending his senses into overdrive. He kept a brave face as he tried to hide it, as he tried once again to free his hands, but I knew he was in pain.

"What the hell is going on in here?"

We turned simultaneously to find Simon standing just inside the door from the ballroom. He shuddered as he looked over Chester then settled his gaze back on us. He was wearing his bartenders uniform, though now the vest was black instead of blue to match the colors of the upcoming Masquerade, but his hair looked matted and unruly as if he'd just woken up.

"Simon, come help us," I ordered, as nicely as I could manage, and he nodded as his feet once again found movement.

"If this is some kind of weird sex thing…." he started, but his words cut off as he rounded the table and saw the markings on the floor. His eyes widened, and he froze in his tracks. "I'm sorry. I didn't know it would be you. You were really nice to me."

My heart sank as realization set in. Of course the young witch who'd learned his craft in Latin would be easily swayed by someone like Aiden.

"Fuck," I grumbled. "Is there anyone at this convention who's not working with him?"

"He came to me a little over a week ago," Simon explained, trying to make himself feel better moreso than trying to make us understand. "Told me he had a spell that could increase the power inside. All he needed was a way in and out of the hotel while the convention was going on where he wouldn't be noticed. He did tell me there'd be a sacrifice, but I just thought it would be one of those assholes like Linnegard or Landry. I really didn't know it was going to be you."

The sorrow on his face was real, yet he still didn't move to help us. I could see his inner turmoil play out on his face as clearly as it would have on mine: the soft angst of a child from a witching family with no Book of Shadows to speak of, no knowledge of what to do with the magic that swirled in their gut; the anguish of being disregarded and spoken down to by all the guests of the Crow's Court who saw him as a lowly bartender who needed a dead language to work his spells; the hope of finally having a grasp on something, having a chance to be able to prove himself as the witch he knew he was. It was heady and confusing and, if we played it right, our way in.

"You cannot trust Aiden Gowdie," I said. "Besides, stealing magic from another witch is not the way to bolster your own."

Simon grimaced, but he didn't move.

"The MAW has countless archives with thousands of family Books," Learco offered. "There's a chance your family's lore is in there somewhere. If you let us out, I can run a check. *That's* how you grow your power. Not by taking someone else's, but by connecting to what's already there inside of you."

There it was again, that nagging feeling, begging me to remember.

"I was adopted," Cernun said. "By those fuckers who made that group outside. I had no idea where my power came from. But once I found my line, Learco helped me find our Books of Shadows. And I feel stronger than I ever have."

"And yet you're still tied to a chair."

We turned quickly to watch Aiden, Félicité, and Zamiah enter from the hallway door. The smug smile on Aiden's face made me wish I wasn't bound if only so I could slap him. He scowled as he blew me an air kiss, still able to read exactly what I was thinking on my expression, then he checked his watch.

"It's almost three," he beamed. "Time to get this witch on the broomstick."

CHAPTER 20

The room felt suddenly dark although the lighting had not changed. Perhaps it was the three witches—Félicité, Zamiah, and Simon—flanking the wannabe witch Aiden with their intense, bloodthirsty stares. Maybe "bloodthirsty" was a little too on the nose for the group, but I could feel my own pulse heralding the descriptor forward as I tried eagerly to figure a way out before the spell could actually begin. Aiden's unruly grin, wild and as desperate as I felt, haunted me when I set my gaze on him. There was no sense of care, of humanity left in his eyes. Maybe vampires truly were real.

"Zamiah," Aiden purred, a feigned niceness on his voice even though the directive was an order, "be a dear and grab those containers from the refrigerators for me. Simon, Fél, if you could, get Chester placed face up on this side of the table for me, headed pointed east."

Zamiah and Simon jumped to their tasks, but Félicité remained where she stood, arms crossed and toes tapping and she squinted her eyes at Aiden.

"How 'bout first you fill us in on exactly what's meant to happen here?" she growled.

Yes! I'd sown enough seeds of doubt in her mind for the sprouts to start growing through the cracks of their plan. And though I had no doubt she'd follow through with whatever it was, hearing what was to come could show me a way out.

"I've already told you," Aiden huffed, squinting to match her gaze. "We bleed these ungrateful fuckers and funnel the power to where it belongs."

"We're gonna need a little more than that if you want us to play lap dogs to your family Grimoire," she hissed.

They rounded their feet to a standoff, both refusing to budge, as Zamiah and Simon froze in their tasks to watch. If my coven and I were lucky, the whole thing would fizzle out before before it even got a chance to begin. Though I didn't think luck would come into play.

My eyes shifted to Learco and then to Cernun. Cernun's fingers quietly worked to breach the knot of his ropes, attempting to keep his movements imperceptible to the show unfolding before us. Learco watched the display intensely, searching, as I was, for a place to jam the knife that wasn't in our chests. I was glad to have them by my side, despite the circumstances, especially with the distracting dizziness at being cut off from my power combining with the nagging push of my mind to remember something that refused to come.

"Fine," Aiden finally conceded. "It's really straight forward, as far as blood magic is concerned, but if it will make you feel better...."

"It really will."

"The spell requires the blood of three unpowered," Aiden started and my mind flashed immediately to Amy and the couple from the roof. "That's what I've asked Zamiah to grab from the fridge. Ironic that garlic is a natural anticoagulant considering the game we've been playing here."

Despite his anger, he was turning on his trademarked charm to try to win Félicité back over to blindly following his side. It didn't seem to be working though.

"Two," Aiden continued, "we need the blood of three who are powered." His hand twisted with a flourish toward me and my boyfriends. "And three, the blood of one who has given his power away freely to act as a conduit. Which is where Chester comes in as his family denied their magic long ago."

It was actually a pretty solid spell, despite being dark through and through. The blood of the unpowered would act as a baseline for the elements to communicate; Learco's, Cernun's, and my blood would be the exciting variable, calling the spell to action; and poor Chester would provide the path for the magic to flow. Something in it did not sit quite right with me though—aside from being forced to give my blood and my power—but I couldn't quite wrap my head around it. Hadn't his little riddle from before contained a fourth element?

"And that's it?" Félicité asked incredulously.

Aiden shrugged.

"We wash ourselves and our blade in the blood of the sacrifice," he said. "Then we use that same blade to cut the power from the offerings, letting it flow through the one who gave it all away until it reaches where it rightfully belongs."

"And those symbols on the floor?"

"Oh, those? Old magic to keep the offerings contained and direct the power to where it needs to be."

He wasn't telling us everything—I wasn't even sure he knew everything—but from what he had, it was a workable experiment, and one we needed to find a way out of before it started and the magic held us in its thrall. Félicité, though, did not seem convinced, and her sister and Simon stood frozen in their tracks.

"I'll make it simpler for you," Aiden snarled. "Knife goes in, power comes out, and I get what should be mine."

"We," the younger sister corrected him, and he rolled his eyes as he parroted the word.

"But no one gets anything unless we get a move on," he added.

Félicité cocked her head as she studied him for a moment longer before nodding and shifting her stance to a slightly more relaxed state. Aiden's smile returned as Zamiah heaved three eight-quart food storage containers, each about half filled, of blood from the refrigerator, attempting to hide the solemn look on her face as she placed them on the table.

I didn't try to hide mine though. That was all that was left of Amy, of the folks I'd found on the roof. I searched Zamiah's face for any hint of sorrow behind her gloom. Like me, she'd seen all three bodies, twisted like grotesque dolls to appear lifelike and horror-filled, after Aiden had murdered them. She had had to face the terror of the plan, urged onward by her sister, for longer than his other two accomplices. Hell, her being the witch on the inside, it was probably her magic that had lulled the victims to the state in which they needed to be for Aiden to drain them. And it was definitely her magic that had blacked out the inset memories of the space around the killings. Though she tried to numb herself to her guilt, I could see the gravity of it all dancing behind her eyes. I could almost feel her hope that when all was said and done, the increase in her abilities would give her a path away from her sister.

Simon grunted as he helped Félicité hoist Chester's body onto the table, laying him on his back with his arms dangling off to the side. Aiden eyed me with a false-pout as he reached forward to angle Chester's head back, revealing his neck to the fluorescent lighting. Chester groaned at the movement, his blood loss beginning to give way to consciousness, and Aiden gasped before he shrugged.

It didn't matter. It would all be over soon anyway.

"What's next?" Simon asked.

I could not tell if his eagerness was a lust for power or a want to get it all over with. Either way, his words made me shudder.

Aiden's lips pushed higher as he peered at the young bartender, and my shiver continued at the evil in my former protégé's eyes.

"For you? This."

It all happened so quickly. Aiden pulled a knife from his belt and buried it to the hilt in Simon's stomach before any of us could blink. Simon howled as he doubled over, his hands clawing at the handle, and Aiden twisted it for good measure before pulling out the blade. Zamiah shrieked and Félicité's jaw dropped but they did not move as Aiden flipped Simon's frame atop the table, his head aligned with Chester's but his body stretched the opposite way. Blood gushed from his stomach as the fight left through his veins. Aiden licked his lips as he wiped the athamé against the fabric on his thighs to clean the blade, and Félicité finally found her voice.

"What the fuck, Gowdie?" she hurled, stepping forward timidly even through the ire in her words.

"What?" Aiden asked innocently. "Oh, that? I suppose there was one more ingredient to the spell I forget to mention before. In addition to The One Who Gave It Up, the conduit also requires The One Who Found His Way to guide the power. And Simon here, even if he didn't spit his spells in Latin, just reeked of a witch who was grasping too hard at something that was trying to scamper away."

The pot-meets-kettle nature of his statement aside, I suddenly realized what was wrong with Aiden's telling of the spell. Like most truly powerful magic, it was based in threes. Three unpowered and three powered. And now Chester and Simon made two. Another piece was missing.

"He's going to turn on you too," I exclaimed, and Aiden shot me a look that made my skin crawl.

"We really should have gagged you," he spat.

"Darragh's right," Learco bellowed. "This is a spell of threes. Three of us, three humans, and now just two on that table."

Zamiah looked ready to bolt for the door, but an open hand raised from her sister stopped her.

"Are they right?" she asked.

"Does it matter," Aiden scoffed, "if you get what you want?"

Zamiah stumbled backwards into a rack of chaffing dishes, and a quick thought from her sister sent a red tendril of her magic out to keep her in place. There was pain in her expression, but she wasn't about to be the only one left to sacrifice. Zamiah's lip quivered as she took in the steely glare of her sister's eyes. The realization that she would always be the offering spread through her every limb.

Félicité and Aiden really were a match made in hell.

"Let her go," Aiden commanded calmly.

"I ain't about to be no blood sacrifice," she growled. "You need blood from our line, you take hers."

Zamiah was crying, tears streaming silently down her face as her mouth fell open but no sound emerged. A lifetime of love and subservience escaped in a haggard breath, replaced by the fear and the hatred that had always bubbled beneath. I almost felt sorry for her.

"Relax," Aiden cooed. "Darragh here, although he thinks he knows it all, doesn't always get it right."

His grin widened once more as he pulled the Gowdie Grimoire from his bag and slammed it to the table next to Simon's face, flipping through the pages to prove himself as his latest victim's eyes fluttered slowly, the pain and the blood loss taking full control of his functions.

"The third element of the conduit is the receiver," Aiden said, tapping the book's thick pages as Félicité peeked over his shoulder to confirm. "So yes, we must perform the ritual thrice to all get what's ours, but you have my word that we will."

Félicité squinted at the ancient text, her gaze traveling from the tip of Aiden's finger to his smug expression as she nodded.

"I'm going first then," she smiled, stating it as fact and releasing Zamiah from her magic to watch her crumble to the floor.

"You can't," Aiden snapped, then, more centered, added, "I need the two of you to hold the circle while I work. I don't…. I can't…." He could bring himself to vocalize the lack of magic in his bloodline. "Once my power is reignited, then I can hold the spell for you."

The room froze as the two scowled into another face-off of wills. I was surprised when Cernun spoke up.

"The problem with getting into bed with villains," he laughed, "is that you can never trust them not to fuck you without lube."

I turned to face him, and I smiled.

With the distraction of their infighting, he'd managed to loosen his bonds! He leapt to his feet pulling his leg free of the final rope before he flung his folding chair over the table toward our captors. Damn it was sexy, watching his smile curve his lips as Félicité and Aiden ducked the chair and he leapt to pull me and Learco from our Fae-bound circles.

Zamiah found her feet first, bolting toward the door as a flick of her hand sent out an orange wave to release the magic she'd used to lock our knots. That was something. Though, when we got out of this, she would still have to face her due. The look on her face as she departed wished us luck even as it promised, one way or the other, we would never see her again.

Aiden shoved himself beneath the table, finding his feet as he reached its edge and tackling Cernun to the floor. My boyfriend's strong arms came up to block Aiden's fists, but the talisman still hanging from his neck prevented his magic from protecting him.

I squirmed as I struggled against my bonds, the wild magic in me surging slightly before I looked down to find my feet still planted inside the Faerie ring. Shit. Although it was stronger, I still couldn't use it to free us until I had total control.

"Cernun, just get out of here," I commanded as he used his weight to shift the balance of power, pushing Aiden off of him and circling to pin him down.

The boy clawed at my lover's face, and he tensed his muscles as he forced his arms to the floor, using his free hand to grip the amulet.

"Or do that," I said.

From what I had seen, his power could outmatch Félicité's any day. And Aiden was nothing more than a sniveling child. A murderous, sniveling child, but weak nonetheless. Before he could discard the amulet to release his power, the bulk of the Gowdie Grimoire struck the back of his head.

Félicité stood back smiling as Cernun went limp, toppling his weight to the still-struggling asshole beneath him. She dropped the Grimoire to the table and moved to push Learco and then me back into place for the ritual. I gasped as the ring claimed hold of my wild magic fully once more, and I winced as I turned my head to watch Aiden squirm his way from beneath my knocked-out boyfriend. At least Aiden had the start of a black eye. Though he deserved so much more.

"Zamiah," Félicité barked. "Help Mister Gowdie get that lump back into his chair."

"She left," Learco smirked as the witch turned to search the room.

"Fuck," she growled starting toward the door before Aiden

told her to stop.

"What if she tells someone what we're doing in here?" she snapped.

"It's fine," Aiden sighed, shaking himself as he tried to regain his upper hand composure. "Once the ritual starts, no one outside the circle can stop it. The only question is, are you strong enough to handle a circle that large on your own?"

Félicité let her scowl answer as she ambled around the prep table to collect the chair Cernun had thrown.

"I guess we need to get started then," she said. "So that there are no more interruptions."

She opened the chair as she walked, kicking Cernun's discarded ropes free of the etchings as she planted his chair back into place. It took both of them to drag his body back to the circle and heave him into the chair, and I was glad the extra time he'd been spending at the gym had forced them to work a little harder.

My eyes found Learco's as I tried not to cry.

"Valiant effort," he winced. "I guess this is it."

Aiden scowled from his perch on the other side of the prep table as Cernun came to, briefly struggled against his newly tied ropes, then sighed back into his chair. I raised my eyebrows—in question and in appreciation—to my boyfriend, and he gave me a wincing nod to let me know he was alright. All things considered.

Simon, on the other hand, was not. His groaning breath had turned shallow and sporadic as he wheezed in his twilight state. Even the flow of blood from the twisted gash in his stomach had slowed, yet plenty of it still pooled on the table between his body and Chester's, still dripped from the rounded edges of the stainless steel to stain the floor. He didn't have much time left, I could tell, and that was making Aiden anxious. I had a feeling the spell required him to be alive, for the blood to be flowing, for the conduit to work, and our attempt at escape had fucked with the timeline Aiden had worked out in his head. If Simon died, he'd be back to square one. Not that I wanted Simon to die. Despite him helping the wannabe witch, he'd been just as much a victim in this as me and my boyfriends had.

Félicité had already placed the candles from Aiden's bag at the four cardinal corners, giving a wide berth around us all for what would end up being one hefty circle. She used a cloth to dip into the buckets of blood, tracing the path of her barrier spell between each candle widdershins: North to West with Amy's blood; West to South with the man's; and South to East with the woman's. It was opposite to the deosil I typically used in my own casting, but I supposed everything about this ritual was in opposition to the magic I preferred. There was hate inside of it. And so much blood. Even with the garlic acting as a natural preservative in the liquid, the blood turned a rusty color as it spread across the white speckled tile. It looked harsh and cruel and deliberate and forever.

"Now what?" she asked, hand on her hip as she nodded toward the final path needed.

"The blood of the recipient completes the circle," Aiden said, resigned to a stoic calm as he pulled his shirt over his head.

His nude torso showed even more of the wear and tear from his months on the run. He was thinner now than he had been when last I'd seen him, though the tight musculature of his politician's son, rugby-every-Saturday upbringing was still there. More scars crossed his abdomen, and there was a just-healing patch of burnt skin tripping over his left pectoral. I wasn't sure if fights had found him as he tried to make his way through the streets or if the marks were the result of attempted magic gone wrong. The burn certainly looked to be the result of magical fire.

He grunted as he pulled his athamé across his left palm, squeezing the stream of blood to collect in the cotton of his t-shirt then shoving it into Félicité's hands. She looked disgusted as she took it and sighed as she stooped to complete the arched line.

I could already feel the energy beginning to build around us. Something dark and primal was excited by the offering, teetering about the edges of the space, lusting for the remnants of the life the blood once held. Or maybe I was feeling the wild magic inside of me. It had existed outside of time, before or beyond the notions of good and bad. And even though I was cut off from using it, I could still sense it wriggling inside my gut.

"You sure you got this?" Félicité asked with a condescending look in Aiden's direction as she tossed his soiled shirt to his feet. "A circle this large, once I set it, it's going to take all my concentration to hold it. I'll be kind of lost in there. But protected."

The last part was a warning, and I thought she was smart for adding it. Though I couldn't really offer her any appreciation.

"I've got my part," Aiden snapped. "Can you handle yours without your big sister?"

Félicité let her scoff be her answer, and she poured herself to the floor, crosslegged just inside the Northern anchor candle. I trembled as she closed her eyes, pushing hard to send the red tendrils of her magic out to ignite the Western flame. The blood between her and the candle sparkled briefly before settling into a dim, crimson glow. She steadied her breathing as her mind pushed to the South and the flame sparked to life behind me. She was panting as she rounded to the East, then pulled the line of Aiden's blood up to kindle the candle at her back. The wick lit quickly, fire shooting high as the circle set, and I gasped at the wave of red energy pulsing skyward.

I could smell the rich aroma of the iron from the blood as it shimmered through the protective barrier. A magic nullifier usually, for this spell it served to keep the erratic mischief of the Fae power from escaping the confines of the ritual. It was a smart spell. Evil, but smart. I wondered how many Gowdies has tried it in the past.

Ever since Aiden's ancestor Isobel had confessed to being a witch and performing dark spells in the 1600s, her family had been obsessed with actualizing the power she claimed was in their line. Like Isobel herself, centuries of descendants had cozied up to witches, learning our ways and passing them down through the Gowdie Grimoire in hopes of one day establishing a true claim to our arts. Now, it seemed, Aiden might actually do it.

I wanted to reach out, to hold Learco's and Cernun's hands as we stared entranced by the display, watching for any opportunity of escape, feeling the magic empowered by the blood. I wanted to promise them everything would be okay, but I didn't believe it myself, and I couldn't have the last words I said to them be a lie. He may have told Dula my lovers and I would not be killed, but the state of Simon and Chester on the table; the plastic containers of blood from his human victims; the memory of Kara falling still on the sidewalk…. It all proved that wasn't true.

Aiden swooned before he steeled himself, nodding solemnly with closed eyes as he tried to take on the air of great importance required by the ritual. His hands cupped as they dipped into the first container, pulling up the blood as they wiped from his forehead to to chin.

"The Blood of the Mother calls to the Ancient," he said, his voice hollow and distant as if he'd rehearsed the words over and over in an attempt to capture their meaning in his mind. "The greatest chasm from which all begins. Her life was given to the creation of new."

He repeated the motion at the second container, smearing the blood to mix in the mess on his face, splashing it over his cheeks and caking the corners of his lips.

"The Blood of the Father summons the Spark," he called. "The blazing fire from which man moves forward. His life was given to the pulse of light."

Although there was no power inside him, I could feel the spell igniting. The blood in the circle mixed with Félicité's magic and pulled through to Aiden to make it work. She shivered, her face contorting in pain, as more and more magic was siphoned from her. But she was locked into the whole of the ritual now. I doubted she could break it even if she wanted to. I imagined that was by design.

"The Blood of the Lamb orders the path," he panted, pushing his hands through the third container as the feeling of new magic began to go to his head, forcing heavier concentration as he tried not to break. "The chaotic youngling; the wild made flesh. This life was given to the duality of the natural world."

His eyes flashed from his own chest to the Grimoire as he marked more Fae symbols on his body with Amy's blood, fingers working slowly to ensure the lines were solid even as the thick blood dripped to elongate the runes.

"Hear me," he yelled, louder than I thought he'd anticipated. "Take of these offerings to grant me the power I desire."

A burst of black energy shot from within him, pushing out to mix with and strengthen the red of Félicité's circle. It was so unlike anything I'd ever seen before, it took me a moment to understand it was Aiden's aura—or the aura of his history—blighted with the tar of his ancestors and their attempts at black magic. Not that Aiden didn't have enough darkness on his aura for himself.

His breath came in gasping pants as his body fought to

equalize the burst of magic now flowing through him. He braced himself on the edge of the table. His chest heaved. A thin, horrid smile curved his lips as his egotistical confidence gave way to the realization that his spell was going to work.

"The fucker is actually going to do it," Cernun gasped.

At the sound of his voice, Learco and I found ours.

"You know, I always figured I'd go out at the hands of some power-hungry dark witch," Learco hummed.

"I didn't," I joked. "I figured I'd inherit Uncle Gardner's Key West condo like I did with HEX and spend my final days overlooking the ocean with the two of you."

"Well, you're not a MAW agent," Learco laughed.

"Much to Leland Hydes chagrin," I said, then to Learco's furrowed brow added, "Depending on the day of the week."

"I never had any visions of growing old," Cernun sighed. "Not until I met the two of you anyway."

My smile was genuine and true in spite of the horrors unfolding around us as I told my lovers I loved them.

"To the stars and back," Cernun responded, all the warmth I was feeling heavy on his words.

"Shut up!" Aiden commanded.

The black of his aura wavered as his break in concentration threatened the spell and he fought to retain his control.

"Are true love and compassion at odds with your blood spell?" I smirked. "Did you expect your victims to sit quietly and await your blade?"

Aiden's eyes squinted as he grabbed his athamé, brandishing it before him as he struggled to steady his hand. Maybe I could goad him into finishing me off early. At least then he wouldn't be able to complete the transfer of power. I didn't want to, but I'd certainly give my life for that.

And so would my lovers. We hurled taunts and insults at the

man as the knife quivered before him, and he switched his grip on the handle. The ire in his eyes was as dark as his magic, and I braced myself for him to bolt around the table and plunge his dagger into my chest. Instead, he pushed the blade across the skin of Chester's ribs, freeing what little blood the man had left within him to pool with Simon's atop the prep table turned spelling table.

Chester's eyes popped open, terror and pain bubbling within them as he stared at the ceiling. But there was no recognition there, only the magic working its way through what was left of his life. Simon's eyes were open now too and filled with the same fear.

"The One Who Left the Path," Aiden yelled, ignoring our catcalls as he opened the conduit to pull our magic from us, "meets The One Who Found His Way to light the course to me."

Shit. We were nearing the end. There was little else we could do.

The Fae letters of our individual circles were glowing now, surging black and red as the power of the ritual arched to meet the source of what was needed. The wild magic inside of me danced, and, even though I was cut off from using it, I could feel its want, its need to reach me, to protect me, bolstered by my witch magic which wanted the same thing.

"That which was beyond," Aiden called, "must find its way within!"

That was it! The thing I was trying to remember!

The Mórrígan's words sang through my mind just as they'd done in the cemetery: *the power is within you, and yet you continue to view it, to use it, as some external thing.... You will learn to use that spark when you've silenced the external and moved to look within.*

The wild was within me, and even if I was cut off from using it externally by some runes scratched in chalk, it remained a part of my being. So, if I couldn't use it outside, I would need to go within.

I just hoped there was enough time to find what I needed before Aiden's blade met my chest.

CHAPTER 21

"I think I might have a way out of this," I announced, my eyes locked on Aiden as he struggled to contain the end path of the conduit opening to him. "But I'm not sure how long it will take."

"I don't think we have a hell of a lot of time," Cernun warned. "But do what you need to do."

I nodded, freeing my gaze from Aiden to take in my boyfriend's faces one last time.

"Just in case I don't make it back mentally," I whispered, my voice cracking as I craned my neck from side to side. "You two have been the happiest thing in the whole of my life."

"I trust you, Darragh," Learco smiled. "No goodbyes. You can do this. You can do more than any witch I've ever met."

That was reassuring. The black billowing from Aiden's eyes was not. We needed a distraction.

As if on cue, the hallway door swung open and Zamiah tumbled into the room, Mehrdad and Layla quick on her heels. Mehrdad still looked wounded, his burns still obvious beneath the layers of newly spelled skin, but adrenaline and those witches at New Orleans Med had worked wonders. Still, awe filled the trio's eyes as they took in the behemoth of the circle, swirling its red and black might between us and them, encompassing the evil that seeped through the room.

Zamiah found herself first, skirting the edge of the space beyond the barrier to kneel behind her sister. Her voice was faint through the circle, seeping through as little more than a whisper even though I knew she was yelling for Félicité to stop. Mehrdad and Layla's bellows were drowned out too, but as they placed their hands on the circle, channeling their magic to break through, a sharp wave struck through the energy, and Aiden stumbled. The wall of magic around us stuttered, its energy trembling in staccato welts as Aiden braced himself once more on the edge of the prep table and tried to keep the energy from spiraling out of control.

He'd promised his co-conspirator that no one beyond the protective barrier of the ritual would be able to stop it, but the concentration he needed to keep it pushing forward was great, and it might just buy me enough time to do what I needed to do.

I nodded solemnly to my lovers, closing my eyes to center my breath, to try to push through the ache of the mugwort and the wormwood and the vetivert and the symbols. But this time, instead of trying to pull my magic out, I was going in.

As I pressed forward, the white darkness behind my eyelids burst with green. Like fireworks. Like leaves unfurling in Spring. The purest form of energy arched through the ether to meet me, to take my hand and say hello. It was intoxicating. It was significant. It was joyous and somber. It was wild, and it was trained. And yet it existed outside of all of that, beyond any notions of duality, of binary thinking. It simply was. And it was far from simple.

As The Mórrígan had insinuated, I was able to go inside my power, to inhabit its source and seek its reaches from within. I smiled into the buzzing, energetic calm as I asked it—asked *me*— to focus on the ritual occurring around me. If I could understand it, comprehend how it was guiding the forces of power, perhaps I could realign their course.

It was a big ask. And it was something altogether new to me, even though a wandering voice in the back of my mind told me it should have been—hell, it *was*—something older than time. As witches, while we had always seen our power as something innate, an element nestled deep within us and passed down through familial lineage, we had been taught its use was an external thing. An outward push. A connection. The voice with which we contacted the elements and asked their help to conduct whatever symphony our desires held. It required learning and training and knowledge. And that showed us how to keep the balance of nature intact as we worked our spells.

We learned that each element needed to exist in harmony— that when we called upon the fire, we needed water to cool it off; that the earth was held in place by the air and vice versa. The water formed the earth while the earth guided its flow. The fire warmed the water while the water fed the air. All of it worked in tandem. Even Aiden's dark spell persisted in balance. The blood of the non-magical countered the blood of the powered, in this case my coven's, and the daisy-chain of witches at the center of the conduit each added their own teetering weight to the scale.

We had to understand that balance in order to use our magic, and our magic responded with that balance in tow.

Yet the wild within me was something different. The Fae believed it was a spark of the very source which had created… well, everything. All the realms, all the elements. The very idea of magic itself. And, if that were true, perhaps it also held the knowledge I was seeking.

My lungs felt heavy, even in the brightness of the wild, and I pressed my concentration further into the green, watching as it began to give way to the black and red of the ritual beyond my closed eyelids. I heard my father's voice warning me to "proceed with caution," just like he had as I'd attempted my first big spells as a teenager, my mother's soothing words echoing him from the other room. I had to get close to the dark to understand it, but not so close I would be consumed.

I needed Learco and Cernun with me. As lovers and as my coven, they were my tether, the kite string that allowed me to wander through the vastness of me and always find my way back. The fear Balor had instilled in me had only served to make me question those bonds, to keep us apart and weaker when I should have been celebrating all that was us and becoming closer in our strength. It was yet another Faerie trick, I realized, and, when we made it out of Aiden's spell, I'd be damned if I let fear stand in the way of us again.

"Uh… Darragh?"

I turned quickly at my name, mouth agape as I took in my lovers now standing beside me. It had only taken a thought—a wish—and they were by my side. The wild was some pretty powerful stuff.

Even in the ether of the magical source, I could feel their bodies as we embraced, pressing hard against mine. We felt as real as if we had been there physically, and I held back tears as my lips met theirs.

"We're in the wild, aren't wet we?" Cernun asked as we parted, and he turned to take in the swirling mass of color. "Inside your wild."

"I think so. Yes," I confirmed, smiling a timid smile as my lovers stared at me in awe.

"This is what The Mórrígan meant by the internal versus the external, huh?" Learco grinned. "This is how we circumvent the ritual."

"If we can figure out the source of how it work…" I started.

"We can stop Aiden in his tracks," Cernun finished. "So

where do we begin?"

I turned to face the wild once more, smiling as it rushed to greet us.

Show us where to go, I thought, and the green swirled to pull us in.

I gasped as the burst of color dissipated into a surreal, mirror-world. It was ever-so-close to reality and yet the hues were slightly off, brighter somehow, or maybe darker. The shapes skewed like they would in reflective glass, but only just so much that when I turned my attention to them they were suddenly proportionate once more. It was dizzying, and I reached to clasp my boyfriends' hands to keep me balanced.

The street before us looked as if it had once been idyllic. A quaintness still rested in its asphalt. Beneath the decades of soot and exhaust and litter, every footprint of every child playing hopscotch, every hopeful young family who had pulled up their moving van to the curb, every heart palpitation in the idling sedan as the caller anticipated their first date, was present and accounted for as time softened and hardened the edges of the vision in turn.

The three of us—Learco, Cernun, and myself—sat on the wooden porch swing of a single-story house, its purple painted siding just beginning to show its wear, but the gray paint of the wooden porch stripped under thousands of footsteps.

"You really should go to the clinic."

In a flash, my coven and I were seated on the steps, staring back at Amy and a young man who had taken our place on the swing's bench.

"Why? So they can tell me shit I already know?"

The man was smaller than his frame wanted him to be, the elasticity of his skin pulling inward past his bones. His shoulders hunched beyond the cage of his chest, and an air of fatigue lingered within his irises. He was so pale, but the thick mauve of his lips matched the lesions peeking from the sleeves of his t-shirt in a stark contrast of color.

"'Your t-cells are lower than they ought to be, Mister Taylor,'" he continued, mimicking the bland diction of a doctor as Amy winced. "'We can try this new cocktail of medications though. The side effects will make you feel sicker, but could give you an extra two whole months to feel like shit.'"

"An extra two months could be enough time for them to find a cure, Seth," Amy insisted.

Her hand reached to clutch his in his lap, but he pulled it away. He shifted his body toward the edge of the bench, and the green of my wild surged to fill the space between them, to highlight the divide. Amy's wince turned to a frown as she stared at her knees, flexing her ankles to send her force to her toes and ticking her side of the swing up slowly. She released the tension in her legs and let her side of the swing wobble back and forth, its chain creaking against the eye hook, and Seth turned swiftly back to her.

He stymied her second attempt with a firm foot downward, but was actually smiling by her third, and he lifted his legs to allow the swing to travel as intended. Despite his pain—and Amy's—it was a joyous sight. I could tell that house, that swing, had known a lot of love. It was just something I knew, as if I had been present for it all along. The wooden bench was waterlogged and gray, pocked with pen-tip carvings of the initials of all the loved ones who'd experienced its journey. They were there, a part of it, even if they were long gone. The green of my wild magic danced along their offerings as I tried to interpret the letters.

"This thing is in my blood," Seth said, suddenly somber again as Amy kicked one more swing from the bench. But he did take her hand this time. "It flows through every single part of me. My body, it's making it. There is no dividing it out. I can't separate the flame from the fire. I have to contain it. Always."

As he spoke, the green of my magic flared around the carvings, trying to catch my attention. They weren't letters I recognized, but there was something in them that was so familiar. Learco and Cernun noticed it too, and we leaned forward to try to get a better view before Amy turned to face us.

"What do you think, Darragh?" she asked, speaking directly to me as Seth continued to look at her. "Is there a way to stop the flow? To divide, to contain what has been started?"

Before I could answer her, the scene shifted.

Cernun, Learco, and I stood in a small bathroom. Deep blue subway tile coated the walls with white grout running like cartography lines between neighborhoods. A small pedestal sink—cream-colored with a silver plated faucet—was before us, but I couldn't see any of us in the medicine cabinet mirror anchored above its drain. I heard the shower cut off, and the man from the rooftop, very much alive now—er, then—stepped from behind the curtain and wrapped a towel around his waist.

At least the distorted mirror image made sense now as we watched him lean in from the other side of the glass. He studied his face, twisting his chin and looking up his nostrils, before he began to slather shaving cream over the subtle growth of stubble on his cheeks. He worked his razor slowly, stopping with each gentle swipe to toss the excess foam into the sink and run the blade beneath the lukewarm water.

"John!" a voice called from another room, shrill and expectant and demanding. "The car is picking us up for the airport in twenty minutes, and you haven't even finished packing!"

John's eyes clouded as he watched himself in the mirror, his mouth scrunching to send strange articulations through what was left of the shaving cream. He steadied himself and then sighed.

"I still don't understand why your sister wants to get married in New Orleans the same weekend as that witch convention," he yelled back, lowering his voice when the woman from the roof appeared in the doorway. "The airport's going to be a zoo."

"Those witches keep to themselves," she sighed. "And the airport's always a zoo. Besides, I kind of feel safer with that many magical people hanging out in town."

John nodded as he took another slow swipe at his indistinct start of a beard.

"I guess what I mean is, you haven't talked to your sister in four years, Alice," he said, the words coming slowly as he continued to shave. "And after this wedding, you'll probably never talk to her again."

Alice shrugged as she leaned against the doorframe, her eyes both distant and resigned.

"She's still my family," she finally said. "She's still blood."

John nodded, forgetting the blade, and gasped as it nicked his jawline.

"I'm just saying," he sighed, "the blood that flows through your veins may be the same as hers, but it's different through and through. Plus, *she's* the one who established that divide. *She's* the one who insists you live separate lives. At least until there's a gift registry involved. Why would you think that invitation contains even the smallest bit of sincerity, of love?"

As he spoke, three drops of blood fell from his chin, and I turned to watch them splatter against the porcelain of the sink. They spread into those same familiar symbols—*flow; divide; contain*—before they washed away down the drain.

"Maybe this is an olive branch," Alice offered, the weak smile she held saying she didn't believe it. "Maybe she's looking to reconnect."

John groaned as he grabbed a hand towel to wipe the remnants of his shaving cream from his face. He grabbed a tiny tear of toilet paper to blot the cut on his chin.

"You can't reverse time," he said as the blood spread through the thin paper's grains.

"If you can't reverse time, then you just have to push forward," Alice shrugged, then centered her eyes on the mirror. "Right, Darragh?"

A flash of bright green pulled us back into the ether of the spell. The red of Félicité's magic and the black of the spell were darker now, more prevalent as they pushed to take control. We didn't have much time.

"I take it those were the three human sacrifices," Cernun said, and I nodded.

"So your wild magic has pulled us into the spell," Learco said, his voice trailing into the low monotone he used whenever he was trying to wrap his head around something. "Their blood was offered first. And your wild is showing us how it works through them."

"I think so," I smiled. "A little convoluted. But at least we know what three of those Fae symbols mean now."

The wild pulsed around us, brightening quickly as if to show it was happy we were figuring it out, learning its language as it were.

"So the conduit must be next," Cernun added. "Chester, Simon, and Aiden."

"And hopefully we learn what we need there before our blood is added to the mix," I winced.

I was glad the wild magic within me had known what I was

seeking, even more so that it was attempting to communicate. Of course, a gentle infusion of its knowledge would have been easier than figuring out the symbology, but nothing in magic was ever that easy. I suspected we'd have more to discern than just what the Fae symbols meant if we wanted to free ourselves and stop Aiden's spell.

"Okay," I called. "We understand. Show us what we need to know."

The green flashed, and we found ourselves on a street in a northwest Atlanta suburb. Behind us, the skyline of the city pressed through the treetops, and I smiled at the solace of the City in the Forest. Normally, from our locale, the skyline would not have been visible, but the skewed and exaggerated state of the visions brought it forth to give us a sense of place. Of home.

The street was picturesque, if a little cookie-cutter for my tastes, and the vast, finely manicured lawns between the near-identical houses screamed "old money" to those without who still thought the size of someone's bank account was what mattered. Still, it would have been a nice place to grow up. Maybe not for me—I preferred the acres of farmland and the way the gravel from the dirt roads of my youth would work its way between my toes—but for someone. There were plastic swing sets in the side yards and badminton nets and bicycles tossed to the sides of walkways with no locks to keep them secure.

"Are you here to play with me?"

The boy who spoke was adorable, with wide, eager eyes and sandy hair and ears he hadn't quite grown into just yet. He was four, maybe five years old, and I sensed a loneliness behind the wonder in his eyes. I knew right away it was Aiden.

"I think we're just here to watch you," I answered his question, then, to his frown, added, "Why don't you play with some of the other children on the street?"

"Daddy says they're supposed to be beneath us," he shrugged. "Even though they look like they're standing on the exact same ground."

It was my turn to frown. Adrian Goldfinch had started his son young. But it made sense. The smooth-talking, man-of-the-people lawyer turned politician had definitely had a superiority complex about him. Well, he did before Aiden's first attempt at wresting our magic had knocked the smugness from his expression.

"Where are your parents?" Cernun asked.

There was compassion in his voice. Although we all despised the man he'd grown into, there was something about the lonely child he'd come from that tugged on my boyfriend's heartstrings. I think he saw a little of himself in him after growing up the adopted child in a family who no longer loved him.

"Daddy's working up in his office, and Mommy just took her medicine," Aiden announced.

The home behind him shifted, opening up like the front panels of a dollhouse, and we watched as Adrian paced the floor of his upstairs den, papers tumbled in his fist as he practiced his diction over and over. Aiden's mother was strewn across the downstairs sofa like a throw blanket, head drooped and legs akimbo with an orange bottle of prescription pills still open beside her half-consumed dirty martini.

Shit. Was my wild magic actually trying to make me feel sorry for him?

If I had to flash back to his past, a glimpse at the Gowdie Grimoire would have been nice, but this was long before he'd discovered it. At least this version of Aiden was closer to the kind young man I'd met all those years before. And if this was what the wild wanted us to see, so be it.

"What game did you want to play?" I asked, squatting down so I could look him directly in the eye.

His face brightened as a smile carved itself over his cheeks.

"Have you ever played Ghosts in the Graveyard?" he squealed.

Okay. That was more like it. There was the creepy Aiden I'd come to know and hate. Still, there was so much glee in his eyes as he pulled us inside the white picket fence of his yard and explained his rules.

"It's kind of like Freeze Tag," he said, "but you only freeze when you get trapped in your grave. And then you can't move, no matter what."

He pulled a piece of chalk from his pocket then used the divisions of the walkway to set up three graves, circling them with the same Fae symbols of his spell.

"I don't like this," Learco whispered.

"I don't either," I replied. "But we need to play along to figure out where this is going."

"Besides," Cernun added. "We're inside Darragh's magic. What could go wrong?"

He didn't mean for it to sound as sarcastic as it did, and I tried to smile at his statement.

"I'm the ghost-catcher," Aiden said, beaming as he finished the final grave and rose to look at us once more. "So I try to chase you back into the dirt. You can run between the mailbox and the porch and the chestnut tree and the bird fountain, but you can't go outside those lines or else the Fae will pop you straight into the ground. Got it?"

"Um… Aiden?" I asked. "Do you know what those symbols mean?"

"That's not how you play!" he snapped, stomping his feet against the ground as the sky rumbled around us.

I held my hands up in surrender.

"Okay," I assured him. "What do you need us to do?"

"This!" he shouted. "One, two, three, go!"

Before we could even move, Aiden's hands had risen to Cernun's chest, slamming hard against the sternum as he pushed him within the first binding of Fae symbols. The lettering— *Contain*—glowed red as it trapped him inside. The magic of the vision trembled, coming lose at the edges as Aiden cackled, and I watched in horror as Cernun's shirt turned red with his blood.

"You better run," Aiden cackled, darting his eyes back towards us without turning his head. "The faster the blood flows, the quicker this all ends."

Learco grabbed my hand as I reached for Cernun's, and we were back in the ether of the spell. Well, two of us were anyway.

"We've got to get out of here," I bellowed. "We need to help Cernun!"

"We will," Learco said, his voice calm though I could hear the tension in its edges. "But we do that by figuring out this spell *before* we go back out there."

I knew he was right, but a part of me didn't care. Cernun was out there, alone and bleeding. And either one of us could have been next.

"Cernun knows we're in here," Learco said, reading my mind. "That we are working to save him. To save us all. The best thing we can do is move forward in whatever the wild has to tell us."

"You're right," I conceded, but I wasn't happy about it. I turned to the magic surrounding us, squinting to single out the green of the wild from the red and the black. "What else you got?" I demanded. "Bring it on!"

It felt like a pinch pulsating through me as the magic pulled us into the next vision.

The library was dark, despite the fluorescents hanging overhead, and the large stacks adorned with tomes cast deep shadows across the gray, low pile carpeting. In the distortion of the illusion, I could not make out the titles or the author's monikers on any of the books, but it didn't matter. I was filled with the same sense of calm libraries always left me with. There was knowledge there, just waiting for me to access it. Maybe the wild was finally ready to reveal what it needed to make clear.

Aiden's laughter, equally as maniacal as it was childlike, echoed through the space, but we weren't here for him. This was Simon's memory. He was the next to give his blood to the ritual. I hoped he would have some answers.

"Over here," Learco smiled, nodding just beyond the end of the bookshelves to a small seating area with less-than-comfortable looking chairs, a stately walnut table, and Simon's face buried behind a sea of books.

I joined him as he stepped from the stacks, pulling him back quickly as Aiden appeared, still in his child form, and screamed "Ghost in the Graveyard!" as he barreled past us.

"Great," I sighed. "Guess we know who's next in the ritual."

Learco's face was serious as he took my hand, pulling me close to him and kissing me on the lips.

"When he takes me," he whispered, "you finish this, okay?"

I nodded, and I meant it. I just hoped I'd be able to.

Rather than expose ourselves to Aiden, we reached to shift the books on the shelving in front of us to provide a clear line of sight to Simon. He was younger—maybe thirteen or so—with a determined look on his pale face and an untamed finish to his hair. It would have been about the age he would have discovered the power inside of him, showing itself as a growling energy right alongside the onset of puberty, and no doubt completing the range of the mountains of confusion those changes brought with them. It had been a trying time for me, and I'd had my family Book of Shadows as well as my parents, uncle, and grandparents preparing me for it since I'd learned to walk. I could only imagine what it must've been like for a witch like Simon who'd lost his family lineage. Or a witch like Cernun for that matter. Fuck, I hoped Cernun was alright.

Simon exhaled heavily as he closed his eyes, pushing the open book away from him.

"*Omnia quae volo venit ad me*," he whispered. "*Parva stella!*"

His hands flourished in front of him, trying to bring the "little star" he had summoned to reality, but nothing happened. He tried again and again to no avail, but retained the steely resolve on his face. At least until a trio of other teens wandered into view.

"Poor little unpowered witch,"one of the boys snarled. "Trying to pull magic from a dead language."

His cronies laughed as their leader announced "*světlo hvězd*" to produce starlight in his Czech-based tongue where Simon had tried. Simon's brow furrowed as a hatred overtook his eyes.

"It's not my fault we lost our Book," he snapped, trying to retain the calm he needed to work his power despite the anger which rose within him.

"If the Moral Authority took your family's Book of Shadows, they did it for good reason," the boy snapped. "They wanted to make sure weak little witches like you didn't fuck things up for the rest of us."

He shot another star through the space between them and smiled as it exploded in yellow shards before Simon's face.

"The MAW didn't take our Book, Marek," he stuttered. "We lost it in a fire."

"Then the Fae took it," Marek snarled. "All the more reason for you to just give it up."

He nodded his unspoken command, and his entourage stepped forth to shove Simon's collection of books to the floor, all of them laughing before they walked away. Aiden's laughter joined theirs, his cackle seeming to come from everywhere as his face shot up through the tunnel we'd made in the stacks and his fist shot toward Learco.

My boyfriend stumbled backwards from the contact, his spine slamming against the shelf behind us as it glowed an eerie red. I hadn't even noticed the arrangement of the books there, their placement forming another of the Fae symbols—Divide. His button-up disappeared from his frame, and a deep gash worked its way across his pecs.

"You've got this," he promised me, wincing as the spell flickered and he disappeared.

"Do you have this, Darragh?"

Aiden was gone too, and I was left alone with Simon in the library as it slowly faded away at the edges of my vision.

"I want to have this," I cried, bringing myself around the stacks to stare into Simon's questioning face. "Can you tell me what I need to know?"

Simon shrugged as he worked at picking up the books his bullies had sent flying from the table.

"It's all about power, isn't it?" he asked. "What kind and how much someone has. How much they deserve. Aiden thinks it's in the blood, but I kind of think it's in the body. Or maybe it's not in us at all. Maybe it's something that exists beyond the body, beyond the mind itself."

I blinked as I tried to figure out what the wild—through Simon—was trying to tell me. It was nearly as circumlocutious as the Fae, but it was trying to learn my language, to speak to me in a means I could understand, instead of tricking me through wordplay. That was something at least.

"Of course, in the end," Simon smiled, "magic is all about what you do with it. *Ignus pompa!*"

The fireworks that flew from his hands were the brilliant green of my wild, and I shivered as they surrounded me to pull me through to my last vision.

Or so I thought.

I'd expected to find a younger version of Chester, all muscles and smiles as he scampered through the brush of the Louisiana bayou. I'd expected some lesson about his family giving up their magic long ago even though he desperately wanted to revive it himself for Félicité—or at least the Lici he thought he knew. A vision to delineate how his approach was so vastly different from Aiden's. I'd expected some insight to wrap up my journey, to let me know what exactly I needed to do.

Instead, I was back in the forgotten prep kitchen in the Crow's Court, Aiden's blood magic spell raging in slow motion around me. But I wasn't in reality. Not physically, not wholly, anyway. I was standing beside Chester, watching his breath grow more and more shallow as his slowing heartbeat forced what little blood he had left against the stainless steel surface. And I was watching myself, eyes closed in my Faerie circle as Aiden finished slicing the wound across Learco's chest.

"There is give in every take," Chester whispered, his voice strained as his breath grew haggard in his lungs. "That's what keeps the balance. Contain, divide, flow."

It felt like falling when I came to, my essence slamming into my body and my eyes snapping open to find Aiden scowling before me, his athamé still dripping with the blood of my lovers. Cernun and Learco were frozen within their circles, the only movement the gush of blood from the wounds on their chests. The Fae lettering of their rings glowed. *Contain* and *Divide*.

So that left me with *Flow*.

"Turns out I'm a pretty good witch after all, huh, Teach?" Aiden quipped, relishing in the strength he felt himself gaining as the spell pushed its way toward completion.

"You're not a witch," I snarled. "A witch doesn't connect with their power by taking it from others. They do the work. They understand the meaning. They find it within."

"Well then. Maybe I'm something new," he smiled. "Maybe I'm something better."

Zamiah, Mehrdad, and Layla were still slamming their fists at the outer circle, but the strength of their power was draining as Aiden's spell worked through. He'd been true to his word to Félicité that no one outside the barrier could break the spell.

But I was inside the barrier. And I knew what I had to do.

The pleasure that spread through Aiden's eyes as he used the knife to rip the fabric of my shirt, the smile on his lips as he kissed the blood-soaked blade before aiming it toward my heart chilled me to the bone. But I refused to let him see my fear, even as the tip of his athamé sliced across the skin of my sternum.

It was nothing at first—a slip, a paper cut—before the burning of the wound took hold. My blood was hot as it dripped down my stomach and pooled across my lap to fall to the chair then to the floor. I watched it reach toward the Fae circle through the corner of my eye as Aiden returned to the far side of the prep table to complete his station in the conduit, to watch us die.

But we weren't going to die. No. I would see to that.

I finally figured out what the wild was trying to tell me. I knew what I needed to do.

He wanted magic? I'd give him magic. All of it.

My lips quivered as I steeled myself.

And then, I let my witch power flow.

CHAPTER 22

It was a strange sensation, feeling the power that had been a part of me for so long—the very core of my being—pull away from me. Stranger still being the one who was doing the pushing. It took every ounce of resolve I held within me to focus as I urged the kelly green of my magic from inside of me. I could feel its reluctance as it coupled with my mind's that I tried to downplay and ignore. Aiden had given me no other choice. If I wanted to save my lovers, to save Chester and even Simon, it was all I had left to do.

Aiden's mouth gaped as my power pulsed around him, weaving its way into his aura to become a part of the fabric of his soul. It was a marvelous sight. I was like Lachesis, braiding the threads which Clotho had spun, making sure the fabric was tight and perfect and expansive as I awaited Atropos' scissors. Maybe I could get a job with the Moirai once this was all over. A witch with no witch magic running a magic shop was not a very good advertising point. I imagined Cal could put in a word for me. And I supposed it was time for HEX to fall into younger hands. In lieu of any children, Madison would make a great heir.

The whole of my body quivered, from the blood loss or the

warmth of my power slipping away, I wasn't certain. The only thing I was sure of, as two-thirds of my magic left my body, was that I had made the right decision. For that moment anyway. Everything that came after would be another cauldron to stir.

As the tendrils of my power flowed through Aiden, I found myself connected to the spell through him. I had a lot to do while I still had some control. I closed my eyes and let my mind reach through the ritual. I searched along the web he had created, finding the connection points of the balance it was attempting to create even as it revoked the natural order. Even a spell as profane as the one we were stuck in still had to rely on the pathways through which all power flowed.

I grinned as my focus fell into place. I could feel them all: Cernun and Learco and Chester. Even Félicité was now connected to me through the muddling of her circle into the magic of the spell. The only one I couldn't meet was Simon. His wound had been so severe, so brutal, I hoped I wasn't too late. Chester's connection itself was incredibly faint as the precursor blood loss that had left him in his compliant state was magnified by the new flow from his arm. But I needed Simon if my plan was going to work. I had to flow through the whole of the ceremony.

Finally, I found him: the tiniest thread, splitting and fraying as it tried to force the ritual through to completion like the knee-bare fibers in my favorite pair of gardening jeans struggling to maintain their shape, like the last ray of moonlight on the shortest night of the year. There wasn't much time left. I had to act quickly.

I exhaled the breath I'd been holding, sending with it the last glimmers of my power to spread along the web of the ritual. Quickly, while I still had some say in the matter, I pushed my magic toward the wounds the spell had wrought, urging a return to wholeness, a reversal. I needed them to be safe. It was the only way I could fully let go.

Yet the reversal, of course, was not for me. I had set my path, and I had to see it through.

My eyes opened slowly to take in the rich green of my power. It was beautiful, the way it poured itself through the space, drowning out the black swirling mass of the ritual, hiding away the red of Félicité's circle. I'd never seen my magic quite like that, even in my mind when I'd centered myself within it. It was fierce and exuberant and so much larger than any witch should be able to contain. I was sad to let it go, but seeing the wholeness of it, I knew I was doing the right thing.

My eyes welled with tears as my thoughts told it goodbye, but I could see the wounds on my lovers' chests already closing. I could sense the returning life-force to Chester. My lips trembled as I opened my mouth.

"So mote it be," I gasped, ending my hold with a shuddering loss replaced so quickly by an emptiness I knew could never be filled. It was massive, and it was solid, and it sent me doubling over my gut as far as my restraints would allow. But it was done.

Well, almost.

The green of my power bevelled upwards as it surged to complete the task I'd set it on, to fulfill its part in the ritual once and for all. The circle surrounding us fell, as did the smaller ones containing my boyfriends and me. The magic in our ropes subsided and the knots released and fell to the tile floors as the power that had been within me found its footing in the world. I watched Aiden's maniacal smile through the teary haze in my eyes as he called my magic to him.

And it agreed, just as I'd told it to before I let go. It funneled toward him like a tornado ready to color his world, swirling to light against his chest and force its way inside. He quaked as it forced through him, falling to the floor from its force.

And then the green was gone, wholly and completely, as if it was just a memory no one had thought to write down.

I hung my head.

I closed my eyes.

It was done.

I heard the rustling of fast movement around me and let my eyes flutter open to find Mehrdad kneeling before my chair, his hand resting on my knee with an astonished and hopeful expression on his face. Behind him, I could just make out Layla and Zamiah tending to the two bodies atop the stainless steel table, checking that my counter spell had worked and the wounds had healed, feeling for the pulses in their wrists. Zamiah smiled, but Layla shook her head.

"Darragh?" Mehrdad asked, his voice low and timid as he squinted to see my face. "Are you okay? Are you with us?"

"Check on Learco and Cernun."

My throat was dry, my words grating as they escaped my lips, and I winced as I tried to swallow.

"They're okay," he assured me. "Lady Z's sister made a run for it, and Learco is out rounding up his MAW agents. She won't make it out of the building. And Cernun is holding guard over Aiden. Whatever you did worked…. What the hell did you do?"

What the hell had I done?

The swelling blankness inside me threatened to overwhelm me again, and I stopped trying to tap the magic that was no longer there. It was a lot to give up, but I did still have the wild magic within me. I needed to learn how to use it, particularly not in tandem with the power I'd always known, but it comforted me to know at least it was there.

I rubbed my eyes as I pulled myself upright, trying to figure out how to answer Mehrdad's question. I couldn't tell him I'd given away all my witch magic. That was a secret I didn't want anyone—except Cernun and Learco when I explained things to them later—to know. At least for now.

"He saved us all," Cernun answered for me, clearing his throat and shaking his head as he noticed the familiar green sparks shimmering around Aiden's unconscious body. "That's what he did." He nodded a graceful appreciation toward me, his eyes promising a much fuller experience once we were somewhere more private, before swinging into protective action to help me cover up what my green had helped him figure out. "Now, would one of you mind bringing over a few of those ropes? We're going to have one hell of a pissed off witch on our hands when he wakes up, so I'd rather get him bound before that happens."

I felt better as I pulled myself to my feet, and Mehrdad helped me study the ropes that had held us to find the ones that were the least magically-zapped. All of them were frayed and torn from where my magic had flown through them, but between them and the cracked amulet Cernun had slipped from his neck and around Aiden's, it should have been enough to keep him contained. Particularly since he was a newly-powered witch with zero real spell experience. And I also had hope my magic would resist him, unnatural and unbalanced as it was within the man.

Zamiah's brow furrowed at Cernun naming Aiden a witch, but I turned my attention to Chester before she could question the calling.

"He needs medical attention," she sighed, caressing his forearm as she looked upon him in pity. "And a few pints of blood. But he's going to be okay."

"How are you?" I asked, and Zamiah winced.

A surprised look as if she'd never been asked before mixed with a sort of solace as she shrugged.

"Simon wasn't so lucky," Layla said, and I took in his body with a solemn nod.

Even if he had played a part in Aiden's plan, the Gowdie had still double-crossed him, and I certainly hadn't wanted him to die. But as unfortunate as it was, the MAW wouldn't have cared about the human deaths. Yet with two witch deaths on his head—not to mention his father's from the first time he's tried this—it would be a long time before Aiden saw beyond the magic dampening bars of a MAW cell. At least I knew he wouldn't be putting my power toward evil deeds.

"I can make arrangements to get the human to the hospital," Mehrdad said, his hand falling on my shoulder in a gesture of simple comfort.

"Take him out the back to avoid the protestors out front," Learco announced, reappearing in the doorway and shifting his eyes to take in the scene. He smiled approvingly at Cernun's knots on Aiden's wrists and ankles. "The agents who aren't guarding the possible exits are sweeping the floors for Félicité and Dula. Once we have the two of them in hand, we'll be able to take them and Aiden into custody."

"And me," Zamiah whispered.

She held a resolved command in her eyes, and Learco nodded. Still, I was sure he'd request some leniency on her part. She had tried to save us, after all. But even if she'd been manipulated into it by her sister, she had been a part of Aiden's plan, and those deaths were on her head too.

"Is anyone going to tell me what the fuck was happening?" Layla wailed, her need for structure and her need to understand finally getting the better of her.

"That's exactly what I'd like to know."

I turned swiftly toward the new voice to find Leland Hyde scowling from the doorway. His face turned red with anger, agitated by the gritting of his teeth as his eyes darted from Learco to Cernun to me before falling to the remnants of the blood on the floor.

It felt good to be back in my suite, away from the death and destruction of the prep kitchen turned blood magic center, even with Leland glaring down at me as I laid back on the couch and he paced the floor of the living room. He muttered to himself as he stomped, and though I couldn't quite make out the words, his Bostonian accent was coming in strong with his anger.

"You might as well have a seat until Learco returns," I huffed, as much to show him I wasn't afraid as to stop the back and forth from making me dizzy as I recovered.

Leland froze. His eyes sent shivers through my body, and I suddenly wished he was pacing again.

"Clarke was a damn fine agent before he got in bed with the two of you," he snarled.

"I'm still a damn fine agent," Learco stated as he pulled himself into the room. "Aiden and his co-conspirators are in custody. They'll be remanded to the local office before their transport to Atlanta."

Leland's face grew even redder at Learco's return, my boyfriend's nonchalance increasing his ire like anise seed in a protection spell. His eyes darted from the doorway to the empty slot on the sofa between me and Cernun, and Learco's smile grew as he ignored Leland's unspoken order.

It was nice to see his confidence back, and real this time—not the feigned aplomb he'd put on when he'd first arrived in New Orleans. He crossed his arms over his chest as he leaned against the doorjamb, his pecs heaving with each cool breath beneath the tattered fabric Aiden's athamé had left of his shirt. He refused to close the door.

I could still see a faint, curved line from where the final push of my witch magic had recoiled to heal his wound. Cernun and I had the same markings on our exposed skin. It was kind of sexy, if I divorced it from the trauma of the ritual that had caused the scars, and the feeling rumbling within me only added to the reasons I wished Leland wasn't there. At least I knew my witch libido hadn't left with my witch magic.

"Is this your excuse for missing our meeting?" Leland spat when he realized Learco wouldn't be the first to speak. "To go galavanting around New Orleans with these two? Getting into Fae-knows-what kind of trouble when you were meant to be begging for your job back?"

Learco's grin didn't falter as he licked his lips and shook his head.

"I believe, Mister Hyde," he purred, the gentleness of his tone edged with a sharp growl, "our meeting was set for you to apologize to me for your impulsive and unsanctioned insistence that I had been relieved of my position. But I'll let that slide."

Leland sputtered, and Learco shrugged as he continued.

"We can consider this that meeting, can we not? And with the pleasantries done, I believe it's time for you to go."

That really didn't sit well with the MAW's resident witch hunter, and his toe met the leg of the coffee table in his tantrum. I couldn't hold back my chuckle as the reverberations from the solid oak slid back up his leg.

"You need to tell me exactly what happened here," he insisted, and Learco rolled his eyes as he cleared his throat.

"What happened here," he said, "is the head of the Southeastern Division of the Moral Authority of Witches performed his duties to the organization and to all of witch-kind. Lest you forget, I do not answer to you, Leland. Or perhaps you'd prefer to discuss my mission with Naimh Fallon."

I'd never heard her name before, but judging by the expression on Leland's face, whoever she was meant Learco's "mission" had been above his pay grade. His wink toward my puzzled expression told me he'd handled the nuances with Naihm as he'd manhandled Aiden's into one of the MAW's black sedans, and I'd smiled. Of course someone higher up in the ranks would want to take credit for being the source behind a Gowdie's apprehension. That her name got under Leland's skin was just the bristles on the broomstick.

"So if that's all," Learco smiled, gesturing toward the still open door, "I think the MAW's witch hunter general may want to make a statement to disperse the Defend Mankind From Magic protesters still gathered outside of the Crow's Court. And be sure to tell Jason that Cernun sends his love."

Leland struggled to keep his head held high as he marched toward the exit, stopping to peer up at the cold warmth emanating from Learco's eyes.

"You're really not going to tell me what happened here?" he asked, his voice gentler this time as his need to know surpassed his ego.

Learco parroted the same lines I'd heard countless times from MAW spokespeople on the news.

"It was an in house matter resolved by the Moral Authority. Humans can take heart that we witches will always keep watch on our own."

Leland's eyes narrowed, but he didn't dare another word.

"Oh!" I called, standing as he took another step past the doorframe. "You may want to check Aiden's spell sign when you get the chance. I think you'll find it interesting. Apart from the fact that it may destroy the basis of your little system."

It was Learco's turn to look puzzled, but he hid it well as he closed the door on Leland's snarling, shocked face and turned back to me.

"Now, Darragh," he asked, the confidence in his voice replaced by care, "what the hell happened in there?"

I took a deep breath as I crashed back down to the couch and closed my eyes. Cernun's hand twined into mine, and I waited for Learco to perch on the side chair before I filled them in on what exactly had gone down after Aiden's ritual had *contained* and *divided* us. It was a doozy, but they deserved to know.

"Are you sure you still want to go to this thing tonight?" Cernun asked, watching me from the bedroom doorway as I tried to wipe away the few creases my suit had accumulated from its time in my bags.

The Yarrow Tooth Suite may have been well-equipped, but, being in a witch hotel, it lacked the iron and the board most hotel rooms had on hand. Of course, most witches would be able to de-wrinkle their clothing with a whispered thought. But I wasn't most witches anymore.

The shower—and the company within it—had made me feel

better though. Plus the suit and mask Cernun had ordered in for the festivities were exquisite.

A part of me had hoped my magic would regenerate inside of me like it did after a particularly powerful spell or a long night of aura play with my lovers. Usually, I'd find myself spent and tired and drained, but a nice Old Fashioned from Aunt Paulina's and a moment of meditation in the Botanical Gardens would leave me refreshed and refilled. That wasn't going to happen this time. And though I'd known it when I'd channelled my flow into Aiden, I was still having trouble wrapping my head around it.

At least I could still feel the wild magic inside of me. That was a small comfort. Granted, I had no idea how to use it when it wasn't tied to my witch power. I didn't think there was a single book on my shelves at HEX that could teach me how. Hell, there probably wasn't one in any of the MAW's vast archives either. What I had inside of me was so old, so distantly removed, that it was new again. I would have to figure it out on my own, and that was exciting. Somewhat.

"Of course he does," Learco laughed as he slipped through the doorway carrying the embroidered linen shoe bag he'd picked up from a courier at the door. "Tonight's party was the entire reason he came to this convention to begin with."

"That and to apparently take part in some covert MAW mission implemented by some higher up whose name I'm probably not even supposed to know," I joked.

"Naihm owes me one," Learco shrugged. "Plus there are plenty of people inside the MAW who'd jump at the chance to knock Leland Hyde down a few pegs. Between his trying to fire me and the sudden discovery that his precious spell signs aren't as accurate as he claims, thanks to Aiden's now reading as yours, I don't think we'll have to worry about him meddling for a while."

"Not to mention what he did to Samara," I added.

Learco winced as he nodded, but smiled once more as he pulled the custom shoes Cal had made for him from the bag. They were gorgeous. Black leather with threaded gold spiraling like ivy across the body and thick wooden soles. Whatever Cal wanted from us, whatever he thought we could give him, he was certainly pulling out all the stops to get there. Perhaps we'd be able to get Cernun a pair in the deal as well. Although, with his Kyteler money, Cernun could definitely afford the two thousand dollar price tag on his own now.

"So I take it Leland won't be the one in charge of Aiden's punishment?" Cernun asked as he crossed to the bed and whispered his *steam* spell to remove the wrinkles I was still absently working at on my suit.

"Fae, no!" Learco confirmed. "I'll handle all of that. That way we can be sure, though it will be known his spell sign and yours are similar, Aiden won't be able to tell anyone he has your magic."

That was good. Not that I thought anyone would believe him even if he did broadcast it, but it was better to not have folks sniffing around and asking questions while I figured things out. Magic fatigue from being involved in a blood ritual would only work as an excuse for so long.

"What's going to happen to Dula and the sisters?" I asked. "Will you be in charge of them too?"

Learco nodded once more.

"I can believe Dula's blackmail story," he said. "But the MAW's forensic accountants will want to open an inquest into her dealings, so her Healing Centers are probably on the outs. Félicité will have the chance to plead her case. And Zamiah will pay her dues. With her help in the end taken into account, of course."

I sighed. I didn't like the idea of any witch—except maybe Aiden—being detained by the Moral Authority, but it did feel better knowing Learco would be the one charged with their incarcerated rehab. And none of the conspirators would come close to paying the price that Simon had. Poor guy. But with four deaths on their hands, and the attempted murders of four more, they all had a debt to settle, no matter who held the athamé.

"We should probably get dressed," I said, shaking off the dread of the past few days and attempting to settle into the reverie. After the day we'd had, we all deserved a bit of fun to calm the nerves.

My fingers traced the smooth leather of the beautiful Green Man mask my lovers had bought me for the trip. It still had two uses of the spell imbued within it that would contour the shape to my face, allowing it to move and express my own emotions through its façade. But I wouldn't be able to invoke it. Not anymore.

"Maybe I won't wear the mask," I huffed, my fingers still tracing the exquisite curve of its features before adding, "I can just go as myself," to try to make me feel better.

"You are one of the only people I know who is utterly *always* yourself, Darragh," Learco laughed. "Besides, after the day we've all had, the three of us deserve a bit of the debaucherous wild these masks have to offer."

I nodded. The freedom of anonymity did sound fun. Especially in a room full of horny witches all expelling the stress of the last few days. But still….

"I can do the spell for you," Cernun offered when my face fell and my fingers retracted from the gift.

"We both can," Learco assured me. "We'll help with anything you need while we figure this all out. If there's a way to siphon your magic back from Aiden, we'll find it."

"And it won't involve blood rituals," Cernun promised.

It felt good to have them on my side. Whatever the months ahead held, I knew we were better off facing them together. The ease that came with letting go of Balor's trick warning was enormous. My lovers and I were a coven, and we were always stronger together. Always.

I smiled a true and genuine smile as I let the towel wrapped around my waist slip to the floor and got ready to face the night. A night that was, finally, free of monsters. A night that was, finally, for us.

EPILOGUE

It felt like an illusion—like I was back inside the wild—as we stepped into the tenth floor ballroom. Mirrors lined the entirety of the chamber, replacing the panelling of the walls but still allowing the woodgrain to show as they reflected back the decor and magnified the grandiosity of the event. Lanterns floated like constellations above the dance floor, and a magnificent oak tree was magicked into being at the center of the space, roots and branches spilling outward with new life and magic, reflected and reflected and reflected into a forest of wonder. It was hard to believe that only a few hours before, just on the other side of the far wall, my partners and I had almost died before I had given up my power in a defunct catering kitchen. Still, it felt good to be here, surrounded by my kind, a lovers' palm pressed firmly against each of my hands.

"These BOG Witches really go out all, huh?" Cernun smiled as he squeezed my fingers. "That's one expensive glamour right there."

"What's more impressive," I whispered back as I caught sight of the performers waiting near the ceiling, "is the base they had built to host the mirage."

In time with the music, six aerialists dropped from the higher branches of the tree, gliding down to reveal swings bolted to the outstretched limbs. Their gowns and tux tails billowed behind them in the air, leaving trails of monarch butterflies flapping out into the crowd. A glamour was one thing: beautiful and of its place. But being strong enough to hold weight meant Mehrdad and his team had worked overtime in building an actual structure. Plus, I could tell as the performers slowed, the ropes that held the swings were reinforced with chains that would allow for a different type of swing to be attached later. They really had thought of everything.

"Darragh? Is that you? I didn't think you'd come tonight."

Speaking of the one who'd thought of everything.

"Layla!" I exclaimed as I turned to great her. "It's a gorgeous party! And I do hope you'll forgive me for being too tied up to go to my seminars today."

"No, I mean…," she stammered as I turned, the green leather of my Green Man mask curving into a wry grin before she laughed at my joke—well, half joke—and took my hands in hers. Although her mask didn't contour and move with her features, I could see a genuine smile beneath its rim as she cocked her head.

"I'm happy you're here. All three of you."

My boyfriends nodded their agreement, and we each congratulated her on the feat it had taken to pull off such an evening.

"I truly hope Mehrdad sees what a spectacular assistant he has in you," I offered. "If he doesn't, I may have to try to steal you for away to HEX. You ever thought about trading the Crescent City for the City in the Forest?"

"You couldn't afford her new salary," Mehrdad laughed as he joined our grouping. "Layla here has just been named the Vice President of Affairs for the BOG Witch Organization."

Mehrdad looked amazing in his pecan-hued suit with the

matching wooden mask elegantly carved to frame his eyes. His burns looked better too; the second skin and the medical witches' spells having worked wonders even since earlier that afternoon. His rich black hair was tussled atop his head, and I could sense a newfound freedom about him as he relinquished a bit of the control he'd tried so hard to maintain throughout the event and handed it over to Layla.

A flourish of his hand brought an eager new assistant to his heels, balancing a tray with an Old Fashioned, a Pimm's Cup, a frothy light beer, and two glasses of deep red wine.

"This is how one starts a party," Learco laughed as we retrieved our drinks, and he offered up a toast to Layla.

"You were right," Mehrdad smiled as he leaned in toward his new VP. "The aerialists are a wonderful touch."

"Just wait until the burlesque show building towards 3AM," she promised.

"Did someone say 'burlesque?'"

I didn't even need to see through the red lace of her mask to know the question had come from Marguerite. She purred as she slinked closer to us, angling the depth of her deep cut satin dress forward to show off the abundance of her cleavage. Ric was close on her heels, decked out in an exquisite black tux with an understated mask tied around his white grey hair.

"Darragh," Ric called as he recognized my features through my own mask. "I do hope you'll be persuaded to join the festivities tonight. We were all so disappointed in your absence at the afterparty."

It was tempting—so very tempting—and I started to answer before Mehrdad cleared his throat.

"Darragh may be otherwise occupied," he explained. "Turns out his partners were able to make it after all. Marguerite, Wulfric. May I introduce you to...."

"These witches need no introduction," Marguerite growled as she threw her arms around Learco's neck, pulled her lips up to kiss his cheek, and Ric reached out to clasp Cernun's hand.

"I know it's a party, Mister Kyteler—" Ric started.

"Cernun's fine."

"Cernun. But could I possibly bend your ear for just a brief moment? What are your thoughts on rideshare services?"

As Ric led Cernun away, Marguerite had already pulled Learco into a conversation about special spells for her coffee shops. I could see their smirks to me as they tried to be polite, and I shrugged a joyful "sorry" in their direction as I turned back to the show. The glory of the evening would put all the business speak to bed soon enough, particularly as the hours rounded out and "bed"—in all its many forms—forced its way to the forefront of every witches' mind.

I turned back to the show and grinned as each swing of the performers sent more monarchs out toward the limbs, landing briefly and shifting into leaves until the tree was nearly full. It was as if the full of Spring was on display for Ostara, and a fitting tribute to the magic that powered us all.

Well, most of us.

I could still feel that emptiness where my power had been, but I tried to ignore it as I watched the reverie. Besides. I had the spark of the wild. And though it had gone silent since the ritual, since the lines of communication through my witch power had been severed, I knew it was still there. And once I figured out how to access it, I knew new worlds of possibility would open.

"How are the shoes?"

"The most comfortable thing I've ever put on my feet," I admitted as I turned to thank Cal for his gift.

His outfit was extravagant. Sequins oscillated between purple, red, and blue across his suit, stretching in elaborate floral patterns that of course extended to his shoes. His mask bloomed with the real life versions of the flowers, each delicate petal swimming against his face. I could tell the flowers were real, not spelled. The mask itself must have been produced for him mere moments before the party.

I couldn't believe I had ever thought he could be the vampire.

"I won't keep you long," he promised as he nodded toward my boyfriends desperately trying to leave their conversations. "I can see you need to rescue your lovers. But we do need to talk. I will be in Atlanta later this Summer. Perhaps our conversation can continue there."

I nodded as he departed, so sure of himself he hadn't even waited for a yes or no. And though I wanted to understand why his aura had been so grating against mine, that he thought I held the answers worried me. I couldn't risk any other witches discovering the wild within me. At least not yet.

But that was a problem for another night.

This night was about fantasy; about dreams. I beamed, my mask curving high with my smile, as I moved to pull my lovers to the dance floor.

NATURAL HEX

**BOOK FIVE
IN THE
HEX'D SERIES**

**COMING SOON
FROM**

ACKNOWLEDGMENTS

As I round out the fourth book in the HEX'd series, I thought it best to utilize the acknowledgements section to pay homage to one thing: love.

Books are a labor of it—the writing of them anyway—and I understand how utterly lucky I am, thanks to the brilliant folks in my life, to get to explore the world of Darragh and his coven.

Amidst all of the book bans and challenges facing authors in our current political environment—and indeed throughout the whole of history—I feel it is as important as ever for writers to tell their stories, to show their differences, and to embrace their love of the world. Between the silencing of voices and the onslaught of AI-generated "books," those who continue to write and tell stories are truly powerful creatures.

As we continue our fight for justice and freedom, I hope my books can bring you some joy. And I hope Darragh's own struggles can show you just a bit of how powerful you are. Of how loved you are. And of just how far we can go: together.

Founded in Atlanta, Georgia in 2023, PARLYAREE PRESS is dedicated to publishing writing that expands, reveals, and interrogates the mainstream. We seek out fiction, creative nonfiction, and poetry that exists in the liminal space between what was and what will be.

The cant of circus performers, freaks, queers, and thespians, Parlyaree is the invented language required to tell the stories of those othered, to keep their secrets, to keep them safe. It is a polyglot of experiences that may only be told in one's own voice. Parlyaree—as an invented language—borrows from what was to create something new.

That is what excites us at Parlyaree Press. Stories that transform; essays that reimagine; poetry that takes us behind the stanza to the core of our being and back again; language that plays as much as it conveys.

Writers: tell us your secrets.
Readers: reimagine your worlds.